PARTY

Arca Book 6

KAREN DIEM

Copyright

Cover art by Deranged Doctor Design.

***

eBook version 1.0.1, published September 2021.

First Paperback Printing: September 6, 2021.

ISBN: 978-0-9975740-9-8

To contact Karen Diem or subscribe to her newsletter, go to http://www.karendiem.com.

Dedication

Dedicated to you. Because you cared enough to read the dedication and because I cared enough to give the very best. Or at least a dedication.

Table of Contents

Copyright 2
Dedication 3
Chapter One 7
Chapter Two 14
Chapter Three 33
Chapter Four 47
Chapter Five 59
Chapter Six 79
Chapter Seven 94
Chapter Eight 105
Chapter Nine 118
Chapter Ten 129
Chapter Eleven 148
Chapter Twelve 172
Chapter Thirteen 193
Chapter Fourteen 206
Chapter Fifteen 216
Chapter Sixteen 226
Chapter Seventeen 259
Chapter Eighteen 278
Chapter Nineteen 304
Chapter Twenty 319
Chapter Twenty-One 330
Chapter Twenty-Two 356
Chapter Twenty-Three 379
Chapter Twenty-Four 389
Epilogue 407
Languages Glossary 421
From the Author 424
Arca Chronology 425

Chapter One

The SWAT teams waiting for her might've been a sign that Zita Garcia needed to rethink her life choices.

In the shape of a hawk, she drifted in and out of the clouds in a lazy circle, mimicking a real bird performing a similar spiral nearby.

The person Zita had come to meet, the Pie Lady, sat on a wooden bench by the water of the long, oval lake that filled the center of the park. As she knitted something pastel yellow, the older woman hummed. Her project matched the cheery flowers of her short-sleeved blouse, her lemon-colored capris, and the bulging tote bag sitting beside her. Even her hair projected her contentment, the fluffy short cut like a peppery halo of baking sainthood.

Go to church, knit baby clothes while humming a happy song, and have the metahuman ability to bake pies so good they temporarily cure mental illness... is she trying to be somebody's ideal mom or something? I bet she's got snacks, tissues, and chanclas in her bag. What's her name again? Irma? Iris? Zita tried to remember while she scoped out the others there.

Beneath the shade of a wide oak, a mud-splattered white SUV sat empty. A tired-seeming man, Zita's age, stretched out on a bench by it. He had Pie Lady's facial structure, the tight body of a serious runner, and hooded brown eyes glued to his phone, making him the only other person in the park who seemed normal.

Everyone else there was wrong. Nicely muscled, but wrong.

When the Pie Lady waved happily at a fit, young couple with a baby carriage, they returned only a curt nod. A dog walker with the balance of a martial artist walked multiple laps, a slight hitch in his stride that might signal a concealed weapon. The canine itself was on alert, with none of the expected joyous sniffing, marking, and dawdling. Two birdwatchers had locked their binoculars on Zita and the other hawk, completely ignoring the smaller birds in the nearby trees. By the shore, a fisherman hung out, busy observing his environs rather than the line drifting in the water. He had no beer, but a three-foot-long duffel lay open at his feet, the bag lumpy with something too big to be a backup fishing rod. Landscapers poked at the dirt as a tray of flowers wilted beside them. The spotless pickup truck nearby lacked any gardening equipment or racks for such. Four black vans and a sedan sat neatly side-by-side next to the handicapped parking spots. Engines rumbled in two of the vans, but the hard-eyed men in the driver's seats didn't even pretend to be doing anything other than watching their surroundings.

Despite the heat and humidity, all the suspicious strangers wore jeans and bulky, plain t-shirts that didn't quite hide the outline of hidden vests on bodies that'd clearly seen serious gym time. They also seemed to share the flat, assessing gazes of cops that moved endlessly over the landscape, as if expecting something or someone to burst out of nowhere.

Someone like Zita.

She laughed at her own self-absorption. *This is pretty far from home. It might not be about me. Maybe they're staking out the park because of drug deals or something. In any case, I promised Elle I'd help her learn to control her shifting, and it's been months since we last managed a meet. Screw it. I need to find out how the kid is doing, even if this place is oozing cops.*

Coasting on a thermal, she looped overhead, plotting the best time and angle to fly down and talk to the Pie Lady.

The idyllic lake took up a fourth of the grassy park, complete with ducks paddling around. A stone statue of a man reigned over myriad flowers and butterfly bushes on a small island, the shrubs bright and oversized with late summer growth. At one edge, a short wooden pier extended out from a cute little dock that held only a pair of pedal boats tethered with chains. Carefully landscaped trees and shrubs forced otherwise straight lines to wind and meander, making the place seem larger.

Not to mention hiding Pie Lady's bench from sight at certain points.

Zita waited until as many of the roving cops were at the farthest end of their respective loops as possible. Trees sheltered her from the parking lot view and whatever hid in those vans as she landed beside the older woman and shifted to Arca. Her chosen form was almost identical to her natural one, save for the face, ears, fingerprints, voice, and long hair. She cleared her throat.

The Pie Lady started.

Both spoke.

"Iris, right? Elle's okay, right?" Zita's voice was thick with the fake Mexican accent that hid her identity and soothed her nerves at the proximity of so much law enforcement.

"Where's Eleanor? It's Irene, actually."

They blinked at each other.

"You don't know where she is? Wasn't she getting surgeries and stuff for her bad heart? Did you just bring the cops with you for giggles, or was there a special reason?" Zita finally said. She adjusted her mask, fingers fussing over the smooth fabric, the same special material as the rest of her vigilante costume, a pair of capris and a sports bra. It was the only clothing she'd found that disappeared when she shifted shape, instead of getting destroyed or tangling her up. When she returned to a human form, the clothing reappeared. Given how weirdly upset people got when their rescuer was naked, that was a blessing.

Their eyes intent on her, the stroller couple and dog walker increased their speed.

The older woman shook her head. "What do you mean police? I didn't bring any. My car's been acting up, so one of my boys drove me here after he got off his shift at the hospital. Nobody else came with us. I haven't seen Eleanor since the last time I texted you her location. DMS took her after that, and nobody will tell me where she is, even though I'm her foster mother and we applied to adopt her. Her doctors said she needed more surgery soon, and I don't even know if she's received it. My son, the one that's a deputy, hasn't even been able to find out. Given how hard Elle practiced what you taught her, I thought you'd set up some other way to contact her. Why would you ask me to meet you about Eleanor if you didn't know?"

Zita gaped at Irene. "You texted me, not the other way around... now the cops make sense. I guess it is all about me. Carajo, I was hoping your town had a drug problem. If you see Elle first, tell her to keep working on her control like we did in the hospital." She sighed. Her back prickled, and she scanned the area.

The fisherman dug through his bag. The landscapers appeared to be attempting to circle around her.

Irene gaped at Zita for a second but then closed her eyes. "What? Then that means..."

Zita took a step away from Irene, preparing to fly.

The stroller couple burst into a run. The female half shouted, "Freeze! DMS! Face down on the ground! Don't move!" Her male partner trained a gun on Zita, and the dog walker released his dog. It ran toward the bench.

"Oye, no need to get upset now. I didn't do nothing," Zita said, raising her hands in the air.

Movement through the trees and the sound of slamming doors made her suspect the vans had just opened up. Somehow, she doubted the occupants were coming to rescue her. The dog was barking and closing in.

Reaching into the carriage, the female DMS agent pulled out a small round item, yanked out a pin, and pitched it at their feet in a practiced move. Under other circumstances, Zita would've admired the throw.

Before her conscious mind identified the grenade, she was already in motion. Shifting to a gorilla, Zita grabbed Irene and dragged the woman to the pier's edge, jumping into the water. Knitting needles clattered on the pavement behind them.

"Wha—!" Irene shouted as they submerged.

Changing shape again to a freshwater dolphin, Zita swam as fast as possible while hauling the other woman to the island in the center. Despite the short distance, she tried to surface a couple times for Irene's sake, but she stayed mostly underwater herself, not wanting to make either of them a target. With a quick switch back to gorilla, she hauled a coughing Irene out of the water and into the partial screen afforded by the statue and overgrown bushes.

Back where they'd been, a thick cloud of weird orange smoke swirled in a ten-foot radius.

Instinct shrieked, and she whipped to the side.

Something whooshed faintly.

Irene stumbled and fell with a thump. "Ow!"

Zita changed to her Arca shape as she tried to haul the older woman closer to the statue for better cover. "You okay?"

To her credit, Irene recovered her breath and composure quickly, even though her fingers dug into Zita's arm as they sheltered behind the warm stone. "Fine."

Standing by the SUV, Irene's son clutched his phone to his chest but stayed out of the way of the cops.

The words DMS SWAT stood out on the backs of multiple people in tactical gear as they swarmed through all forty acres of the park. Some covered the sky while others combed the underbrush. The landscapers were tearing off vests and boots by the shore.

"Goodness gracious, why does my arm hurt so much?" Irene slurred.

Spotting a dart protruding from the other woman's shoulder, Zita plucked it out, setting it aside. "You got hit with a dart." *Air guns! Whatever they've put in there is taking effect awful quick, too. That can't be good. Dios, how did I miss that they've got at least one sniper out there somewhere?*

"I didn't know... trap. Just wanna... help Eleanor. Go." Irene collapsed onto the grass, her eyes sliding shut.

Her grip gentle, Zita eased the other woman over to rest propped up against the statue.

"Eleanor?" Irene half-reared up, eyes opening.

Zita nodded, worried about the way the older woman was panting. "I'll find her."

"Uh-huh. 'Ppreciate that. Nice girl," Irene replied, one hand rising to sloppily pat Zita's head. The older woman's words trailed off, and her eyes fluttered shut as her arm dropped. A soft, congested snore followed.

Across the water, the breeze brought words to her. "Dose Arca now with the meta gas! We need her controlled. Find her friends!"

The stroller woman pulled out a grenade launcher.

Zita bellowed, "You hit the old lady. She's having some kind of reaction! Get an ambulance! Don't shoot!"

"Mom!" His weariness apparently forgotten, the normal guy from the parking lot grabbed something from his car and sprinted to the edge of the lake. After dropping a big duffel with a red cross on it, he unchained one of the boats.

Freed of their vests, landscapers dove into the water and struck out for the island. The fisherman sidestepped along the shore, trying to get a better angle on Zita with a long gun.

Although she hated to abandon the sleeping woman, Zita leapt up, exploding into golden eagle form. As she rose through the air, she glanced below.

The stroller woman lowered her grenade launcher, while the fisherman tracked Zita with an air gun. A dripping landscaper bent over Irene while the other had a gun out. The boat was just reaching the island.

Zita's instincts screamed. She banked hard to the left.

A dart buzzed by.

No mames. They ain't playing. If those things can knock out a woman who's got at least thirty or forty pounds on me in human form that fast, it might be fatal in this form. Please let her be okay. I'll have to bring Wyn back and see if Irene needs her healing spell. Zita pumped her wings harder and let the clouds hide her. She circled, changing to a white-bellied sea eagle, and peeked through her cover to check on the Pie Lady.

Irene's son bent over her, his bag open beside him as he grabbed something in it. One sodden landscaper remained nearby. All the other DMS agents mobbed the lake shore. Someone in a suit and glasses did a lot of gesturing and stomping. With relief, she saw an ambulance speeding down the road, lights flashing.

Just in case, Zita lingered overhead. Once Irene was safely in the vehicle, she let herself drift higher and teleported home.

Chapter Two

For once, she knew where her friends would be.

After getting home, Zita went to the webcam already open in her browser and studied the live feed of the desert zoo. She shifted to a golden eagle and teleported to the very edge of the visible area.

She searched for Andy and Wyn from above, praying they'd avoided attracting attention if they were here. If a lone animal shapeshifter rated all the people in tactical gear in the park, she hated to think about the force that would be sent against a powerful witch and a nearly invulnerable bird shifter.

The difference in humidity was immediately obvious. While both places were hot, here the air was light. Flying felt right, rather than swimming with wings as it had back home. Absently, she noted the brilliant bursts of colorful foliage—red and sage and silver bright against orange dirt—with symmetrical man-made shapes interrupting it. A small crowd gathered around one building surrounded by umbrella-shaded tables, leading her to guess it was some sort of coffee shop or restaurant.

Zita dismissed that section of the park. *Not there. Too many people swarming around as if there's free food or some celebrity. They'd avoid that area. This was supposed to be our chance to hang and check out the wildlife without making Wyn hike.*

To be certain, however, she did a quick loop over the parking lot. Her worry eased when none of the vehicles seemed likely to hold a military team. The people she saw acted normally, down to the toddler screaming for ice cream. Finally, she spotted a sign with a map and perched on it, checking where her friends had said they'd be. Once she'd gotten her bearings, Zita followed the trail markers until she reached a spot where cord marked off a section of the path as closed. Like any other experienced trespasser, she flew over it without really paying any attention and scanned the area for her friends.

To her delight, they were not only safe but almost an hour early.

Andy paced, revealing the easy balance granted by his martial arts training. His gaze was on the mountains. His cape flared behind him, bright purple against his long black braid of hair. Other than that, he wore the male version of Zita's costume: a purple mask, bike shorts, and a tank top.

Enthroned in a collapsible camp chair, Wyn sat in the shade of a large desert hackberry with three empty chairs around her. Instead of a costume, Wyn had cast her usual illusion of Muse, a too-perfect icy blond woman dressed to go dancing at a club, complete with impractical high heels and amethyst-studded tiara that matched her illusory eyes. Privately, Zita preferred the warm beauty of her friend's natural form... a pretty brunette.

Wyn spoke. "Nervous?"

"Wouldn't you be?" Andy said, rubbing the sides of his thighs.

Swooping in, Zita shifted to Arca and landed on her feet by her friends. "Nervous about what?"

A startled laugh burst from Wyn, and Andy jumped. They exchanged glances, and their smiles faltered when their attention turned fully to Zita.

"Goodness gracious, you surprised us! We weren't expecting you for an hour, Arca. What happened? Why are you all wet?" Wyn's hands fluttered.

Andy wrinkled his nose. "And why do you reek of dead fish?"

Zita glanced down. The aridity of the Arizona desert rendered her clothing comfortable rather than clammy, so she'd almost forgotten about her impromptu dip. "That's probably from when I jumped in the pond to escape the grenade. On the bright side, I'm drying off pretty quick."

"Grenade? Weren't you supposed to tutor that poor child in shapeshifting? What did you do to anger a girl with a heart condition so much that she would hurl munitions at you? And why? Never mind the why, it's you." Wyn shook her head.

Unhelpfully, Andy added, "And you smell like fish."

She rolled her eyes. "You said that before, mano."

"You stink. It was worth mentioning again," Andy said. "Maybe this wasn't the best time to pick..."

Frowning at him, Zita shook her head. "Best time for what? Elle was never there. Pie Lady—that's her foster mom, Irene—and I were set up by DMS. They tossed a grenade at us, so I grabbed Pie Lady and jumped into the water before it hit. They kept shouting something about using some meta gas on me before I could escape, so I'm assuming that's what the weird orange smoke was that came spewing out of the explosion."

Both of her friends frowned.

"Whatever that is, I dislike the sound of it. What do you think it does?" Wyn said, nibbling on her lower lip.

It was Andy's turn to shrug. "It could be anything. Based on my extensive study of comic books, it could stop our powers from working, disable us, mutate us in some unpleasant way, control our minds, or maybe just kill us."

"Just kill us? Ay, buey, I like how you downplay that option," Zita groused.

Wyn blinked at Andy. "That doesn't really narrow down the possibilities, and all of them are dreadful."

"Sí, I don't like any of those choices. I vote we avoid the funky gas," Zita said.

Andy nodded. "Sounds like a plan."

"Motion passed. The Department of Metahuman Services runs on their own twisted logic, but they haven't attempted entrapment before. Have you done anything lately that we don't know about?" Wyn queried.

Zita frowned at her. "Why does it have to be my fault? Maybe they got tired of endlessly harassing quarantine victims to agree to be guinea pigs and have moved on to kidnapping awesome folks like me. Do you think you could find Elle with that spell of yours? I only have her first name..."

After a pause, Wyn shook her head. "I don't know her, so I need more than that. We could search the papers for mention of an Elle in her state and combine it with keywords... a lot would depend on if her local newspapers thought it worth carrying and if they're digitized."

"It was a pretty small town. They might not be that fancy." Zita grimaced. "I need to find the kid, though. All this time, DMS had her spirited away somewhere when she should've been getting medical treatment... if she hasn't gotten it, she needs to go see a doctor right away. Also, it'd be good if you could check on Irene. Normally a tranquilizer takes a while to kick in, at least in animals. I assume people are the same, but Irene dropped right away and was breathing funny."

Wyn nodded. "Of course. If you know her location, I'd be happy to go assist her, though she should be fine if she received prompt medical attention."

Tension lessened in Zita's shoulders. "Good. She's a nice lady. I don't know where they'd take her, but there can't be that many hospitals close by where we met."

"Why don't you see if Chevalier can help find Elle and Irene? You took care of his koi when he was out of town, so he should owe you a favor. Search engines are his jam. And his bread, considering how he made his money off search algorithms," Andy suggested.

"Good idea. I should've thought of it myself. I'll call him right now." Zita pulled her phone and its battery out of her pocket.

Wyn made a small hand gesture toward Zita and stared at Andy.

He shook his head.

The witch raised her eyebrows.

Although suspicion itched at whatever telepathic conversation they were having without her, Zita let it go. The kid was more important. She had to try a couple times to get the battery to connect. "If he gets her full name, can you cast that tracking spell as soon as possible? Poor Elle's been missing for months. While a few more hours might not matter, I won't abandon her now that I know. Plus, Irene might need healing..."

"Understood. Helping both of them isn't a problem. I don't suppose I could convince you to upgrade to a better phone? That one seems a bit battered." Wyn wrinkled her nose.

Zita switched on the little device, smoothing her thumb over a crack. "It's a cheap little prepaid. All it has to do is get calls and texts and be easy for me to separate from the battery so it can't be tracked. I don't need an upgrade, just a replacement."

It beeped at her. Two texts.

The first made her grunt in surprise. A warm feeling curled in her stomach as she read the second text, and she smiled a little.

"Good news?" Wyn asked.

Aware of how her friend felt about the mercenary she was dating, Zita hesitated and tried feigning indifference. "Ah, people. They like me. I'm likable."

Her friend narrowed her eyes.

Before Wyn could protest, Zita waved the phone at her. She remembered to use Jerome's fake name at the last minute, since they were technically in public. "Chevalier texted. He wants a meet with all three of us as soon as possible. Must be important. He used a lot of exclamation points. His place, knock on the back gate. We're specifically not supposed to try to sneak in and be creepy. I think he means Wingspan."

"Me?" Andy raised his eyebrows.

She nodded. "It's the cape. Freaks people out, probably because it's always catching on fire and getting shredded and stuff. Totally bad luck."

"We agreed not to speak of the shredder incident," he said, though one hand rose to touch a shoulder where the cape fastened to his costume.

Wyn's expression was still suspicious, but she allowed herself to be diverted. "Very well. Let's schedule an appointment with Chevalier."

"He said 'as soon as possible.' We can always sneak back here and give ourselves the grand tour after-hours or another time, so why don't we see if he's available now? As much as I hate to miss a good bird of prey flying exhibition, Irene and Elle are probably counting on us," Zita said.

Wyn widened her eyes and twirled her fingers at Andy.

His shoulders hunched.

Zita fidgeted, recognizing the stare the other two exchanged. "If you're going to talk behind my back, do I need to be here for this? I got things to do, people to help."

He sighed, his gaze drifting to the trail. "I had a friend who was going to join us, but if we need to go see Jerome, let's get on that now. Probably better given the fish stench, anyway."

"It seems as if our plans for today have been derailed." Wyn sighed and murmured something under her breath that sounded a lot like, "Yellow."

"Yellow what?" Zita asked.

"Nothing," her friend said, smiling too sweetly.

Andy glanced down the path and then at the women. "Could you collect the chairs? I'll meet up with you in a sec. I need to tell my friend we're taking off. They went to grab something from concessions."

Her face softening, Wyn patted his arm. "That's fine. Arca needs to shower anyway before spending time in close proximity to anyone, so we'll go to her place. You can join us there whenever you've finished talking. Tell your friend we're hanging back until you can leave."

Zita tapped her foot. "If I'm going to shower, we need to go."

"Oh, you're definitely going to shower." Wyn wrinkled her nose.

***

Forty-five minutes later, a newly showered Zita and her friends were in the park behind Jerome's house. While they saw a few others in the distance, the heat kept down the number of people in the area, so no one came close enough to react to the three vigilantes. The shade of the trees along the trail cooled the humid air to an almost pleasant temperature, making it into a relaxing stroll in the woods for her friends.

Even if their speed was torturous to Zita. *So slow.*

She trudged along and tried to enjoy the sound of the birds and the rich, green scent of the flowers in full summer bloom. Finally, she gave that up and settled for jogging back and forth in front of them. With relief, she spotted the stone walls surrounding Jerome's lush little garden through the trees and opened her mouth to point it out.

A phone rang nearby.

Her friends stopped and stared at Zita expectantly.

After a second, she rolled her eyes and answered it. "Diga."

"Stroll by without stopping, but be back in five minutes, thirty seconds. The rear gate is unlocked. Come in through the back door fast, and don't let anyone see you. Turn off your phones and pull out the batteries," Jerome said. He then hung up.

Andy and Wyn waited. "Problem?" he asked.

Zita frowned and continued walking, forcing them to follow. After transmitting Jerome's odd instructions, she concluded with, "He sounds like he's been watching too many movies. If you want to go to the second mark, even I know you got to synchronize watches, assuming you wear them."

"Perhaps he has a guest he needs to usher out the door first?" Wyn lifted one shoulder and let it drop as she strolled along.

"Why would we care about that? It's weird, but whatever." Zita turned off her phone and pulled out the battery before slipping it into her pocket.

They followed his directions, though she was pretty certain they'd missed the exact time target.

Jerome met them at the sliding glass door, waving them along with a big hand. Once they were in, he drew the blinds.

Zita blurted out the question that'd been burning at her. "What was that about with the gate and the time?"

He shrugged and ushered them away from the door. "Someone—probably a government agency—hacked my security camera feeds. I've been letting them, mostly. The shorter the camera loop, the less chance they have of realizing that I know what they're doing. While I don't mind if they catch a burglar or my psycho ex coming to visit, I'd rather have some privacy when I have someone of your..." He paused for a moment, then snickered. "Let's just say guests of your particular caliber."

"Lot of government action these days," Andy muttered.

Jerome snorted and led them toward his office. "You don't know the half of it. Also, while you're all here, I'll install an app on your phones that encrypts communications. Only text me using that. They won't be able to trace it or tap into it."

Wyn and Andy handed him their disposable phones.

His lip curling, Jerome said, "What, did you buy the cheapest things you could find? No matter, I'll get the apps installed. You can talk securely with anyone else who has the same program without being traced or tapped into. I'd suggest you pick a password more complicated than the numbers an idiot would use on their luggage. I mean you, Arca. Where's yours, by the way?"

Andy giggled.

"In my pocket. I don't think mine does apps. It only does texts, crappy pictures, and phone calls. I'm going to get another one once I get the chance." Catching a whiff of a delightful scent as they cut through his fancy kitchen, she inhaled deeply. Last night's dinner or this morning's breakfast for Jerome had clearly been a nice Panang curry that had her licking her lips.

Jerome shuddered. "Luddite. I'll be contacting one of the others until your phone leaves the dial-up era. When we're done with our chat, Arca, would you change into a cat or something and sit on the camera near the roof in my backyard? Get it angled to the side and down so the view is only the side alley and the neighbor's yard. I'd like to be able to come and go from my house without messing with the feed."

"I can do that," Zita said, "But I want the number of the place where you got that curry."

Other than the toy shelves being even more cluttered, little had changed since her last visit to his office. Even the weird green boar-woman in the metal bikini remained frozen on one screen, though now she wore a headdress like a Vegas dancer and appeared to be mid-swing at a dinosaur.

Jerome seated himself in his oversized, black leather chair. He tapped a couple keys and smiled. "Nice of you all to show up without any explosions or violence surrounding you, for once."

"You said it was an emergency. What's up? Are the koi okay?" Zita asked.

He gestured at them. "It's not about the fish. They're fine. I'm calling in that favor you three owe me."

She snorted. "Favor? What favor?"

Wyn and Andy wore dubious expressions she probably mirrored.

"You know, from all those times I helped you out." Jerome leaned back in his chair, folding both hands behind his head. Their skepticism did not appear to faze him.

Her eyebrows rose, and she scrutinized him for any obvious signs of illness. "What? Do you mean when you refused to give us key information until we let you tag along with us to Brazil?"

Andy pointed out the other alternative. "He could mean the jailbreak on the highway, when he joined the battle without being asked."

Wyn simply arched an elegant eyebrow at him and folded her arms over her chest.

Jerome gestured toward himself, running a hand over the smooth, brown top of his head. "I understand. You have your pride and don't like to admit to needing my help, which is why I had to make you accept it. I even got shot helping you. In the face! I'm far too foxy to have people doing that. It's a waste of a national treasure."

"Good thing you heal faster than... faster than..." Zita faltered, searching for a comparison. "Faster than I can eat a box of donuts."

"I would've said Wolverine, but that's even faster," Andy murmured. A grin tugged at his mouth.

"Ludicrous speed, yes," Wyn concurred with a small smile.

Jerome sighed and did something to Andy's phone. "It's the principle. And it still hurt. Anyway, I'm calling in my favor. I need your help to find some people DMS kidnapped. We're going to save millions of people. Possibly only thousands, but probably millions."

All joviality fled.

Zita squashed down the urge to smack Jerome on the back of his head. "Why didn't you lead with that? Of course, we'd help prevent a catastrophe like that. What's going on? We need to find a nuclear bomb or something?"

The big black man hesitated as he handed Andy's phone back. "To be honest, I'm not certain. I have a confidential informant who told me DMS is up to something. If we take too long, they're going to fumble it, a meta will make stuff explode, and people will die at a major port city."

Without hesitation, Zita said, "While we're looking into DMS, can you see if you can find someone in their system? They've got this kid, a girl named Elle, and they won't tell anyone where she is or even how she's doing. She's supposed to be living with her foster mom and getting medical treatment for a bum heart, but DMS stole her from the police. They won't give her back or tell anyone how she's doing."

Jerome sighed and sent a quick text. Then his hands flew over Wyn's phone. "Lot of missing people these days. You have her full name for me, preferably with her birth date and where she was born? Social Security number would be even better."

Zita snorted. "You wish. Wait... she might be listed as Eleanor. That's what the Pie Lady called her."

"One name, like a rock star?" Jerome grumbled and reached for his keyboard. "You've got to give me more than that."

She raised her hands in the air. "I get texted where to meet her when she's stable enough for a lesson. Elle was at the Pediatric Cardiac Unit of the Saint Martha Hospital in Springfield last time. She's fourteen. I'm pretty certain she's got charges up the wazoo for property damage stuff and probably endangerment. Maybe assault... Pues, she stole a cop car, so I guess grand theft auto too." Zita frowned, trying to figure out what else might be helpful.

"That's your student?" Wyn asked.

She shrugged. "I'm just helping train her powers, so they don't kill her, and she doesn't throw any more cars through high-school scoreboards. Football fans get cranky about stuff like that. There might be a special charge on the books for that, but I don't know."

Jerome's hands stilled for a second before they resumed a rapid clatter. Words flashed on nearby screens in a dizzying display. "You picked quite the little delinquent for a protégé. Why does that not surprise me? That might narrow it down, though. What's her power? DMS keeps track of that, though I've signed multiple agreements that say I can't tell you how."

She squinted at him, still uncertain how he typed so fast with all his fingers while not looking at the keyboard. "Elle turns into a twelve-foot-tall fuzzy pink bipedal monster with googly eyes and a serious case of drama. The kid's not my student or nothing. I'm only helping a little with her control."

Jerome grimaced at his screen. "Pink monster shapeshifter. Can't be too many of those."

"With googly eyes. One shouldn't forget that detail." Wyn seemed to be trying to hide a laugh behind her hand.

Andy didn't even make an effort to hide his snicker.

With a snort, Jerome conceded the point. "Yeah, that might be distinctive. I'll add it to the parameters. Maybe I can get in from an associated network. You said she has foster parents? Family Services will have records of that. Do you know their names?"

"The foster mom's name is Irene. She said something about wanting to adopt the kid." Zita scanned the room. Spotting a set of weights, she grabbed one and started to do slow bicep curls.

He all but rubbed his hands together in glee. "That means tons of paperwork. That'll get me data. Irene what?"

"Beats me. I can tell you what church she goes to though."

He sighed. "Right. Elle and Irene, no last names. It's a good thing I'm a miracle worker, but this is going to take time. Can you give me any more details on Irene?"

"Not a ton. Pie Lady and I don't talk much." Zita switched to a heavier barbell.

"Pie Lady? Is that a business name?" Jerome's fingers raced over the keyboard.

Zita lifted her hands in the air. "Not sure. She makes amazing pies."

The big man snorted, glancing up from his computer. "Thus, explaining how you know her."

"Even Chevalier picked up on your weakness, Arca," Wyn said.

Dismissing her friend's comment with a wave, Zita said, "Shut it, Muse. She's real nice and might be a meta."

"What can she do? Can she attack people with it? Or is that a euphemism?" Jerome never paused his typing, but his grin was wide.

Zita rolled her eyes. "Don't be ridiculous. She's not Vaudeville. If I'm right, Irene's pies make people less messed up in the head."

Her face freezing, Wyn stiffened. *If this pastry is that efficacious, why haven't you passed along some for my aunt? Or mentioned it before so I could request some from her?*

Andy glanced between them and took a step back.

Zita recognized that expression and launched into her own defense. *It was on my list of things to do, but it didn't seem right to ask Irene to bake while she's hovering over the kid in the hospital... It's also only a temporary fix, not a permanent one, from what I can tell. I figured it wasn't any better than the spell you've been using on your aunt to maintain the status quo. Quentin's first piece didn't solve his problems, but it got him to agree to therapy and stuff. I've only been able to get one more piece for him since last Thanksgiving, but it seems to help when he starts looking like he's going to jump off the no-sex wagon and onto some willing mujeres. Sorry. We still cool?*

Wyn's expression softened. *Understood. Yes, we are good, though I'd like to follow up on this later.*

I always intended to, Zita sent.

Oblivious to their conversation, Jerome snapped his fingers in the air. "I don't know why you all started spacing out, but do you have anything other than the pie angle?"

"Would Irene's cell number help? She texts me with Elle's location and if the kid is well enough to meet. DMS has it though, so don't call it. They imitated her number to trick me into a trap earlier. That's why I have to get a new one," Zita said.

"Bury the lede, will you? And it's called spoofing when they pretend the number is something it isn't. Give it to me." His keyboard clattered.

Hauling the phone from her pocket, she reattached the battery before reading the number to him. As soon as she was done, she removed the battery and tucked it away again. She picked the weight back up and switched to the other arm.

The air popped. Remus appeared. An outfit similar to Andy's hugged the speedster's impressive runner's body, but the fabric was a subdued navy and included what Zita guessed was his business logo. "I came as soon as I could get away, Jerome."

Remus spotted the trio and spoke again before they could react. Even in English, the words came out as rapidly as bullets. "What? Oh, no. Why are you all even here?" His voice rang with dismay, and his shoulders drooped.

Zita blinked at him, lowering her barbell. "Dude! Hey there!"

Jerome beamed at the newcomer, standing and thumping him on the back. "Remus! Great to see you, man."

Wyn and Andy smiled and waved.

"He randomly rolls in and out of your house, and you hug him, but you been on my back for hanging out in your garden and knocking? I mean, he's cute and all, but at least I wait for an invite." Zita winked at Remus.

He didn't return it or smile.

As he reclaimed his seat, Jerome said, "He doesn't hang upside down from my statuary as a tree sloth. And I invited him."

She crossed her arms over her chest. "That could've been anybody. Or a real animal resting after a walk."

Wyn shook her head.

"Unlikely," Andy said.

Jerome snorted. "No proof otherwise, either, and I doubt it. Remus, my friend, I have a favor to ask."

Oddly enough, Remus took a step back, his too-handsome face crinkling. "Whatever it is, no. Every time Arca and her friends do something, I end up under a microscope or otherwise paying for it."

Without stopping her workout, Zita raised an eyebrow and glanced at him. "Drama much? I mean, yes, you helped out a couple times in the past, but it wasn't anything that should've gotten you in trouble."

Andy lifted his hand in the air and wiggled it. "Eh. You kind of are trouble, Arca."

Wyn and Jerome nodded in agreement.

Remus kept talking. "Maybe it shouldn't have, but it does. I'll give you this much credit, Arca. You were right when you warned me the meta tax laws were brutal. I think I'm paying almost more than I'm making. Not that it matters when I spend more time dealing with your problems than my own sometimes. For example, your Grecian vacation or whatever that was? That meant increased government interrogations and surveillance for me, plus the anti-metahuman protestors went nuts."

Zita frowned. "What's there to protest?"

"Their only worthwhile point is that powers shouldn't put you above the law. I can't say that I disagree with them there. The rest is the usual anti-metahuman rhetoric, from us needing to spontaneously stop existing to requiring all of us to be locked away until the government requires our assistance." Remus ran a hand over his ebony hair, a single lock flopping rakishly over one eye.

Wyn winced. "Ah, yes, the nastier clauses of the Metahuman Regulatory Act that allow for the possibility of metahuman-only areas that we can only leave to perform DMS-sanctioned tasks."

"They going to take kids away from metahumans and put them in special schools too? That and the camps worked so well before," Andy said, glowering.

Zita crossed her arms. "No mames. I figured the meta haters were just a few crazies or bored racists."

"Maybe you should read the news once in a while," Andy said.

"That's what I've been trying to get you to take more seriously. If that new Everyman party gets enough of their candidates elected to the Senate and House in November, the Meta Act could pass. The wording is convoluted, but camps are one option it opens up for consideration. The President has not officially commented on the topic, so his office cannot be relied upon to veto the bill, should it pass." Wyn rubbed her forehead.

His face still set in angry lines, Andy said, "Probably waiting to see what would make opinion polls rate him higher. We really need to avoid bad publicity."

"All the pressure has turned my nonprofit from a business booster for metas into a support and legal resources group, and we are running short on both. As if it wasn't enough fun to have those idiots camped out in front of my house and business, let's not forget about the lawsuit. In addition to being annoying, it consumes valuable resources we'll need to contest the Metahuman Regulatory Act if it passes," Remus said. His handsome face almost seemed to age with worries as the conversation continued.

"Lawsuit? Someone's suing you because of us? That I hadn't heard." Wyn gaped.

"Technically, I'm involved in multiple litigations right now. You guys are specifically named in one. You didn't see the notices in the paper? Arca didn't pass on my texts? An elderly man died. His family is contesting his will because it leaves money to his caregiver and property to you guys. My nonprofit was made trustee on your behalf. If they'd claimed anything other than you're metahumans who probably coerced or otherwise used unknown powers to force him to change his will, I would've settled and given up your rights to the property."

After a second, Wyn gasped. "If they win with that, it sets up a precedent where no metahuman will ever win a court battle because they might've used unknown powers to influence things in someone's favor."

"Exactly," Remus growled.

Zita frowned. "Sorry, I thought you meant those texts to go to someone else, and then I... forgot about them. Why would anyone leave us something?"

His face thoughtful, Andy suggested, "Maybe a person we rescued?"

"The wording of the will implied the gift was more to annoy his family than to reward you. Thanks to some court cases from the Seventies, we could win, but all we really want is them to throw out the argument that a metahuman can't inherit. DMS is all over the case and me. I've given them almost everything I know about you, including how to reach you, and they still won't leave me alone. Or my family." Remus' fine body tensed more with every word, and his fists clenched.

"Is that why I've been getting so many hang-up calls? They leave long, empty voice mails too. I definitely need a new phone. Actually, all of us do because I called you guys, and now they'll have your numbers." Zita frowned.

Wyn perked up.

"Just new ones. Not fancy ones." Zita rolled her eyes.

Her friend hmphed. "I'll see if I can find some low-cost replacements."

Remus shrugged and paced a few steps, limited by the number of people crammed into the room. "That's probably why, yes.

Among the many cases we have in court regarding civil-rights violations is the fact that they don't get warrants, at least not that they've shown me or my lawyer. They've been going through my phone, my office, my taxes, and probably my underwear drawer whenever they feel like it... when they're not interrogating me about you."

Wyn's face was grim. "I'd heard they'd been taking liberties, but I didn't know it was that bad. That sounds like a ton of legal bills."

Remus ran his hands through his hair and gestured as he continued to speak. "Even at discount rates, it's incredibly expensive. Jerome, you said I should come here for something to do with my missing people?"

Andy lifted his head from where he was examining a comic book. "You lost people?"

"Over the past few months, several members of my nonprofit have gone missing, including witnesses we needed. A few were arrested for offenses like speeding, so we know DMS has them, and others are just gone... coincidentally after we added them to the witness list." Remus made a face.

Rubbing her temples, Wyn said, "Not to disparage your associates, but is it possible some simply left or perhaps chose to start over somewhere their abilities were unknown?"

Remus dug out a photo from his pocket and set it on the desk, his handsome face grave. With a parakeet hand puppet on one arm and a mischievous grin, a skinny black man stared up from it. "No way. This is the latest one, so add him to the list. He teaches kindergarten. A neighbor finally admitted that they witnessed him being carried off in manacles and shoved into a prison-type transport van last week. His only power is he can make up to five kids take naps whenever he sings a lullaby. It doesn't affect adults. Anyway, was there something you wanted, or did you just need to see how much worse their presence can make my life this time?"

"I thought you'd want to be involved in the search for your friends," Jerome said.

With a frustrated huff, Remus said, "I would, but Arca and her friends are involved now. Their mere existence is illegal. I can't afford to touch anything they're doing. Last time DMS came around asking questions, they had surveillance photos of my parents and siblings to encourage my answers. If they ask me about this meeting, I'm not certain I can—or want to—stop myself from telling them everything. I won't risk my family."

Wyn touched his shoulder. "I'm sorry you've been put through so much trouble on our behalf."

"What she said." Zita nodded.

Andy nodded.

"If you want to help undo some of the trouble you've caused, talk to my lawyer and show up in court sometime. Don't contact me directly. Please." Remus' tone was bitter.

The air snapped, and he was gone.

Another pop, and the speedster was back. He pressed a business card into Wyn's hands. "Here's my lawyer's contact info. Jerome, you have my number if you have a completely legal and aboveboard question for me that you don't mind DMS hearing."

The air cracked again, and Remus was gone.

"People come and go so quickly here," Wyn murmured.

Chapter Three

"**Going back to the possible port disaster,** do you think the explosion happens because DMS tries to grab the wrong meta?" Andy broke the silence following Remus' departure.

Wyn touched a few fingers to her mouth. "Possible. However, the problem would be identifying the target with the ability to do so. Their choices in captures so far seem rather indiscriminate. Arca's friend Elle has charges against her, but Remus' acquaintances seem a more varied bunch."

"Remus' people are largely upstanding locals with nothing worse than a few speeding tickets," Jerome confirmed.

Wyn tapped an elegant finger on her own lips. *We may be limiting our searches unduly. Whoever they grab must either have abilities connected to explosions, or they have to be very powerful. Remember what Chiron said? When a meta he would consider a god dies, their power explodes.*

Well, so much for narrowing it down to metas who blow shit up or who might blow up. Zita sighed.

Jerome's hands continued to fly over his keyboard, the constant click of keys almost rhythmic. "If there's a literally explosive metahuman, they've kept a low profile. The closest I've found are the Living Flame, the Icelandic madman who burned down his asylum, and that Pretorius guy who threw lava blobs."

"Plasma. Pretorius threw plasma," Andy muttered. "There's a difference. Lava is molten rock. Plasma is an entire fourth state of matter, basically super-heated gas."

Jerome canted his head at the shorter man. "The Geek Force is strong in this one."

With a wave of her hand, Zita cut through the blather. "Whatever. It's all deadly hot goo. It'd be bad if DMS got their hands on any of those three."

Wyn shuddered. "Given what we've witnessed with two of those, it would be best if we could prevent their capture."

After setting down the weight, Zita said slowly, "I'd hope the news would've mentioned if Pretorius was anywhere other than that Brazilian jail. Several ports are near volcanos or in earthquake zones... or both. Jen Stone might be missing and all, but what if she triggered one of those? She's not wound real tight without her meds. Somebody I know would have heard she'd been spotted, so I can ask about her."

Just someone? Or a heartless mercenary you like to ogle? Wyn arched an eyebrow.

Be nice, Wyn. She doesn't need our help to mess up her relationship, Andy sent before Zita could protest. Aloud, he said, "True. Jennifer Stone could resurface. We did. Add her to the list of possibles."

The black man only grunted.

Her eyes narrowing, Wyn said, "Who were you searching for, Jerome? Who's your missing person?"

The only signs he'd noticed the question were how his body tensed and the studied nonchalance of his answer. "What's that?"

"You said we all have people we want to find. Remus wants to find his missing associates. We came to you to find the girl and Irene. Who are you looking for?" The witch narrowed her eyes at him.

Although the typing stopped, words continued to scroll by on one screen. Jerome studied the heavy onyx and gold ring he wore on a finger before answering. "I've been getting tip-offs from this woman. She's the one who told me I needed to be there to help when Zeus freed those prisoners last year, and she's warned me off a couple of things that ended badly for those involved. While I can't verify everything, she's been pretty accurate. Anyway, DMS has her, and we need to get her out before they move her. She said corporate or government hands upon her would cause an explosion in a port city when they reached it." Jerome sighed.

"What's your friend's name, Jerome? I can work a finding spell if I have her full name. If you have one of her belongings, that will work even better," Wyn said. One hand dipped into her purse and retrieved the arrowhead she used for the spell. Another quick check resulted in a large, folded map.

He cleared his throat, and his entire body radiated tension. "I don't know. She shows up in my dreams."

Andy and Wyn groaned in unison.

Zita rolled her eyes. "Dude, you were razzing me for not knowing last names and Social Security numbers, and all you have to go on is Dream Auntie? Black lady, dresses like she's going to church, interrupts fun dreams with cryptic hints of impending doom and demands for you to pay attention?"

"You know her? That sounds like her other than the pay attention part." Jerome's shoulders relaxed.

Her tone dry, Wyn said, "I suspect the admonition is specific to Arca."

"Preventing us from getting a good night's sleep is one of her favorite hobbies," Andy added.

Jerome rubbed a hand over his mouth. "Glad I'm not losing it. I'd hate to be as nutty as Arca. This is why I asked you to come here. I can't locate Dream Auntie without your help. We're missing necessary information, so before we can make any plans, we need to gather intel."

Her face unhappy, Wyn said, "What do we need?"

"The location of the prison and DMS' databases. While the original law designating truly impressive funds is a matter of public record, very little is available on DMS' inner workings. Their data services and prison contracts were awarded to some corporation nobody's heard of. And I mean nobody."

"Surely, with the amount of government paperwork required to do anything, they can't be that obscure," Wyn said.

"DMS has all kinds of waivers, so they can. I'm still digging, but it's a shell company of some sort. It's remarkably obscure, especially since the prison alone has an obscene budget allocated to 'create a corrective facility to provide for unique metahuman challenges and allow rehabilitation.' The Senate Advisory Committee that receives their reports doesn't enter them into public record or share any information."

Her attention wandering, Zita lost track of his explanation until Wyn stepped on her foot. *Pay attention.*

Jerome continued, "So. Our goal will be to find the server farm where they're hiding the data. Once we find that, we can mine it for information on the prison and our missing people."

Wyn held up a hand. "It's possible we could skip rifling through their databases. One of my spells could locate Elle if I had her full name and preferably a picture. Perhaps we could try with the full names of a few of Remus' missing people?"

His expression conflicted, Jerome took a minute before he finally nodded. "Remus gave me names and birth dates, so I can pass you a few of those. We can try that first, but we should plan for what we'll do if that doesn't work."

"It's never failed before. Give me one. Remus' teacher friend would be a superb choice since we know he was recently captured." Wyn's tone was serene. She glanced around the cluttered office. "Perhaps we should move this to your kitchen table? I need space to open up a paper map."

They all trooped into the kitchen.

Wyn carefully spread out a map of the United States. She cast her spell while dangling an arrowhead over the center of the map, the golden magic sending the arrowhead spinning...

And then darting off the edge of the map.

"Is it supposed to do that?" Jerome whispered.

Zita frowned. "I don't think so."

"You're gonna need a bigger map," Andy said.

Jerome snorted.

Wyn frowned, and the glow vanished, the arrowhead falling still. "I'll have to recast with a world map, but I don't see them building a federal prison in another country. It's far more likely they've got a magic-blocking charm so they can better handle magic users. Unfortunately, my world map was accidentally destroyed, so I'll have to buy a new one, unless Jerome has one?"

He shook his head.

Shoulders slumping, Wyn tucked away her spell supplies in her purse.

"Well, shall we go back to my study and see what Irene's phone number netted us? We'll plan to find the databases and the prison, and if Muse can cut the search short later, we'll run with that."

"Why is it so hard to find their data?" Zita had to ask.

"They didn't want what the rest of the government uses for whatever reason, so they hired excellent technology consultants, including one who may or may not be one of DC's most eligible and charming bachelors three years running." Jerome winked at them and ran a hand over his smooth head.

"Subtle," Andy said.

Jerome ignored the other man. "They came up with their own solution by picking and choosing pieces from their assorted experts' suggested courses of actions. As a result, they keep their records completely separate from the Internet and even from the government. Other agencies basically incorporate placeholders that refer to DMS, and that's it. However, I've got a good guess how it's set up, so once I get into the system, it'll be my bitch."

"But you don't know where it is?" Wyn's eyebrows rose.

The big man cleared his throat. "Not yet. DMS is really strict with their prisoner records. From what I can tell, their data is downloaded every Friday to wherever they keep their server farm, and then it all drops off the Internet until the next update."

Andy wrinkled his nose. "That seems a bit iffy."

"Theoretically, that communication is kept separate from regular traffic on government lines with a secure VPN and RSA encryption, but who knows? I got the feeling their decision-makers didn't understand technology nearly as well as they thought they did." Jerome shrugged.

"Boy, that sounds familiar," Andy muttered.

Wyn nodded.

Zita blinked. She lifted a finger. "Uh, what?"

With a half laugh, Jerome continued. "To keep things easy enough for even Arca to understand... if we could find a few agents who will connect to it, we can insert a file that'll send me the server location before it disconnects. Our ultimate goal is to get the data we need, so the only alternative to my little MITM attack program—that's the file I mentioned—is to see where their people have gone lately, which their phones might tell us. When DMS agents want to access information, they have to go to a secured database site and view it there or submit a request and wait. Any data they get the second method is wiped within a week or two."

That'd explain part of why Miguel has been complaining how long it's taking him to solve cases. Zita asked, "Are you certain?"

Jerome nodded. "Mostly. They might have a bit of code to make the data self-destruct after the set time period, though since I haven't seen it, I can't swear on it."

Andy hummed a bit of a song.

"Bingo," Jerome said and joined in.

Wyn's tone was distracted. "Enough movie theme music, boys. I don't think Tom Cruise is going to come rescue us."

"Is he a vigilante too?" Zita asked.

Someone threw a wad of a paper at her, but at least the humming stopped.

Zita caught it and tossed it into the recycling bin. "What? That was a legit question. That level of paranoia can't be helping them do their jobs. They're blinding themselves, which is why Parzarri was able to operate his little drug empire."

His attention mostly on his screens, Jerome nodded. "Bingo. It's good data security, but hard to use given the necessary national distribution of DMS agents."

Don't get angry, Zita, but I have to suggest it. It's the easiest way. Wyn bit her lower lip. "So, we need a DMS agent's laptop? What if we could get you a single DMS agent's phone?"

As she comprehended which agent her friend meant, Zita stopped moving, alarm shooting through her. *Leave my brother out of this! This is exactly the sort of stuff Miguel needs to keep far away from!*

Andy grimaced. *What if—*

No. He stays squeaky clean. Zita glared at her friends.

Jerome rubbed his head. "That's a great idea. Their GPS might give us the location too if they've been to one of the secured sites lately. Both phone and laptop would be better than only one or the other, though. The problem is finding someone who is actively chasing down metas and might need to submit an update soon."

Before she could stop herself, Zita laughed, a sharp bark of sound. "Oh, that's easy. DMS sent teams after me today, and they caught Irene. She might be in a hospital or under surveillance or even under arrest."

Jerome seemed hopeful. "Did they arrest her? If I can get even the phones of the people arresting her, I should be able to track where they took her. I already started a trace based on the number you gave me earlier."

"I don't know. She went down fast and hard under some dart that was meant for me, so I left to avoid them dosing her again. One of her sons works at a hospital, and he was doing something with a medical kit when I left." Zita switched to doing curls with her other arm.

Jerome hmmed. "We need to move fast, then. If they arrested her, she's going to disappear off the local radar in less than a week. Her injury—and I hope she'll be okay—might help us though, if they took her to a local clinic or hospital. When today was it?"

"Maybe an hour and a half now," Zita guessed.

He brightened. "Then we have a chance. Can you tell me where the park was? If I search in a radius for all the local hospitals and police stations in that general area, I should be able to find her."

"Sure." Zita dutifully recounted everything she knew.

Ten minutes later, Jerome waved his hand, and an image of the Pie Lady appeared on a screen. "Is this your Irene?"

"Sí," Zita said.

He stretched and cracked his knuckles. "Excellent. I should be able to follow the trail from her to find the kid, but it'll take a while to cruise through all the records. When I have something on that, I'll tell you. In the meantime, Irene's in the hospital overnight. So, we need to see if any DMS agents are buzzing around her... ones whose electronics I can play with."

"The hospital's keeping her? That's not a good sign." Zita sped up her lifts, and her leg vibrated with suppressed energy.

Wyn touched Zita's shoulder. "They might have kept her for observation given the unusual response to sedation. It's also possible they're keeping her for a medically preferred but unnecessary procedure just to prove obstructionist to DMS. Small towns and their hospitals tend to close ranks to protect their own."

After a moment, Zita twitched her shoulders, trying to loosen the tension that seemed lodged in the muscles. "True, and DMS does have a habit of alienating pretty much everyone."

Andy snorted. "I can't think of anyone else who does that."

"You shouldn't talk about Chevalier like that, Wingspan. He's not a pompous, self-serving windbag like DMS, even if he had the poor taste to take their paycheck," Zita said.

Jerome folded his arms over his broad chest.

"Ah, I didn't mean you, Chevalier, I meant—" Andy sputtered.

The other man snickered. "We all know who you were talking about."

Zita raised her eyebrows. "Do we? Or are certain people just hating haters? Seriously, though, we need to check on Irene."

Wyn covered her mouth with a hand, and her voice trembled with suppressed laughter. "We'll verify Irene's recovery first or heal her if necessary. She can give us more details on Elle, and then perhaps we can find her without pilfering anything. If she cannot provide sufficient detail, we'll see if we can identify the DMS agents in her vicinity and figure out how to get hold of their electronics."

Pointing his finger at her, Jerome nodded rapidly. "Yes! Exactly what I was thinking. Beautiful and smart. That's why you're in charge of these two."

Zita harrumphed. "It's rude to point, and she's not the boss of us."

Jerome snorted. "You all succeed far too often to be the rolling ball of chaos you present to the world."

"Maybe we're just really good at chaos," Andy said.

After checking one of his screens, Jerome typed something. "If you say so. Getting back to my plan, then. DMS might increase their security or change something if they were aware of a breach. So, we borrow. Muse, you can be our femme fatale. While you're drawing their attention, Arca can steal their laptops. Maybe pick their pockets for their phones. She connects to my special web page, clicks on my virus link, and then puts their stuff back."

Wyn nodded and toyed with a lock of hair. "I can do that."

Zita had a problem. "Dude, I don't know how to pick pockets."

"What do you call what you did to that creepy witch in Brazil?" Jerome paused in his typing, though his attention appeared to be on the screen, skimming lists.

"Tiffany basically distracted herself with all her ineffective fighting tactics. I took advantage of that. Anyone competent would have noticed. I mean, not you because you were shot in the head at the time and lying around, and Wingspan might've been playing in the quicksand—"

A hand touched her shoulder, interrupting Zita's commentary. "Perhaps you should stop before you completely chew off that foot you have stuck in your mouth," Wyn murmured.

Zita grunted.

The big man rubbed his hands together. "Great. We'll keep the details flexible until we know what the exact situation will be. Once we've got our information and the location, we move to the second act."

I have a bad feeling about what he's hinting at. Andy visibly braced himself before asking aloud, "I'm afraid to ask, but I'm going to do so anyway. What is that?"

Jerome smiled. Practically purred. "Rescuing Dream Auntie and Elle."

Wyn held up a finger. "Wait, you don't just want to borrow a laptop and phone or break into an office building. You're talking about breaking into a high-security penitentiary."

"Yep." Jerome enunciated the final P, almost snapping out the letter. "Dream Auntie, as you call her, needs to get out of there. She showed me what would happen. It's bad. Very, very bad, and we can't let all those people die. I'm assuming you won't leave the kid behind if she's in rough shape too."

Andy hit his own forehead with a smack. "Of course. Why didn't I see that coming?"

With a groan, Zita shook her head. "That's why Remus left. It's not us. It's this nutcase. He wants nothing to do with anything even remotely illegal since they're riding his ass so hard."

Wyn shook her head.

"Not that his idea isn't terrible, but I'm pretty certain Remus left because of us. Maybe just you, Arca," Andy said.

She punched his shoulder gently with the hand not holding a barbell. *This is such a bad idea.*

Andy sent his agreement but couldn't resist teasing her. *When Zita thinks something's too risky...*

Wyn frowned and massaged her temples. *But do we have any alternative? Not if Dream Auntie—why have we never asked that woman's name?—is right. She has had uncanny accuracy with her previous predictions.*

Vague-ass ones, Zita sent. *And we don't really converse. She usually just barges in and starts bellowing doom and gloom.*

Andy asked, *Do you think she's been trying to avoid talking to us other than to give warnings?*

That's a legitimate question. My assumption has been that her power is weak enough she won't waste words on conversation, but perhaps she's hiding. I wonder why? Perhaps we could help Jerome find the databases. Then breaking into things might not be necessary. Wyn brought a finger to her lips and bit the tip.

Zita grunted. *I'll go in on that, provided it's not my brother's stuff or someone we access through him. Miguel stays out of this.*

His hands rubbed nervously on the sides of his shorts. Andy nodded. *Agreed.*

"Hey! You guys are making faces at each other again and zoning out. What's going on?" Jerome asked. "You're awful picky about this for folks who moonlight as vigilantes."

Wyn sniffed and moved her hand from her mouth. "That's different. We react to obvious power imbalances. We do not purposefully seek trouble, and we generally obey as many laws as possible."

Andy snorted and elbowed Zita. "Most of us, anyway."

She poked him back. "Don't pick on Muse like that." *She's an only child and doesn't know how to defend herself.*

"Hey!" Wyn said. "No fighting, children."

Andy snickered. *My bad, Wyn.*

We all know you didn't mean me. Wyn tossed a long pale lock of hair over her shoulder.

His eyes dark, Jerome stared at them. "So, are you guys in or what?

"We'll help you with the first part, but we're not committing to burglarizing any DMS installation, let alone a penitentiary," Wyn said.

Andy and Zita nodded.

Jerome shrugged. "I don't see a way around it later, but if it helps any, it's technically owned by the contractor. If it were regular government, there'd be enough paperwork to track it better. However, when you're up against a secretive government agency with no oversight and fewer scruples, sometimes you have to crack a few eggs."

"Or break into a few prisons?" Andy's brows raised.

"You say tomato, I say tomahto. If you're not willing to even consider the idea of a jailbreak, how exactly were you planning to help your girl or Dream Auntie?" Jerome stopped typing, but he rested his hand on a desktop machine as he waited for their answer.

Her stomach twisting, Zita had to admit, "I don't think we'd gotten a chance to think that far ahead."

I really don't like this, Andy sent.

Again, what are our choices? Wyn chose not to speak aloud.

Zita sped up the rate of her bicep curls. *I don't see any.*

"If we were to participate in this, we cannot be caught. That'll mean keeping as many of our abilities hidden as possible. It'd be horrible publicity, and with the metahuman bills and the elections in only a few months, we can't afford to seem..." Wyn let her words trail off.

Andy supplied the words. "Like supervillains."

Jerome relaxed. "Wanting to not get caught is a given. I'm too pretty for prison. I'd rather not face treason charges for hacking my way through ultra-posh super-secret databases either."

"Is that the technical term for the DMS system?" Andy asked.

The other man snorted. "They wish they were that cool."

Unhappy with the conversation, Zita scowled. "We can discuss what happens later when we've all had a chance to think things through. You know where the hospital is, so tell us, and we'll go check on Irene."

The big man laughed. "It's not that I don't trust you... actually, that is the problem. You'd probably run off without me if you thought you could."

She opened her mouth to protest his all-too-true statement, but another tap on her arm stopped her.

Allow me. Focusing a brilliant smile on Jerome, Wyn said, "How about a compromise? We check on Irene and get the names of any agents in her vicinity. They've likely accessed DMS' files on Irene and Arca in the past week and would make good targets for you should my spell... be blocked again."

Jerome snapped his fingers. "Fine, but you're helping me if I need to get the data. It's unlikely they'd overlook a big, handsome guy like me pawing through their things."

"Well, then. If you tell us the hospital, once we've verified Irene's health, we'll get those names for you. You can stay here to begin work on your program while we're doing all of that in case it's necessary to get information later. Or perhaps something that would allow us to anonymously deliver a few of DMS' secrets to the media." Wyn smiled at him.

Multiple screens suddenly went blank. Jerome grinned. "Oh, I'm coming with. The code's ready to go. I need to set up a few things to hide our tracks and get the physical gear ready to go. We can be all set in maybe a half hour."

"That's very prepared of you," Wyn said, her eyebrows arching. Party line went down for a moment, and her eyes seemed distant.

He nodded. "I need to find a portable system. Might have one in the garage. Be right back. I'll see if I have any good satellite tracking devices too, in case we need those. If not, I'll have to see how fast I can order them." Springing from his chair, he strode out of the room.

Zita and her friends exchanged glances.

Warmth spread through her mind as party line returned.

Is anyone else frightened that he has equipment like that readily available? I skimmed his mind. He did seem sincere in his goals and mostly truthful. What he didn't mention is that he has a gap of a few days in his memory when he was working for DMS. He's planning to check his own files to see if they contain any information about the missing time, in addition to acting on Dream Auntie's warning. Wyn didn't speak aloud, instead studying her hands.

Well, I'm not letting him handle my electronics again, Andy sent.

Zita had one final comment. *So, you going to keep making fun of me for not having smart phones anymore when Jerome can pull a customized virus out of nowhere?*

Honest as always, Andy sent, *Yes.*

Absolutely, Wyn agreed.

Chapter Four

A couple hours later, Wyn and Zita marched down the hall of the hospital in disguise, gripping Bibles. Just before they reached Irene's room, a trio of men swept out of it.

Two had the musculature to fill out their suits in a flattering way and the habit of repeatedly scanning the area that made Zita suspect they were cops or military. The buzz cut on the tallest had her leaning toward the latter. Unlike his companions, the third moved with a lanky, uneven gait exaggerated by his too-large clothing in an oddly familiar manner. His attention was on whatever he was typing into his phone. As she watched, one of the others had to grab the awkward man to keep him from bumping into a wall.

Wyn pulled out her phone and made a show of displaying it to Zita as both women turned their heads away from the agents.

Zita barely stopped herself from groaning when she recognized the protuberant eyes and baby face of the clumsy man. *What's Justin Smith doing out here?*

Who? Oh, the psychiatrist whose nose you broke on a blind date? I remember him. He interviewed us and wanted his associates to arrest you, more from spite than any concrete reason. Her friend's mental voice held a laugh.

Yes, the junior shrink who I rescued from a bunch of high schoolers who were kicking his butt. It's not my fault he has a grudge against me. Zita kept her head lowered.

After their gazes passed over Wyn and Zita, Justin and one of the others left. The third, Buzz Cut, planted himself in the empty chair outside of Irene's room.

Good thing you're not you, then. Right now, you're a man on a mission of mercy. Her friend reminded her of the illusions that masked them both.

Zita caught a glimpse of herself in the glass as they went by. While Wyn appeared to be a crisply dressed blond woman in her twenties, Zita was a short, middle-aged white man with a craggy face, an ill-fitting suit, and a fedora. In reality, she wore her Arca form, and she idly wondered if Wyn's current illusion layered on top of her usual Muse one or not.

Seated in a visitor's chair, the guard pulled out his phone after another quick scan of the hall. The tinny sounds of a baseball game emanated from it until they approached, and he lowered it with an irritated grunt. His posture had a slight hunch to the left that she associated with a gun holster too close to an armpit. After a moment, Zita recognized Buzz Cut as a landscaper from the park.

No laptop. Wyn sighed in her mind.

Did you really expect it to be that easy? Zita held her Bible a little closer.

Her friend sauntered beside her. *No, but wouldn't it have been enchanting if it had been?*

The man at the door eyed them. "You look familiar."

Caramba. Did you make us people from a movie again? Zita sent.

Wyn giggled. "I modeled in an ad for the local paper? Perhaps that's where you saw me?" Over party line, she explained, *Illusions are easier to hold when I can picture them clearly, like when I've watched a motion picture. Most people have poor recognition of images out of context, so the odds of being recognized aren't high.*

Unless he's seriously an old movie buff, we should be safe. Most people wouldn't have seen that particular film.

I certainly haven't. How much trouble are we in? Zita checked the hall, picking out the easiest escape route. Without releasing her friend's arm, as she'd been repeatedly warned that would break the illusion, she eased sideways into a more defensive pose.

Her friend sniffed mentally. *It's a given that you wouldn't recognize anyone who wasn't in a kung fu flick. We'll be fine. Both of the actors I chose died of old age years ago.*

He shook his head, his brow furrowing. "The ancient guy with a mohawk at the motel only offered us a national paper."

Zita remembered the clerk. He'd been supremely uninterested in his customers, or working, or anything other than the tiny laptop he'd hunched over. *Sounds like they're staying the same place Quentin and I did when we drove through last Thanksgiving. It's the only motel within thirty miles, or at least, the only one listed on the app my brother checked.*

Well, if we have to steal a computer, we'll know where to find them. Wyn simpered at him. "If the ad's been picked up by bigger papers, perhaps I'll get a bonus! I'm saving up for an apartment in the city. Anyway, Dad and I came by to see how Miss Irene was doing. We were going to pray with her; hospital visits are part of Dad's duties as a church deacon. Can we stop in for a minute?"

Zita tried to seem suitably grave and serious and fatherly. She brought the Bible up higher to cradle it against her chest and struggled to think of what her papá would've done. *Given he's been dead since I was five, I don't remember much more than his smile and laughter. Tell a bad joke maybe?*

Before she could come up with a suitable piece of humor, Buzz Cut spoke again. "Can I see some ID?"

Wyn gazed deep into his eyes, and party line dropped. She touched his arm lightly and passed him a piece of paper. It looked like some kind of receipt. "Our IDs are all in order."

His gaze trapped in hers and his face oddly blank, the guard nodded as he returned the paper. "So they are. No more than five minutes. She's under sedation, so she may not wake up."

With a smile, Wyn withdrew her hand and tucked away the paper. "We'll be quick. Thank you."

"The Lord will hear our prayers. Bless you, my son," Zita murmured as she passed by, managing not to startle at the gruff man's voice that had replaced her own. She stopped herself from making the sign of the cross with effort.

Wyn paused to wink at the man. Once the door closed behind them, she released Zita's arm. "Are you okay? For a moment, your expression made it seem as if you were contemplating a trip to powder your nose."

"I'm fine." Zita rolled her eyes and tried to focus on their surroundings.

The hospital room resembled every other one she'd ever seen. Beige speckled linoleum, rattling air conditioner by the window, and the sting of antiseptic unsuccessfully hiding the odors of illness. It was tiny, barely spacious enough to hold the metal bed and assorted beeping machinery around it. A cheap, metal chair with lumpy padding was the only concession to visitors.

Her attention fell on the huddled shape in the bed, and Zita swore quietly in Spanish.

Irene lay quiet, far too pale and still for the vibrant woman she'd met with in the park. Tubes wound in and out of her nose, and an IV dripped nearby.

"She wasn't that bad earlier! At least this isn't intensive care... I think." Zita hurried to the bed, setting down the Bible on the edge. Her hand, reassuringly brown again, danced over the sleeping woman's wrist, pressing for a pulse. The slow, steady throb against her fingertips relieved her more than any of the fancy equipment nearby could have.

As her friend joined her, Wyn nodded toward the door, letting her magic fall and revealing her usual Muse illusion underneath. "Remember, you're visible as Arca unless we're touching. Keep the door shut, and I'll see if my healing spell can help. I'll put our disguises back up once the spell's over."

With a worried glance at Irene, Zita wedged the visitor's chair under the doorknob. She lowered her voice to a whisper as she returned to her friend's side and grabbed her arm. "That'll buy us a few seconds, far better than trying to barricade it against armed people. Given that DMS is a dumping ground for the rejects of other agencies, make that paranoid, armed people."

Your brother Miguel works for DMS. Her friend whispered words in the usual cadence of her healing spell, lifting her hands in a familiar, fluid series of gestures. A gentle green glow came from her fingers and twined around Irene.

Zita nodded and concentrated on her answer rather than Irene's state. She clutched Wyn's upper arm. *Only because he upset some politician and his FBI boss said the transfer would either give Miguel the political savvy he needed or let DMS take the fall for his political gaffes.*

Despite her obvious focus on the magic, Wyn had enough attention left to tease Zita. *Ah, so your lack of diplomacy is a family trait, then, that Quentin somehow overcame. Would you mind allowing circulation in that arm? It'd make spell casting easier.*

Oops, sorry. Zita eased her grip and tried not to wiggle and distract her friend. An interminable length of time that was probably only a minute later, the spell ended.

Irene's eyes fluttered open.

As Zita watched, Wyn's Muse illusion turned to the dainty form she'd used to enter the room, and her own arm appeared to grow and pale.

Patting Irene's hand, the witch said softly, "Quickly, Irene... what's Elle's name?"

The older woman gazed fuzzily at her. Her voice was raspy and rough. "Why would Lauren Bacall ask about little Eleanor Johnson?"

The doorknob rattled.

"Hallelujah!" Zita exclaimed loudly, in case someone was listening. Over party line, she groaned. *Johnson?*

I'll need more than that for the spell, but it may be sufficient for Jerome's searches. Wyn smiled at Irene and gave her arm a little squeeze. "Eleanor Johnson, what a lovely name. Do you know her middle name?"

As the door pushed the chair back a few inches, Zita whispered, "We need to go."

In the hospital bed, Irene's face wrinkled. "Her middle name? Are you with Humphrey Bogart? Am I dead?"

"No, you'll be fine." A thought slipped onto party line. *Nobody will recognize us, my little brown culo.*

Hush your mouth. As the man outside pushed it open and the lightweight visitor's chair skidded out of the way, Wyn said, "Amen. We'll see you at church."

Irene struggled to focus on them. "Church?"

Folding his unimpressive arms over his chest, Justin demanded, "Why was that chair there?" While the psychologist hadn't drawn a weapon, his companion's hand hovered over his holster.

Her eyes wide, Wyn said, "We needed more space to pray. I'm sorry, we slid it over there and didn't pay attention to where it ended up. I'm sorry."

"Fine, but you can't be in here," Justin said.

Irene moaned.

"We'll leave her to rest. It's a miracle that she's waking up, though! Hallelujah! Jesus rules!" Zita said. As she gathered up the Bible she'd dropped on the side of the bed, she tugged Wyn to her feet and sailed toward the exit.

"Amen, Daddy. Let's go," Wyn said, drifting along beside Zita as if she didn't have a care.

Justin typed something on his phone, suspicion on his face as he watched them go. Even though his expression never changed, his partner subtly tensed as they edged out.

When they stepped into the hall, Buzz Cut grabbed Wyn's free arm. He said something in a low, urgent voice to her.

Zita started to slide into a defensive position but remembered at the last minute not to let go of her friend or seem too suspicious. *Kick to the head and run?*

No. I've got this. With a giggle, Wyn winked at him. "I could be free later. We'll see."

He grinned.

As the two women walked toward the meeting place they'd arranged with the guys, Zita managed not to ask until they'd made it out of the hospital. Once they were clear, though, she blurted out the question. "What'd he want?"

"A date. He said they're eating dinner at the motel bar later and invited me to join him. So now we know when he won't be in his room." Her friend flicked her hair over her shoulder.

Aloud, Zita said, "The motel's familiar to me. It won't be a problem to get in their door unless they've added locks or alarms. I know where the restaurant is too."

"We expected nothing less of you." Wyn giggled.

Zita elbowed her.

"Time for phase two," Jerome crowed, popping out of the bushes. "Did I hear we're meeting back up tonight for some quality computer time while Muse goes barhopping?"

Andy followed him out, frowning. "He's enjoying this far too much."

***

While relatively secure, dates in inaccessible places weren't terribly convenient.

With only a few hours to spare before the night's mission to grab electronics, Zita was almost late to the date she'd already postponed twice before, thanks to work and vigilantism. Per the description she'd been given, the western Pennsylvania clearing had one lightning-struck tree, two stumps, and a small gritstone cliff sheer enough to make her hands itch to climb it before she even took a form with fingers. At least the greenery seemed free of poison ivy and sumac, and it was the type of hidden nook she delighted in.

It appeared deserted, but that didn't bother her. He was here. Some visceral part of her recognized it, thrilling and comforting her. For fun, she tried to spot her date before he emerged from hiding.

As she landed on a stump and switched from a golden eagle to Arca, Freelance materialized from the second of the three spots she'd narrowed it down to. Every motion of his finely honed physique held that inimitable, predatory, and economical grace she'd only seen otherwise on a stalking cat. As usual, he wore fitted body armor, goggles, and a balaclava that hid his face, with a belt dripping with all kinds of pouches and doubtless entertaining tools.

"Hey. Sorry if I'm late, especially after we had to move this a couple times!" Zita tossed a pair of canvas shoes on the ground and stepped into them, then removed a handgun from her cleavage. Digging in a pocket with her free hand, she pulled out a plastic bag with bullets.

His focus on the weapon was visible. After a second, he tapped his goggles, zooming in on the gun before lifting his gaze to her.

"About this... Oye. Yes, it's yours. I owe you an apology. Sorry." Zita rubbed the firearm nervously, trying to clean it a little. She strode toward him, holding the items out, and coming to a stop a few feet away.

To her dismay, stupid gabble poured from her. "I grabbed it after it got dropped because I didn't want some kid tripping over it. Then, we didn't start meeting up on the regular until February, but I forgot about it. This should've gotten back to you months ago."

He didn't reply, but he drew closer.

Her mouth curved downward and kept running for some reason. "I don't know if it's got sentimental value or not for you, but I know how important little things can be. My... a friend had her belongings stolen from the quarantine warehouse in DC and never got any of them back. It wasn't anything fancy like your gun, but it was one of the few remembrances they had of someone... special." Remembering the loss of her father's medallion made her twitchy. Her one leg vibrated with the need to move, to hurl herself into climbing or freerunning or something. Anything would do, provided it wasn't standing around talking about problems she couldn't see a way out of.

Rough fabric brushed over her naked hands as he accepted the items. His posture relaxed slightly. Even though he automatically ran a rapid check on the weapon, his gaze didn't appear to waver from her, as if he could tell by feel if it were loaded.

"Anyway, sorry for the delay and if it's sweaty at all. It won't fit in my pockets." She waved her hand at her Spandex-like outfit and gave him a half-hearted smile, tilting her head back to keep her gaze on his face. "I guess that's a downside to secret identities."

He tucked the baggie and gun into the small backpack he wore. "Thank you."

Relief loosened the knot that had been in her stomach, and she flexed her fingers as she relaxed. "It's a sweet gun, even if the grip's a bit too big for my hands."

Freelance was still. His head canted to the side, but he didn't retreat. "Your accent."

Zita blinked, realizing she'd stopped using it during the conversation. She never dropped it in any form other than her natural one. Except for now, apparently. After running a hand over her hair to verify it was Arca's long, tumbled mass instead of her short, uneven one, she grumbled and gave his shoulder a light tap. "Weird, I always use that when I'm Arca... I blame you for making me all comfortable and shit."

He remained motionless.

Nerves flared, and she stepped back. Zita dropped back into the accent, laying it on even heavier than usual. "Now you're making me jumpy, and it's going to get thicker and thicker until I sound like the comic relief on a telenovela. Ay."

A strange sound escaped his voice changer as if he hadn't known whether to laugh or clear his throat.

Zita watched him. "We're good, right? Not going to tell on me?"

"No." His answer was a whisper of sound.

She smiled and bumped his elbow with hers and let the accent drop again, this time on purpose. "Good. Speaking of funny, I need to get a new number, and you have to ditch Wingspan's old phone. DMS squeezed my number out of someone, so they're probably reading all our texts."

To her surprise, he dug another phone out of one pouch and offered it to her. It was very similar to the cheap model she'd been using, but the screen was bigger and more complicated. He spoke again. "Text with app. Found footprints here, multiple men, military. Two days ago."

Zita groaned. "Wasn't that when we were originally supposed to climb until I canceled last minute?"

He nodded.

With part of her mind wondering if it was the same app Jerome had put on her friends' phones, she accepted the small device. "I am so sorry. This is really thoughtful, thanks."

"Not your fault. Who?"

With a slash of her hand, she dismissed Remus' culpability. "It doesn't matter. He didn't have a choice. You should know that DMS is apparently kidnapping metas left and right, so keep yourself and your team safe." She exhaled slowly, trying to decide how much to tell him. "We found out about that whole chingado mess when we went looking for a kid. I've been helping her control her shifting off and on, and they've hidden her somewhere. You want to stay far, far away from all that."

Freelance tilted his head at her. "Trouble?"

"A ton of it." She ran a hand over her hair, back and forth, and her leg started jiggling again. "If it goes badly, your reputation may end up being better than mine. Did you want to... stop dating? I don't want to drag you into our problems."

Quiet stretched between them for a minute.

His mechanical voice split the silence. "Available 8 August, 1700 hours?"

Relief flooded her. "I'll keep you out of the mess, no worries. And yeah, that's after work, so I can make it."

"Not helpless." Somehow, his voice changer seemed almost insulted.

A smile snuck out at the ridiculousness of the concept. "No, and I like that about you. However, you don't need to be dragged into this. Someone's already gotten hurt just meeting with me. Anyway, I don't want to talk about it no more. It's bad enough I have to meet up with my friends and probably do something stupid later tonight."

The mercenary padded over and lifted a rope. He gestured to the cliff.

"Oye, you read my mind! Then again, maybe we shouldn't climb here if they're hiding somewhere nearby." Her spirits fell, and her shoulders slumped. *I only wanted time...*

He shook his head, a slight, sharp movement. "Checked. Camera suffered accident."

Good humor restored, Zita rocked on her feet and grinned. She flexed her fingers. "Convenient. Funny how these things happen around us. Let's get to it, then."

Chapter Five

Goodness, what have you been eating? You weigh a ton, Wyn complained over party line.

A tiny bell and the sway of movement told Zita they'd entered the bar, and she tried not to move, despite the several uncomfortable objects piled up around her capuchin form. *Only because you've got wimpy arms. If you'd move up to a larger barbell...*

I'm fine with what I have. Your weight is the issue. Despite their mental conversation, Wyn's voice lilted in a greeting, her words ending in a giggle.

A man's voice hailed her. It sounded like Buzz Cut, the guard from the hospital.

The point is to go to heavier weights, not fart around with the lowest possible one forever. Besides, it's not me. That's all the other stuff you crammed in here, like the big-ass hardback books. I'm six pounds max right now. You're lucky you didn't have to lug the mobile wireless spit thing too. Zita tried not to wiggle, but the edge of... something... bit into her side until she was certain her kidney would bear its imprint for the rest of her life. Her ear itched. Voices were muffled by the fabric, so she had to listen hard to follow their conversation.

Wyn sniffed mentally, though the voice of her illusion continued genteelly flirting. *This character would prefer the solid heft and weight of the hardback versions of a book. And it's mobile hot spot, not mobile wireless spit.*

You're not even trying to get the terminology right, Z. Even though he wasn't visible, Andy's tone made it clear he was rolling his eyes.

Seriously? You're making up book preferences for an illusion? Couldn't you make her at least like audiobooks so I could sit on earbuds instead? Why do you need two books as props, anyway? Now that she was trying not to scratch herself, one of her ankles was unbearably itchy, too.

Even as she bantered with a man inside the diner, Wyn answered without hesitation. *Why would I carry a massive tote bag without reason? Besides, you learn a lot about people from what books they enjoy.*

Now Andy sent a laugh over party line. *Zita doesn't read.*

She harrumphed mentally. *I listen to educational books on tape when I work out. And I read when I can't find no free audio version and if I can prop it up while I'm on the treadmill. At least audiobooks are meant to be tools, unlike certain people.*

Wyn sent amusement, edged with something else. *Let's not traverse such dangerous territory. Now, remember what you practiced with our phones.*

Zita grumbled—mentally, anyway. She wanted to scratch her knee now, too. *I make the phones connect to the fake DMS website and click on the logo to infect the phone with Jerome's computer virus. When the browser closes itself, I put the phone back wherever it was. Am I there yet? Can I get out yet?*

Giving into the urge, she scratched her ankle.

Justin's suspicious voice broke through the flirting. "Did your bag just move? Do you have a dog in there or something?"

Zita froze.

The entire bag moved up and down as Wyn shrugged and giggled. "It might've slipped down my shoulder and the contents shifted a little. I may have stuffed more than I should've into it again."

More solicitously, Buzz Cut said, "Why don't you come join us and set the bag down for a while. I'd love a chance to get to know you."

Even without seeing him, Zita could hear Justin's impatience. "You know, we should be working and discussing our strategies while we eat. Perhaps you could carry out your pointless flirtation another time when we're not busy?"

Even though she was royally bored with the conversation as well, Zita noted, *He doesn't like you in this form. You must be losing your touch.*

Maybe he doesn't care for classic beauties. Or is jealous that his companion has significant charms that he lacks. Aloud, Wyn said, "It's fine. I wouldn't want to interrupt your dinners, especially if it's a working one."

After Justin's comment, Zita didn't dare move even to scratch that spot behind her ear that was driving her mad. *Aren't you supposed to be getting to the table so you can slip me their phones?*

Patience, Wyn sent.

"I insist. You'd be doing me a great favor. We're not going to get any farther with our work tonight. Bob's on guard duty until nine. It'd be far faster to plan any kind of strategy when we're all together and can then communicate it to the rest of the team."

"I suppose," Justin said.

"Great! Then it's settled. Let me get that for you!" The bag jerked and swung through the air.

After a disorienting moment of freefall, it hit the floor and a wall with a thud. A book slid out. The other squashed Zita.

She choked back a squeak at the impact. *Hey!*

Buzz Cut said, "Oops. Heavier than I thought. What do you keep in there? Rocks?"

Sorry. He just grabbed it. Aloud, Wyn said, "Books. I have a textbook and a bit of fun reading tucked away."

Wyn's target laughed.

The bag lifted, and the missing book was dropped back inside. Onto Zita.

Involuntary tears came to her eyes, and she had to bite her tongue to keep from crying out.

The world tilted and swayed again, bouncing her against something hard before dropping the last few inches to the floor.

Pinche chingado... She bit back another exclamation as the books settled on top of her small frame, and she just panted for a moment.

Her friend sounded worried. *Are you okay? The bag's under the table now, so you should be safe to work.*

Bruised, but I've had worse. Zita fought her way to the top and peeked out.

She was under the table in one of the vinyl-padded booths that lined the small restaurant attached to the motel. One of Wyn's delicate shoes brushed a much larger foot hidden in men's dress shoes. Across the table, another pair of legs sprawled wide. A desiccated fry and some crumbs marked where someone had missed sweeping the poured cement floor, right next to a pair of laptop bags. The bar smelled of alcohol, sweat, and... she sniffed. *Mmm, buffalo wings.*

Forcing herself to concentrate on their mission, she eyed the cases. *These two are carrying around their computers. That's why we only found one in their motel rooms when we know there are three of them.*

Wyn sent her agreement. *It's fortunate we chose to do this first instead of breaking into their car.*

After verifying no one was seated in easy sight of their table, Zita relaxed a little. *We chose that mostly because I refused to pick the locks before checking here. They parked right under a camera and a light. This looks promising, though.*

Slipping out of Wyn's purse, Zita sent a mental prayer of thanks when she checked the first bag and found a phone right away. She shielded it from the rest of the bar with her body and edged under the red duct-taped bench. The floor was tacky underfoot, and she tried not to think about it too much.

"So, what are you studying?" Buzz Cut sounded interested.

With a giggle, Wyn enthused about the imaginary degree she was planning to get.

A man—Justin?—snorted. The other made the kind of interested noises that made Zita suspect he was humoring her friend.

As the conversation continued above her, she discovered the phone was unlocked. She tapped keys, barely following the discussion above.

"Don't you think that's fascinating, Justin?" Buzz Cut asked.

"I'm checking email," the psychiatrist replied.

The guard sighed. "Put the stupid phone away, Justin. Nothing's going to happen. The poor woman's in the hospital for the next day or two, so relax."

Zita could've cheered. *This job is pan comido. One phone down. Going for the other as soon as I can get my paws on it.*

Don't jinx us, Andy warned from where he and Jerome hid nearby.

Justin sounded annoyed. "You know, your persistent aggression toward me might indicate an underlying issue that you should address. Is it because I'm more intelligent than you? I'm smarter than most people, so you shouldn't feel singled out." A hand slid down and dropped a cell phone into the laptop bag.

Setting the first phone back where she'd found it, she scampered across and peered into Justin's bag for the new phone. A faint glow came from the bottom of the bag. *Por supuesto, it couldn't be resting on top where I could grab it real fast, but if I hurry, it might not lock. No big.*

The other man sighed. "And sometimes, Freud, a cigar is just a cigar. It's rude to play on your phone when you have company, even if it's way, way out of your league."

Zita reached into the bag. Her arms weren't long enough, and only half her attention was on the conversation overhead.

"Out of my league? Speak for yourself." Justin snorted.

Her voice hesitant, Wyn said, "I'm sorry, maybe my joining you was a bad idea…"

Frustrated, Zita climbed into the bag and grabbed the stupid phone. It took both hands to maneuver with it, the phone made bulky by a thick, rubbery case. *I need more time, Wyn.*

I do not intend to depart until we're done, but the offer had to be made. Her friend reassured her.

Buzz Cut was quick to soothe Wyn. "No, you're fine. Big City shrink here's just cranky that things didn't work out the way he predicted today, plus he didn't get his afternoon nap."

Justin snorted. "That had more to do with you locals than me. My predictions were correct. Your team failed to catch her after I made sure she'd show. Whatever. I'm going to the bathroom."

The bag tilted as it was yanked off the ground and moved.

A squeak escaped Zita. She curled up in the bottom of the bag, hugging the phone to her chest, and swore mentally.

The bag's movement stopped. "Did you hear something?"

"No, nothing," Wyn said.

The guard scoffed. "No. Your nerves are way too tight. Should've had a beer like I suggested."

Justin sighed. "Then who would drive us back to the hospital if something comes up?"

Motion resumed.

What's wrong? You jinxed us, didn't you? Andy's mental voice had that fatalistic tone.

I'm in his laptop case, Zita admitted.

Said bag wobbled back and forth before it was finally set on the ground with a thump. Rustling and muttering came from outside.

Wyn caught on. *The one he took to the lavatory?*

Sí. I'll do my best not to get an eyeful or let him catch me. I don't know which would be worse. Zita peeked out.

The bathroom had a row of dingy white urinals that terminated at two tall stalls with rust-spotted metal legs holding up maroon privacy panels. While neither of the doors was shut, they hung mostly closed. Three sinks and a couple half-empty containers of soap took up most of a counter that matched the stalls. Rough brown paper towels straggled out of a white holder that had been hung crookedly on walls papered with mallards in flight. A window ran the length of the stalls, dark with no sunlight.

Justin had set the bag on a plastic counter, and now had his back to it. He released a long sigh as the sounds of urination began.

Avoiding the mirror, Zita dropped back down to finish her task. She dragged her finger across the screen, frantic to get it done so she could escape as soon as he returned to the table.

The screen lit, requesting a fingerprint.

Seriously? Do we really need both phones? Had quarters not been so cramped, she might've chucked the device.

Wyn replied, *You're working on Justin's phone? He's both a psychiatrist and apparently one of the organizers of that ambush on you earlier. He's far more likely to have reviewed Elle's file recently than my ersatz date. His entire DMS team was borrowed for the operation today.*

Bowing to necessity but hating it, Zita bit the edge of the case, feeling the silicone give a little under her teeth, and hung onto the phone with one hand while she leapt out of the bag, scurried across the counter, and jumped seven feet to land on a stall door.

It creaked.

The peeing sounds stopped.

Zita didn't stop moving, swinging over the top of the door to the side that would not be visible at the sink. Hanging from the top, she put her feet against the door and leapt again to a side wall. She eased down to drop soundlessly on top of a toilet paper holder. Even with her slight weight, she could feel the metal flex slightly underfoot. *Dios, please don't look in the stall. If he does, I'll make a run for the window. He'll need a ladder to get up there, and I can escape when he goes to fetch it.*

The phone vibrated in her paws, the screen lighting up.

She slapped the Reject Call button as fast as possible.

He muttered something as he zipped up. Below the divider, she saw his feet move the length of the room, but he didn't touch the stall door.

Water gushed sullenly. A few footsteps later, the door to the bar opened and closed again.

Even though she listened, she didn't hear anyone else in the bathroom anymore. Zita risked a quick check to verify she was alone. She was, but the door was stuck an inch or so open. *Carajo. Dude moves fast. That can't have been more than a splash of water on his hands. Gross. If he heard the buzz, he's going to be looking for his phone. I need to hurry.*

She climbed along the wall and jumped to land on the counter. After a quick shift to Justin's form, she crouched by the sink and pressed her thumb against the screen. *Dios, let this work and let the counter hold out. No way do I want to stand on that nasty ass floor in bare feet.*

The phone unlocked.

As fast as she could, she opened the browser and began laboriously typing the website address into it.

Shouting from outside the room drew her attention.

Wyn fretted over party line. *He can't find his phone. I'm guessing you left his bag at some point. Can you hurry so we can go? He's really upset.*

Zita bit her—his—lip as she concentrated on the phone. *Doing my best.*

The page finally loaded, and she clicked the icon. While she waited for the virus to work, she eavesdropped shamelessly.

Justin was panicking, his voice high and shrill and carrying. "Where's my phone? I put it into my bag! You know I'm a DMS agent and could have you taken to jail for this! That's why she's been hanging on you! She's some sort of... agent! You should've known she was far too high class to be in this hole!"

An unfamiliar voice said, "Hey now! Don't start anything you can't finish, kid!"

"Agent of what? She's a college student! Justin, check your bag again." Wyn's guard did not sound sympathetic.

The soft voice of Wyn's illusory self spoke softly. Even if Zita couldn't make out the words, the tone was soothing. Despite that, hints of Wyn's natural Southern accent were creeping in, a sure sign the witch was stressed.

The psychiatrist did not seem interested in reason. "It's not here! I know I had it! What did you do with it?"

A wash of panic flooded party line.

Andy spoke first. *Wyn? Do you need me to bust in?*

Zita winced. As the browser closed itself, she locked the phone and set it on the floor by the sink he'd used. *You okay, Wyn? Tell him to retrace his steps. Maybe it fell out in the bathroom. I set it where anyone should be able to see it. They won't find me.*

Shifting to a Brazilian gecko so her mottled gray skin would blend as much as possible, she scurried along the wall and hid under the counter behind the sturdy chrome pipe of a sink trap.

Sorry, he grabbed my forearm and leaned over me, and for a second... never mind. The bartender is coming your way, Zita. The blind fear receded, but an unsteady tone vibrated through Wyn's mental voice.

Zita clenched her front toes as if she could punch Justin with the tiny digits. *Already hidden. Feel free to leave without me. I'll meet up with you at the rendezvous point we set up with the guys. I've got a handy window I can get out of once you're clear.*

The bathroom door creaked as someone pushed it open.

Muttering as he went, an unknown man neared. "Moron. Is it too much to ask that I get a peaceful shift without some big-city asshole causing a fuss?" He had the same voice as the person who had protested Justin's comment before, so she assumed it was the bartender Wyn had mentioned.

She stayed very still. A flash of color moved nearby.

The footsteps retreated. With a creak of the heavy door, the unknown guy exited. "Hey, buddy!"

Zita checked the floor. The phone was gone.

He got his phone. I will depart now. While it helps that he looks like he's fifteen, I'm not at my best when people are shouting at me, and this provides an obvious exit justification, Wyn sent.

Zita heaved a sigh of relief before teasing her friend. *Justin's buddy is going to be mad at him.*

Amusement ruffled along the line back at her. *As well he should be. Not that he ever had a genuine chance. Even if I hadn't been playing a role, I would never seriously date anyone that cavalier with books.*

Deciding the walls by the sink were probably cleaner than the floors... anywhere... in the bathroom, Zita ran along them to the high windows. A teleport later, she was gone.

***

Chortling gleefully about the information coming into his laptop, Jerome was all too ready to be dropped off. He promised he'd let them know as soon as he had more answers.

By silent agreement, Zita and her friends said nothing aloud until they were back in the safety of her apartment. Andy and Wyn had even waited patiently outside while she verified no one else was in the apartment before letting them in.

Wyn dismissed her Muse illusion.

Andy removed his mask and shoved it in his pocket.

"Momentito." Stashing her own mask, Zita shifted to her natural form and checked her apartment for a note or a duffel showing that her eldest brother was there.

Finding it empty, she tossed an oversized t-shirt over her costume and returned to her friends. "We're good. Miguel was supposed to spend the night here on his way back to New York from somewhere in the South. He had a date with his girl today, though, so it must've gotten steamy or something."

"Good thing. We don't need him hearing our conversation," Andy said.

Wyn murmured her agreement.

"We should eat while we have the chance. You guys want to join me?" Zita said. Without waiting for their answers, she padded into the kitchen and opened the fridge. She grabbed the ingredients that'd been marinating overnight and a container of leftover rice.

The witch sank gracefully into her favored chair. "What should we do about the metahumans that DMS is likely keeping prisoner? If Dream Auntie's right about the looming catastrophe, and her precognition has yet to fail, DMS can't keep her. I doubt you'll want your little friend to stay there either if they're mistreating her."

Zita grimaced. After switching on the stove, she set a pan on it and splashed some oil into it. "De verdad. Assuming it's not a coincidence that Dream Auntie says vague things and then stuff that sort of fits happens eventually."

Wyn bit her lip. "I don't think we can afford to risk that she's wrong. Now Jerome has the data, he's going to want to go to the next step in his plan."

Andy shuddered and took his own seat. "I've been trying not to think about it."

"A prison break. That's... huge. I mean, we skirt the law, but that's been necessary. We'll lose any leeway we've gotten in the past. Before, sure, they were out to get us, but they weren't going to make an effort or nothing. It wasn't worth it to them. This changes that." Zita lined up ingredients next to the stove.

"That's already changing. They sent an armed team after you today, Zita," Wyn pointed out.

She huffed. "And that's just the US government. If everyone we've pissed off figures out the Man would be happy with us dead, they'll up their attempts to get us too. I'm the lowest value target in this group, so you two better watch your backs."

"It's disturbing that you know our approximate bounties. I blame the company you've been keeping," the witch said.

"Does Wyn still have a higher price on her head than me?" Andy asked. "And Z, I totally would've expected your bounty amount to be way, way higher. You're the best of all of us at annoying people."

"Thank you, I think so too—wait..." Zita narrowed her eyes at her grinning friend.

He smiled, but it faded. Hesitantly, he said, "Speaking of jailbreaks, I heard DMS is bringing Pretorius in early Thursday to a special secured location in western Pennsylvania. There's a stretch of road with no cell service that they're particularly nervous about should someone decide to spring him loose. If we could make sure he doesn't escape..."

"Back up DMS? I hate to help them, but he's real dangerous and deserves to rot in jail. I guess I'm in," Zita said.

Wyn nodded. "Perhaps assisting in this will deflect attention from us should we be forced to other actions later."

"Are we really going along with what Jerome's planning?" Andy asked.

"You try your spell on those people Remus was looking for. If that gives us a location, we check it out. The missing metas need to be found before the port city gets destroyed. By the way, if anyone talks to Dream Auntie, we need to pin her down on the details and a timeline. Latitude and longitude would rock."

"I never knew you were such a dreamer, Z," Andy said.

She made a face and a rude gesture at him. Tested the pan. Dumped in the meat and veggies. "Set the table and kiss my culo, mano."

Silverware clinked as he chuckled.

Wyn steepled her fingers. "Reward amounts are unimportant."

Busy poking at the food with a cooking spoon, Zita realized no one had spoken after a minute or two. She glanced between her friends. Some instinct told her she couldn't ignore the question. "Last I heard, Wyn's bounty is the highest. Freelance and I don't talk about it much."

Andy's eyebrows rose. "He talks?"

"Regardless of what they do or do not discuss, Zita's contretemps at the park today suggests that the period of leniency we've benefited from previously is ending. Especially if DMS gets that bill passed." Wyn pressed her lips together.

"So, what do we do? Sitting around talking ourselves into inaction won't help anyone. Maybe you could use your spell to locate Elle if Jerome gets her full name," Zita suggested.

"I could not locate Remus' missing associates even with a larger map. We can only hope that finding Elle will allow us to find Dream Auntie and the others. If we are truly lucky, no intervention will be necessary. Or an obvious solution will present itself other than what Jerome expects. Perhaps what we've heard about DMS is merely rumor," Wyn said. She slid into her usual seat at the table.

Andy set down a stack of napkins and stared at them. He spoke slowly. "While I'd like to think so, the reservation still talks about the horror of the boarding schools. Zita's parents fled their home countries for scary reasons. I doubt we have the luxury of sitting back and not doing anything. That can't be allowed to happen again."

Zita splashed in more seasoning and then added the rice. She stirred with more vigor than necessary. "It's not rumor. We know people are missing. We know DMS took at least a few of them and are being very secretive about who they have and what they're doing with them. That never ends well. Not in the Argentina my mother fled, and not now. At a minimum, we should try to warn people what's happening." *Maybe somebody smarter than me will solve it once they know there's a problem. I don't want to be anywhere near this one, but I can't abandon Elle now I know she's in trouble.*

"While the upcoming bills and election frighten me, I'm not convinced we should take so drastic an action as a prison break. However, warning others is a sensible precaution." Wyn curled her fingers and brought them to her mouth.

After a snort, Andy said, "It's at least a start. How do we do that? Do either of you know a reporter or anyone else who can get the word out? My... friend... might be able to spread the word a little, but that can't be all we count on."

"Not as far as I know. Remus already knows, and you can bet he'll have warned people in his meta business group. I told Freelance, so his team will be fine, but I don't think they talk to many people. At least, he doesn't." Zita threw some leftover beans into the pan.

"Dmitri!" Wyn said. "His club has a special night every week for metas, and he's the de facto head of the local vampires. He's in a perfect position to ensure the information is widely disseminated."

Zita grimaced. "Plus, the last thing he'd want is a prison cell with a view."

When they caught her meaning, both of her friends winced.

"We'll go tonight then," Wyn said. "Let him know as soon as possible."

Andy grunted. "That's a good start, but what's the next step after that? Jerome's plan seems to be the only alternative."

"If we got to do a jailbreak, we need to be certain we don't get caught, or we're chingado in the US. Wyn won't be safe healing on the sidelines anymore because they'll haul her off, and if they have one of us..." Zita let her words trail off.

"They'll have a matching set eventually because we won't abandon each other," Andy said as he fussed with the napkins.

Zita tilted her head. "Or a huge mess to clean up because I'm not into living in a cage. Or being dumped in a grave."

"Cheery." Wyn flattened her hands on the table and stared at them. "So. We shall hope my spell works or Jerome finds the information in the data we assisted him in obtaining. Once we have a location, we'll scout out the prisons. They are required to allow convicts a minimum number of hours outside daily, weather permitting. It would be easy enough for Zita to sneak close during that time to have a brief conversation and ascertain their status. If Elle and the others are healthy, that will do a great deal to allay fears, and perhaps no further action would be warranted beyond attempting to legally spring Dream Auntie. We have to get her out, and it'd be far preferable to do so via legitimate avenues. Your little student needs to be removed from their custody as well if they're not granting her the care her medical condition requires."

"If we can't go the legal route, what's a safe place to stash a teenager with heart problems where she can get treatment without letting DMS know her location? You already said you can't heal her heart because it's a genetic thingy. At least with Dream Auntie, we could give her a lift to another country or something where she could hide. We don't have the cash to pay for Elle's care, and I doubt Pie Lady does either." Zita poked at the food with her spoon, frowning at it.

Pinching between her brows, Wyn said, "My biggest concern is that they don't exist in the criminal justice system, so we can't clear them of charges. We'd have to get DMS to agree to release them. Who knows how hard that is?"

"What if they're already dead?" Andy interjected.

Wyn winced.

Then I will have really failed the kid. Zita sniffed the air above the pan, then added more spice. "If they're already dead, we need to know. Bury them right if we can and prevent the same thing from happening to any other metas. It would also mean that the Dream Auntie catastrophe can't happen."

"Unless her powers include revivification and animated corpses wreaking horrible vengeance on the living," Wyn said darkly.

Andy groaned. "Can we not have a zombie apocalypse? We have enough to deal with already."

"Vampires exist, so I guess the zombie thing's possible. Still. Let's assume they're alive. We find them first and then figure out what to do." Zita snapped her fingers. "Hey, what about that clinic in Brazil? Doctor Mwangi's not a fan of ours, but he wouldn't turn away a sick kid. You can heal her, so she's not in need of immediate surgery even if she's in terrible shape. It'll give the kid a quiet place to lie low and not exert herself while we figure out how to fix things, even if his clinic isn't set up for heart surgery."

"While it's not a permanent answer, it'll do for a bit. It's not like we have options," Andy said.

Wyn nodded. "If additional actions are required, well, we will have to concoct an alternative that doesn't end with us appearing on the Most Wanted Criminals list."

Andy grunted. "Sounds as much like a plan as we ever have."

Zita tapped her nose. "De verdad. We'll need to refine that not getting caught bit."

"I agree. Caroline was asked to bring us in once. She refused, but if we participate in a jailbreak, that gets a lot harder for her." Andy fussed with the napkins and sighed.

Wyn bit her lip. "Oh, you—we—definitely do not want to go against her."

"Caroline? You mean the tool? Was she threatening you? Was that why she told you something like that? I mean, I agree we don't want to fight her, but that's rude," Zita said.

"No, she wasn't threatening me," Andy said.

Zita scowled. "She must've been threatening the rest of us then. We'll have to watch our backs, so she doesn't stab them."

Andy closed his eyes and took a deep breath. "You need to stop, Zita. Don't say things like that."

"Maybe she should be less of a tool, then. You know she'd hand us over in a heartbeat if somebody told her to." She waved her hand.

Andy stepped forward. "She wouldn't! The last thing she'd do is hand us over to DMS. Zita, Caroline and I... we're dating."

The world seemed to flip upside down and then right side up. Vaguely, she felt her jaw moving, as if it was opening and closing. A strangled sound came from somewhere.

"I think you broke her," Wyn whispered, poking Andy.

As soon as it registered that she was the source of the strange noise, Zita took a deep breath and shut her mouth. Then, she realized she'd made a terrible mistake. She relaxed. "Ay, I misheard you for a second. Why are you dieting? You don't need to lose no weight and given how good of a cook your dad and stepmom are, not eating their food might be a sin. You don't want to make Baby Jesús cry, do you?"

He sighed. "Caroline and I are dating, not dieting, Zita. And it's serious."

"Here we go," Wyn murmured. She removed the flask from her purse and set it on the table.

Zita blinked and laughed. "No. No, you're not that stupid. You wouldn't put all of us and our families at risk for that piece of—"

Andy hissed before she could finish her statement. "Shh! Don't go there. I know you're upset, but you need to stop insulting her, insulting us."

"Insulting you? I don't need to do that. If you're with her, you're insulting yourself already! I hate her and her stupid face, and I don't know how you can stand to be around her." Zita caught her voice rising and stopped herself with a growl.

He ran a hand through his hair. "Dang. I knew you'd be pissed. That's why I put off telling you for so long."

She stopped. "Wait, so long? You've been with her for a while? When we were in Greece?"

"Yes," he said.

All the little conversations she'd ignored came back to her, and Zita whirled to face Wyn. "And you knew? Wait, what am I asking? Of course, you knew. And didn't say anything. Because you'd rather let her ruin our lives and endanger all our families, even your aunt, to her bad choices than tell me?"

"Actually, I've been pushing him to tell you for a while so we could get this over with," Wyn said coolly. Her apparent nonchalance was spoiled by the big gulp she took from her flask.

Her lips tightened, and Zita turned away. "Seriously, mano, you could do so much better! Were you just lonely? I'm certain I can find a nice geeky chick to hook you up with if you give me a chance. I don't know *all* the dojo owners in Maryland. There's got to be one you'd like."

Wyn nudged Andy and whispered, "Bargaining, already. Probably a good sign."

Zita overheard it and frowned at the other woman. "What are you talking about?"

Andy seemed just as confused.

"Never mind," Wyn said. "I believe you were about to head into depression next?"

After scrubbing his hands on the sides of his pants, Andy exhaled. "Z, I might... love Caroline. I don't want another woman. I want her. She's fun, and sweet, and amazing. The reason she works with the government is because she believes in using her talents to help people, which is the same reason almost all her lawyer work is pro bono, and she spends a ton of time fundraising for kid's charities. I don't see you doing that."

She made a scoffing sound. "It's easy to do stuff for free when you're sitting on piles of money and have other people to sweep up any mistakes you make along the way. I work for a living."

Andy shook his head. "If you gave her a chance, I think you'd recognize how hard she tries to contribute to everyone. We don't need your permission to be together, but you're like a sister to me, and I'd like you to be okay with it."

Her heart hurt, and she had horrible indigestion. Zita groaned. "Her hooks are in deep. Mano, she's going to break your heart and send all of us to DMS jail. Or worse. And our families will be helpless against Pretorius—"

"Who's in prison," Wyn murmured.

Zita continued, "Halja, Zeus, and—"

"Missing in action," Wyn said. "Should the food be smoking that much?"

After pulling the pan from the burner and turning off the heat, Zita growled. "Stop it, Wyn. We have enemies, bad guys who will go after our loved ones. That will include the Man after the stunts we're considering with the prison and Dream Auntie and all. Our families will have to go into hiding and give up their whole lives when she tells everyone who we are. You can't expect anything better of a chingado tool like that."

"Grief, with a bit of a backslide into anger, but that's better than I was expecting, really," Wyn mumbled to herself.

Andy crossed his arms over his chest, expression pained. "What'd I say about insulting my girl? Dang, Z! How is this different from you dating the mercenary? And for the record, I wasn't going to tell her who I am yet."

The food didn't seem burned, only a little blackened around the edges. *More than good enough.* Zita waved the big spoon at him. "Freelance barely talks to people he likes! He considers all the angles before acting, and he doesn't do collateral damage. I know Caroline. There will be a lot of damage, and she won't be the one taking any of it. You will, and we will, and our families. Have you spent any time thinking about how vulnerable your family in particular is? Dude, you're making a massive mistake. And Wyn? Please stop—whatever it is that you're doing."

Andy flinched. He opened his mouth, but Wyn set her hand on his arm. Anger and hurt darkened his face, and his slumping posture shouted his unhappiness.

She hated herself for doing that to him, but her emotions churned and boiled and threatened to pour more caustic words. Instead, Zita slapped their plates down on the table, sliding into her usual, permanently glittery chair. "Dinner's ready."

"We don't have time," Andy protested.

Zita shot him a look, swallowing hard to keep from hurting him further. "Mano. There's always time for food. Eat."

"Now you sound like my family." Andy set down his fork and pushed his untouched plate away. "You know, I'm not hungry. Wyn, do you really need me at the club? Room to breathe would be good."

Wyn touched his arm, eyes searching his face. Whatever she saw had her nodding. "We'll be fine without you for a night. Go flying."

He gave a curt nod and stalked out onto the balcony. With a hop, he flew away.

Zita's emotions swirled in an uncomfortable mess. She picked up her fork and stared at the table. Something finally registered. "Did he fold my napkin into the shape of a donkey?"

Chapter Six

"Of all the gin joints, in all the towns, in all the world, she walks into mine."

Wyn had that tone that meant she was quoting something as she toyed with the stem of her wineglass. Shadows crossed the too-perfect pale face of the illusion she used as a disguise.

More than a little curious and concerned at her friend's statement, Zita pulled aside the curtain that half-shrouded their booth, the fabric velvety against her calloused fingers. The square shape of the upper floor where they waited had small tables and luxurious curtained booths on three sides, with the center open to below. Fog billowed and flowed down to the lower floor from the bar that took up most of the fourth wall. In the center of the room, thick, high railings allowed patrons in the VIP area to watch those on the Danz Mizer dance floor below without fear of falling, even if they chose to imbibe the often glowing or bubbling specialty drinks.

Most of the booths were full tonight, and a handful of people loitered by the railing, watching the packed dance floor below. The first floor had smelled like sweat, alcohol, and a thousand offensive chemical perfumes. Here, incense and the scent of the smoke machine almost hid the more human odors. Tiny coffin speakers piped music along the railing, currently a fast-paced, cheerful electronic beat that clashed with the cynical lyrics.

Zita squinted at the chandelier and adjusted her mask to ensure it wasn't blocking part of it. Shaped like a cephalopod in a top hat, each arm of the light fixture held a glowing glass that splattered flecks of light in jeweled tones on everything below. "This is Dmitri's nightclub, not yours. Speaking of, why is there a squid on the ceiling?"

"I was quoting a movie, and you did burn his last chandelier. Perhaps he felt a water-based totem would be appropriate for the new one," her friend replied, a small smile fluttering to her lips. For once, her usual Muse illusion of a sparkly dress fit into the surroundings.

Zita harrumphed. "Órale, you can't blame that on me. The flying skull burping fire did that."

"It was aiming for you at the time. Close the curtain before they see us. They're over by Incubus." Wyn flicked her fingers in that direction.

Tearing her gaze from the chandelier, Zita glanced that way.

At the polished wooden bar, a familiar psychic vampire with a man-bun was handing drinks to and chatting with a pair of women in short, sparkly dresses. One woman giggled at Incubus over the beverages, a curly-haired brunette in the sort of heels that either belonged to a stripper or cost a lot of money. Either way, the stilettos would make a great weapon. The other woman had sleek, black hair in a pointy cut, sensible heels, and a purse that matched her ruby garment. She held herself with a dignified reserve despite smiling at something being said.

"Who do you—oh. Rani. Earning millions seems to agree with her. Her biceps have improved from when you guys were together. I bet she's not afraid to go up another five pounds in weights when she plateaus like some people." Zita grinned. Absently, she noted the three people with military-perfect posture who hovered near the women.

As if sensing her stare, Rani turned.

Zita could tell the instant the other woman identified them by the way she paled beneath the warm topaz of her skin and stiffened.

Wyn pursed her lips and yanked the curtain closed, cutting off her view. "Indeed. Can we talk about something other than my ex-girlfriend?"

Shrugging, Zita obliged her. "It might be an octopus on the chandelier instead of a squid. I can't tell if there are hooks on two of the arms or not without getting up there and checking more closely. That's probably the most reliable way of telling them apart."

With a groan, Wyn shook her head. "While fascinating, let's pass on that topic too, and definitely do not climb this chandelier. Neither of us has the money to throw at a new one. Next subject?"

Zita glanced in the chandelier's direction. "Okay, though it would've only taken a second to check," she grumbled.

No reply. Party line disappeared, and Wyn's gaze changed, becoming focused on nothing.

I guess it's my turn to hold up the conversation while she does whatever telepath-y thing she's doing. "We're here on a mission, right?"

Her friend nodded, still focused elsewhere.

"Then why are you drinking?" Zita asked.

Wyn absently sipped at the last of her wine. "No reason I can't combine business with pleasure. Besides, I am not the one with the penchant for lodging her feet in her mouth."

Zita sniffed. "I'd be all offended if that weren't true. Pretty certain you could tweak the President's nose and be invited in for tea and stale, fancy cookies."

Awareness flooded back to Wyn's face, and her mouth firmed. "Don't look now, but Rani's coming over."

"Seriously? Were you spying on them?" Zita whispered, wiggling fingers near her forehead so her friend knew what she meant. "Oye, amiga, that's not going to end well."

Wyn didn't reply, but party line returned.

The curtain rattled faintly as it was drawn back and tucked into a bat-shaped hook on the side of the booth.

"Muse, Arca, it's been a while. I'm glad you both look well." Rani took a deep breath. "Dare I ask if this is simply a social event for you or if you're performing some foolhardy vigilante task?"

"It's a bit of both," Wyn said cautiously, her gaze intent on the other woman's face.

Rani and Wyn stared at each other.

Zita wondered if the third wheel ever got the grease or at least snacks. *Jalapeño poppers would be a great reason to let them talk it out without me. That's helpful, right?*

"I see. Then we'll go—" Her words were cut off when another woman cuddled up to her side, slipping a golden arm through Rani's darker one.

"Where'd you sneak off to, honey? Oh! Wow, is that really Muse? Hi!" the giggly one from the bar burbled at them.

Rani took a deep breath. "Muse, Arca, this is my girlfriend, Brie. Sweetheart, you're familiar with Muse and Arca."

Zita bit back the urge to cheer for cheese. Because food.

The smile on Wyn's illusory face never faltered as she rose and extended a hand graciously to Brie. "Pleased. How did you two meet?"

Releasing Rani, Brie grabbed Wyn's hand and pulled her close for a hug. "I'm so happy to finally meet you! You're even more stunning in person than on television. Rani and I met at work. I'm a product liaison there."

While surprise vibrated for a second on party line, Wyn gave the other woman a genteel hug back and a gracious smile before stepping back.

"Brie's the Senior Vice President for General Aetherics Energy Division Public Relations," Rani said, her voice dry.

Her cheeks turning pink, Brie said, "It's a fancy title so that when I tell high-ranking politicians the billion-dollar SNARC ball they've waited years for isn't ready, they don't insist on speaking to my manager. It doesn't compare to what any of you do, of course."

Wyn directed her words at her ex-girlfriend as she reseated herself. "Affectionate, intelligent, and lovely. Rani, she's charming. I'm truly happy for both of you."

Brie clapped her hands and turned toward Zita. "And Arca, I'm beyond delighted to meet you too!"

Forewarned by her behavior with Wyn, Zita remained safely seated and waved. "Hola."

Still smiling, Brie touched Rani's arm. "Isn't she even more adorable in person? Is Wingspan here somewhere too? I've watched the video of your song a million times. Actually, most of upper management are fans. Speaking of which, if the three of you ever want employment in the private sector, get in touch, and we'll be happy to discuss possible positions. We have generous salaries, four weeks of paid leave, and retirement funds to die for!"

Rani rolled her eyes. "Honey, do we need to recruit on our weekend off?"

"Sorry, but how often do I get the chance to talk to Muse in person! And Arca too! This is such an honor, not to mention anyone who gets them to join the company gets a very nice bonus." She winked at all of them. "Would you mind if we shared a table with you? I'd love to get to know you better!"

With identical uncomfortable expressions, Wyn and Rani stared at each other.

Zita stifled a snicker.

"Of course not. Please do," Wyn said faintly. *Would you want to wager that her emails contain a great many emojis and exclamation points? Bless her heart.*

Maybe she thinks you can show her hilarious and embarrassing photos of Rani, Zita teased as she slipped out of her seat and joined Wyn on her side of the booth. She bumped her friend with her hip. "Move over."

"Seriously, Rani, did you know they'd be here?" Brie elbowed her girlfriend and sank onto the bench Zita had just vacated.

Wyn made noncommittal noises. She and Rani were now avoiding eye contact.

Rani shook her head.

Her amusement fading, Zita realized she had no idea what she should be doing. While Wyn had claimed the breakup had been amicable, the atmosphere had her wondering if she had to be supportive or something. *I got your back, amiga. You need me to hold your earrings while you go after her? I'd offer to punch her for you, but she's not in my weight class. I don't want to be a bully, even for a friend.*

A small smile touched Wyn's lips. *Indeed not. Brie only has thirty pounds and almost a foot of height on you. That wouldn't be a fair fight at all.*

Zita agreed. *De verdad, she doesn't move like a fighter at all, though I notice she makes it to arm day at the gym at least once in a while. Still, do I hate this chick for stealing your woman?*

Wyn tossed her hair over her shoulder and murmured something noncommittal aloud. *Thank you for the offer, but no. Rani was right to break up with me. The life of a vigilante's significant other is fraught with pressure and unwelcome attention. It also endangered her highly lucrative new position. Over time, that level of unhappiness would lead to resentment, and we both preferred to part with no animosity.*

Plus, her new girlfriend is all kinds of exhausting. I don't think I've ever met anyone who can talk so fast without taking a breath. Other than Dmitri, but he doesn't breathe except when he's talking, Zita sent.

Amusement rippled along party line. *You find her exhausting? Pot. kettle.*

Before she could reply, a waitress came over and set a tray down on the table. Four crystal goblets glowed lurid chartreuse in the dim light. A reddish stream of fizz wound through it, and a long, wooden pick speared triangular chunks of pineapple and cherries. "Complimentary drinks, courtesy of the owner." She whisked off without waiting to see if they needed anything else.

"Oh, how thoughtful of him!" Wyn said with a smile. "I can't wait to try them. Have you tried their drinks, Brie? They're delightful!"

"Odd. Dmitri knows I only drink bottled water in clubs." Zita frowned at hers. She bit her tongue before she could ask if Wyn brought her magic rock.

Her friend sighed and set down the glass she'd been about to put to her lips. She hauled her purse into her lap and dug into it. Murmuring softly, she said, "Paranoia must be contagious."

"Speaking of which, are those people with you?" Zita nodded toward the military or ex-military lingering near the booth. "They got cop eyes and are following you."

Brie nodded. "Bodyguards."

Zita relaxed slightly. "Cool."

Rani's girlfriend threw back a long, appreciative gulp of her own drink. "These are great!"

Wyn set a purple obelisk on a silken cord on the table. She muttered a few words, and the amethyst glowed a deep, rich purple for a moment. "Don't make me regret giving that to you. Again."

Zita collected it, rubbing her fingers thoughtfully over the smooth stone. She pocketed it. "Glowy means it's all charged and ready to go, right? Thanks."

Brie watched, wide-eyed. "What did you do?"

Rani seemed focused on pulling the fruit off the sword and then stabbing it again.

"The stone purifies the body of inebriation and chemical influences, and yes, Arca," Wyn said softly.

"That's pretty neat. No hangover? You could make a fortune on it! If it's just a matter of figuring out how to produce them, I could get you a meet with our director of new technology…" Brie's eyes sparkled.

"It's a short-lived spell, unfortunately," Wyn said.

Rani cleared her throat.

Her girlfriend gave Rani's forearm an affectionate squeeze. "That's a shame. Why is that?"

Wyn tilted her head. "Enchanted objects require magical batteries. If the person using the object doesn't have magic, it must call upon its own resources or drain something from the user."

"That's why crazy-ass Halja kept stabbing people with the knife that had magic she wanted to activate. She thought murder would power it up," Zita added.

Rani hacked at a chunk of pineapple. "Gruesome example."

Brie gulped down more and set down her glass. She steepled her fingers and leaned forward. "That's fascinating. So, the issue is the power source? You know, we could set you up with a research lab and look into hybridizing a solu—"

Wyn demurred before she could finish the statement.

"Pity. It's your decision. If you change your mind, you've got my card. With my personal cell phone," Brie said with a wink. Before they could say anything, she fished two cards from her purse and slipped one in front of each of them.

Cheese-girl got some recruiting moves on her, Zita said, sliding hers over to Wyn.

"Thank you," Wyn said graciously, putting both cards into her purse. *Indeed.*

Tiny chunks of pineapple floated in Rani's drink as she kept up the assault on the fruit.

With a glance at the electrician, Brie tapped a finger on the top of the table, her polished nail set with tiny crystals that sparkled in the light. "Whew, this air needs a bit of clearing. Rani misses you. I'm sure you miss her, but you've both moved on. I know it's a stereotype, but we can all be friends, can't we? We're all just happy lesbians out for a night on the town, right?"

"Actually, we're not. I like men. With penises. Especially if they know what to do with them. Muse and I definitely aren't a thing. We only stopped by here to talk to someone real quick about some vigilante stuff," Zita said.

Brie straightened and grinned. "Oh? What mission are you on now? Is someone planning to sacrifice everyone here? Or steal another SNARC ball?"

Zita snorted. "No such luck. We're just here to pass along some gossip about DMS. They're getting all heavy-handed with metas, arresting and hauling them off unprovoked. Once they've got them, they're gone. No lawyers, no letters, no legal recourse."

Wyn stomped on Zita's foot.

"Ow! Hey, we should totally tell them. Rani's—Rani knows metas she could warn and wasn't the point to make sure people knew? Gossip or some boring crap like that so people could be safer?" Zita said.

Her friend pinched the spot between her eyebrows. *The more people who know we're looking into DMS, the more likely they are to connect us with Jerome's jailbreak, even if we decide not to go along with it.*

I didn't say we're doing anything about it. I said we're here to talk about it. Zita rolled her eyes.

Neither of these women is an idiot. Wyn shook her head. "We'd appreciate it if you didn't mention you heard it from us. We heard it from another friend and are just trying to alert others in case it's true."

"Of course." Brie crossed her heart with her fingers. "Thank you. We do know a few people we could pass that along to, and we'll leave you out of it. Sweetheart, you take me on the best dates." She beamed at Rani.

After swirling her drink and taking a hesitant sip, Rani tugged on her date's arm. "You know, I'm a bit more tired than I thought. Maybe we should go dancing another night. My supervisor did recommend a romantic couples' resort in the Caribbean. We could grab a quick flight there. DMS won't run into another country with guns blazing, plus there's sunshine, sand, and ocean..."

"Which we won't be exploring by boat after the last time," Brie giggled.

Rani turned green. "No, definitely not."

"Fine, but I'm finishing my drink and getting at least one dance out of you first. It was wonderful to meet you two!" Setting aside the fruit on a stick, Brie chugged her drink and dabbed daintily at her lips with a napkin. Her eyes sparkled.

Polite as ever, Wyn protested, "You needn't leave. We will leave as soon as we speak to someone..."

Rani flashed Wyn a tight smile as she took her date's arm. "Yes, I've heard that before. Nice to see you two again. Let's get you your dance, precious, and be gone."

"Bye!" The two women disappeared down the steps.

Zita looked around. "If Dmitri sent the drinks, where is he?" She spotted the waitress standing by the bar, one hand on her ear, watching their table. Something niggled at her about the woman's posture. The way she was leaning, her gaze checking each quadrant of the room...

Noticing her gaze, the waitress turned away and picked up a tray, carrying the empty object toward the stairs with purposeful strides. The back of her work blouse had a faint bulge to it.

"I need a drink and perhaps to swear off dating entirely." Wyn lifted her glass.

Zita snatched the liquid away. "Don't. If you want another drink, we can order it, but you can't have that one. The waitress has a gun and checks the room like a cop or a criminal." Honesty propelled her to admit, "Or like me."

"So, she's trouble, then. Can't we not be paranoid for one night?" Her friend sighed.

"Given the whole vigilante thing and our history? No, not really," Zita said.

The curtain was drawn back and tucked into an open position.

An amused baritone voice, thick with an Eastern European accent, interrupted before she could say more. "We must stop meeting like this. People will talk."

The Vampire Prince of DC stood at the entrance of their booth, leaning against the carved wooden post. Dmitri smiled, his fangs tinged faintly pink from the club lighting. As usual, smoky makeup emphasized his stunning face. His shirt was red lace and ruffles, hanging open to the waist and showcasing perfectly toned pectorals and abdominals. A pendant hung from his neck, blood-red gems against the extreme pallor of his skin.

Music swelled from the lower levels of the club.

Zita frowned. "You suddenly mind chatter about you?"

Wyn stepped on her foot. "Good evening, Dmitri."

He set a dramatic finger to his lips, lace spilling out of the cuffs of his coat with the movement. A shiver of crimson glitter sparkled on his coat. "True enough, it does not bother me. What man would not wish to be linked via rumor and hopefully deliciously salacious gossip to two such lovely ladies? We should meet more often! Now, what brings you in? Normally, this would be my night to entertain the crowds, but something came up at home. So now I have only until my chariot arrives, but Incubus said you needed to speak to me about something?"

With his entrance in the enclosed booth, the scent of cologne, incense, and death washed over Zita. Her nose wrinkled involuntarily. "Chariot? You mean your mom? Tell her I say hi!"

He sniffed. "Ride-sharing service, if you must know. However, I will pass along your greetings to my maternal parent. She remembers you fondly for some reason. Now, what did you need, and are we all still on for movie night?"

Lashes lowered over amethyst eyes as Wyn smiled. "We are, though Wingspan has something else going on that night. Your shirt is magnificent, by the way."

The vampire bowed. "Thank you, and if he has other obligations, it will be my turn to choose the film, which is excellent."

"Actually, I don't think I've had a chance to pick for a while. It should be my turn. I'll get one with subtitles this time," Zita said. *Is he seriously ditching us for a date with the tool? You think you can check and see if there's something wrong with his brain?*

Wyn ignored all of her comments. "We came to give you a warning that metas are disappearing. Given your status, your staff, and the number of metas who visit this place, we felt you should know."

"That is grave news indeed." Dmitri's expression sobered.

Zita snickered. "Grave. That's funny because he's dead... never mind."

"As I was saying, do you have any idea who it is? It's not happening at my club, is it? We watch very carefully for that, given the way it was used in the past." Dmitri crossed his arms over his chest, brow furrowing. His eyes glowed red for an instant before returning to their normal deep violet.

"DMS," Zita said.

"Possibly," Wyn amended, kicking her ankle.

The vampire glanced between them. "Very well, then. I shall tell the staff to be especially wary of strange men in boring suits bearing gifts of paperwork and pass that along. If I hear something, should I contact you?"

Zita opened to mouth to answer, then closed it.

Fortunately, Wyn interceded, leaning forward and gazing into his eyes. "It couldn't hurt. We all need to band together if someone's preying on metas."

"Quite so." He stepped closer, his regard intent on the witch.

"Does the music sound different to you?" Wyn lifted her brows.

Dmitri seemed fixated on her. "Quite. While I enjoy Broadway, it's not the style I would choose for the club, especially on a Saturday. Perhaps a future theme night? I shall speak to the DJ."

Wyn nodded.

Music is music. Maybe it has fewer drums than what they usually play here. Or it's a little off-key? Whatever. Zita had that third wheel feeling again, and the staring contest between her friends had her growing uneasy. She cast about for something to say that wouldn't get her kicked again. Finally, she elected to change the topic and confirm her suspicion about the waitress. "Thanks for the drinks and all. Even if we're not drinking them."

That broke Dmitri's focus, and he shook his head as he glanced at the table. "I would tell you a moment in your company would be worth bankrupting myself with a million glasses of the most expensive of liquors, but these are not from me. Nor am I so fiscally irresponsible, but that is irrelevant. I might send one of our special drinks to the always exquisite Muse, but for Arca, never. For you, I would only send offerings of food and bottled water to keep you from swinging from my very expensive and not easily replaced ceiling decor."

"For the last time, the flying skull broke the old one, not me. Speaking of weird, the waitress who brought drinks to us walks like military and was wearing a gun, you know. New girl, I think." Zita rolled her eyes.

Dmitri jerked back, all humor gone from his face. "New staff do not work the VIP floor. Only long-term staff. Carrying weapons is against club policy and probably illegal as well. Where is she? Can you point her out?"

"You don't know?" Zita raised her eyebrows and scanned the upper floor for the server. "I don't see her right now."

Wyn leaned forward and checked. "Neither do I."

His face darkened. "Incubus is my manager, and such things are usually left to him. He's normally an excellent judge of character. Had I listened to him, Domina wouldn't—It matters not. Pardon. I must clear this up before I leave."

"Of course," Wyn said.

"Hasta."

He gave each of them a nod and strode over to the bar. After an exchange of words with the man behind it, the vampire strode down the stairs.

Zita practically vibrated with the urge to move. "Who's paranoid now?"

Her friend shook her head. "I dislike this. Even if they planned to leave soon, let's make sure Rani and Brie aren't suffering any ill effects from their drinks. Then we should go."

"Sweet!" She bounced out of her seat. Despite her glee at getting to leave, something wasn't right. Her instincts were clamoring for attention.

More slowly, Wyn stood. She wasted time fussing with her illusory hair, or maybe the real hair under the magic.

Zita touched the magic rock to her friend. She tilted her head. "Where'd all the people talking noises go? All I hear is music?" She checked around them.

Most of the patrons of the upper area were gathered along the railing, watching the first floor of the club.

Must be someone really good or funny dancing, Zita thought. I hope Miguel's not here again. Then again, Wyn might have a camera if he's actually dancing.

Wyn shook her head, and they headed to the lower level.

As they descended the carved wooden stairs, a spotlight flashed on, focusing on a figure posed flamboyantly atop the bar.

Dmitri.

Chapter Seven

The spotlight really brought out the sparkles in the vampire's outfit.

If anything, his accent seemed even thicker as he flashed a fanged grin at the audience. A catchy beat rang out. "Welcome to the club! I am Dmitri, your humble host. You may know me as the Vampire Prince of DC, but I bid you all welcome and hope you find the love tonight in my little club that I have yet to find."

With that, he launched into a full-throated song, something about loneliness and eternity and the difficulty of finding the right outfit.

Wyn came to a dead stop in the middle of the staircase.

Darting around her to see better, Zita peered below. Words fell out of her gaping mouth, loud in the club. "No manches... I thought he was leaving, not doing karaoke?"

When Dmitri hit the chorus, six men in black club uniforms took up positions around him and danced in eerie syncopation, lifting their own voices in support as they danced around and on the bar. They spun in perfect unison, Dmitri's cape a dramatic swirl of striped crimson and black around him.

Her friend blinked. "This is new. He can sing, though. I wonder how long they had to practice that choreography?"

"Sí, he's got great lung capacity for somebody who doesn't breathe. Standing on the bar's got to be against some kind of hygiene code, though. Think about the food, man!" Zita was aghast.

"Hush," Wyn said.

Zita considered the scene. The club was packed. Dmitri, his staff, and random club goers sang and danced, but they were forced onto tables and chairs and suspiciously convenient openings for the more flamboyant steps. Others waved their phones over their heads or made no attempt to disguise the fact that they filmed everything, including herself and Wyn. Incubus appeared to be going through a rapid progression of yoga poses on top of the bar. She allowed herself to be impressed with the bartender's flexibility before she focused again. "Guess they stepped up the drama here. Is this going to delay us leaving?"

Her friend shushed her. *We're being filmed. Rani dislikes the limelight, and her contract requires a lower profile, so we will have to catch them outside. Perhaps we can linger out there long enough to catch them departing.*

Dmitri dove dramatically off the bar and his employees caught him, carrying him over to the stairs. He righted himself on the polished banister and threw out his hand to Zita and Wyn. He burbled, "And she sang..."

Zita frowned at him. Her words rang out in the club. "I'm pretty certain nobody wants me to sing." Despite that, she felt music bubbling up in her throat and a rising desire to move. Her hips twitched, and she started to slide into a ginga. She forced herself to be still and scowled.

Both of Wyn's hands drifted to her throat, and she swayed in place.

His eyebrows rose, and the vampire bowed. Sotto voce, he looked at Wyn and said, "I don't know why you're doing this, but it's quite diverting. Just not every night, yes?"

Eyes wide, Wyn said, "I'm not doing it." Party line dropped and her face slackened.

Almost drowned out by the music, a waterfall of bell-like notes sounded.

Dmitri straightened up and pulled out his phone. He held it to his head. "Alas, my ride is here!" Launching into a spirited musical farewell, he threw roses to the crowd as he headed out.

Zita surveyed the singing and the dancing while she waited. "Where'd he store flowers in that outfit? Well, it's lame, but they all look like they're having fun." Her feet itched to move as she watched two women inexpertly attempting to pole dance with building supports. *I could do better.*

Her friend snapped back to attention and poked her. "Someone's using a mental coercion power to have people sing and dance. If it were magical, it'd be easier to dispel, but I think I have to either try to trace it back to the source or disentangle each person."

That squelched most of the urge to dance. "Seriously? A happy singing and dancing hypnosis power? I thought squirrel control was weird."

Wyn bit her lip and wrung her hands. "We have to stop this! I enjoy musical theater, but it doesn't always have a happy ending. I'll see what I can do without hurting anyone. You find the waitress."

"You're out of it when you do that kind of thing. I should stay and guard you," Zita said.

"No time," Wyn said. She sat on the steps, her gaze already unfocused. She started humming, a pretty soprano descant.

"Carajo. At least get out of sight first, so you're less of a target. That way, people can't make out the words if you start singing our secrets." Zita hauled her friend to her feet and steered her back up to the second floor. She tucked her into the booth closest to the steps and closed the curtains.

Other than a pause in the humming, Wyn didn't acknowledge her.

Her mind already on her next task, Zita returned to the lower floor and scanned the room, searching for the waitress. Everyone was on their feet, even if not performing. She shook her head when standing on the banister didn't help in the search. Hopping down, she thought, *Need more height, but also not to scare anyone.*

She did the obvious thing and shifted to a giraffe, eliciting more cheers from the crowd.

Slowly, she swiveled her head, searching for the woman. When she didn't spot her, she plodded carefully through the crowd and lifted her head to double-check the VIP floor above. The crowd was even more enthusiastic, waving their cups at her as four women and Incubus danced on the bar.

Zita dodged a bead necklace that'd been thrown at her. *Maybe the waitress went into the kitchen? Too many people crowding around here.*

Shifting back to Arca, Zita grabbed the railing and pulled herself up to stand on it.

Incubus stopped in his tracks and held out his hand as he sang to her. "Not the chandelier! It's a custom work of art!"

A chorus of feminine voices echoed his words in a descant.

The bartender went back to his song and dance routine, spinning through partners.

"What? Squid chandeliers aren't popular? Color me shocked," Zita muttered to herself. Unable to get through the crowd, she climbed high enough on the stairs to vault over the railing onto the end of the bar. She flipped over it to bounce off a wall and somersaulted to her feet in the doorway.

For some reason, she threw her arms up in a flourish she hadn't used since her days at gymnastics meets.

The crowd cheered.

The pull to dance was enormous, but she made herself focus and barreled into the kitchen.

Startled staff members stared at her. One man had a single leg up on a stool and held a soup ladle to his mouth like a microphone.

"The new waitress! Which way did she go?" she asked.

Soup Ladle Guy pointed toward the loading dock and then began singing something about giant carrots.

That's how Sobek's crew got out when they kidnapped Dmitri. Is there a sign telling bad guys to escape through that exit? Zita shifted to a cheetah and put on a burst of speed.

The waitress was trying hard to open the big garage door. The lock lay nearby, the shackle broken.

Quietly, Zita shifted to Arca and pulled up the back of the busy woman's shirt. She plucked out the gun and danced backward, this time falling into a ginga by habit. She pulled the magazine, letting bullet cartridges chink musically on the floor. "What did you put in the drinks?"

"I'll never tell you! Give me that back!" the other woman trilled as she attacked Zita.

As she danced aside and pulled the remaining cartridge from the chamber, an odd urge to sing her reply rose. Zita swallowed it back down. Even if it would get her out of movie nights, she didn't want to be banned from the club. "Not until you tell me!"

Music trickled in, quiet at first but fast.

Zita tossed the gun back toward the kitchen.

They both sprang forward and...

Grasped hands?

They leapt backward again, spinning in unison.

She shook her head, trying to clear it. *That's not what I meant to do.*

The other woman feinted forward twice, then turned around and shook her rear at Zita. Behind her, multiple hands gripped the bottom of the big garage door and began manually pushing it up.

"Caramba. What is going on?" Zita swore as she flipped over the other woman. After a quick switch to a gorilla, she dove onto the garage door handle and dragged it closed. She hurried but tried not to break any bones.

A series of yelps sounded outside, and all the fingers withdrew.

After stomping the broken lock in place, she shifted back to Arca and whirled into a series of spinning capoeira kicks nowhere near the other woman. She ended near the interior door.

Apparently, the faux waitress felt like singing as she ran through a series of moves that seemed like an odd cross between contactless Krav Maga and dancing. Her lip curled. "I'm just a soldier and might never grow older. Obeying orders from higher up, offering others a drugged cup." She went on singing about uniforms.

"Why does this keep happening here? What about this club makes people think that drugging others is a good idea? Maybe they should turn it into a hamburger place or something!" To her horror, Zita's words held the cadence of song.

"Not likely. The vampire takes away their bread before he drinks them down for dead." The waitress-soldier took a deep breath, as if preparing for a big chorus, and she dramatically kicked the lock out of the latch.

"He left already. What did you drug them with? Can you at least drop the rhyming? This is all very bad timing..." Zita cut herself off.

Multiple hands grabbed the loading dock door again. It banged and sped upward.

Wyn and all those people! Zita retreated, slamming the door to the loading dock shut. After a rapid shift to an ox, she pushed a pallet of potatoes in front of the door. *That won't hold them long, and there are still other ways in.*

She ran to her friend, changing back to Arca midstep. As she passed through the singing and dancing kitchen staff, she called out a warning in English and Spanish about the raid.

While some of the workers continued their singalong, a few began a panicked chorus as they grabbed multiple items and ran for the exits.

When Zita emerged from the kitchen, Rani grabbed her frantically. "Where's Muse? I need her!"

"Last I saw, singing while she looked for the source of whatever crazy is going on right now," Zita said, gesturing to everything around them.

Most of the room appeared to be participating in or filming a synchronized dance of some sort. A group of waiters and waitresses passed, carrying a reclining Incubus, who waved as they carried him up the stairs.

"I need her help! Something's wrong with Brie." Rani gestured to a chair against one wall, where her girlfriend was slumped against a mirror.

Sweat ran in rivulets down Brie's face, and her attention was glued to the show. Her skin had paled, and shivers wracked her body.

"Muse is in the booth closest to the stairs in the VIP section," Zita said.

Rani nodded and darted off that way.

Swearing internally, Zita checked Brie's pulse. It beat far too fast and erratically under her fingers, and her pupils were dilated.

A conga line formed with the bodyguards leading the way as they danced through the room, knocking over chairs.

She dug in her pocket for Wyn's sobering charm and touched it to the other woman.

Brie sagged as if her strings had been cut, eyes closing.

All the singing and dancing stopped. A man leaping through the air landed on a table with a crash.

Voices hummed in multiple conversations as the disoriented crowd disentangled from each other and tried to figure out what had happened. A path opened for Rani and Wyn to come running through, like a pair of light and dark supermodels in a movie.

When they reached her, Zita tapped Rani with the rock. "Someone spiked the free drinks, and we've got soldiers of some kind incoming. Brie's not in good shape."

Wyn frowned, her hands and lips already weaving the familiar patterns of her healing spell. Soft green light twined around Brie. "This is... this might be the same stuff that Sobek was selling, the amped-up meth. She's got serious internal damage. It's as though her system was burning from the inside."

A camera flashed somewhere nearby.

"Freeze! DMS. Let us in!" Someone bellowed from the front door area.

The crowd shuffled about, but only flashes of color and the occasional tip of a long gun could be seen through the press of people.

Brie giggled. "Cheese it! It's the fuzz!" she shouted, before coughing. "Ow."

Rani kneeled beside her girlfriend, despite the sticky floor and her short skirt, taking her hand. "Are you all right, precious?"

"I can't leave her. She's barely stable. I don't want her to die," Wyn said, concentration on her face.

Rani muttered, "Finish healing her. I owe you."

With that, she rose and stepped in front of a DMS agent. "Is there a problem, Officer?"

The DMS guy told her to get out of the way and reached to push her aside.

"No, I don't think so." Rani plucked a glass off a nearby table and dashed it in his face.

He tased her.

Around them, the crowd hissed. Someone screamed. Multiple phones glowed as they were held up in the dimly lit club.

Her immunity to electricity clearly still working, Rani batted away the prongs. "Hey! That hurts! Help! Police brutality!"

The other one tased her.

A few more people screamed, and partiers finally ran for the exits. The crowded club was a press of bodies going in every direction. Zita couldn't see the exits or the DMS forces, save for the two already closest to them.

Warmth spread through her mind as party line returned. *I need more time,* Wyn sent.

Zita stood and lifted her hands. "Oye, if you want to dance, you should ask nicer."

"The vigilantes! Get them!" someone cried from within the throng.

Around them, partiers booed.

A DMS agent surged toward Rani, handcuffs readied, only to be met by a bodyguard.

Someone threw a drink. The plastic goblet bounced off the other DMS man's head and spilled liquid all over his face.

Another person shrieked and tossed a beer bottle.

Brie's eyes were glassy. She cooed at Rani and slapped her lightly, her hands floppy. "Are we vigilantes now? So tired..."

A bodyguard forced his way through the mass of people and pulled Brie to her wobbly feet.

"Just arrest all three of them," someone barked.

Wyn lifted her hands from her patient. "I'm done. She'll be fine, but she needs rest."

"Bye now!" Brie called out from where the bodyguard appeared to be supporting most of her weight. "Keep that job offer in mind!" With a giggle, she shakily tipped a chair in front of another agent who was lunging toward them.

The third bodyguard appeared to be bulldozing a path for the women to follow, pausing only to allow them to keep up.

With a sigh, Rani squeezed her unsteady girlfriend's shoulder as she was half-carried by. She tilted her head toward the exits. "Go," she whispered. "Goodbye, Muse."

Wyn's lips parted. "Goodbye, Rani."

The electrician nodded and darted after Brie. The bodyguard who'd been waiting for her closed in behind her.

Zita grabbed her unmoving friend and shoved her toward the largest mass of partygoers. *Sneak out with the crowd?*

They ducked into the mass of people.

They'll probably arrest everyone and sort it out later, Wyn sent. She kept looking back.

This is a lot of people. Play our cards right, and we'll slip through. If necessary, you do that mind trick thing where you convince them we can go on our way. We won't be the only ones running for it. If we can make it to a dark alley with no lights and cameras, I can teleport us back to your place. Zita pulled Wyn deeper into the throng of now-panicking people.

I want to go home. Muscles moved beneath Zita's hand as Wyn cast a spell.

Zita saw her own hand change color, paling and becoming larger. Hairier. *I see I'm the dude again.*

Her friend shrugged, now appearing as a freckled redhead in short shorts. *You make a better man than I do.*

Verdad. I can't argue with that. When we get outside, follow my lead. To her annoyance, even seeming to be a much taller man did not help to open a path through the panicking mob, though she suspected she got shoved far less.

Works for me. Wyn stumbled beside her, looking back as they were carried out the doors and into the cooler night by the wave of people.

A thought struck Zita. *We're going in on Jerome's mad plan now, aren't we?*

Unhappiness filled the party line. *I'm afraid so.*

A few minutes later, in a dark alley blocks away, Zita remembered and grumbled. "I never did ask what cephalopod was on the chandelier."

Chapter Eight

For anyone else, driving the people in their dreams to throw mugs of hot chocolate might have been interpreted as a sign of displeasure. Even if she'd been surfing the marshmallow waves in the cup at the time, it didn't bother Zita. For her, it just meant her brain was keeping it real in her sleep.

"Chill. Don't upset the narwhal." She gestured to the creature on a similar surfboard beside her, an ivory fellow with brown and black speckles all over his back.

The big mammal shrugged, an interesting trick that it managed despite lacking shoulders. "I'm cool. You could even call me Arctic."

Zita snickered. "I see what you did there. A friend of mine would love you." She held out her fist to him.

"I get that a lot. Before the orcas show up—party poopers, all of them—I'm going to do another run," he replied, bumping his fin against her hand. He set up his board to surf again.

The person who had thrown the cup, Dream Auntie, hovered above the surface of the hot chocolate. She made an impatient gesture with one mahogany hand. The narwhal, surfboards, and everything else disappeared so that the two women drifted in a void. Exasperation flattened her deep voice and emphasized her melodic African accent. "Enough of your foolishness! You need to listen. You need to—"

"Oye, I liked him. For a whale, he was pretty awesome. You don't find many willing to go cliff diving and then surf to shore." Zita stared mournfully at where her buddy had been. A thought struck her. "If you got rid of everything, does that mean if I did yoga or something here, it would react like I was in space? That might be cool."

"Stop! Focus!" The other woman gestured dramatically at her.

"Lady, people have been saying that to me my entire life without it working. You think that's going to change in my dreams?" Zita snorted and folded her body into a physically demanding pose. In her dreams, it took no effort. *Disappointing.*

A clicking noise came from somewhere nearby, and she checked to see if the narwhal had returned. *No. Pity.*

"So, you realize you're dreaming?" Dream Auntie narrowed her eyes, but the answer seemed to mollify her. Unnecessarily, she smoothed the front of her old-fashioned pastel pink skirt suit and patted the tiny hat pinned in her hair.

Her attention on which position to try next, Zita replied absently, "Of course. We fall asleep, then you come tromping in with commands and warnings and such. Ruining awesome dreams, I might add. You never show up during nightmares, just during the good ones."

Dream Auntie considered her. "Sleepers rarely wish to recall nightmares, let alone the advice dispensed during them. You must remember my words."

Zita waved a hand. "Whatever. Just saying. Why do you always come talk to me or Wingspan? Muse would be happy to talk to you. Not only does she have a better memory, but she also doesn't use a dreamcatcher."

"Is that the web that makes you harder to reach? As much as your friend may be willing to speak when she is awake... when she is asleep, her mind protects itself too much for me to enter without risk. Your Muse is the only person other than my twin who has been able to keep me out of their dreams, and I am weakened right now. You are simpler. In many ways."

"You got a twin? Do they invade people's dreams too?"

"No. That is solely my gift. Theirs is apparently to keep me out, so I may never apologize for my foolishness in an argument about her life. It is a great sor—Why do we speak of this, anyway? This is not why I came to you. We must discuss more important things than my problems with my sister's choices." Dream Auntie frowned as if confused.

Zita shrugged. "People tell me personal shit all the time for no reason. I must have one of those faces. If you're here about the danger to the port city, my friends and I are working on that. I don't suppose you came to give us some tips? Something more useful than badness is coming? You know, if you gave us practical details, we might do better. Instead of 'fire will burn in the sunlight,' you could say 'Fifth and Main on Tuesday at 1:23 p.m. Bring fire extinguishers and burn kits because of the flamethrowers.' Straightforward shit we can use."

The other woman sighed, her forehead wrinkling. "I've tried. It doesn't work like that."

"It should. Where are you?"

Dream Auntie paused. "I don't know."

"How can you not give even a rough ballpark? Were you lost when you went to sleep?" Zita raised her eyebrows.

"No, but I've been asleep for quite a while, and I know I've been moved."

Zita's mind drew a blank on what to ask. "Like eight hours?"

The other woman gave a tight smile. "Longer. I've been resting since the blackout."

"Last May, when people passed out, and bunches woke up as metas? That qualifies as a coma."

Dream Auntie shook her head. "No, it was July when I went to sleep."

"Also qualifies as a coma when you've been asleep for a couple months. Do you know what hospital you were near?" Zita asked.

"Longer than that, I think. It was July, July 1977 when the blackout happened. I'm uncertain what the date is now, but I was closing a shop on Broadway when they came and brought the violence and the fire. The trauma... I didn't wake up from that the way I did from the coma that gave me my abilities a few years earlier."

Zita held up a finger as she did the quick calculation. "That was thirty-seven years ago. You didn't wake up once?"

Her expression haunted, Dream Auntie looked away. "It seemed for the best. I do much good this way."

"Sure, be more cryptic. That's just what this dream needed. Well, tell me what you came to say. Oh! And do you know a girl named Elle or Eleanor? Is she with you or near you?" Zita leaned forward.

Another click. This time, she recognized it.

"Wait... those are my door locks. I need to go."

Dream Auntie made a clawing gesture, and webs surrounded Zita. "Stay! Many are in danger! I came because you need to—"

"I need to check who that is," Zita said, tugging against the webs. A bright turquoise door appeared.

Dream Auntie dismissed the door. "No, let us finish this first. You must—"

Click. Her internal alarms blared. *Someone's here.*

"Only one lock left! I need to get up. I can't help nobody if I'm murdered." Zita teleported to where the door had been and concentrated.

The door reappeared.

She grabbed the handle and hurled herself into a psychedelic void. Before she woke to the sound of the last lock, she could've sworn she'd heard Dream Auntie use a very unladylike curse.

Her eyes shot open in the real world.

A faint jingle and shuffling sounds came from the living room.

After grabbing the knife from its hidden sheath behind her headboard, she vaulted out of bed. She crouched beside the closet, weapon in her hand. Her heart pounded. *My brothers and Wyn are the only ones with keys. None of them come in the bedroom when the door's closed, so if whoever comes in, they're not anyone I know. Has DMS found me?*

The footsteps drew closer. Not Wyn or Quentin.

Hunkering down even lower, she shifted partially to a cat, just enough to improve her senses. The dark shapes of her bedroom resolved into familiar detail. Bed, desk, chair, tiny wicker nightstands. *Not enough space for fighting.* She pressed her back against the closet so if they approached the bed, she could pounce on them.

The door to her room opened.

Light flared as a phone flashlight snapped on, and she involuntarily brought up her non-knife hand to her face. Inhaling, she recognized the intruder's scent. "¡No mames! Miguel! Why you always got to be breaking into my apartment?"

Her oldest brother lowered his phone so it wasn't in her face, instead shining it on her weapon. "I bought you a Taser and a stun gun, but you're crawling around with a knife? What are you going to do, stab a burglar? Is something on your face?"

Carajo. I hope he didn't see anything inhuman on me. I don't have fur on my hand or a tail, at least. After a hasty shift back to being fully human, she lowered the hand from her face and stood. She pointed the knife down and switched on the light, a cheerful plastic turtle on the closest nightstand. "Only thing on my face is drool. You woke me up. I grabbed something. You're lucky I didn't stab you. And yeah, probably would've gone for a hamstring. Nonfatal and all that."

He scanned her with a puzzled expression and then eyed the weapon, a fixed blade several inches long. "Maybe you shouldn't sleep with a machete."

With a snort, Zita rolled her eyes. "You know perfectly well it's a nice KA-BAR knife. The machetes are in the closet with my camping gear. And I don't expect guests to waltz into my bedroom at... what time is it?" She glanced at the clock. "Three a.m. Date with the vet ran long, did it? She seemed more like the breakfast and cuddle type, but people got their kinks, I guess."

Despite the poor light from the lamp, she caught the flush that temporarily stained her brother's dark skin, only a couple shades lighter than her own. Deep circles underlined his eyes, and the chiseled Quechua lines of his face seemed engraved with worry. He switched to the rapid-fire Spanglish that they'd used as kids. He scratched his neck. "Work had me on planes almost every day last week. You know I'm staying here, right? Were you going to fillet me if I went to the bathroom?"

She spun the blade in a practiced circle as she replied in the same language. "No, because the toilet is not in my bedroom. I was expecting you to sleep on the sofa. If you were here, I'd expect to hear you moving around. You said you'd be back before too late, and I figured you'd at least call. What's with that?"

"I called. Actually, I stopped by, too, but you weren't home, but your phone was. That's why I came in here, to see if you ever came home. Why did you leave without it?"

"It didn't rin—oye." Zita picked up her phone off the bedside table and pressed a button. "Sorry, I forgot I turned it off while it was charging. I had dinner here, so you must've just missed me."

Miguel folded his arms over his chest and tapped his foot. "Did you also forget to take it with you when you went out?"

"Sounds right. Since we're up, you want a snack before you go to sleep?" She yawned.

Her brother frowned at her and yanked at the loosely knotted tie around his neck. "Zita, I really don't like... you've always been erratic about your coming and going, but you've been extra flighty since the quarantine. What did Mama always tell us?"

Zita tried to pick one of the more common phrases. "Stop touching that?"

He frowned. "Not that. You know."

"Climbing is for monkeys. Children should walk? Try to hold still for a moment so I can see if it's an earthquake or just you bouncing around? People aren't trampolines?" She ran through the first few that came to mind.

Miguel scowled at her. "I can't tell if you're serious or not... I forgot for a minute how much she said those things to you."

"Can it be a bit of both? I'm not sure which one you're going for," Zita said.

Lifting his hands, he intoned in Spanish, "Keep your head down..."

"And be ready to run. That's a good one. My go bag's always packed," she finished.

Her brother nodded. "Listen, Zita, I don't know what bad idea you're currently chasing, but you need to play it safe and boring for once in your life."

She made a rude noise to let him know what she thought of that.

"I shouldn't tell you this, but DMS has you in the database of possible metas. Everyone who got quarantined and hasn't been cleared is in there. Right now, that means email and phone campaigns to get you to agree to basic medical tests to prove or disprove it either way, but it won't stay that way forever if certain people have their way." Miguel ran a hand over his hair, back and forth, frowning.

Zita fought hard to keep her muscles from overtly stiffening, even if she could feel her heart rate increase at his admission. "Can they tell that?"

"They have a blood test, but I guess it requires special equipment or something because you have to go to the test site... at least for now." He shrugged.

"I'm not going nowhere with or for them," she said.

He sighed and somehow seemed to age another decade. "You may not always have a choice if those bills pass Congress. With meta crime going wild these days—in the past month alone, the reports have doubled in number—they've got a lot of support, and some of it is pretty high up. If that Everyman party wins the midterm election, their votes will definitely support anything DMS does to control and possibly eliminate metas. Or possible ones."

Zita didn't bother to hide her skepticism. "Like they're not doing that now? They're pretty much unsupervised thugs, you excepted."

Her brother quirked an eyebrow at her. "You've been paying attention to something other than sports for once? Good. You understand why I don't want you caught in the middle, so if you've been engaged in some stupidity, you need to stop. Please."

Zita scrubbed a hand over her short hair, making it stand on end.

Miguel took a step closer to her, his eyes glinting. "And if you've been doing something illegal, you should not only stop but also tell me right away so we can figure out how to get you amnesty for turning in others you've been associating with."

Every curse she'd ever learned ran through her mind. *He's guessing. And no, I won't turn in my friends, ruin their lives, my life, and end your future in law enforcement, especially when you're getting settled with a girl and everything.*

"Little sister, I can practically see steam coming from your ears. What's going on?" His face softened with concern.

And it's not like I set out to be a vigilante. Revealing my identity is not an option. She forced a smile to her face. "Nothing. You're too suspicious. I haven't been doing anything but some climbing and stuff, and I'm a grown-ass woman. DMS can look at me, but they won't find anything, so that's that."

Her brother leaned forward, a flash of triumph on his face. "Excellent. They're offering tests to see if you're a meta to quarantine victims and DMS staff. They gave me the V Test last week when I was on travel."

"V Test? They got through the rest of the alphabet already? That's not real confidence-inspiring." Zita raised an eyebrow.

He shook his head. "It stands for Virus Test, and it's supposed to be more accurate than any of the others. Apparently, the doctors inject you with an inactive virus, like a flu vaccine, and they can tell if you're a meta or not based on a small blood sample after a few minutes. You should offer to take the test. When it comes back negative, they'll lose all interest in you."

She rolled her eyes. "No mames. I'm tired of people jabbing me with needles. Plus, the virus thing sounds hinky. Besides, I never agree to do anything more than I have to with the government. You're the one who told me never volunteer."

Miguel paused, shook his head, and said slowly, "Maybe this once..."

Zita slid the knife back into its hidden sheath and folded her arms over her chest. "No. When it comes back negative, they'll just keep calling me back again and again in case it was wrong. When I start refusing to go, they'll claim that since I was willing once, I should ride the carousel every time until they finally find a test that says that everyone who was quarantined should be in their power. That's what they really want, isn't it?"

He paused.

Struck by a thought, she said, "Besides, I heard DMS is disappearing metahumans. I'm not getting anywhere near them, other than you."

Miguel closed his mouth on whatever he had been about to say. "You have? What have you heard?"

"All I heard is that metahumans get arrested for jaywalking or speeding, DMS takes the case, and they're gone. Plus, they've been searching houses and phones and stuff without warrants and raiding homes in the middle of the night, arresting any metas inside even if they didn't do anything. No court cases. No last phone calls. Nobody hears from them again."

His face was grim, and he rubbed his eyes. "I hadn't heard all that, but clearly someone should follow up to see if they're really warrantless. That's all the more reason for you to avoid their notice."

Zita pointed a finger at him. "Exactly, and going in for a blood test, even one that would be negative, wouldn't accomplish that."

He frowned but didn't negate her comment. "Every time a meta does something splashy and bad, DMS and their backers get more currency. Rumor has it that the head of the Congressional committee providing oversight, Senator Chivington, is even considering a presidential run in the next couple years on the Everyman platform, which includes expanding DMS."

Zita raised her eyebrows at him. "¿Neta? They already class metahumans as terrorists. I got to say, if they come for me, I'm out of here and moving someplace sunny. So, if that happens, prepare to rent out your condo to someone else. I'll expect you to send me my stuff though because you're family and don't want strangers pawing through my sports gear." As an afterthought, she added, "Or my underwear, I guess."

He nodded. His gaze turned to her window, and he said, "If someone, particularly another government agency, were looking into it, they'd need to collect pretty strong evidence and win significant public support before acting against DMS."

She relaxed a little, though something about his last statement had her wondering. "I guess. It's late. Early, whatever. Are you crashing here or what? You look terrible. You getting sick? I'm going to catch another hour, maybe two, before I get up for my morning workout. Some of us got lives, you know."

He nodded. "I should sleep. It's been a really long week, and I'm so drained the last few days are a blur."

She frowned. His body language wasn't just tired. "Something's bugging you. Did you talk to your girl or a bud about it?"

Miguel shook his head.

After rolling her shoulders to loosen them and wishing for an alternative, Zita braced herself to be a good sister. She forced the words out, "You want to talk about it?"

He said nothing.

She waited. Managed not to glance longingly at her bed... much.

Finally, he spoke. His face was sour, as if he'd bitten a lemon, but his eyes grieved. "I walked in on a meta attacking men in a satellite DMS office. Because of all the blood, I thought he'd murdered everyone, so I killed him when he attacked. Now I'm on desk or training duty only until they clear the shooting."

Zita punched his arm and leaned against him. "No mames! You going to be okay?"

He slung an arm around her and hugged her.

She didn't say anything, even when he held on a bit too tight.

Miguel released her and paced, hands gesturing as he spoke. "It turns out the guys weren't dead, just unconscious. What bothers me most is that I'm the only one who seems to care that the meta died. Everyone else is acting like it's a huge inconvenience because he was an informant, and now they have to find a new one. DMS is pretty quick to find any shooting justified, or so I've heard. It's not right, and I've applied to rejoin the FBI. Not that I didn't have cause to shoot him, but... I can't work with an organization that's so callous about a life."

"Of course not."

"That's actually why they gave me the V test. They wanted to ensure I wasn't infected by meta blood. I didn't even know that was a thing before this."

"I haven't heard anything about metas being contagious, even when it was all comas all the time," Zita said. "And you couldn't tell Linnea any of this?"

Her brother sighed. "I'm unsure about a lot of things, but she's not one of them. She worked a double shift and was so dead on her feet that she fell asleep during dinner. I couldn't… I won't dump on my girlfriend when she can barely hold her head up without one of those overpriced sugary coffees she likes."

Zita thought ruefully of her own relationship. The one where she wore a literal mask to hide a face that wasn't hers. Even her voice and accent were wrong. "You know you got to tell her all this sometime."

"I don't want my work to touch her." He frowned.

She chuckled. "Mano, if you're serious about her—"

He met her eyes, the deep brown of his eyes identical to the shade that stared at her in the mirror. "She's the one, Zita."

"Carajo. Congrats, I guess. In which case, you get ahead of it and tell her at least what you told me. All that's coming home with you, whether or not you say something about it. If you want her to be a part of your life, you got to tell her sometime. Maybe not tonight when she's all double shifted, possibly high on caffeine, and sleep-deprived, but soon. Not like the gory stuff like the brains all over or anything. Then again, she's a vet. She's seen some super gross stuff."

Her eldest brother fell silent and stared at her. Finally, he said, "That's surprisingly good advice from someone who's as bad at relationships as you."

"After the first hundred dates or so, you learn a few things. Like being honest upfront either ends things real quick or at least starts everybody on the same page." Zita shoved down her own guilt. *Or as honest as possible, anyway.*

Miguel hugged her again, before ruffling her hair.

She batted him away.

"Ah, there's the sister I know. I'm going to grab a few sack hours. While I think any conversation about the man I shot should be in person, I'll call to warn Linnea about DMS before I head back to New York. If what you heard is true, she needs to be careful as a known metahuman. We'll need to work out something to keep her safe."

She nodded. "Yes, you should definitely keep your future baby mama safe. Blanket and pillow are already there for you. Night, mano."

His voice tart, he said, "Next time, pull the stun gun, not the knife."

Zita snorted. "With DMS on the hunt? No promises."

Chapter Nine

A few days later, Zita found herself in her Arca form and spending her lunch break alone in a janitor's closet. Over party line, she sent, *Are we certain this is a good idea?*

I'm positive it's not, but Remus has been dealing with this case on our behalf. We owe him, Wyn sent back.

A tall, vaguely familiar black woman peered into the closet where Zita had been hiding for the past half hour. She snapped her fingers. "Be quick. Understandably, we don't have much time."

Zita flexed her fingers and squared her shoulders. Smoothed the long hair of her Arca disguise. "Sí, sí, I got the message," she muttered, but the stranger was already gone. Taking a deep breath and dodging the rolling mop and bucket, she strode out into the well-lit courthouse corridor.

Down the hall, the woman was holding open a door.

Inside, Zita found a small wood-paneled courtroom, thick with the scent of sweaty bodies, industrial cleanser, and slightly moldy air conditioning. Her nose wrinkled as she followed the lawyer down the stained, maroon carpet.

A heavyset woman behind a massive wooden desk took center stage. To one side of her, a man armed only with some odd little typewriter sat, flexing his fingers. An empty chair sat by the desk. Two tables faced the judge's seat.

Remus and a slender African American woman were side by side at one table. Luis, who she knew as a live-in nurse and aspiring music (or movie, she couldn't remember which) critic, sat immediately behind them. Weariness lined his face.

Three people sat at the other table. Two wore expressions so sour that even their obvious and extensive plastic surgery could not fix them. A plump middle-aged man in a suit scribbled something on papers beside them. Given that he was the only person smiling in the room, she assumed he was a lawyer, filling out his billable hours during slow moments.

Visitor seating was mostly empty. In one corner, a pretty guy in makeup exchanged whispers with a camera person. Two elderly women sat on the benches in the back of the room. One was asleep, and the other was lovely enough that Zita didn't need the wink and elegant toss of silver hair to tell her which was Wyn under an illusion. A man in a uniform stood by the entry doors.

The woman behind her closed the door and murmured, "Keep walking. Make it good."

Zita glanced at her, then at the front of the room, and did a double-take. She didn't, however, pause in her slow stroll down the center aisle.

Beside Remus, the lawyer had risen, and she had the exact same face as the woman next to Zita, though the suits were different.

Zita gestured toward Remus' attorney and then at the lady beside her. "Twins?"

"No, I'm a meta. One of me is home playing with my kid right now, too. Go sit in the square box by the judge." Copy One—the woman who had summoned her from the closet—said, remaining by the door.

Beside Remus, the lawyer—Copy Two—said, "We call the individual known as Arca to the stand."

The guy taking notes straightened and pulled out his phone, texting like mad. The camera turned in her direction.

Taking a deep breath, Zita stepped forward and waved as she strolled toward the judge. "Hey, that's me!"

The bailiff by the door immediately grabbed his walkie-talkie and stun gun.

At the front of the room, Copy Two stood beside Remus. She waved a hand at the bailiff. "Wait! Don't call security. She's a witness."

"Objection! The witness is masked and claiming to be someone unverifiable," the cheerful guy—Suit Guy—at the opposite table said. "I don't think she's tall enough to be Arca, either."

"I'm known as Arca, and people know what I do well enough that I can prove it," she said, reciting the defense she'd been told to memorize. She couldn't help noting the only exits from the room were the one she'd come in and a concealed door behind the judge's chair.

The odds of escaping capture went down if they could cage her in the room. Zita sent, *Wyn, where are the closest windows?*

Leaving so soon? They're in the judge's quarters, per the map Remus' attorney showed us, her friend replied.

Copy Two stood. "Per Paladin v. Cattivo Nostro, 1977, masked individuals with meta powers may testify provided they can verify their identities through a demonstration of powers or other acceptable means. Clockwork v. the United States, 1980, further demonstrated that individuals so identified may own and manage property."

"Can you prove you're the person known as Arca?" the judge asked. Her eyes narrowed as she eyed Zita.

"Am I going to be attacked if I do? I'll demonstrate if he's not going to come after me for it," she replied, glancing at the bailiff.

The judge squinted at the guard and waved a hand. "I'll allow a quick display of powers for the purpose of determining identity, as I'm assuming legal identification is out of the question?"

"No shit," Zita muttered. At the judge's frown, she amended her statement. "I mean, yes, yes, it is."

"Nothing dangerous. I'll allow it," the judge barked.

The bailiff moved his hand away from his weapon but hooked it nearby.

"Tell you what. You name an animal, and I'll turn into it. That way you can't argue I set up nothing in advance. Just, you know, nothing water-breathing or tiny. I also don't know what your floors are made of, so you probably want to keep away from elephants since this is the third floor of the courthouse and all," Zita said. She came to a stop in the widest area available, the empty space between the judge and the lawyers' tables.

The judge said carefully, "Are you the only shifter who can assume multiple forms?"

She shook her head. "No. I've heard of or seen others with up to three shapes, but I haven't met and asked everyone, either. Assuming they'd tell me, which they might not. Far as I know, though, nobody other than me can do more than three."

The judge tapped the gavel. "Very well, then. I will require you to shapeshift to five different animals and will call out each form when I am satisfied with the preceding one. The attorney for both sides will step forward and give you a pat on the head to ascertain if you have truly taken the form."

Zita shrugged and straightened up to her full five feet of height. "So long as they don't get fresh or beat me, I'm cool with that."

The judge might've sighed. Both attorneys waited by their tables, though the portly man opposing Copy Two lost his cherubic smile. Remus' handsome face seemed pinched... as if he'd eaten something sour and was trying not to react.

With a bang, the judge began the test. "Please only speak when asked a question. You may begin. Sheep."

Since she'd been warned in advance that this would be required, Zita obediently took each form as it was called out. In the end, she took six shapes: sheep, giraffe (the ceiling was almost too low for that one), chimp, sloth, tortoise, and pig, the last chosen by the old lady in the back of the room, who had woken up in time to cheer her on.

As she demonstrated, more people slipped into the room, including two more bailiffs, a guy who almost certainly had a gun hidden under his jacket, and several people who appeared to be filming her with their phones.

The judge banged her gavel. "Return to your human form. Is the plaintiff satisfied?"

Dutifully, Zita returned to her Arca shape.

Suit Guy rose. "Your Honor, we still protest her presence in this court."

Copy Two cleared her throat. "Her demonstration should have adequately proved her identity, and you were a witness. Given that your clients called said abilities into question, I find her presence relevant."

"In which case, we request a thirty-minute recess to review notes." Suit Guy wasn't giving up that easily.

Without waiting for approval to speak, Zita said, "I don't got that long. DMS will come busting in soon, so if you want to question me, it has to be fast. I'm all you're getting, too, because Muse isn't the only witch out there, and Wingspan could prove himself, but he'd need to be outside to do so. Also, he makes guard types real itchy. I'm the only one of my friends who spoke to the dead guy, anyway. I think."

"This is all highly irregular, but very well. I have no wish for DMS to turn my courtroom into a circus. Remember, I do not tolerate lying or tomfoolery in my court." The judge shot Zita a flinty look.

Suit Guy and his clients glared at her.

"What? Did I forget to wear deodorant?" Zita asked, sniffing at her own shoulders.

The judge banged her gavel. "Arca, please refrain from speaking unless you have been asked a question. Restrict yourself to the question and no other commentary. Swear her in so we may begin."

Wyn laughed over party line. *The judge has heard of you.*

All good things, I'm sure, Judges like honest. I'm honest, Zita replied.

Amusement vibrated over their connection. *To an extremely awkward fault.*

Someone hurried forward, escorted her to the witness box, and swore her in on a Bible.

Zita asked the question she'd forgotten before. "Your Honor, judge lady, can I stand, please?"

"Is it necessary?" The judge raised an eyebrow.

She hadn't planned on answering quite as honestly, but the words seemed to tumble out of her mouth. "Only if you want me to pay attention. I get distracted trying to hold still if I'm sitting."

"Then you may stand, but do not leave the witness box."

Idly noting a door almost hidden in the paneling behind the judge, Zita rose to her feet. "Thanks! So, what'd you want to know?"

The judge sighed. "Defense, your witness."

✱✱✱

Remus' lawyer, Copy Two, stood. "Arca, you've proved beyond any doubt that you are a shapeshifter. Do you have any abilities that allow you to force or charm others to do your will?"

She snorted. "No. I can barely convince people I rescue not to attack me sometimes."

A few people in the increasingly crowded audience tittered.

Copy Two smiled at her and set a photograph in front of her. "Have you met this man? Exhibit Three."

Zita glanced at the picture. "Sure."

Remus' lawyer waited a beat, then said, "For the record, the witness has identified Mr. Stanley Shivers. Can you describe your relationship with the deceased?"

"Didn't have one. We—Muse, Wingspan, and I—rescued him once. At least, I think that picture was the dude who owned part of a knife. One ancient white guy looks a lot like another, you know?"

The lawyer did not comment on that, instead proceeding to her next question. "Were you or any member of your team involved in a short- or long-term relationship that could be viewed as romantic or sexual?"

"Eww. You got problems. He probably grew up stabbing dinosaurs or something. Besides, the one time we met, his helper dude... that guy in the seat behind Remus there... was right there. No way the old guy could piss in that little house without him knowing. Right, Helper Dude?" She nodded to Luis.

He nodded.

"Do not address anyone in the audience, Arca, and please answer using only facts, not conjecture. I'm allowing considerable latitude given the situation, but I demand decorum in my court," the judge said.

Zita sighed. "Okay, but I was answering the question. I don't want to find out how many novenas I'd have to say if I broke a promise I made on the Bible."

Copy Two gave her a brief nod. "Did you or your friends request a reward or gift at any time or in any manner?"

"No. We don't do that. We go in. We help people. We leave before the paperwork starts." More words poured out, though she'd intended to stop there. "Mostly, we just told him to go hide and stuff like that. He asked if we had some kind of Hallway of Justice or something, and I told him we didn't have that kind of cash. His reply was that he could believe it because our clothes sucked."

A few people snickered in the audience.

"And that was the extent of your conversation?"

"He told us where the thingy was the bad guys wanted."

"Are you referring to part of the Key of Hades, part of a dagger that was the focus of a robbery and hostage situation at the Carter Shuster Museum of Design and Innovation?"

"Yeah. Old dude owned part of the Evil Knife of Evil."

"The witness will stick to facts," Suit Guy protested from the plaintiff table.

"It was evil, though. That's a fact," Zita protested.

Perhaps to avoid the judge becoming upset, Copy Two shoved another photo in front of Zita. "Is this the knife? Exhibit 15-A."

She squinted at it and made a face. "Maybe. I never got a close-up on the knife and only saw it when it was being used to stab people. That could be part of it."

Copy Two spoke again. "Witness has tentatively identified Mr. Shivers' portion of the Key of Hades. Did you have any further communication with Mr. Shivers?"

"No, we only met the one time. Oh! He said something about his relatives being all up in his grill and not liking that they were only after his money. How rich could he have been, anyway? He had this tiny-ass house in the woods. Might have had termites. Oh, I'm sorry, the termite thing is a guess. You maybe shouldn't write that down, but it'd be good if someone sent out exterminators to check."

While their faces never changed expression, both of the cranky people at the plaintiff's table stiffened, and the man's fists clenched.

"The property in question is valued at several million dollars," Copy Two explained.

"No mames. It was a bunch of trees, a broken-down airfield, and a small house. Was there like an underground bunker made of gold or something? Or did he upholster his house in diamond-studded velvet or some crazy shit like that? I mean, the airport was pretty run down."

The judge hit her gavel against her desk. "Enough. Restrict your answers to answering the questions only."

"It's located in a high property value area," Copy Two explained.

"Whatever." She waved it aside. Glancing at the judge, she said, "Shushing now."

Copy Two said, "Your Honor, we rest."

The judge massaged her temples. "The plaintiff may question the witness now. Again, the witness will refrain from offering opinions and restrict herself to answering the questions, or I will find her in contempt of the court."

Suit Guy eyed her and spoke. "What's your name?"

Even though she had no intention of lying, she wiped sweat off her forehead. "I'm known as Arca."

The lawyer's eyes glittered like coal. "Your full, legal name."

Zita leaned closer to the microphone and articulated each syllable clearly. "None of your chingado business."

Copy Two leapt to her feet. "Your Honor, he's badgering my witness. If we're going to discuss anything actually connected to the case, he should focus on that."

"Did you or your friends use your powers on Mr. Stanley Shivers?" Suit Guy snapped.

"I'm a shapeshifter. My powers only work on me, same with Wingspan, other than he can carry people places. We didn't take the old guy or his helper anywhere. Muse stuck a shield on them during the fight, and she healed them, I think. She does that. She does that a lot. That's the only powers that got used on them by us."

"What pay do you accept from those you've rescued?"

"We don't usually, though occasionally they'll give us a sandwich or cookies or something. Normally we run off, so the cops don't waste their time or ours chasing us around instead of handling the bad guys."

The question snapped across the distance separating them. "Sources claim Caroline Gyllen refused to bring you and your friends in. What is your relationship with her?"

Copy Two was on her feet. "Objection! Relevance!"

Words tumbled out of her mouth, far harsher and more truthful than the simple no she'd meant to give as her anger reignited. "I don't have one. Maybe she refused because we generally help people and leave. Our paths happen to cross because we do good work. Then she likes to show up to claim the credit for it. She's an entitled rich girl who gets her jollies being a government tool and ruining people's lives. You going to ask me about anything that has to do with this case or just run through every meta I ever met?"

"Sustained. Keep to the case being tried, councilor and witness," the judge warned.

Urgency ran through Wyn's message. *You can't afford to stay any longer. Incoming DMS. Go. I'll leave party line up so if either of us gets caught, the other will know.*

"And I got to go. DMS is on their way, and I don't want them shooting nobody here. Last couple times I ran into them, they attacked innocent people who happened to be in our vicinity." Zita put her hands on the rail and vaulted over it. "Uh, nice to meet you all. Except for you three. You're kind of assholes." She nodded toward Suit Guy and his two companions.

A murmur started in the audience. Someone shouted, "Arca, can you show any proof that DMS has been shooting bystanders?"

"Sure, ask the people at Saint Martha Hospital in Springfield about the poor lady I ran into in a park. I hope she's okay. They also were tasing people left and right at Danz Mizer a couple days ago in DC."

"You have not been dismissed. Order in the court!" the judge said.

The bailiff put a hand on his stun gun.

"Sorry! I'm not going to stick around and get people hurt." Zita edged toward the door.

Four men in combat armor burst in through the doors. "DMS!"

Revising her original escape plan, Zita darted behind the judge's desk and pulled open the hidden door.

It opened into an office. Most importantly, the room had a window. A small, narrow one high up. She locked the door.

Something hit the thick door with a thud.

"Good thing I haven't had lunch yet, or I might not fit." She eyed the window. After climbing onto a bookcase, she leapt up, grabbed the sill, and pulled herself up. Once she got the window open, she pocketed her shoes, switched form to a hawk, and flew away.

Chapter Ten

Jerome was not a gracious winner. "I knew you'd come around. I even turned down an invite to go yachting with these twins... Twins! If anyone deserves a fun date, it's me. The most interesting thing I've done lately is changing a storage facility's records. How sad is that? Speaking of sad, why are we meeting in a closed restaurant?"

In a booth at the very back of an empty Greek restaurant later that night, he had set up two laptops. Zita, Wyn, and Andy sat with him. While the shades were drawn, enough illumination leaked around the edges to light the interior, however dimly. Tables and chairs, stacked in tidy piles, striped the room with angular lines of shadow. The scent of grilled meats and mint lingered under the astringent sting of cleanser. Other than the noise of traffic outside, their voices were the only sounds.

"We needed somewhere to meet. DMS knows about the air park. Given they're watching your house, that was out. This place is closed indefinitely. The owner inherited some money, so he's busy deciding if he wants to be some kind of shipping magnate or go back to selling the best stuffed eggplant in DC. Since his security system stinks, and I overheard that little tidbit, it seemed safe and unconnected enough to use. Just don't mess with any of their stuff and pick up after yourself. Hopefully, nobody will come by to check on the place while we're here," Zita said. *While I'm happy they don't have to worry about going bankrupt, I'm going to miss the free lunches they were giving me for winning that bet. If he comes back, I'm going to get Quentin to sell him better security at a discount.*

"If they've questioned Remus again, they know we came to see you at your house. This seemed safer," Andy explained. *Don't get too distracted mourning missed meals, Z.*

"Why would they question him again?" Jerome asked.

The food was incredible. You'd be sad too, she sent back.

Wyn cleared her throat. "When we endeavored to assist Remus with the disputed will case—"

"Technically, isn't it yours since you'd be the beneficiaries?" Jerome asked. At least half his attention was on the information on his screen.

Her eyes narrowing, Wyn's voice held a prim edge. "While we can do little to assist him without revealing our identities, it seemed prudent to do what we could... given the importance of the case. Even if any ruling is likely to be appealed."

"Rich people hang out together, so you got to know lawyers and stuff like that. Talk to some of your friends and see if they'll help bail out Remus' group. From what he said, they don't have the cash for long lawsuits, and this kind of shit is the sort of thing civil liberties people live for, right?" Zita said.

Jerome frowned. "Not all wealthy people know each other. I mean, my dad's a lawyer, but..."

Zita crossed her arms over her chest. "Wouldn't it be fun if all your clients refused to pay your invoices because you might have used a secret meta power to get them to agree to your contract? And hey, your house is sweet. How do they know you didn't use your abilities to get it?"

Even beneath the warm brown of his skin, Jerome paled. "Fine. I'll see if Dad knows someone who can help Remus and his group."

After clearing her throat delicately, Wyn began, "Right then. Now legal aid for Remus has been procured, what I had begun to say before I was interrupted—"

"That was totally rude of you, Chevalier." Zita nodded at Jerome.

Wyn raised her eyebrows. "Really?"

Zita pretended to zip her lips shut but smirked a little.

Jerome glanced around. "I get we had to meet somewhere neutral, but did we need to come here? The dancing guys in that mural are staring at me. The guy with the huge shoe pompoms is extra creepy."

"I like Arizona," Andy said. "We could meet there."

Zita nodded, bouncing a little on the bench seat. In the heat of the barely air-conditioned restaurant, the bare skin of her legs came away from the bright blue vinyl with a loud sucking sound. It stung a little too. "Death Valley's good too. We would just tell you to dress for heat after we found a place with a picnic table, shade, and enough elevation that the temperature is a little below where the Devil likes it. You'd also have to go without any cell access."

The big black man sighed and typed something on a laptop. "Objection withdrawn. A closed restaurant is fine. This would've been easier to show you on my big monitors at home, though."

With a toss of her hair, Wyn said, "What I've been trying to ask was if you found any useful information?"

"We got lucky. One agent had not only pulled up some files of interest, but he'd actually gone to what I think is the prison in the past few weeks. With the information from his phone, I was able to locate the prison and even the approvals for the renovation required to turn it into a prison." Jerome angled one computer to allow everyone to see the screen.

"What was it before?" Wyn asked.

Jerome grimaced. "Former missile launch site. The weapons are long gone, and the entrances are extremely limited. I think they're hoping that even superpowers won't be able to get through the concrete plus all the dirt to escape or contact the outside world. On the bright side, it limits the number of people they could be holding there."

Andy shuddered. "Everyone's stuck below ground?"

Absently, Zita patted his shoulder. "That'd backfire with Jen Stone."

"So, you want us to break into a secure, underground prison and do what?" Andy frowned.

"This first run will just be scouting. We need to pull out Dream Auntie. Without her real name or direct database access, I can't locate her or even discover when she's supposed to be moved." Jerome hesitated. "We might also want to consider taking your Elle with us, too."

Zita stiffened. "What'd you find out?"

"Nothing directly…" Jerome wouldn't meet her eyes.

"Just say it."

"The agent looked at the files for Elle, Irene, and the three of you."

"They have a file on the Pie Lady?"

He nodded. "Yes, and at least I have some good news there. They know what her ability is, but they're leaving her in perpetual house arrest rather than transferring her to the prison. Apparently, the psychologist felt her abilities might suffer in a prison environment. She might either be unable to use them, or her desserts could have a negative effect rather than a positive one. She'll be required to bake a certain number per week, which DMS will then take into custody and study or distribute as necessary."

Air hissed out through Zita's teeth. "Food thieves and perpetual house arrest!"

Wyn bumped her shoulder, an easy task in the confines of the booth. "At least she'll get to stay home with her family."

Zita grunted. "Still shady, though. What about Elle? And our files, you said?"

The big man nodded. "They divide up meta prisoners into different groups and subgroups. I'm guessing at the designations based on the names. No explanation was given for anything, of course. All three of you are set as High Gas. Elle, Wingspan, and Muse are also marked for a Science group. Arca is assigned to General Population."

Her lips pursed, Wyn said, "High Gas... Do you think they're referring to the orange smoke Arca mentioned?"

"I'm hoping it means a healthy bean-based diet, but your guess is probably the right one," Andy said mournfully.

Zita's stomach rumbled. "I could eat. You brought those burrito bowls I made, right? I cleaned this booth before everyone else got here, so it's okay to eat as long as we take our trash afterward."

Although she removed the food containers from her purse and set them on the table with some silverware, Wyn otherwise ignored their comments. "That label would argue for the theory that the gas does some form of power suppression. If not inhibited, our abilities would allow us to more easily escape imprisonment than someone with a more limited subset."

The first bite of the spicy mixture turned to glue in Zita's mouth. "That would make a jailbreak more difficult. Do you think they pipe it throughout the whole place?"

Andy shrugged. "Given they're marking files with amounts, I'd assume they only have it in certain areas."

"So, we can't count on our abilities necessarily when we do the scouting run?" Zita frowned.

Jerome lifted his palms in the air. "I don't know. Hence why we need reconnaissance before acting. We don't even need to get in too far physically if we can get into their computer system and get a look at the security in use."

Worry accompanied Andy's thought. *This is too dangerous.*

We are without options, Wyn sent.

Can we let people die if we can stop it? Zita started pacing, carrying her bowl with her and shoveling in bites as her mind ticked through possibilities. "We'll need to change up the plan."

"It's a good plan," Jerome said.

She shrugged. "If we can't depend on our powers, then we need to move our pieces around a bit. Muse, you'll need to wear a physical disguise, not just an illusion, and you probably can't go too far from the truck. If your illusions go down, it's bad. Wingspan and Chevalier probably can't come inside at all. You're both recognizable. Me... I'll have to be the one on the inside since I do locks the old-fashioned way, not with my powers."

"Wait, you actually know that stuff, and it's not an ability? Are you certain you're not a burglar?" Jerome raised his eyebrows.

She nodded. "Yeah. I'll hope they cheaped out and didn't install anything too fancy. If they have standard locks, I'm good. If they've got laser beams or movie-style stuff, we're screwed."

Jerome winced. "Let's hope the government's funds ran low when they were buying locks then."

After another mouthful—the next batch needed more cilantro—Zita had to agree. "Yeah. We'll hope they sank so much into remodeling the place and making their orange gas that they're using standard locks. With the lack of info, we have no choice about making this a scouting run rather than a jailbreak."

Jerome breathed out. "If I can't go in, I'll have to put a virus on their system and figure out a way to broadcast the results. That or copy what they have."

"If I need to put it on their computers, don't make it too complicated," Zita warned him.

The big man laughed. "Don't worry, my little Luddite. It'll be easy." He grabbed a bowl and stuck a fork in it, taking a mouthful. "Ugh. Other than the soapy taste I'm guessing is cilantro, it's not bad for beans and... beans."

"The secret is bacon fat. I keep a little jar in my fridge," Zita said.

Jerome glanced over at Wyn. "Are you going to have some? Wait, did I take yours?"

The witch made a face. "No. Beans and I have an ongoing disagreement. That bowl was yours. I'll have yogurt later."

"So, we'll work on our respective parts of the plan? I've prepared a folder for each of you. It's paper, so you can burn it when you're through with it. Also, that way, I don't have to tell Arca how to use a computer."

She would've defended herself but didn't bother. "You're giving me a floor plan? That helps, but they don't have a lot of details."

"The one phone led me to where I could find the money request, and that had a preliminary concept floor plan which I scooped for you... so it's likely not completely accurate."

Andy skimmed his. "This is pretty sparse. I'm going to have to do a flyover, won't I?"

Jerome nodded. "Sorry. I wanted to get working on the parts of this as soon as possible. I have a drone watching the place, but it's been too sunny to do flyovers without being detected. The place seems to run on a skeleton staff."

That gave Zita pause. "Are we talking the usual meaning where they're short-staffed, or do you mean actual bones walking around doing stuff?"

He started to laugh and then stopped. "That's actually a legit question these days. As far as I know, all their staff are standard humans."

Andy wiped sweat off his forehead and gave Zita a meaningful glance.

She nodded. Tilting her head down over the documents, she considered what she needed to do.

Jerome pointed to his laptop screen and rested his hands on his keyboard. A diagram of a small compound appeared on half of the small screen, and a video filled the other side with a slow pan of the facility. "So, here's the site. I would've preferred more than a few days to arrange things, but since we don't know when that port city's going to go up in flames, we've got to act soon. It's in the swamp right by the Everglades. The bulk of the facility must be underground, with more above-ground development to start at a later date because right now they only have the original entrance to the missile silo, half of which appears to be a loading dock, three bunkers, a tower, and the parking lot. Around all of that, they have a fence with barbed wire at the top and a few guard posts. Only the stations by the road are manned, and two patrols walk the perimeter hourly, so I'm guessing they lean heavily on cameras."

Andy frowned and gestured toward the video. "Is that a wire fence? Electrified?"

"You'd think so, but it wasn't hooked up as of the other day. A few of my drones caught animals sliding through or under without harm." After a quick pass of his hands over the keyboard, the video changed to show a fox squeezing under the fence.

Zita raised her eyebrows. "So, it's half-built? Do they have workers coming in and out? Construction's one of those professions where people bop in and out of a project all day long. We could fake that pretty easy."

Jerome shook his head. "Good thought, but no. As far as I can tell, they have very little traffic in or out. Trust me, I wish they did. My drones recorded a handful going between the main building and the northernmost structure at what I'm guessing are regular shift times, so guards are likely housed on-site. They've got to have staggered shifts to account for all the cars."

"Have we any idea of how many guards are there?" Wyn asked, frowning at the images.

The big man lifted his hands in a gesture of helplessness. "If they're following federal standards, they'll have about ten guards per hundred prisoners, plus the regular entry and exit guards. If they're following state standards, they'll have twice that. Since we don't know how many metas they have... The lot has fifty cars, of which only three or four changed position over the course of multiple days. So, we'll assume a minimum of fifty guards or staff in there."

Andy murmured, "Personally, I'd assume fewer prisoners per guard with powers in the equation, but it is what it is. Fewer guards is better for us, though."

"It is, but this whole situation is still chingada," Zita muttered.

***

"Remember, this is a scouting run only," Jerome intoned the next morning. For some reason, he stared at Zita.

She raised her eyebrows. "I can follow a plan."

His expression was dubious. "We're only going in for information to use later. At this point, we don't even have a ballpark head count of staff or prisoners, let alone any way to accommodate a mass escape, unless Wingspan wants to fly around with them on his back forever."

"Not really, no. I have a life, and feeding my bird form would be prohibitively expensive, even for you." Andy shuddered.

Jerome inclined his head. "Muse, you're the key to getting in. You'll intercept the daily laundry truck, put the driver to sleep, then drive the truck pretending to be him. We'll put him back in his vehicle before he wakes up and park him at home, so he thinks he ran his route. His recycling bin has enough liquor bottles to make me think this wouldn't be the first shift he can't remember. Arca, you'll be hiding in the truck. Slip off when they're dealing with the laundry and do your part. Do you remember what that is? Do you need to practice?"

She was quick to nip that in the bud after he'd had her practicing for an hour on a laptop earlier, not even allowing her to jog while she did it. *Inhumane.* "I got it. I sneak in, plug in your dingle dangle so you can reach their computers without being there."

Wyn made a choking sound.

Andy hid his laughter behind his hand.

Jerome rubbed his forehead and shot her a grin. "I'm not letting you play with that, though I understand why you'd want to."

After a second, she realized what she'd said and tried to guess the correct term. "Oh, I meant your dongle?"

This time, Andy didn't hide his laughter.

"Not the time, children," Wyn said primly.

"Always the time," Andy assured her.

Zita rolled her eyes. "His stick? Whatever. The little electronic thingy with the bad computer programs on it that'll let him steal information. It'll send it out if there's a connection or store it if there isn't. I wait for the light to turn green. Then I sneak out with it. It's a scouting mission, so no jailbreaking anyone unless death is imminent because we don't have a place to put them yet or a way to get them out without revealing our identities. I should also try not to talk, not to snack, and not to be me."

Jerome nodded. "You might not even need to do more than hang out on the top level for a bit, depending on how they're set up. Once I'm in, if they've looped in cameras and automatic doors, I can open everything to let you through and lock everyone out of your way once my little programs have time to work. It'll be a breeze."

Andy snorted. "You had to say that. We're doomed."

Jerome shook his head. "I don't have to be here. I could be on a boat with twins. Did I mention they're models?"

***

The computers were a lie.

Or rather, they were fake.

After checking every apparent computer in the above-ground level, Zita huddled in raccoon form under a desk. She held a useless flash drive in her paws and plotted out her next move while mentally growling more than a few impolite words.

Amusement and concern carried over the mental connection from Wyn. *Should we assume from that colorful exhibition of linguistic ability that Jerome's stated ease of access did not prove prescient? He's complaining that he hasn't gotten any data yet.*

It's not real. None of it. Zita caught herself before she could growl out loud.

Andy groaned. *Too high tech for you? Maybe Wyn should convince them to let her into the main room so she can tell you what to do.*

No, she has to stick to the routine, which means she never leaves the dock. The cameras there are real. Beyond that, there's cameras on entry and exit doors, but that's it. Everything else on this level, including the cameras, is... is... like somebody set up a house for sale and wanted to make it look fancy. The computers are basically screensavers, and that's it. Zita sniffed the data stick and tried to figure out if she could stay out of camera view if she shifted back enough to put it back in her pocket.

It's staged? Why would they do that? Puzzlement accompanied Wyn's words.

Zita resisted the urge to slap herself on the forehead as her friends finally got the problem. *Sí. That's it. Nothing actually works except the cameras and the door to the next level. It's super-heavy steel with a fancy keypad lock. If I had the time and the right tools, I could disassemble it and get through, but I doubt the distraction will last that long. If a guard goes through, I can hitch a ride.*

The distraction's ending, and they're coming back. Given the nonchalance with which they reacted, they must get a lot of people joyriding along their boundaries, Wyn sent.

Most of their guard stations are unmanned, and they've got all that swamp. They're probably depending on the local wildlife to scare off most trespassers. We have to do Plan B. I'm going as far underground as necessary to find a machine with useful information. Zita glared at the table, where a pack of cards, two books, and half a sandwich waited. Even from her hiding spot, she could smell that the mayonnaise had gone rancid in the mercilessly humid heat that the underpowered AC units couldn't keep up with. Her raccoon instincts didn't care that it was bad, so she crushed the impulse to steal and eat the food.

Andy sent, *We should've made that Plan A. Then when it went off the rails, we might've been able to implement Jerome's plan. I'm enjoying telling him so, though I don't like you being stuck in there any longer than necessary.*

Zita nodded, forgetting he couldn't see her for a moment. *You and me both, mano. Wyn, can you convince one of these dudes they need to use the bathroom? Somebody here ate part of a sandwich, and the mayo's bad on it.*

Did you eat the rest? Andy knew the challenges of being shapeshifted better than Wyn.

She ignored the temptation still nagging at her. *No, the mayo's gone off, I told you.*

Wyn stayed focused on the mission. *Even the bathrooms are fake?*

Yup. No pipes. Whoever ate that sandwich is going to need to spend quality time in a bathroom soon anyway, so can you encourage him to do it now before you have to take the truck and go? Think of it as a service to his coworkers. Crawling as far as she could under the desk, she switched to Arca and stuffed the drive in her pocket. She darted over to a large (plastic) potted palm by the heavy door.

Ugh. I despise using such base motivations, but necessity insists. Be ready—when party line returns, he'll be on his way back, Wyn sent. The mental link dropped.

Hoping her friend managed to hide her distaste for the suggestion from the target, Zita shifted to a brown jumping spider. After a precious few seconds acclimating to the very different sensory input of an insect, she climbed the fake plant. She prayed that whatever was on the other side would allow her to stay hidden until she could dismount her unknowing ride. If she had to, she could go smaller, but she hated being an insect. They had two very important disadvantages: the smaller she got, the harder it became to understand what was going on around her, and the more likely it was that a passing predator would eat her.

Party line returned with a torrent of words from Wyn. *He's on his way! His distress started before I even did anything. I just reinforced it. His buddy is staying here with me and helping with the truck since the man I appear to be threw out his back.*

You got out of doing any heavy lifting as usual? Andy sent.

Wyn replied only with the sensation of smugness.

The loading dock door burst open, and a guard ran through. He stabbed buttons with his fingers, muttering under his breath.

Zita hoped she wouldn't need to know what code he used, though she tried to remember how it sounded, as the man was a huge, blurry, moving shape. She jumped onto his back and scurried up it to hide under his collar. With delight, she noted the fabric of his charcoal shirt was coarse and thick, perfect for her to cling to without being felt. After she'd crammed as much of herself as she could into hiding, she peeked out.

While he absently scratched at his back once, he seemed too preoccupied to notice his passenger.

With a harsh buzz, the wide steel door swung open, revealing a set of stripes that she guessed were bars.

I'm on my way. Let's keep the chatting down while I concentrate on not getting caught. She would've squinted if she could but instead tried to relax back into interpreting what her senses told her, other than the taste of sickness from the sweat soaking the back of the guard's uniform. That she tried not to notice.

The guard slammed his hand against a black square on the white wall. "Come on, come on," he muttered, his body jiggling with need.

Based on the amount of air the first door displaced, Zita estimated its probable size and weight. *Carajo. We'll need Andy to get through that monstrosity if we have to force it. That's a thousand pounds of steel at a minimum. I take back what I said earlier about getting the door myself.*

When the light turned green, the plexiglass door buzzed open, and the bars withdrew into the wall.

The guard darted through. They went down a steep, dimly-lit flight of cement stairs, based on the sound. Given the limitations of her size, she couldn't tell if there were any cameras. She kept still just in case, hoping her mottled hair would blend with his. By the time they reached the base of the stairs, the temperature had dropped several degrees.

A blur stopped any further forward momentum.

The guard punched in what sounded like the same sequence of numbers. After emerging into a much brighter corridor, he turned left and repeated his actions to open another door.

A couple steps later, he stopped in front of another set of black lines. Her senses told her it was another hall, but this one led to an open area.

A man's voice boomed. "Roberson? What are you doing down here?"

Her ride bounced in place, groaning and bending nearly double. "Bathroom break! Landry's with the truck."

"Be quick. Chaniclas is here, and you know she doesn't like deviations from the schedule," the other guy said.

A buzzer sounded, and the bars disappeared.

Roberson (and his passenger) rushed in and down a hall. "Will do my best," he called over his shoulder as he ran through a few rooms. He paused long enough to open a locker and toss a few things inside. Metal clicked, and then something heavy thumped.

His stomach gurgled, and he bent double.

Praying it was a plant, she jumped off onto something brown. It had the hard flatness that suggested furniture, and she scurried into the first patch of shadow she could find beneath it. *I need a form that'll give me a better idea of what's going on.*

The ground vibrated as the sick guard slammed the locker door shut, dropped something metallic, and went into another room.

She stayed still, feeling for the air disturbances that would tell her if someone else was in the room. After a minute, she shifted to a brown gecko and peeked out.

Her hiding spot was a metal and wood bench in between two rows of tall, gray lockers. One hung open, with a combination lock abandoned on the floor below. Another set of uniform clothing lay inside, including a pair of boots and a belt laden with keys and other objects. The scent of sweaty, unwashed men and the guard's sickness filled the air.

She shuddered and checked for cameras.

None apparent.

Creeping over to the open locker, she studied the belt. To her delight, it included the man's security badge. It only showed the face of a sour-faced forty-something white man and not his build. *Score!*

Her unwitting ride was still being noisily sick in the next room.

Making a quick decision, she shifted to match the badge as much as possible. Since she could only tell that the clothing was big... but didn't know if he was heavy or muscular... she went for the muscles. *A prison guard wants to be fit, right?*

Well aware that someone could enter at any moment, she yanked on the clothing, a camp shirt and cargo pants in a boring shade of dark gray, and all the matching accoutrements: belt, flashlight, and boots. When the belt wouldn't stay up in the hole with the most use, she shifted again to more of a muscular dad-type body. *That makes sense, I guess. After all, if he hadn't hated missing a meal, his stuff wouldn't have been available for me to steal.*

She flexed and did a few quick warm-up punches and kicks to get used to the unfamiliar form. *Better reach, less overall fitness. I hate being male. It throws everything off balance, and I have to be careful not to squish myself.*

As she was about to close the locker, she spotted a ball cap. It was damp and smelled like the sick man's sweat. With a grimace, she put it on anyway, pulling it low over her face to hide it better from the camera. After rifling through the belt quickly—the handcuff key and pepper spray seemed the most useful—she took a deep breath. *Now, I need to get going and find a real computer that nobody's using. I've had some lucky breaks so far, but that won't last.*

With a muttered prayer, she strode out of the men's locker room.

She found herself in a small break room with spartan tables and chairs padded in a dull green fabric. The walls were a dull off-white as if they'd been coated with a primer and then never painted. A sink and an ancient fridge bookended a counter cluttered with dirty dishes. Most importantly, no cameras were visible anywhere, and the lights were dark. Across from the men's was a women's locker area. The hall outside the break room looked well-lit and industrial, done in the same white walls and gray-speckled linoleum.

Andy's mental voice broke in. *Z? How are things?*

I'm in a break room. Haven't found a working computer yet. Wyn, just go if they send you on your way. Don't wait. This may take a while. She checked the hallway.

The corridor outside had cameras mounted in the corners, but they were angled down to record people passing. As Zita studied them, she hoped the recording angles and distances would be about the same as the very similar civilian systems she'd installed for her brother's locksmith business.

She mused over escape routes. *Given the tight spaces and camera angles, a small bird or lizard might slip by unnoticed if I stick close to the ceiling. Nothing can be done about the lack of windows, given how deep underground this is.*

The boring color scheme continued for a short distance in either direction, though some helpful soul had hung small signs on the wall with arrows to direct people. A hum of conversation drifted down a stairwell to her left, marked as Administration on the sign, and two guards stood sentry over the steps. They held shotguns and had Tasers belted at their waists.

And Roberson only had pepper spray and a handcuff key. It figures I'd get a loser to imitate, but on the bright side, nobody pays attention to the little people.

The opposite direction—the Prison and Infirmary, according to the sign—held only a single guard, seated by a set of bars. On the other side of the bars was a heavy steel door. Armed only with a baton and a Taser, the guard flipped idly through a series of black and white security camera views. Someone's radio buzzed, but the words were too soft for Zita to make out.

An infirmary should have computer access to prisoner records and be less guarded than the actual cells or administration. Decision made, she stepped out of the break room, turning toward the infirmary.

One guard behind her said something to his partner and strode down the hall toward her. "Roberson! Hey, Roberson?"

Belatedly, Zita remembered that was her and stopped.

As he came up beside her, she noted his uniform was similar to hers but had more rank bars on his sleeve. "You're sick, huh? How bad is it? Do you need the infirmary?"

I have no idea what this guy sounds like. She nodded, rubbing her stomach and keeping her head down.

He sighed. "Fine. I'll go stay with Landry while you go. Be quick about it. Try not to wake the creepy hottie. Last thing we want is her caterwauling while we're being inspected. You're not contagious, are you?"

She grunted, bending over as if her stomach had gotten worse. "Bad mayo," she whispered, fighting the urge to use her fake accent.

"Figures. Try not to puke on anything else. Geez, Roberson." Her interrogator strode toward the infirmary.

Obediently, she fell in step behind him.

He waved and showed his badge to the guard at the door.

Zita copied the motion, keeping her hand on her stomach.

The door guard hit a button, and the bars slid open.

Her chatty interrogator went through and stopped in front of the big door.

She trailed behind him.

Once the bars closed again, the new guy punched in a set of numbers.

Zita memorized the sequence, noting that the series of beeps sounded identical to what she'd heard earlier. *Pues, if they all use the same code, at least the real Roberson is less likely to get blamed for anything I do.*

When the thick door banged open, the other guard walked through.

She followed him, stepping into another well-lit white hallway. This one slanted downward and had no visible end or alternative exits. While cameras were liberally placed along the hallway, they had two different types installed, with half either far cheaper or fake compared to the ones she recognized as a common brand.

When he turned off and went through a door labeled Stairs, a whiff of fresh air escaped.

She hobbled down the hallway, forcing herself to shamble slowly as if in pain. *At least I know the way out now. Same angles on these cameras as in the other area, so the ceiling is my best exit strategy.*

Finally, she got all the way to the other end. A big metal door with a number pad read Prison, while a normal steel door with a tiny inset window was marked Infirmary. Both had badge readers beside them. The cameras pointed at the doors appeared real.

Her heart sped up when she glanced in the tiny window and saw the back of a computer monitor. *Perfect. Let's hope the local doctor or nurses will leave me unwatched long enough for Jerome's toy to do its job.*

She slapped her badge against the door.

A light turned green, and she went inside.

Chapter Eleven

While Zita had been in countless hospitals and clinics, and even once woken up strapped to a bed in a defunct hospital, she'd rather return to any of the others than go to the DMS infirmary.

She left the lights off and navigated using what little illumination came through the hallway window and from a tiny green LED on a refrigerated cabinet. Sterile and cold, the room had six spotless steel examination tables in a row. Each had wheels, a thick iron bar underneath, and manacles dangling from both ends. A long counter with a sink ran the length of one wall, with cabinets guarding the space above and below. Humming came from a small refrigerator in the corner. Almost everything had locks, with the exception of a large utility closet marked First Aid. Twin monitors sat on a desk near the entryway. Posters warning about various health hazards and a strange collection of floor lamps, aimed at an open interior door, were the only decorations.

In case someone watched, her hands were clenched over her stomach, and her head was down as she trudged toward the first-aid cabinet. Once there, she opened it and pretended to peruse it while she checked out the rest of the room with her peripheral vision. The only camera was aimed at the door; it wouldn't catch anything other than the exit and a corner of the workstation. To her delight, the towers for the computer were both housed under the desk on the side the camera didn't cover. A few quick calculations had her grinning. Even in the larger, unfamiliar form she wore right now, she could sneak over to the towers and do what was necessary without being filmed. In the back of the room, a door hung open with an odd, lumpy shape inside.

She closed the cabinet and drifted toward the back room. *Don't know why they wasted all that space on the first-aid stuff when they've got hardly anything in there. If the exam room has a computer and no cameras, that'd be ideal for avoiding questions...*

When she reached the inner doorway, she paused. It was too dark to see much other than a series of irregular shapes scattered through the room. Old blood, musky perfume, and antiseptic combined in a swirl of scent that had her shoulders tightening. Her stomach roiled. Skin prickling, she felt along the wall until she found light switches and flipped them on.

An unearthly howl came from nearby, followed by a thud as the room lit up, temporarily blinding her.

Zita stumbled back a step, her eyes watering at the sudden glare. Once she'd recovered, she peered inside and shuddered. The main centerpiece of the room was an odd, vinyl-covered chair, like that of a dentist with a bondage fetish, placed directly under a large, open black grate and surrounded by more floor lamps, all brilliant white and radiating heat like the sun. Brown stains marred the white-painted walls under the grate. Cabinets lined all the other walls. High-pitched wailing, accompanied by thumps and creaking sounds, came from somewhere nearby. No cameras were in this room.

She hastily hit the light switches off.

The creepy shrieking stopped.

"No mames. I'm not doing nothing in there." The masculine rasp of her voice reminded her of her mission.

If those sounds were a horror soundtrack or something, someone's seriously messed up. I hope nobody heard that alarm or whatever that was. As she backed away from the creepy room, she dug out

Jerome's virus-laden drive from beneath her borrowed uniform and crawled over to the computer, below what she hoped was the camera line-of-sight. She plugged it in and took a cautious peek over the edge of the desk. Judging it to be safe, she grabbed the closest monitor and turned it toward herself. She grasped a keyboard cable and pulled it slowly over until she could reach it without crossing the camera's view.

Zita tapped the POWER button and waited. And waited. After a minute, she wondered at the lack of whirring or any other sound from the machine. She checked the monitor.

It remained resolutely dark.

Another long minute later, she tapped the POWER button again.

The machine stayed silent and lightless.

She tried again. *My friends can never hear of this or I'll never live it down.*

Hear of what? Andy asked.

Nothing, everything's good. I'm doing boring computer stuff exactly the way it should be done, she sent back, tapping the button again.

A hint of laughter danced in Andy's mental voice. *Did you check that it was plugged in?*

Of course, she lied. Her cheeks burned as she traced the power cord to the closest outlet. Or rather, to where it lay a few feet below the outlet, next to the first-aid storage. Another cord snaked its way to a wide phone jack beside the obvious power outlet. *No, wait, that's an Internet cable. Or a charger cable.*

She plugged both in to be safe. *Everything's fine. The computer's just taking a while to start, that's all.*

Light wavered as someone blocked part of the window at the door.

Zita tried to dart into the first-aid cabinet, knocking over a few supplies. It was too small for her current form.

The door buzzed as it unlocked.

After snatching up a fallen box of bandages, she shifted to a chimp and leapt into the cabinet again, this time fitting. She fell in headfirst as her now too-big clothing and boots tripped her, hitting her forehead against the back. Something broke underneath her as she scrambled to turn around in the tangled mess of clothing and basic supplies. Despite the involuntary tears that came to her eyes, she yanked the door shut, all but a small crack.

A woman in a long, white lab coat and scrubs swept into the room. Although her stride showed confidence, she lacked the finesse or muscle that would've come from military service or serious dance or sports practice. Short, dark hair in a no-nonsense cut was held back from a round, serious face by a pair of plain metal barrettes. After locking the door behind herself, she set a briefcase and a Taser on the desk and glanced at the computers. She turned a monitor to face away from the door and the camera even more.

Well, that's convenient. Zita eased into a position that would let her peer out more easily. Despite her care, things inside the cabinet shifted, and a box of bandages fell on her. The scent of rubbing alcohol increased and she suspected that one leg of her pants was marinating in the stuff.

Instead of sitting, however, Lab Coat Woman twisted Zita's direction. "I heard you moving around in there. Get away."

The pain in Zita's throbbing head increased proportionally to her heart rate at the scientist's words.

Lab Coat Woman strode forcefully toward the back of the room.

Bracing herself, Zita prepared to spring out and surprise the woman if she opened the cabinet door.

The scientist walked past her hiding place.

After a couple of clicks, bright white light spilled over the room from the exam room area. The lamps hummed.

A faint shriek sounded through the wall.

"Ha. Ghoul. What is she even doing awake?" Metal clunked, as if the scientist had closed the vents on a wall grate, and then a door shut. As she returned to the computer, she grunted. Fortunately, she either didn't notice or didn't comment on the small stick inserted in the machine. She tapped the POWER button.

It obediently lit and whirred.

Zita remained huddled in her hiding spot, watching the lady log on. When she calmed down, the soreness in her head began receding. Her leg definitely was wet, cold, and stunk like rubbing alcohol.

A tiny blue LED lit on Jerome's little device, but Lab Coat Woman didn't appear to notice.

Done yet? Andy sent.

Someone came in. I got to wait to retrieve Jerome's stick, but it's plugged in and glowing blue. Let me know when Jerome's got what we came here for, she replied.

Worry in her mental voice, Wyn sent, *They've almost finished loading the truck. Do I need to delay leaving? The original plan didn't have you going underground.*

No, don't draw attention to yourself. I'll just get the stick back and check on Elle before leaving, Zita replied, her attention distracted by the computer.

Andy sounded unhappy. *That wasn't part of the plan. You're already doing far more than we were supposed to today.*

Fuck the chingado plan. Maybe I didn't know she was in trouble before, but now I know. This horror show is all sorts of wrong, especially for a kid. I need to see her and make sure she'll be okay until we can get her out, Zita sent back.

And if she's not? Wyn asked.

The woman at the desk twisted the second monitor around to face her. Other than when Lab Coat Woman leaned forward to type something, Zita had a near-perfect view of both screens. Exterior views of the facility displayed on the first monitor, flipping from camera to camera after a set few seconds, and the other was just a blank screen with some icons, as if the scientist were waiting for something to load.

I'll figure it out. Teleport if I have to. Some science or medical lady is settling in to do something. Not sure what. If I'm lucky, she'll check on Elle's cell. In any case, I'll wait her out if I can, she sent.

Oh, yeah, winging it never gets us in trouble, Andy sent. *Jerome says he's got data coming in.*

A second later, the computer rang, sounding like an old-school phone of the sort she hadn't seen since her last trip to South America.

"Finally. They've got to hardwire in more lines, so I have more options for private meetings," the scientist muttered, and she clicked something.

A man's face appeared on the formerly blank screen. He was an old, white guy with a conservative haircut, navy suit, and too-perfect teeth, bared in an expression that might've been pleasant if his eyes weren't strangely flat and cold. A jaunty American flag pin held his scarlet tie in place.

"Took you long enough," the scientist said.

The online guy sniffed. "Need I remind you of my position and all the duties incumbent? Is the room secure for our discussion, Dr. Chaniclas?"

Zita pressed her face against the door to see better. *Lab Coat Woman is talking to someone over the computer. Her buddy has the hair, vocabulary, and insincerity of a politician.*

"Of course. As usual, you forget I'm not an idiot." Chaniclas' posture stiffened.

Politician said, "What's the status on our outstanding projects?"

Both of her friends spoke at once. *Who?*

No clue. Old, white guy. Science lady is Dr. Chaniclas, Zita sent back.

Andy groaned. *So, of course, the one member of our team who wouldn't know who he was is the only one watching...*

If I didn't have to drive this truck out now... I'll peek as soon as I get some place I can pull over, Wyn fretted.

Chaniclas sighed. "No change on the gas project. It's effective on all prisoners that breathe. Progress remains slow in speeding up the production without using the metahuman chemist. He's working seventy-hour weeks, though, so we should be able to distribute the grenades nationally to all DMS offices soon. We've begun a stockpile for future military use."

"Can we get any more hours out of him?" the politician asked.

"No, his batches fail after the ten-hour mark each day," the scientist replied.

Shushing her friends, Zita sent, *Cállate, guys, I'm trying to listen here. If either of these jokers wants to say what the chingado gas does, I don't want to miss it. A meta creates it, which makes sense, even if it increases the odds that whatever it does is probably weird.*

With a wave of his hand, Politician dismissed it. "Fine. Keep him at it. How about the testing?"

"On schedule. The focus has been possible Strike Force team members and support staff. General McCarten would like to create two more drones so he could begin emptying the military of metas, but..." Chaniclas shook her head.

Politician grunted. "I'll speak to Thad and throw him another Strike Team as a consolation prize, maybe for this week's big bang. We have three testers now, right? The Queen and the two drones?"

Zita tilted her head, her fur prickling. *Why does this not sound more science-y?*

Probably a good thing if they're keeping it simple. It's always a pain to untangle political technical babble to figure out any real science underneath, Andy sent.

Wyn shushed him over the mental link.

Chaniclas sighed again. "No. A visiting DMS agent killed the West Coast one. Apparently, he walked in during a test and believed the meta to be murdering the subject. No word on why the drone's handler was not in the room to stop him."

A big knot settled in Zita's stomach. *Wait. That sounds like the story Miguel told me...*

"While I can't fault his eagerness to shoot one of the creatures, that's unfortunate. Can we transform him into the next drone?" Politician raised an eyebrow.

The scientist shook her head. "We flew him in and had the Queen test him. He's human, so he can't be converted. After she fed off him, he was given the usual story and sent on his way."

Zita fought the urge to burst out of the cabinet and start throwing punches.

The politician straightened his tie. "Pity. It would've been such lovely symmetry. Fine, pick a disposable meta to be the next drone. Perhaps one with a family so they're more malleable?"

Chaniclas nodded and made a note. "And McCarten's request?"

The man onscreen nodded. "We'll replace the West Coast drone, but that's it. Since some of those things are contagious, we don't need to take the chance of accidentally creating another queen or king. If he remains insistent, we'll collect a list of his top targets and up their testing priority. What about the Vigilante Project?"

Her body tensed as she watched. *This can't be good.*

What can't? Just hearing your comments is killing me, Andy sent.

Shh. I'll tell you later, Zita sent. Her stomach dropped at Politician's next question.

"Do you have Wingspan and Caroline Gyllen chipped yet?"

Before she could relay that tidbit to her friends, Wyn sent a hurried message. *Need to do something. Be right back.*

Party line dropped, and Zita was once again alone in her own mind.

Purple-painted lips turned down as the scientist leaned forward. "I still believe you're too aggressive with the timeline on that project. The chips cannot yet trigger targeted power usage, nor do we know of any weakness that would allow us to implant it in the male."

The politician scowled. "Excuses! Controlling those two should be paramount. Do we at least have the vigilantes? Any of them?"

Zita's fingers curled into fists, and she flexed her long chimp toes.

"No. The attempts to capture Arca were unsuccessful. She escaped the trap baited with the older meta woman, never showed up for the forest meeting, and teams were not fast enough to catch her in the courthouse. Her companions were never sighted." Chaniclas seemed bored with the topic.

Her words clearly did not please the politician. "DMS has as close to an unlimited budget as we can give them, and multiple teams made up the finest veterans we could pry loose from the military. How hard can it be to catch some pole-dancing imported trash who can barely speak English?"

Zita bit back an annoyed squeak. *Seriously? Show up naked to a few fights, and everyone assumes you're a stripper. It's probably good they're so far off base, but he's just being nasty.*

The scientist shrugged. "Ask McCarten. They're his strike teams. It's their job to run the captures and do the PR projects. My end is the science and the prison. The cages are ready for all three vigilantes when we get them, assuming that we can keep the male sedated or otherwise under control. The females shouldn't be a problem."

In the cabinet, Zita made a rude gesture, even knowing they wouldn't see it.

"Yes, he'll need to update me as to why those attempts failed. Continue to leave those projects off the official reports sent to the

Oversight Committee. What about Gyllen?" Politician folded his arms over his chest.

Chaniclas idly flipped through a few of the security camera views before answering. "The Air Force is keeping her very close and is not... amenable to losing their asset. Given they have the support of POTUS, we have not pushed the matter, especially as she may be necessary to defend against Wingspan or Dragon. We have prepared a custom tool to handle Gyllen's implantation when the time comes, however. She obeys orders well enough that it shouldn't be a problem to collect her."

The man online's face darkened. "Most orders. I've heard she sometimes refuses them."

Chaniclas shrugged. "She's not really on our side. What do you expect?"

Although red crept up the politician's face, he kept his tone level. "Frankly, more than I'm seeing. If we're to get the bill passed, DMS can't afford to keep allowing dangerous creatures free rein to do anything they please. Our ship will be truly sunk if we don't keep control of when and where they strike."

The woman in the lab coat held up a hand. "Save your rhetoric for the cameras. As for the rest of the projects, we're working on them with mixed results. The Ice Project is probably a no-go. Only one weapon seems to work at a time, and only for a couple shots for anyone other than her. She'll get one more week of solitary meditation before we give her another chance to try again. After that, we might want to abandon that project and concentrate on the Health Project. Initial results on his blood are promising, and McCarten said he plans to pick up that subject within two weeks. He's just waiting for a viable excuse given the visibility risk."

The man onscreen nodded. "Fine. The Youth Project?"

"No progress, but no protest either." While Chaniclas' expression, reflected in the monitor, seemed uninterested with the subject, one of her hands tapped angrily against her thigh below the desk.

Politician snorted. "If only all the metas could have remained in comas or could be coerced to blindly follow orders."

"Speaking of which, I object to your focus on General Aetherics in the staged attacks. We would've had more impact if those raids had been public places, rather than their warehouses and offices. They hushed everything up."

"Not wasted. Those 'unfortunate metahuman attacks on industry' netted us gear they refused to sell. Say what you will, Clockwork's company is still the best source for certain necessary supplies. Besides, soon enough, we'll go so big that they won't be able to keep it quiet. General Aetherics is the largest and wealthiest company in the world, and we will need sponsors. After this week's upcoming tragedies, we should be able to switch from using the stick and see if they'll bite at the carrot. They've been nosing around, practically panting at hints they might get the Youth project."

Everything in the lines of Chaniclas's body shrieked her unhappiness and anger. Beneath the desk, her clenched knuckles turned white. "What?"

The politician lifted his hands and beamed like an old fallen angel through the screen. "Right now, we need at least one or more major corporations onboard to proceed with the next steps once we get our bill passed. These projects are expensive and delicate. Managing them will grow increasingly complicated as we remove more metas from circulation."

Chaniclas growled, "You can't do that. I'm the preeminent doctor on this project, and that subject's genes could be the link to determining how they were made! I thought we were a team!"

The man on the other side of the screen took a step closer to the camera, bringing the sharp lines of his face into focus. "We are allies, even if I do not subscribe to your conspiracy theory."

The scientist growled. "Reptilian Supplantation was not my idea, but it's the most likely explanation for their existence. Your inability to accept the evidence only shows how badly you need a scientist. I'm the most obvious and best choice for the job."

Why does that theory sound familiar? Where have I heard it before? The politician's next words cut Zita's musing short.

"You are a valued member of a team, but no one is irreplaceable. Some thought that Singh would've been a choice, but his untimely passing gave you control of the research division. Given your tragedy last year, you might snap under the pressure of this job. Accidents can happen to anyone, Doctor, so perhaps you should focus on the projects you've been given and leave the political decisions to me. That's my business. Though, I suppose I could be dissuaded from handing Youth over to them... if..."

Brown eyes narrowing, Chaniclas drew closer to the screen. "Leave my late son out of this. I do not need your false condolences. You'll let me keep Youth if what?"

"If you can seal the deal with new allies." If the politician had batted his eyes, Zita wouldn't have been surprised.

"Not Clockwork." The scientist folded her arms over her chest.

The name struck a chord with Zita. *Isn't he dead? Or missing? I think he's the meta from the Seventies who invented SNARC balls and started General Aetherics before losing it on TV.*

Politician shook his head. "After his little tantrum in Las Vegas, no. His values never truly aligned with ours anyway, despite his supposed belief in your alien invaders. These are new players. They want living metas, preferably from the top and bottom of the barrel."

Chaniclas made a sound of protest.

"Of course, I wouldn't give them anyone too powerful, but we could pawn off some of the weakest ones, like those we farmed out to Parzarri, or better yet, the teenagers. You've complained that your guards are too lenient with them, and they're mostly useless.

Our potential allies claim they won't come back to the US, so we could skim off the most useless ones and have valuable foreign partners."

"What exactly do you want me to do?" Chaniclas said. "I wouldn't mind getting rid of some inventory, provided I could choose which ones we lost."

"Simple. Pick out what you're willing to part with and arrange for the buyers to pick them up. I've already negotiated payment from their management on a per-meta basis, so you needn't worry yourself about negotiations. Do make sure anything we part with includes those implanted explosives we've been working on. In case they turn on us."

Chaniclas nodded slowly. "The implants will require healing time and extend the hand-off timeline."

"If you want to keep your pet projects, you will make this happen ASAP. I'll give them your personal number to contact, if you are agreed. Forward momentum on this and sufficient progress with our other projects would be a considerable incentive to allowing you to keep Youth in house and put off General Aetherics." Very white, unnaturally even teeth flashed in a smile, and the politician straightened his tie.

The scientist snarled. "Fine. I'll deal. Your new buddies get their pick of the trash, but if we have to transfer prisoners, it needs to go through Miami, not the main facility. We don't need more eyes there."

"That's the kind of response I was hoping for. Agreed." He checked his watch. "I have another meeting in five, so summarize the rest for me."

Her face was bland, but Chaniclas' form trembled with fury. "The inspections for the month are complete. Everything is functioning within our parameters, and they've corrected the glitch that was making one image flicker. Nothing else to report. And, by the way, one would hope no accidents befall me, as that would cause certain financial information regarding Singh's unfortunate accident to be released to the press. I've heard the odds of gaining the Presidency drop significantly when one has been convicted of hiring assassins."

The man online stared at her. Finally, his lips curved upward. Paired with his dead eyes, it seemed more of a declaration of war than a sign of happiness. "Good talk. Give me better results next time." He hung up.

Chaniclas rose and yanked the Internet cable from the wall.

Something plastic snapped.

She massaged her forehead and took a deep breath, raising a hand to her eyes. Although she muttered to herself, Zita still heard every word. "Petty, small-minded dictator. This is for the good of humanity. I'm going to save us, no matter what. Eventually, I won't need him anymore."

Save humanity from what? Morality? The Reptilian whatevers she mentioned? I don't recognize the theory, but Claire might. I'll have to ask her later. Zita exhaled and tried not to squirm or move, no matter how badly she wanted to.

Someone tapped on the door.

After straightening her lab coat, Chaniclas strode over and jerked the door open. "What?"

A guard outside cleared his throat. "You asked to be alerted when the laundry truck exited the boundaries. The elderly joy rider at the fence appears to be repeating his loop but has not approached any closer. Continue to hold action?"

"We can't afford the publicity, so obviously, yes. Hold unless they attempt the fence." Chaniclas growled. "Anything else?"

"Understood. We'll continue observation only. We might have one other issue, a minor protocol issue. One of our men has bad food poisoning, so he's being taken to the barracks to sleep it off. However, he lost his badge somewhere."

Oye, looks like my good luck is wearing off. Zita wiggled her toes cautiously to wake them up.

The scientist snapped, "Must I do everything? Have someone retrace his steps and search for it. Use the cameras if you need to. I'll finish up my paperwork here and meet my escort in administration. Let me know when it's found. Oh, and order another Ethernet cable for this room, and have it here before the next inspection. The existing one broke."

The guard all but saluted. "Ma'am, yes, ma'am."

After a moment, Chaniclas said, "Well? If that's it, why aren't you on it?"

The guard rushed off.

With a shake of her head, she whipped the door shut. She stalked past the computer and to the back of the room again.

Warmth spread through Zita's mind as party line returned.

Wyn sent, *My apologies for the abrupt departure. Have you completed your tasks?*

The bad guys are done talking. Did Jerome's program have enough time to send him everything? Did he get that? Tell me he got that chingado conversation because even without knowing what they're talking about exactly, it sounded bad. Murder and selling people bad.

Wyn sighed. *We're so out of our depth in this. Andy, can you or Jerome assist me in setting up the laundry truck driver for when he wakes up?*

Jerome's on his way, Wyn. He says the flow of data stopped, and we don't, as far as he can tell, have Dream Auntie or Elle's location yet, so it's up to whatever gets downloaded on the stick. I'm staying with the airboat in case Zita needs a daring rescue, Andy sent.

After a pause, a burst of amusement preceded Wyn's next question. *You've been wanting to say that, haven't you?*

Maybe, he admitted.

Metal rasped as the door to the exam room swung open and then clunked. Half of the extra light shut off, leaving the room dimmed.

A throaty female voice drawled, "Leaving the lights on like that was mean. I hear your hearts beating in there. I do hope you're about to bring me something pretty and muscular today. The last scientist gave me contact acne and had me picking nerd out of my fangs for days. You could always bring back last week's spicy hunk of an agent. A little Mexican food from time to time is tasty."

Zita had a sinking feeling that she recognized the voice, and anger burned when she made a guess at the agent.

While she couldn't see the scientist from her hiding spot, Chaniclas's words held disdain. "You have had sufficient food given that we had you testing multiple people this past week. Tomorrow, you'll get two metas, and we'll let you feed and program them every day until they're deployed. After that, we'll let you make another drone, plus you'll get whoever's up for testing next or the agent who brings them. You won't starve. I will send documents with the exact instructions to give them."

"All work and no play makes me a very dull girl. Did you come by just to let me know my schedule? If that were truly the case, you wouldn't be talking to me. You'd shove a piece of paper at me and leave. What am I getting for helping with this?"

The scientist paused. "Food."

"Ah, no, that's my price for the testing. It's far more effort to implant commands. Has anything been done about Dmitri yet? The Prince of DC needs to suffer, and I need proof of it. If you kill him, I want his head brought to me. Preferably mounted in a glass case so I might decorate the walls of this hellhole with it," the woman hissed.

Zita closed her eyes. *Domina. Guess we know where Dmitri's vamp ex-girlfriend is. We'll need to warn him that DMS is gunning for him specifically.*

After a pause, Andy sent, *Jerome says to let his device run a couple more minutes to grab as much data as possible. It was transmitting before, but the connection died, so it should be copying files as a backup measure. You need to bring it back out with you.*

Chaniclas said, "Not yet, but DMS has raided and closed his club indefinitely under suspicion of aiding and abetting meta terrorism. If you aid with the programming, I can have pictures brought to you. Perhaps even a video."

The vampiress squealed. "Excellent. He doesn't have the funds to support the club or its employees without it being open, so the longer you keep it closed, the better. I will accept that price along with a copy of the listing if he puts his house or the club up for sale."

"Fine. Have you thought about what we've discussed?" the scientist said.

"You've carried through on your promises to me, even though you're dreadfully dull. If you continue to do so, I see no reason to trust a stranger." The vampiress heaved a sigh.

Chaniclas said, "Excellent. I will have your orders sent, then. Goodbye."

Zita started to relax.

Domina wasn't done complaining. "What, are you pretending to be a man now? Getting what you want and leaving me all alone? At a minimum, you should leave your friend here. I don't even need to bite him provided he stays and amuses me for a few minutes."

Carajo. Guess my luck just ran out. Zita bit her lip to keep from swearing aloud.

"Friend? I'm alone," the scientist said. A drawer rattled as it was drawn open and then slammed shut.

The vampiress snorted. "Hardly. It's you and another. His smell is all but hidden under antiseptic, but I can hear his delicious little heart beating away so very fast. Even faster now. It's not a child, is it? If that's the case, take them with you. Children are dirty hassles."

Zita touched her chest. *Time to stop hiding and move!*

Footsteps loud and rapid on the cold white tiles, the scientist scurried past her.

With the intention to grab her and put her into a choke hold before she could resist, Zita hurled herself out of the cabinet.

Her body was too tangled in her clothing to do more than burst out and fall face-first on the ground. Medical supplies flew in all directions. Kicking off her pants, she shifted back into the guard. Even though the much larger and heavier male form threw Zita off her usual stride, she tackled Chaniclas' lower legs and sent her crashing down in a pile of tangled limbs.

The scientist cried out, and something fell from her hand to the floor. A long, evil-looking needle rolled across the floor.

Zita recovered first and pounced, pinning her down. After easing back on her knees, she caught the scientist's arms in a hammerlock.

Chaniclas shouted.

"Shh!" Zita hissed.

Maintaining control of the scientist's bent arm, Zita pulled her up. They spun in a circle until they faced the direction of the exam room—and the only manacles she could reach without letting go or allowing her prisoner to see her clearly.

"You're breaking my arm!" the struggling woman said.

Fearing she'd miscalculated the strength in the unfamiliar body, Zita loosened her grip.

Chaniclas broke free and ran for the syringe.

Instead of trying to race to the device, Zita ran for her pants, yanking the belt free and spending a precious second unsnapping the spray holster.

"Where are your *pants*?" the scientist screamed as she charged at the shapeshifter with the oversized needle.

Zita rolled, popping back up on her knees as she squirted the pepper spray at Chaniclas.

It hit.

Shrieking, the scientist reared back, free hand going to her face.

After leaping to her feet, Zita grabbed the other woman's weapon-wielding arm with both hands and forced it down by sheer strength, banging it against one of the hard metal cots.

With their combined weight and the hit, the examination table rolled, tilting sideways.

The struggling pair went with it as it crashed against another of the metal cots in a huge clang.

Zita whacked the scientist's arm again.

The syringe dropped.

Zita pinned her opponent against the table. With effort, she remembered not to use the accent. "Don't fight. I don't want to hurt you."

Chaniclas struggled harder. Tears rolled down her inflamed face, and she made little gagging noises in her throat.

Even if she missed using her own familiar form—or Arca's, as it was identical save for appearance—Zita had to admit being a big, stocky man had advantages. It made forcing her prisoner into the little examination room and dropping her into the creepy bondage chair much easier. Before the scientist could recover, Zita locked the shackles around her wrists and ankles.

Chaniclas stared at her through swollen, teary eyes in a reddened face. Her nose ran.

Zita snorted and poured a cup of water over the bound woman's eyes and face to lessen the pain. *I better hurry in case someone comes running at all that noise. Speaking of which, I can't have her letting people know she's here. Don't want her to get cold either.*

A quick visit to the other room later, she'd bound gauze over the scientist's mouth and spread a blanket over the woman's lower half.

Metal creaked and silver-tipped fingers slipped through the gaps. "Wait! If you open the grate and push her a little closer, I could feed. If I'm busy, I certainly won't tell anyone about your little scuffle in there."

Revulsion coiled in her. Zita shuddered and glanced at her prisoner.

Even with Zita's attempt to soothe some of the pepper spray pain, Chaniclas's face was red and puffy. The scientist let out a muffled protest. Or swore at her.

She flicked at the vampiress' hand until Domina withdrew it, and then Zita snapped the grate shut. Just in case, she shoved the creepy chair a little farther away from the vampire.

Pausing by Chaniclas, she unclipped her badge and put it into a pocket.

Then she slipped out of the exam room and closed the door. *That should buy me some time before people realize she's missing.*

Glancing around the room, she groaned. Medical supplies, her pants, and tables were strewn every which way. She ran to shove all the supplies back into the cabinet and put the tables back in place. Finally, she put on the pants again, returning the pepper spray to its holster. Every few seconds she checked the door to see if anyone was coming.

No one came.

Belatedly, she realized one benefit of being underground— thick earth to insulate sound. With another glance up to ensure the camera couldn't see her corner, Zita sat down at the computer. The camera screen switched to a different cell, and she mentally groaned.

Unlike all the other camera views, this one had what looked like a luxury hotel suite after a knife fight. While no obvious knife slashes marred the queen size bed or Jacuzzi tub, stark gashes like claw marks striped down one cream-colored wall. Blood splattered the silky-smooth tangle of what might've been white satin sheets. Something lacy peeked out of a black lacquer dresser, upon which was an enormous, flat screen television. In the center of it all, a familiar vampiress kneeled on a brocade chair and caressed a familiar grate, set into a barred window.

Metal creaked in the examination room.

"You linger near my prison. Come play with me. I promise it'll only hurt in a good way." Domina's words slithered out despite the closed door. While her long, claw-like nails flashed silver and black in the room light, a few inches of dull brown roots showed above the flat black of her hair where it had grown longer in the months since Zita had last seen her.

Zita grimaced. *Dmitri's girlfriend has special digs with a TV and everything. And she's even creepier than before.*

Ex-girlfriend. Domina belongs in a prison, or perhaps staked out in the sun for what she did to those people. Wyn's tones held no sympathy.

As Zita stared at the lab setup and the grate on the screen, her stomach tightened into an unhappy ball. *No argument there.*

She glanced down at the stick, shifting from foot to foot uneasily. The light still shone blue. It took a moment, but her brain put a few facts together. Her stomach twisted, and she fought back the urge to vomit. *I'm guessing she's their foolproof lab test for metas. Dios help him, Miguel said he'd gotten the V Test and showed up normal. They told him it meant Virus Test, those lying pendejos.*

Domina whispered something else, her voice husky.

Her words unintelligible, Chaniclas made an angry muffled sound.

With an involuntary shudder, Zita swore mentally and tried to tune out anything else. *I hate vampires.*

Even Dmitri? Wyn asked.

She allowed the exception. *He's okay. Hard to hate a guy who always has snacks, even if he can't eat them, and laughs at his own cheesiness.*

Fumbling with the keyboard, she checked on Jerome's device. It was only half full. She let it keep copying files.

Slowly.

I need to speed things up before someone else comes in here, either looking for Chaniclas or for an aspirin. Impatient but not daring to move much for fear of being caught on camera, she clicked a few feeds to get the layout of the prison and see if she could find their targets. For now, she ignored the set labeled outside and only clicked through the interior ones. The surprisingly scarce hall views focused downward on tall, narrow corridors with few exits. Most of the shots were views of small, almost identical cells, none of which had any personalization, save for Domina's indulgent nest.

And they wanted me in one of those cells? They're not even big enough to cartwheel in wearing my own body, and I'm not a big person. She twitched, more unhappy in an unfamiliar human body than an animal one, but then her eye caught something that made her freeze.

Andy interrupted her thoughts, just as she checked a few other feeds to verify what she was seeing. *Did you get anything good? Jerome says he got a streamed conversation, but it slowed down online file transfer, so he needs you to let the drive fill as much as possible.*

Her mind whirled. *I don't know. It's still saving files. I need to cut it off though, get away from Ms. CreepyFangs, and see what's going on. This whole place might be a dummy system? I don't think they're actually storing any prisoners here, or not many.*

What do you mean? he replied.

A wash of curiosity came from Wyn.

Zita fought to arrange her thoughts, so they'd make sense to someone else. Saying that the setup gave her an icky feeling wouldn't explain her position. *Computers aren't my thing, but I've set up a lot of security cameras, so I was trying to scope out the place via those. They've got a ton, but most are useless. A bunch are outright dummies, but even some of the real ones are useless.*

How so? Andy asked.

Zita chose her words carefully. *The lab, Domina's hotel room, and the administration area all seem accurate. The problem is in the prisoner area. One cell has a crack under the bed around the right size for a skinny rat to get through.*

Distaste came from Wyn. *Disturbing, but so?*

Her mouth had the sour tang of acid as her stomach clenched. *According to the time stamp, these videos are live, but I've seen the same exact flaw in at least nine different cells with a different prisoner in each. They're looping footage. The only reason it's not more obvious is these cells don't have windows or anything.*

That's... no coincidence. Andy sounded as nauseated as she felt.

Even though he couldn't see her, Zita tapped her nose as she studied the cells. *Exactly. Something's being hidden, and you can bet it isn't cookies. Sadly. On the bright side, I've got a better idea of where the live cameras are and know what to avoid. I need to find out what's going on. I haven't seen Dream Auntie at all, and Elle's one of the prisoners on the looped footage. At least we know Dream Auntie's alive as of a couple nights ago.*

She visited you? Wyn sighed. *Of all of us to visit... Did you get anything helpful from her?*

Sí. It ended quick though because my brother woke me up, so I didn't get any useful data other than she's been asleep since 1977. Didn't I tell you?

The witch's tone was sharp. *No, you neglected to mention that tidbit. She may be the only surviving Seventies super then.*

Other than the scary Cambodian lady and Dragon, Andy pointed out.

It's a pity we don't hear more about some of the less evil ones, though I think Zita mentioned something about Joe Paladin being spotted in South America, Wyn allowed.

Occasionally, and I haven't heard anything about that for a few years now. They mentioned something about Clockwork on the call, too, so he might be around still. Zita tidied up her uniform as much as possible and pulled the ball cap low over her face again. She picked up the clipboard that Chaniclas had carried and pocketed Jerome's device.

Clockwork's reputation tended toward the sinister, Wyn sent.

As she ran through a mental checklist, Zita focused on preventing her thoughts from reaching the others. *I've got a uniform, badges, and a clipboard. Hopefully, no one will notice that I smell like rubbing alcohol or spot the giant wet patch on my rear if I look like I know what I'm doing.*

Before she left, she set the monitors to display the vampiress' quarters again and hung Chaniclas' Taser on her own belt.

Domina stood at the grate, stroking it as if it were a pet. Her nose was pressed close, and her shoulders rose and fell as she inhaled and exhaled.

Sniffing Chaniclas and me like Wyn picking truffles at a fancy chocolate shop. Zita shuddered, drew herself up straight, and left the room.

Thankfully, outside of the infirmary, she could no longer hear the vampire's whispers.

Chapter Twelve

It was a good thing that numbers were Zita's jam. And she was a fan of jam. Especially with peanut butter.

She punched in the guard's code and slapped her badge against the door to the prison area. The need to hurry burned inside of her while she lowered her head as if to study her clipboard. *Ring 3, cell 5, maximum security for a kid with a bum heart. Walk like a woman—err, a man—on a mission so no one stops you.*

Suspicion flavored Andy's words. *Z, what exactly are you doing right now?*

The light turned green, and the massive steel door unlocked and slid open. Behind her, feet marched down the corridor.

She pulled the door shut rapidly and found herself face to face with another set of bars and a guard in a little box. This one was a bald, African American guy in his fifties, with laugh lines around his mouth and the lean, wiry build of a lifelong runner. He had an unused shotgun and a coffee-stained mug both resting in easy grasping distance. Monitors that flicked through views of all the cells by his chair.

While she considered lying to Andy for all of a second, Zita decided to go with the truth. *Probably the stupidest thing I've ever done in my life, but I'm going to find Elle. I know her cell number and block, so I'll go right there. Then I'll leave as soon as I know she's okay.*

The camera feed is too hinky to trust. Just in case, can you have Jerome use his flying robots to check for… for signs of digging lately?

Solemnity accompanied Wyn's quiet voice. *Have the drones check for disturbed earth? Excellent idea, which is why I already had him on that. He found a small area he wants you to sniff around once you're done endangering our mission. Do you really need to take the risk of searching for her? The plan was to perform a simple scouting run. Retrieve some data. Get out. This is foolish, even for you, especially since we have to hide our powers, so they don't identify us if we're spotted.*

As she held up Roberson's badge for his inspection, Zita growled internally. *Even for me? Nice.*

The bald guard tapped a badge reader on his desk she'd missed.

Yes, we need to do this. If that poor kid is dead because I gave her too long to heal between lessons, that's on me. I thought at worst she was in a hospital in juvie. If she's alive and suffering, I need to know so I can fix it as soon as possible… You guys don't have to help if you don't want. Zita slapped her forehead and ran the badge through the scanner.

Reluctance curled around Wyn's reply. *Fine, but attempt to show caution at least. Complying with Jerome's plan was foolhardy to start and grows only more so as we deviate from the initial limited scope.*

If it helps, I don't sense people in immediate danger. And yeah, we can't leave her now we know she's in trouble, but be careful, Z. Andy sent.

His face wrinkling in confusion, the door guard paused, his hand over a button. "Roberson? What're you doing here? Aren't you supposed to be topside today?"

Doing my best. She coughed and clipped the badge back on her belt. Tapped the clipboard. Remembered at the last second not to use her usual fake accent when speaking. "Chaniclas. Following up on an inspection item."

"That woman and her inspections. Frog in your throat?" the guard asked.

"Bad food," she replied, pounding on her manly chest as if she had heartburn.

The other guy shook his head and buzzed her through. "Juan's chili get you again? When are you going to learn not to eat other people's food? You're old enough to know better."

She shrugged and stepped through. "Gotta eat, right? Sorry, got to go. Boss is all up my ass."

"Don't let me hold you up, man. It's all just the usual snooze here," the guard said, relaxing in his booth as the doors locked behind her.

Zita strode forward pretending to know where she was going. Jerome found plans of the original base, but he hadn't known how it had been modified for the DMS prison, so she tried to orient herself based on what he'd been able to find.

This must've been the missile silo, she guessed. Wide black steel catwalks ringed a round room, with an eight-foot-tall fence preventing access to the center, which was left open to below. Everything smelled like sweaty people, metal, plastic, and stagnant water. Stairs led up and down to higher floors at the midway points on the walkway that circled the level. A freight elevator was across from the barred entry guard booth.

No telling what security they have on that to keep prisoners from taking it over. Then again, why would they bother with an elevator when they've got perfectly good stairs nearby? If all the floors are the same size, I've got at least five to check.

The same small cells she'd seen on camera filled the walls, separated from the walkway by thick bars and transparent plastic that removed any possible privacy. All the cells had visible pipes at the bottom, that a constant slow stream of a low-lying, sickly orange mist in some of the occupied cells. The only obvious separations were by sex—men appeared to be on the left side of the ring, with women on the right. To her delight, the helpful sign-maker had struck again and marked not only what ring and cell she was on, but also where Maximum Security was—down. Something called Overwatch was up.

Already suspecting what that meant and not liking it, she glanced that direction.

Catwalks crossed the wide circular area, and guards roamed up there with long guns.

Nice shooting gallery. Getting caught is definitely a bad idea. Even though she hated the delay, she walked the circle of cells, stopping and pretending to check her board at random. Relying on her memory of the walkways from the cameras, she stayed near the railing by the big center hole so she would hopefully not be visible on camera often.

Every third cell held one or two people, but all the rest were empty. Little placards listed specific prohibitions for some prisoners, some of which were odd, like the one preventing anyone from giving a bland, middle-aged woman any dolls. None of the faces stood out as anyone Remus had said was missing, nor were any of them Dream Auntie or Elle. The only ones she recognized were a tattooed man and a woman with bristly hair and a surly expression in two of the orange gas cells. Tiger had tried to use the massacre of patrons at a nightclub that'd fired him as a way to sell drugs. Sheriff was a badger shifter who had worked as a bouncer at the same club and been mind-controlled into assisting Domina with her assorted plots.

Zita had hoped DMS would consider the coercion when determining Sheriff's sentence, but there were no obvious signs of leniency. With a shake of her head and a sour taste in her mouth, she headed down the stairs.

"Hey, where are you going? You know nobody's down there," her buddy in the booth called out.

Zita picked up her pace and hurried down as if she hadn't heard him. *Maximum security is down. Elle's supposed to be there. If they're all empty, I need to see this. What have they done with all the metas who have disappeared? Remus' list alone is like twenty people.*

The next floor down was identical in layout to the one above, but it was empty of people. The cells hadn't appeared on any of the screens she'd viewed in the infirmary, and their arrangements varied widely. One had thick black curtains outside of the bars and a set of the same floor lamps she'd seen in the infirmary. Three had extra thick manacles attached to the walls with chains of the sort that she expected to see used for ship anchors. Two were identical to those above but had what looked like chicken wire covering the holes in the plastic.

Domina didn't like those lights, so maybe the one is another vampire cell? And the manacle cells are for super strong metas? I'm guessing the wire ones are to stop shapeshifters. All empty. Dios, what have we stumbled into?

Her breath caught in her throat, and she couldn't resist a strangled hiss at the last two rooms on the floor. Instead of a bed, these two cells had versions of the bondage chair in the infirmary, but with a toilet replacing the seat. Markings circled the furniture, incised into the ground with a dull gray metal. Still more dotted the chair restraints.

Even though she hated to do it, she needed to confirm what she was seeing. *Wyn? You need to tell me if this is what I think it is. You've got my permission to use me to see.*

A moment later, party line disappeared. Weight built up, as if someone pressed too close, and she felt the weird sensation of someone else looking through her eyes.

After a moment, Zita glanced around so Wyn could take in the rest of the floor.

The pressure behind her eyes ended, followed by the warmth—and blessed distance—of party line touching her mind again.

Wyn's voice was tight. *Yes, those are spells meant to prevent magic use. I recognize the large circle. It's partially my work.*

Of all the things her friend could've said, that wasn't something Zita had expected. *What?*

Remember that project I've been working on? The one where I loved the work but had issues with the professor? That's what we were working on. I thought it was an academic exercise in the combination of magical styles...

Ah, is he, uh... Andy let his words trail off.

Zita didn't share his reluctance to be blunt. *Is that the guy you banged once who's drooling for a repeat? The one you don't want me to punch for you yet?*

Her friend sounded irritable. *Yes, but that is irrelevant right now. What that means is the circle might actually work to restrain someone. If said person didn't figure out that having the toilet built into the chair creates a gap in the circle continuity. Have you seen enough? Can we go?*

Zita checked the camera installations and tried to stay in a blind spot. *Haven't found Elle. Or Dream Auntie. Assuming Jerome's missile silo floor plans were accurate about size, I've got four or so more floors to go if they're all similar, but at least one needs to be for exercise unless they're letting people rot in their cells. Entering maximum security now. Clearly that's where you keep teenagers with bum hearts instead of in the scary infirmary or a cell closer to it.*

She scurried over to the maximum-security door and swiped her badge. The light shone green, and the door opened with a hiss of noisy hydraulics.

As she prayed nobody caught that sound, she peered down below. Beyond the doors... was nothing but junk. Other than the obvious supports that had been put in place for the upper floors, nothing seemed to have been touched for years. Rickety, rusty metal stairs leading downward, the occasional step missing, making her suspect that even her normal form's weight would be too much for it. The smell of mold and stagnant water was much stronger, too.

They're not keeping anyone down there. I can leave this weird-ass place. She lifted her hand to close the door, but heard footsteps clattering down the stairs.

A guard jogged toward her, a shotgun ready in his arms. "Hey, hey! Why'd you open the door, Roberson? You know nobody's down here."

She waved the clipboard and coughed, remembering not to use her accent at the last second. "Inspecting cells."

He came closer and looked around, lowering the weapon and pointing it to the floor. "Then you've seen all of them unless you haven't done the topside ones yet. You have no need to open that, making work for Overwatch."

Outside? There are more cells outside? I'll have to check there too. Zita swallowed and nodded toward the big iron door with Maximum Security plastered on it. "Just... making sure the door locks. For the inspection. Locking doors are good in a prison."

The other guard frowned. "Why would Chaniclas want to check that door? For that matter, she came through at the start of first shift for inspection."

Zita swore internally.

He peered closely at her, studying her. "Hey, you're not—"

She tased him, kicking the gun away when it fell from his arms. "Not much of a liar, no."

After a long moment of fear that someone would notice the snap of the weapon or his long, drawn-out breath, he fell.

Catching him before he hit the ground, she hesitated before finally dragging him under the stairs, another spot she hadn't seen when flipping through the camera views. *I'd buy more time if I shut him in the faux maximum-security area, but I doubt it's stable enough to hold his weight. Plus, I need to hurry before his absence is noted and I end up an endless parade of dudes needing tasing.*

After cuffing his arms behind his back, she tore off one of his shoes and removed his sock, stuffing it in his mouth. When she went to take his cuffs so she could keep him from running up the stairs, her hand paused.

He jerked and pulled against the restraints.

Zita pressed a hand into his chest to keep him down, reaching toward his belt.

His eyes widened, and he made a strange sound. He kicked at her.

"Don't flatter yourself, buddy. Relax," she whispered as she removed his cuffs, the key for them, his badge, and the pepper spray. After attaching one of the cuffs to the underside of the stairs, she linked it to the ones she'd already put on him to keep him from running off or alerting anyone. The rest of the stuff she tucked into her own increasingly heavy belt. His gun she set on the dangerous-looking stairs of the abandoned section.

Zita closed the door. The red light reappeared over the badge reader. *That should buy me a couple minutes, but between him and Chaniclas, someone's going to figure out I'm here soon. I need to hurry.*

After straightening her shoulders and pulling out her shirt a little to make her seem broader still, she strolled the stairs, sticking to the areas without cameras as much as possible. Zita kept her head bent over the clipboard. If the cameras caught her, they wouldn't get a good shot of her face, even if it was borrowed. Although she wanted nothing more than to run, she kept to a sedate pace.

The friendly guard at the entry box waved to her as she passed through. "Done? Where's Brown?"

She shrugged and coughed to buy another second. "Tied up. He'll be back soon, I'm sure."

"Treads coming loose again? It figures. See you in the barracks! Stay away from the chili." The guard cackled at his joke.

Her laugh wasn't convincing, but that only made the comedian in the booth cackle louder as he buzzed her through. Rubbing her stomach, she nodded and left.

Zita made it down the hall and had almost reached the stairs to the top level when a squad of six men stepped into her path.

The guy in charge had the short, sturdy structure of a human bulldog, the alert gaze of someone in a war zone, and a voice like a drill sergeant. He also had more stripes on his shoulder than her. "Roberson!"

"Sir!" Zita said.

"Have you seen Chaniclas? Why aren't you in the barracks? Didn't we send you there sick?" He stared at her, as did the men behind him.

Sweat beaded on her forehead. "Chaniclas caught me and told me to check the cells for the inspection. I don't know where she went after that."

He remained silent, his gaze on her.

"Sir?"

His posture eased. "I can almost see the weight you've lost. You don't look right, you're sweaty, and you smell. Not to mention you've never called me sir before, let alone twice. Give the remaining checklist to someone at the upper holding cells and get back to bed."

"Okay," Zita said.

"That's better. Drop off your clipboard at the jail before you go back to the barracks. Stay there until you're better. Nobody wants to cover your shifts or clean up after you." The sergeant or captain or whatever he was continued down the stairs past her.

As the group of DMS guards thundered by, she stepped aside to let them pass, keeping her head down. Then she strode up the stairs and into the faux office.

Her back itching with the knowledge that the others there watched her, she walked through the room with all the fake computers. As much as possible, she avoided eye contact. The one time someone seemed about to say something, she gagged a little, and they backed away.

She exited the building. Her uniform clung unpleasantly to her body, sticky with sweat and still redolent with the rubbing alcohol she'd spilled. Despite that and the sticky heat that had wrapped her in its miserable embrace, tension eased from her shoulders. The breeze didn't cool her so much as it brought slightly different odors, that of swamp, exhaust, and something meaty cooking.

They must've started making lunch. Now, if I were a creepy DMS above-ground prison, which building would I be in?

Jerome's insistence that they waste time studying the overhead view of the compound came in handy. As she recalled, there had only been four above-ground structures large enough to possibly be a prison. She'd just come from the one of them. The parking lot was to the south, and a single building stood alone to the north. Zita guessed that was the barracks since it was the only unguarded building. Two long, half-buried buildings huddled together, and each had a pair of guards. Big, sleek dogs barked and ran around in a fenced area between the two buildings. Absently, she picked out cameras as she headed toward the guarded buildings. A tower platform loomed over it all, but it was empty. In the distance, swamp beckoned.

Way better camera coverage up here than below ground, but it's a relief that the shooting platform is empty.

Tension knotted in her shoulders while she plodded along, fighting the urge to speed up. One building had obvious reinforcement done to the walls and was the source of a bland but meaty smell. The other had garage doors and a nasty chemical odor emanating from it.

Well, that narrows it down. Garage doors for vehicles, regular doors for prisoners. Despite the temptation to visit with the dogs, she trudged toward what she hoped was the jail. She made sure to rub her stomach as if feeling unwell, surreptitiously using the motion to fluff her shirt out around her stomach and make herself seem stockier.

Shotgun-wielding guards at the door watched as she approached. One was openly curious; his companion seemed bored. Sweat stained their uniforms, but both seemed alert and fit enough to be a problem.

Is the guy I'm imitating the only person here who isn't carrying a shotgun? This place probably got inspected earlier today too. When she reached them, she held up her badge. She coughed and said, "Chaniclas wanted a double-check on inspection results."

Curious Guard snorted. "You look green. I swear you look like you've lost weight since breakfast this morning."

His partner grunted agreement. "You look like crap."

"Juan's chili," Zita muttered.

While neither laughed as much as the guard in the underground prison, both cracked smiles. Curious Guard said, "Should've known. Go on."

With most of her attention on monitoring the guards, Zita typed in the passcode.

The number pad gave a harsh buzz.

Both guards straightened.

"You're really off today, Roberson. I know we just got the code Monday, but you should be used to the weekly code changes by now," one guard said.

"You have no idea," Zita muttered. Licking her lips, she eyed the pad and wondered if she'd mistyped or if it was a different code. She leaned against the door frame, wondering if she could pry it open enough to force acceptance.

"Are you sure you should be working?" The talkative guard eyed her.

Between the relentless, sticky heat and their scrutiny, her clothing would be dripping with sweat soon. She shook her head. "Chaniclas insisted."

The chatty guard grunted. "Get whatever you're here to do done, and if you're going to puke, aim for a trash can. Or Jones."

His partner reached over and punched his shoulder before returning his gaze to Zita. "Go on, Roberson. Enter the code."

Licking her lips, Zita stabbed at the panel, carefully watching this time.

To her relief, the light turned green.

Both guards relaxed.

"Good, now get it done. No reason to linger," Bored Guard said.

With a nod, Zita stepped inside.

It was no surprise to find herself in another airlock-type room. Yet another guard, this one a stocky, sleepy-eyed white guy, waited in a plastic-walled booth surrounded by bars identical to those of the man in the booth underground. He also had a shotgun.

Familiar with the drill and impatient to be done before she was discovered, she slapped her badge against the reader.

It beeped and glowed green.

"I thought I heard you ate yourself sick." The man inside leaned forward and stared at her.

Zita deliberately made her voice hoarse as she slouched and tried to seem unwell. "Chaniclas doesn't care if I explode... as long as the inspection follow-up gets done first."

The guard rolled his eyes. "Of course not. She must be nervous about the new shipment we're supposed to get in any day now. I heard they're hoping to use the creeper cells on Level Two for some of them. Have you heard anything about that?"

Even though she was dying to know what he meant, she made noncommittal noises and tapped the clipboard. She eyed the room beyond the box she was stuck in. An aisle separated two columns of cells, culminating in an open shower area and a room with a big sign: Kitchen.

His face crumpling at her lack of an answer, the guard leaned back. "Yeah, I guess all we can do is our jobs. They keep claiming we're going to get someone famous but not coming up with anything better than the pair they're trying to get work out of. Would you believe they had us wash down a few of the max-security cages for tomorrow's big double event?"

"Craziness. What do they do with all the metas that leave here?" she muttered, wondering if solving the mystery could be as simple as a chatty guard.

He waved off the question. "Who knows? Who cares? It doesn't affect us, though I wish they'd leave the harmless sexy ones here longer. Last week's hottie was only here a few hours before she got shipped out on the Sunday afternoon van. I've got a twenty in the betting pool against the teams coming up with anyone we'd recognize from the news for the rest of the month."

Again, she tapped the clipboard.

"Fine, fine, go on." He sighed, hit a button to open the airlock, and resumed flipping through the monitors.

With the board clasped close to her chest, she exited the box and walked down the center. It stunk, an odd combination of meat, sweat, and cheap cleansers. It lacked air conditioning, but big fans were aimed down the aisle, which lowered the temperature from sweltering to merely unpleasant, at least in the aisle. While similarly outfitted to the prison below ground, more of these cells held prisoners. Wear showed in even the empty ones. Each was little more than a cement stall, with the top and visible front walled in with transparent plastic. Air holes were at the very top, and the cells had the same sparse furnishings she'd seen before. A metal pipe ran along the floor of each, with orange smoke drifting lazily out in some of the occupied ones.

Neither Elle nor Dream Auntie were there.

Most of the prisoners had worn cards and paperbacks and nothing else even close to personal. Of the visible prisoners, most seemed to be in their twenties. Two exceptions stood out, however, both spaces lacking the orange gas. The most luxurious had extra blankets, a fancy pillow, and a television propped on a row of books—all chemistry, she noted. A gaming system with a single controller rested on the ground beside the TV. The occupant was missing. In the other cell, a middle-aged woman stared at the photo of a chubby, cherubic teenage boy in a golden frame and flipped listlessly through a paperback.

Almost done, she sent to her friends.

Good. Let us know if you need a pickup.

I might. They've got a lot of outside surveillance. Way better than inside. She paused at the last cell before the big cafeteria door. A large placard prohibited touching outside of it.

Incubus lay on his stomach in a yoga pose and stared at her dully. Like all the others, he had a plain orange jumpsuit, and his hair was a frizzy, messy braid down his back. The psychic vampire seemed drawn, with dark circles beneath his eyes. His arms trembled in even the basic cobra position that should've been no trouble for him.

Surprise made the words slip out, and she took a step or two toward him. "Incubus? What are you doing here?"

"You know my court name? Please, you've got to let me out. All the negativity here is playing havoc on my chakras, and I didn't do anything." He rose in a fluid movement to the door and stuck his fingers out of a waist-high slot. "Please. This is killing me. I need people. I need contact."

From his little cubicle, the guard called out to her. "Roberson? What are you doing? You know regs don't allow us to talk to them. Especially that one. He's only still here because the van was full last Sunday. He's been on a hunger strike since he came in."

Zita bit her lip to keep from mentioning the truth, but her face must've showed something.

Incubus' eyes widened. He reached through the doors. "You do know. Please, help me."

Others in the cells pushed to the front of their cells and added their pleas, creating a loud, miserable cacophony.

The guy in the booth opened the door, shutting and locking it behind him as he stomped toward Zita, a baton in hand. He banged it on cells as he passed. "All of you, get away from the doors. If you don't, I will punish you. Damn it, now they're all going to be whining. Why'd you have to set them off?"

An alarm blared and a red light began flashing, alternating with a yellow one.

Swearing internally, Zita stepped away from Incubus, restraining herself from freeing him now with the silent promise that she'd come back for him later. Feigning a shrug, she said, "It was an accident. He looked like an old buddy for a second."

"Maybe that's his power. You can't trust them, you know," the guard said.

Radios buzzed, including the one at her waist and that of her interrogator. "All Bob Robersons are to be arrested on sight."

"I knew something was off! Surrender!" The guard lifted his baton and charged at her without waiting for a reply.

Zita rolled to the side, but the unfamiliar body made it clumsy. She pulled her Taser and shot him with it.

He jerked, jiggled, and fell.

With a glance at Incubus, she dragged the guard up against the cage, within reach of the psychic vampire's arms. Out of habit, she took his badge. "Don't kill him or do the mind thing. I'll tell your boss you're here," she whispered.

Incubus nodded and set a hand on the man's hair. "You poor man," he crooned. "Let me take some of that pain away."

Zita ran toward the cafeteria, praying it had a window she could use to escape. As she passed, she pushed over the floor fans, hoping it'd buy her another second once the men got through the entry.

She slammed up hard against the door.

Locked.

The doors burst open, and the guards from outside shouted commands for her to stop. They didn't put down their shotguns, and one was on the radio as they tried to get through the airlock thing.

Zita slapped the guard's badge against the reader.

The door clicked, and the light flashed green.

His face glowing with health, Incubus pulled back his hand and retreated to the rear of his cell. The guard she'd tased snored.

Zita hurried into the kitchen. To her dismay, someone was there, a young man who stood in front of a long, steel table with a huge, steaming tray of brownish-gray mush and an array of cooking tools in front of him. His back was to her.

Radios buzzed in unison, both hers and the one at the cook's waist. "Williams is down! Take any and all Bob Robersons into custody immediately!"

"Surprise inspection!" Zita barked out, darting over and tasing him. The door locked shut behind her.

He fell on the table, muscles spasming.

Zita ran forward to ease him to the floor so he wouldn't hit his head on the hard, beige tile. Out of habit, she relieved her victim of his badge and Taser, tossing the weapon into the sink of greasy water. Sadly, he didn't have any handcuffs she could steal, having used her own.

She ripped the badge reader to the interior door off the wall and pulled the wires so the door to the cell area would stay locked.

With guards now delayed, she glanced around, hoping for an easy out and no cameras. The room looked like a school cafeteria in a poor neighborhood with a dented commercial fridge, a rusty warming oven, and the other normal accoutrements of an industrial kitchen, but everything had enough dings and stains to seem secondhand. The clouds rising from the big steam table smelled of mold and meat and beans. To her dismay, cameras silently filmed, one aimed toward the wide door she assumed was the equivalent of a loading dock, and the other on the cooking area. Red light glared at her from the reader by the exterior door. An unfamiliar black screen, a foot high, was mounted above this one.

She hurried over to the badge reader by the outside door. Roberson's badge still didn't work, so she discarded it and used the cook's badge instead.

Something banged against the interior door.

The reader beeped and turned yellow. The screen above it lit with a hand-shaped print and a request for authentication.

"Seriously? On a kitchen door?" Zita swore inwardly and glanced toward the cell area. *The guards will get through there soon.*

After abandoning the clipboard, she got a good grip on one end of the long, heavy table. Cooking implements rattled and jittered, and metal screeched in protest as she huffed, puffed, and pushed one end to block the door.

The cessation of sound was such a relief that she almost missed the whisper of noise behind her.

Eyes red and angry, the cook staggered to his feet. His movements were stiff and slow, still recovering from the jolt she'd given him.

Zita tried to tase him again, but her weapon just clicked. Empty.

He drew the baton from his belt.

She threw the useless Taser at him.

He batted it aside and charged at her.

Dodging to the side, she fumbled to release the baton from her belt as she skidded away from him. Her fingers ripped at the unfamiliar closure with no success. Blindly, she grabbed for a utensil with her free hand, trying to remember where the knives were. Her hand closed around smooth, cool metal. "Don't make me hurt you," she said, waving her new weapon at him.

The man facing her laughed. "With a spoon?"

Stupid longer arms. I hate fighting in someone else' body. She reached for something else and came up with a second of the same weapon in a different color.

"Technically, it's a spoodle, and I have two! Back off!" she said, feeling stupid.

He lashed out with his baton.

She blocked his hit with one chunky ladle and slammed the other against his kidneys.

Even if his baton didn't strike her, both of her weapons bent, and the painful impact of the hits vibrated down her arms.

She tossed the utensils aside, backing up and grasping blindly for another weapon. Nothing met her hand.

He swung at her head.

She ducked, but not enough, and it grazed the top of her head.

Gasping at the unexpected pain, she kicked his knee. *Need to treat this like fighting someone my own size. I'm too used to fighting bigger people.*

His knee buckled, but he remained standing. He swiped at her again.

Worry infused Wyn's words. *Fighting? Are you okay? I thought you were leaving.*

This time, she managed to dodge, rolling over the table and landing on her feet in a noisy cascade of falling kitchen tools. She grabbed something—a knife, at last!—and hurled it at his shoulder. *Busy! Trying to. Be ready to pull me out.*

He shouted an imprecation as it hit, staggering back.

Something thudded against the interior door.

Her friends sent quiet assent through the link and the image of where to meet.

Arm bleeding, the cook growled and tipped over the massive tray of steaming beef hash at her.

She danced backward but failed to escape all the scalding meat. Even through her stolen pants, it burned her legs, wringing a yip out of her. Under her boots, the floor was slippery with food.

The table shuddered and skidded on the greasy floor as whoever was on the other side banged on the door again.

Her attacker ran around the end of the table, his feet sliding and costing him a second.

Zita bashed him over the head with the empty hash pan, once, then twice.

The cook went down.

With a shrill screech, the table inched away from the door.

After checking his pulse and loosening her baton in the stupid holster, she dragged him over to the door and swiped the cook's badge. She slapped his palm against the reader.

The blessed light turned green.

"Thanks"—she checked his badge—"Jorge Georges." She propped the cook up against the closest cabinets and peeked outside. *I'm going to head for the fence. Can somebody meet me? Or at least lay down tracks so it looks as if I got away like that instead of shapeshifting?*

Dogs barked and ran around the kennel with bright eyes in a swirl of gold and black fur. A uniformed man had opened the door and was trying to calm them down in German. More guards ran her direction, but most hadn't reached the alley between the buildings yet. Robots flew overhead, little more than flying cameras.

Andy sent, *Be there soon as we can without obvious powers.*

"Come on, make yourself useful," she told the cook, who was stirring beside her. Pulling her cap low over her face, she dragged him out the door, toward the kennel entrance.

"Hey! Georges needs the infirmary! You grab him so I can go help Jones and Williams," she called out to the guy dealing with the dogs.

"Sure thing!" the guy said, closing the gate to the dog pen and hurrying toward them. Inside the wire fencing, the dogs wagged and crowded close to her.

She dumped Georges on the kennel guy.

He said, "What happened? Hey, wait, you're—" Dropping Georges, he stepped back and threw open the kennel door, shouting in German for the dogs to attack her.

The animals rushed at her, pausing in confusion when they drew close. Their ears went up and down and they brushed her aside as they poured around and past her in a tidal wave of fur. One straggler, a younger dog with the leggy cheer of immaturity, stopped to give her a play bow and lick up the meat dripping off her pants.

Not one to question her good luck, Zita pointed at the kennel man who had just brought his radio up to his lips. "Jump," she said in German, hoping the dog had been trained in the command.

The licker ran over and jumped on the man gleefully, knocking him down.

He sputtered as the animal covered his face in kisses.

Unwilling to waste any more time, she jogged down the alleyway between the buildings. As the shouts to stop began and people started chasing her, she switched to full run. A flying robot caught up to her and kept pace, soon joined by two others.

Zita ran toward the fence. Her legs burned, her head hurt, and her current form lacked her usual stamina, so she was panting and had a painful stitch in her side. She pitched a rock at a robot, but the attack missed. *Guys, is that pickup close? They're going to catch up if I keep running in human form, and I can't tell which of these spy bots are Jerome's and which are theirs. The only thing that's stopping me from getting shot is most of these guys have shotguns.*

I'm on my way, Andy said.

At the first gunshot, she changed her path to a crazy zigzag. A glance back revealed several guards chasing her, and someone climbing the tower. Zita forced her aching legs to move faster.

Another flying robot joined the three following her. All four stopped following her and sped in different directions.

Jerome says to tell you that if he gets his drones close enough to theirs, they're all his, Wyn sent.

A dot appeared in the swamp, rushing toward the chain-link fence. An airboat slewed to a stop nearby. A man with a knee-length, dirty white beard hopped out and began cutting through the fence with an enormous pair of bolt cutters.

"New look? Doesn't suit you," Andy said from behind his Santa beard and baseball cap.

Zita slipped through the hole he'd made, jumped into the driver side of the airboat, and adjusted the seat. She bent double, hands on her knees, catching her breath.

"I could say the same," she gasped.

Her friend slid into the passenger seat. "Limited resources, and I wasn't using my Hagrid beard for this," he reminded her. "I could've driven."

Zita revved the engine. It roared and vibrated beneath her, and she grinned. "Not like I can."

Andy gulped and held on tight as they raced away.

Chapter Thirteen

"If you inquire if they are here one more time, I shall commit grave acts of violence upon your person that will leave you a cowering and broken woman. Do not think that I have forgotten your narrow escape yesterday."

Wyn didn't even glance at her when issuing the threat. While they waited for the prison convoy, the scholarly witch sat cross-legged behind a large mountain laurel and made no pretense of being on watch. Instead, she frowned down at the e-reader in her lap.

Her friend's (probably) joking threat made Zita close her mouth around the query that had been about to slip out. One leg jiggled with impatience, and her bare toes curled into the rough bark of the massive tree towering over Wyn's hiding spot. She resolved to be patient and checked below.

Their target, a length of narrow road snaking along a mountain, remained stubbornly empty. Thin belts of scrub brush and trees lined the ridges in the otherwise sheer cliff walls that bracketed one side of the road. The women hid on a natural terrace, behind the exuberant summer foliage rioting with growth in the humid heat. The other side of the road tapered off to another steep drop. From the stone tunnel that swallowed one end of the road, a lone man in a construction worker's bright vest and a hard hat leaned a sign telling oncoming traffic to slow against the wall beside him.

Thunder growled from above where Andy circled, high enough up for Zita to glimpse his avian shape but not discern details. Even without preternatural acuity, she knew he appeared to be a giant golden eagle, with glowing eyes and a tracery of lightning flickering over his feathers.

Zita's patience lasted perhaps two minutes. She scoffed quietly and reiterated her concerns. "Real construction would be louder. There'd be more than one piece of heavy construction equipment and three vans that ride awful low. Also, who ever heard of a crew filled with young, beefy, white guys who all look like active duty soldiers watching their sixes? We should block off the tunnel. Fake construction or something."

When her friend didn't react to her repeating the situation, she waved toward the lone visible man standing outside the tunnel. "That flagman's standing at parade rest. If we're not going to block off the road, I should do another loop, maybe as a bird, and see what else they're up to. Maybe they're discussing their plans right now. You know how bad guys randomly start describing their plans for no apparent reason these days."

Without looking up, Wyn murmured, "Wingspan's keeping watch above. He won't miss anything. Given that I cannot get to the ground without one of you to assist me, your presence here is necessary."

"He can't see what's going on inside there, and his people-in-danger alarms only start once people are in danger. If you need down, he's the best choice anyway. I could cut through the tunnel just to scout. Even with your big illusion up warning people about the trap in the tunnel, the transport might ignore it and go in. Then all the additional scouting will be invaluable." Zita gestured toward the magical billboard that seemed to glow even in the bright sunlight.

They are not here. Andy crushed her hopes, his tones the male chorus of his giant bird shape.

Zita sighed and swung around so she could watch the road from an upside-down position. *Fine, but I don't have to like it.*

Below her, Wyn glanced up from her reading and shoved a lock of long hair out of her face. Because she wore her usual Muse illusion—that of a too-perfect woman with ghostly pale hair and skin in a short, glittery silver dress—the vivid amethyst of her eyes stood out in stark contrast. "Were I not a strong, self-confident woman who knew the real reason for your complaints is that you hate sitting still, I would feel unloved given your eagerness to abandon me."

Zita's phone buzzed in her pocket with a text. She dug it out. *I thought I had switched that off.*

Wyn frowned. As always, she was careful to use Andy's false name when speaking aloud. "Wingspan said there was no cell service up here. Wasn't that the whole reason the prison transports would be in danger? Chevalier needed a few days to go through the data we retrieved yesterday, so he couldn't verify it one way or another."

"I know. Weird, right?" Zita couldn't help a spurt of excitement and a smile as she opened the phone and checked the app. *Freelance? Ah, verifying our meet tomorrow.*

Her friend's gaze raked over her. "Wait, what's that look?"

"My usual one?" Zita tried, tapping out her reply.

With a snort, Wyn said, "I beg to differ."

A text sprang up. "Brazil?"

Wyn studied her. "Are you texting the mercenary? I figured you'd have messed that up by now."

"No, US," Zita laboriously typed, her nose wrinkling at Wyn's comment.

His reply came back almost immediately. "P in Brazil. Been monitoring."

She frowned at his words.

They come. Andy's avian chorus of male voices sang over their mental connection.

"Well?" Wyn said.

Zita glanced at the road, finally picking up transports in the distance. She did a partial shift to an eagle, using the vision and ignoring how the long, thick black hair of her Arca form changed to a waterfall of feathers. "No time for personal stuff. Wingspan's right."

Wyn stood up, a hand shielding her eyes from the sun as she squinted down the road.

Are you ready? I think that's the convoy. Andy must've switched to his human form because it was just his usual voice on party line.

Below her, Wyn raised her pale brows. "Are you evading my question?"

"Not now," Zita hissed at Wyn. She closed the phone, most of her attention on the convoy. *Two armored transports and one escort each preceding and following.*

I see them, Andy sent.

Wyn would not be derailed, but she put away her e-reader. "Are you two still together or what?"

Zita sighed as she separated her phone from its battery and dropped it back in her pocket. "Yes. It's only been a couple months since we agreed to date, so we haven't had a lot of time together. So far, the only change is that occasionally we'll stop doing fun stuff to stare at each other for a really weird and awkward moment before we go back to being awesome. We agreed to meet tomorrow night after work. Whether I make it in time depends how long things drag out. Are they slowing down?"

"Perhaps they'll turn around when they see my sign," Wyn said hopefully. The billboard grew several feet in every direction and developed an air horn.

Wincing at the noise, Zita frowned and promptly forgot her friend's question as the convoy barreled past the sign and toward the tunnel. *Guys, Freelance texted that Pretorius is still in Brazil. Given that he might not be in the trucks, the suspiciously military construction crew, and the dead cell phone zone that isn't actually dead, this setup has gone from stinking to truly foul. Andy, how much do you trust the person who asked us to be here?*

Caution infused Andy's tone. *My friend's trustworthy, but it's possible she received bad info. Or Freelance did.*

Zita tapped her fingers on the tree branch, most of her attention on the convoy. *Unlikely. He gets a payday if he finds Jen Stone, and Pretorius knows where she was living. Wyn, can you stay farther back than usual until we make sure everything's okay?*

Wyn bit her lip. *Not that I mind staying back, but isn't all this a bit paranoid? Perhaps they've upgraded phone service to this area. Could you lift me down to the road now?*

For once, Andy agreed with Zita. *Possible, but I'd feel better if you stayed back more than usual too. It could just be Zita's paranoia rubbing off, but...*

Fine, I will remain farther back than usual. One of you must help me down from here, though, as I cannot get down on my own. Wyn smoothed her dress.

Zita couldn't resist. *Without an ice brush.*

Wyn huffed and folded her arms over her chest. *We agreed not to speak of that. If someone gets hurt, make sure you let me know so I can get closer. I don't want people to die just because the locals built another cell tower.*

Fair enough, Andy agreed.

With his sign encouraging drivers to SLOW, the flagman waved the convoy into the tunnel.

The vehicles proceeded inside.

Tossing aside his sign, the construction worker hauled wooden ROAD CLOSED sawhorses and orange cones into place and disappeared into the tunnel.

It's going down! Zita sent.

Wyn straightened her purse and stood at the ledge, frowning at the tunnel. *That does seem suspicious. Let's go.*

Andy sailed to them and scooped up Wyn, his expression grim as he flew.

Finally! Zita shifted to a great gray owl and soared on silent wings toward the tunnel. Even if lights were set at fixed intervals, it was still dark enough to have her choosing an animal that could see in the dimness. The highway held one lane in either direction, with a narrow shoulder on either side. Horns blared and brakes squealed, followed by ominous metal screeching sounds.

Andy set Wyn down by the entrance. Loose gravel crunched under their feet as they jogged toward the cacophony.

Zita pulled up before she crossed into the light spilling around the bend from work lights. Her wings beat against the air to keep her aloft while she waited for them to catch up. *The noise is coming from around the first curve.*

Gunfire sounded.

Andy picked Wyn up and dropped her right at the bend.

With a few gestures and a whispered spell, a magical bubble appeared around the witch. *I won't go any farther unless I have to heal.*

Keeping low in the hope that any gunfire would be well above her feathered head, Zita zipped around the corner, with Andy running close behind her.

The convoy and a construction crew appeared to be in a firefight.

Both lanes were impassable by car. Convoy trucks blocked the road closest to Zita and her friends, with the rear of the vehicles turned toward the fake construction site as if they'd tried to turn and run but had been stopped. People crouched behind vehicles.

Andy ran toward two grappling men near the back of a truck.

Another burst of gunfire sounded, and someone screamed. "Medic! Help!"

For all her dislike of battles, Wyn ignored their plan for her to hang back. She ran around the bend. Her protective bubble was almost invisible in the poor lighting.

Under one of the yellow lights, a woman wearing a DMS guard uniform tended to a fallen man. Red stained her hands and a towel as she pressed the fabric against the man's stomach and called out. While the sharp, painfully loud retorts of guns drowned out most of what she was saying, a pause in the shooting let her words echo down the tunnel. "Medic! I'm losing him!"

Wyn stopped a few feet away, the bubble between her and the downed man. "If you want me to help him, you need to move away from him," she said clearly. *I need backup. After Greenie's stunt in Greece, I modified my shield spell. Now people can only get through it if they don't intend harm to me or those with me. Unfortunately, I cannot reach the injured fellow because of it. It could be the woman with him is the aggressor, but... In any case, I can't cast while the shield is up.*

Zita headed toward her friend. *I got Wyn. You do your thing, Andy. Or I could be right, and this is all a big—*

Someone shouted, "Now!"

Her feathers ruffling, Zita threw herself aside as air guns popped nearby.

Men flung open the doors of the other truck, and someone shouted "Wingspan!"

Although he'd been about to reach a pair of battling men, Andy pivoted to see who had called him.

A glob of goo with five trailing tentacle-fingers hit him. A long goopy strand of blue connected it with the rear of the truck.

He staggered back in surprise. "Eww! What the?" When he lifted his arms, the goo expanded around them.

A fast winching sound came from the truck, and Andy was yanked off his feet and into the vehicle.

He squeaked.

Men slammed the doors shut behind him and dropped a bar across it. "Start the gas! Get the gas going! Take away his powers!" one shouted, pounding on the side of the truck. Now that they'd made their move, the "construction workers" and "convoy guards" had abandoned all pretense of fighting.

The truck's engine fired up.

Wyn squealed.

Three people, including the "injured" man, surrounded her, but none seemed able to come closer than four feet. Showing no signs of being hurt, the hurt man pounded on her bubble shield as if he could get through by force while the woman soldier who'd been calling for help picked up a syringe off the ground. A crumpled black piece of fabric and extra cuffs hung from the belt of the third man who held an air gun.

Zita zipped in between the trucks to limit the number of shots that could be taken at her. *Mano, you OK? I'll get Wyn.*

A loud crack assaulted her ears, and her instincts blared warnings as a blocky, black object flew toward her.

She tried to whirl to the side, but in the narrow corridor between vehicles, it hit.

The weighted net tangled in her wings and dragged her downward.

While Andy's cranky confirmation of his health was reassuring, it was also distracting. *I'm fine. The goop makes it hard to move, but I'm almost out of it now. It's like I was assaulted by the slimy love child of oobleck and quicksand.*

Zita struggled to stay up for a beat or two before she changed tactics and shape again, landing as an elephant. Her sides brushed both of the trucks, and she bugled defiantly. Behind her, she heard more feet approaching.

From the inside, a fist punched through the wall of the truck that held Andy.

The guy running up to her pulled a long gun from his back. Someone shouted, "More gas! More gas!"

Curling her trunk, she yanked off the net and hurled it at the man following her. She couldn't turn to see behind her, but the sparse hair on her back prickled.

Someone fired an air gun.

Already shifting to a hog-nosed skunk, Zita darted under the trucks. She peeked out, careful to avoid the swearing people surrounding the vehicle.

Wyn hadn't moved.

The fake injured man was circling the bubble. The woman and the other guy were unfolding what looked like a big net.

Zita frowned. *Can they drag you using the net?*

I don't know, maybe? This would be an excellent time to leave, Wyn sent.

You want me to bust out and steal their attention? I'm not quite free, but I can move again, Andy sent.

Growling, Zita slashed a long claw at whomever thought it was a good idea to grab her. The arm retreated. *Work on getting out of the goo before you escape. Be ready to bounce once we give you a signal! Wyn, can you darken this place?*

While what little she could see of Wyn appeared serene, nerves ran through her words. *Easily, but you'll need to retrieve me before these people notice my shield is down.*

Andy sent, *I'm free. They're piping in some kind of gas, so don't take too long. We still don't know what this stuff does, so I punched a hole in the side of the truck I'm in and am breathing out of that.*

Zita crouched under the truck, scurrying to the edge closest to Wyn as she eyed the chaos around them. Once she spotted her friend and verified which truck had the hole in it, she sent, *No worries, mano, this won't take long. You trust me, right, Wyn?*

Caution threaded through her words as Wyn replied. *Yes, though I already regret my answer.*

Lights out, then. I've got an awesome plan, she sent, hissing at someone who was trying to poke her with an air gun. She batted it aside.

The gun withdrew, and someone peered at her. "Found Arca!"

Ah. We're doomed. Andy moaned over party line.

The tunnel darkened to almost black. With the skunk's night vision, she could see that Wyn had placed illusory bands of black over the tunnel lights and the visible headlights of cars.

Men shouted commands. Some made sense. A few conflicted with others. The woman and her helper threw the net at Wyn, who backed up as she struggled with it. The fake injured man charged at her and missed.

Zita turned and sprayed the person foolish enough to remain close.

He screamed and backed up, flailing around wildly.

She slipped out from under the vehicle and ran between the floundering people. Switching to a gorilla, she jerked the net out of the hands of the DMS guards and picked up Wyn. With her friend in her arms, she sprinted to the truck holding Andy.

Setting down Wyn, Zita yanked the driver's side door open.

A man in camouflage sat in the driver's seat. Keys dangled in the ignition.

The man inside turned toward her. "What—"

She pulled him out and shoved him toward one of the fake construction workers, who had been standing nearby with an item that looked like an enormous cattle prod. The pair went down in a tangled mess.

More gently, Zita set Wyn inside, and then shifted to Arca. Without checking the settings, she slid the seat as far forward as it would go while she eyed a strange, black box attached to a bulky machine. She flipped the switch to the off position. "Get your belt on."

Oh, no. This was your plan? Wyn grabbed the belt and banged it against the receptacle.

No hay bronca, I got it all under control. Remove the illusion from this truck's lights but keep the others out as long as possible. Hang on, mano. Zita put on her own belt and stomped down hard on the accelerator, crossing the median to avoid the shouting people chasing her.

The truck's moving. Should the truck be moving? Andy sent.

I don't want to die. Goddess, save us, Wyn prayed.

Andy's thought was almost a mutter. *I felt safer before I knew Zita was driving.*

As did the entire world. Watch out for the—Ah! Wyn shrieked. As much as her seatbelt would allow, she curled into a ball, arms over her head.

Zita rammed through the wooden ROAD CLOSED sawhorses at the entrance to the tunnel and roared down the road.

Haters. Hang onto something. After about a mile, Zita jerked the wheel, letting the truck drift sideways to a stop, blocking both lanes. It had a bit more horsepower than she expected in something so bulky and did an extra revolution, slamming into a metal barrier at the edge of the precipice. Something thumped repeatedly in the back of the truck. Wyn's screaming was incoherent.

Hey! If I'd been a normal person, I'd be all black and blue in here! You're rolling me around like a pool ball, Andy complained.

Applying a little gas to back away from the edge, Zita rolled her eyes. *I told you to hang on. It's not like I'm driving too crazy with Wyn in the car.*

The truck came free with a loud screech, bringing part of the barrier with it, and she backed it up to block the road.

"Good enough," she said. *Okay, we're clear. You want me to break you out, mano?*

Metal ripping from the rear of the truck accompanied his answer. *You've done enough.*

Wyn whimpered.

"You okay, Muse?" Zita asked.

"Never drive again," she said.

Zita unbuckled her friend and hopped out of the car, leaving the keys in the ignition. "It was your idea, and look! I moved it back so you could get out without falling."

"I thought you'd free me, and we'd run!" Wyn struggled to get out.

Already running around to the passenger side, Zita blinked as she opened the door for her friend and pulled off the net. "Oh. You hate running. My way was more fun, too. And you know I'd never crash it with us in it. At least, not you and me."

Wyn brushed off her clothing and then stopped, her eyes wide.

Andy's clothing covered in blue goop. He waddled over to them, plucking at himself, and tried to pull off the slop. "I officially hate this stuff. Whatever it is."

Her nose wrinkling, Wyn recoiled from him. "Is that as disgusting as it appears?"

"More," he replied, grimacing.

From the direction of the tunnel, she heard multiple engines racing.

"They're coming, and I'm willing to bet they've got cameras on the trucks," she said. "Grab Muse and take a long walk off a short pier. I'll catch up to you at my place," Zita said, nodding toward the steep drop-off.

Andy ran to Wyn and scooped her up.

Grabbing at his shoulder, Wyn lifted her hand. "Hey! Ask first! I prefer—"

The sound of engines grew louder.

"Sorry," Andy said.

"I could have jumped off the edge with you and trusted Wingspan to catch us in his claws or done a long, high-speed truck chase, but I thought this was better,' Zita said. She leapt off the edge, shifting to a golden eagle and circling back to her friends.

Wyn shuddered and wrapped her arms around Andy. "Permission granted."

Chapter Fourteen

"Why is it that everything we do lately ends up as a felony?" Wyn moaned, burying her face in her hands fifteen minutes later.

Zita patted her shoulder and tried to be comforting. "If it helps, you'd probably just get a few misdemeanors. Actually, Andy was mostly out of action, so he might only get a misdemeanor, too. Depends on how seriously they take the hole in the truck."

Andy coughed. "Thanks to someone bouncing me around like a ping pong ball when she drove the truck, I broke the thing in the truck too... I don't know what to call it, but it looked expensive. A sticky hand harpoon gun?"

That seemed to distract Wyn for a moment. "That was interesting. Perhaps a combination of a Claw of Archimedes and a harpoon gun with a chemical component. I haven't any words for the sticky material."

"I have plenty. Gross. Disgusting. Hard to get out of your hair. I'm going to need so many showers to get clean." Andy picked a bit of blue goop from his hair and flexed his fingers, staring at the stretchy stuff with a disgruntled expression.

"No hay bronca. What's a little grand theft auto and assaulting an officer of the law among friends?" Zita tried. "Today wasn't our fault, though. We meant well."

Andy muttered something about wishing they'd been playing a car theft game instead as he scraped goo off his clothing. He reached back and checked his own shoulders. "Lost another cape, too."

Raising her head, Wyn's lips compressed into a thin line. "I do hope our future attorneys can provide a better defense than good intentions gone catawampus."

"It was a trap, specifically for us. Weighted nets and darts could be standard issue, but they can't have many harpoon goop things. How did you hear about it again, Andy? Who told you?" Zita asked.

He refused to meet her eyes. "A friend asked if we could guard this part of the trip because it was the highest risk section," he mumbled.

"A friend. Who? Either they're a danger or they're in danger," she said, suspicion curdling her stomach.

"I'll talk to them. They could've been the intended target," he finally said slowly.

Zita growled, "Who?"

His expression mulish, Andy took a deep breath. "Caroline told me."

I should've known I couldn't trust her, not even for his sake. Zita rubbed at the tip of her nose. She could swear she still felt dirt there from when she'd sniffed around a remote section of the prison grounds after escaping DMS pursuit the previous day. Her usually robust appetite died at the memory of the foul, sickeningly sweet odor of decaying humans. Her temper flared. "And you believed her? This all makes sense now. Stealing the credit for your hard work isn't enough anymore for that pinche glory hound. She wants us stuck in cages. Or dead, like the people I sniffed out after Jerome's drones found the grave site."

Andy slashed the air with his hands. "Caroline's not like that. Someone probably gave her bad information. I'll ask her when I see her."

"We should all take deep breaths and calm down," Wyn tried.

Ignoring her, Zita's eyebrows raised. "Is that supposed to help, Andy? That she's so entitled that she didn't check it out? Someone in the government told her to recruit illegal vigilantes to guard a truck instead of sending troops, and she doesn't even question if it's legit? Seriously, think this through. Don't be a Caroline."

Fists clenched, Andy glared at her.

"We got away this time, but if that gas had started working sooner and you couldn't bust out... At least you guys know now not to trust anything she says," Zita said.

"She didn't set us up! She wouldn't!" His fists clenched.

Zita snorted. "She totally would."

"Look, Z, I've put up with plenty from you, but you need to get over your stupid vendetta. Are you done now?" Andy said.

She growled. "She literally just sent us into a chingado trap! How can you defend her? This isn't about vengeance. Some people aren't trustworthy, and she's one of them!"

When Andy opened his mouth to say something else, Wyn stepped in, placing a hand on his chest. "Would you please excuse us a moment so we may discuss this, woman to woman?"

He glanced at Zita. The corner of his mouth trembled, and his entire body practically vibrated with tension. With a curt nod, he spun on his heel and walked out onto the tiny balcony. The overflowing plant life almost hid his slim form, but the tilt of his head toward the sky was visible even from the kitchen.

Folding her slim arms over her chest, Wyn frowned at her. "How do you want to do this? Because the time has come to deal with you."

"Out loud and in my exercise room. If you're going to nag, I'd rather it not bounce around inside my skull." Zita headed there.

"Don't attempt to distract me with belligerence," Wyn warned as she followed her into the room.

Zita shut the door. After removing her martial arts dummy's enormous hat so it wouldn't get damaged, she began the slow build of movement. "I'm listening. Say your bit."

"Did you really look at Andy? Did you see how upset your words made him? How difficult it was for him to admit what should be a good thing—a healthy relationship with a clever, attractive woman who recognizes his value—to someone who should be one of his biggest supporters?"

"I support him except when he's an idiot. What kind of friend would I be if I didn't tell him when he screws up or lets someone lead him around by his dick? This morning was typical Caroline!" She kicked the dummy with extra strength, making it rock and her foot sting.

Nibbling her lower lip, Wyn said, "You know, you should give her a chance. She's really quite nice."

"Caroline's a tool. She's always been one." Bitterness filled her mouth.

Wyn ran her finger on the table. "It was just a competition, and it was over a decade ago. Maybe it's time to let it go."

Anger ignited, and Zita sped up her strikes on the wooden dummy until she heard an ominous crack and her hands were sore. "It's not about the chingado Olympics."

"No?"

Zita smoothed the wood as if it would make the small crack go away. "Sure, I wanted to prove I had the skill to sweep the gymnastics events, but that was a side thing."

"The Olympics were trivial?" Wyn's eyebrows rose.

"Compared to my family, yes! My coach knew a guy at INS. If I did well at all the meets and got into the Olympics, Mamá was going to get her US citizenship. They'd even started the paperwork. She was taking all the required classes. Papá died before we ever met Coach, so he was never part of the deal."

Wyn's eyes were sad. "You never mentioned any of that before..."

"The first rule of avoiding family getting deported is not talking about them being illegals, even to otherwise awesome friends. Anyway, citizenship was the prize for getting in. If I won any medals, the money from that and sponsorship deals would've supported all of us, so my brothers could've gone to any college they wanted. I'd been working toward that since I was five or six! Once I started winning stuff, Coach even pulled me out of regular school so I could concentrate on practicing."

Wyn crossed her arms. "They just let him remove you from school?"

Zita's aching fists clenched, and she forced herself to release them and calm her breathing. "There was paperwork, but he handled it all. His wife taught me the stuff I needed to know to pass the tests while I ran gymnastics drills and stuff. Honestly, the school stuff was way easier when I could move while doing it."

The telltale line between Wyn's eyebrows showed her friend's unhappiness. "That explains your eclectic range of knowledge. Why was your coach so desperate?"

"He had black marks on his record, and he needed a winner to get the money clients and his good name back. All that crumbled though when Caroline reported me for doping." Zita hit the dummy a few more times, avoiding the cracked area.

Wyn's eyebrows rose. "You? On drugs?"

The words tore out of her, still painful after all the time that had passed. "I wasn't! Those were the first rounds of my cancer meds. Entitled rich girl didn't bother to ask me why I had drugs. She didn't even read the labels and look them up, just assumed they were for funsies or an advantage. Like I'd do that. I spent more time practicing than anyone else on our team."

"I'm sure you did," Wyn said.

Zita threw in a few kicks against the dummy. "We'd known each other for years at that point, spent hours together every day. We were friends. Maybe not best friends because everything was handed to her before she knew she wanted it, and I had to work my culo off not to burden my family. She couldn't take five minutes to ask me, or better yet, stay out of my chingado locker that she shouldn't have been opening in the first place. Nobody punished the golden girl for that, by the way."

Wyn made a sympathetic noise.

She swiped at the air with a hand. "Anyway, once she said steroids, all those years of work were wiped out. Gone. She didn't only tell Coach, either, where it might've stopped. No, she informed everyone, all the organizations, everything. Pues, even when I explained to him, my coach dumped me. I was a charity project, and he wouldn't risk his reputation on a suspected doper. Nobody else would take a cancer patient on, not on a scholarship basis, and we didn't have the money to bankroll it ourselves. Oye, my wins were most of our income."

Zita had to take a deep breath before continuing. She kept her hands moving, the pattern of strikes soothing her, even when tempering her strength. "Caroline's mom—who's hardcore enough that Satan thinks she needs to tone down the evil—got INS to lose Mamá's paperwork and go after her. After us. We had to move from state to state and live in a car for a while. We lost everything. As soon as Miguel was a legal adult, he took guardianship to keep Quentin and me out of the foster system. Of course, he had to join the military to get health insurance and a steady paycheck to do so, and I doubt that was in his fifty-year plan or whatever."

"It's typically a five-year plan," Wyn pointed out.

Zita grunted. "It's Miguel. His plans have extended families, with junior plans, grandbaby plans, and third-cousin-once-removed plans."

That won a half smile from her friend. Wyn licked her lips. "I better understand why you were upset with her, but you two were barely teenagers. She couldn't have known."

Zita pounced on that, emphasizing her point with her hands. "She could've. That's the problem. She didn't even question if it was the right thing to do. If she'd asked me instead of reporting me that night, I would've explained. If she'd waited to get me kicked out, one year later, even six months, it wouldn't have mattered. Mamá would've been a citizen, Miguel wouldn't have had to join the army, and Quentin wouldn't have spent two years bouncing on friends' couches. While my tía taught me useful stuff about fighting and surviving, I wouldn't have had to go live in Brazil once I got out of the hospital. My family wouldn't have been separated for years from each other. All because Caroline couldn't pretend to be a person instead of a tool for a few minutes. How can I forgive that?"

While her friend digested that, Zita couldn't resist adding, "The fact that Caroline won gold in the Olympics was only salt in the wound, especially given how sad her second half was. Totally all safe moves. Boring! We'd been neck-and-neck for years, practically trading off wins, and she slacked off once I was gone. They gave her a gold for it anyway because she's Caroline chingada Gyllen."

Wyn hmphed. "Glad your self-confidence is healthy."

"Sure. I know who I am and what I'm good at. And what she's good at. She's going to hurt Andy and screw us all over! And, sí, it might be an 'innocent' mistake again, because she doesn't even live on the same planet with the rest of us. Caroline had every advantage, all the private coaches, lessons, gear, even private gyms. A team of people did her makeup, and fashion designers competed to do her costumes. She has no concept of consequences because she's never suffered from her own mistakes. Someone else always does. It was me and my family before. I don't want to see them, you, your aunt, or Andy and his family hurt because of her. We've paid enough for her mistakes already."

Her friend closed her eyes for a moment. When she opened them, Wyn said, "I understand your anger better now, but think about this—neither one of you is a kid anymore, and Caroline's smart enough to have a law degree. The trap today might've awakened her to the dangers of blind trust in her handlers."

With a snort, Zita said, "Doubtful."

Wyn touched her arm. "I recognize the trauma of her past decision, but maybe you should consider forgiving her. It was a long time ago."

Zita shook her off. "Now you sound like the priest I went to this past week."

Her friend tilted her head. "You actually spoke to one about this? What did he say?"

"Well, obviously I couldn't give him no details, and I got Confession out of the way beforehand. But first he was all 'you must decide what Jesús would want you to do and act accordingly.'" She shook her head, remembering.

Wyn quirked a brow at her. "Just at first?"

"When I told him it'd be hard to knock enough tables over to keep her away from Andy, he said I needed to reread the Bible and forgive, treat her more like a prodigal son. Not happening. Why can't Andy be sensible and cut our losses now? Even without what she did to my family, Caroline's already tried to hand us in once."

Her friend studied her. "Are you scared of her?"

For good measure, Zita snapped out a kick to the dummy's head. "Of course not! I'm... I'm appropriately cautious, given the woman's history."

"We knew this would be a big deal with you, but she matters to him. If it were only one or two dates, do you think he would've told you at all?"

Bitterness rose in her throat as she put together Andy's recent odd behavior and the furtive conversations with Wyn. The dummy received another kick, this one low. "They've been dating for months, haven't they? All his disappearances when I thought he found a sparring buddy, all the canceled climbing trips..."

Her expression wary, Wyn nodded. "Yes. They've gotten quite close. And do you know what? He doesn't have to be scared around her. Other than the mask, he can just be himself."

Zita gaped at the witch. "What's he got to worry about? He's nearly invulnerable!"

"Himself. She's one of the few women who can withstand his strength. He can't hurt her accidentally. You know how upset and worried he was with Brandi. He refused to meet her for months after we first got our powers and only agreed once you and I could accompany him in case of an emergency."

Zita swore and held up a hand. "That's still bugging him? I told him enough practice would make it innate." She shook her head. "And he's happy? With her? Even after she set us up?"

Wyn enunciated each syllable. "Absolutely thrilled. You need to give her at least the same benefit of the doubt you'd give someone else. For his sake. He'd do no less for you."

She swore. Stuffing down the urge to just keep punching the battered dummy, Zita marched into the other room and yanked open the screen door.

As expected, Andy stared at the distant horizon as if he were mentally flying there.

"Answer this," she said, staring at him. "When we were in Greece, the stuff you said about me and Freelance. Do you actually believe all that or were you playing me to get me on your side now?"

He actually tore his attention away from the sky to eye her. A flicker of hope shone in his dark, shadowed eyes. "I meant it."

"I love you, mano, but this is hard. Wyn can tell you what Caroline did to my family. Today didn't help. Maybe it'll help you understand why I can't... why I haven't been your wingman." She paused, trying to get her scattered thoughts to focus. "I got an afternoon shift, so I should go. I need to work out before it."

"Work through it or work out?" he asked.

Zita shrugged. "There's a difference?"

He didn't seem to know if he should smile or scowl. "This shouldn't be a difficult thing."

Silence hung awkwardly between them.

Wyn finally broke in. "You know, I have work I should get to. Andy, would you please be so kind as to escort me home?"

After another glance at Zita, he nodded. "Sure. I should probably make sure Farnswaggle's still knee-deep in physics and doesn't need me. Given it's a relatively new job and all, it'd look bad if I never show up for it."

They headed toward the door.

As they passed, Zita gently bumped Andy's shoulder with her fist.

He hesitated, but kept walking.

Chapter Fifteen

Her date had texted the three little words that always made Zita's heart race: "Don't be seen."

In the shape of a crow, Zita circled a building the next day, coasting on the warm breeze as she searched for him. Several large roads met and spilled into each other around a big park, with a tiny triangle of green where three roads met on one side. Across the street from the park, her target building was one of many, with expensive-looking stores at street level, and office or residential places on the higher floors. The pavement seemed to seethe with movement as people jostled each other to fit around a fenced-off crane without falling into the slow traffic.

It took her a few loops before she figured out where they were to meet. After a cautious perch on the window ledge to ensure it wasn't a trap, she hopped through the open window. If anticipation had her cooing, well, she hoped he wouldn't notice. *Any date that started with a challenge is sure to be interesting. Not that any of our meetings have ever been dull, and not just because the man makes body armor look sexy.*

Shifting in midair, she landed on a splattered white drop cloth in her Arca form. She grinned to the man waiting nearby and eyed her surroundings for a clue to what they'd be doing. Absently, she pulled dollar-store shoes out of her pockets and slipped them on her feet. Even if the sneakers meant she had no room for anything other than the necessities, it was worth giving up the space to have her feet unpunctured.

The room was demolished. Literally. Drop cloths hid the floor, and wires hung out of the ceiling and dangled listlessly in the wall framework. Assorted building supplies lay in piles all around. Construction dust, stale air, and the lingering odor of glue and burned plastic tickled her nose.

The only source of light and fresh air—as fresh as it came in New York City, anyway—came from the open window. Sections of wallboard blocked all the others, throwing shadows across a pair of spotless folding metal chairs parked an arm's length apart at an immaculate card table. Atop the table, a sniper rifle pointed down out of the remaining opening. The weapon divided the table in half. Two bottles of sealed water and four protein bars were in a tidy stack beside a set of binoculars and a folded piece of paper on one side, with water and a single protein bar on the other.

Even though she'd arrived exactly on time, managing to squeak out of work, assist someone, and find the place just in time, she felt as though she should apologize for not being as early as usual. "Sorry to take so long getting here," she said. "This girl got stuck in her mermaid form at a public pool. I had to help her out before DMS locked her up for being fishy in public or something."

From where Freelance stood by one seat, he inclined his head.

Zita grinned and winked back. She gestured to the snacks. "Órale, you cooked for me! Sweet. So, what's our plan for this week? I'm guessing we're not renovating this joint."

Freelance turned to face the view outside. He waved a hand toward the binoculars. As usual, he wore a mask and body armor, so not one inch of skin was exposed. While the bullet-resistant material hid and blurred the specifics of his body, she couldn't help but notice (and inwardly drool over) the perfect balance of stamina, dexterity, and strength in each economical move.

A more practical corner of her mind wondered how he'd set all this up unseen in a heavily populated building in a large city in daylight. *He's wearing black, long-sleeved body armor in August and has at least two obvious guns. Since he wore the same thing in the jungle, it must be breathable, but it's August, and I'm warm in my costume. Then again, it is rush hour in New York. It's possible nobody said anything if he didn't dawdle.*

Zita couldn't imagine him dawdling.

She joined him by the window, choosing her steps carefully so none of the construction debris injured her feet through the flimsy shoes. "Nice to see you, too. You were right about Pretorius not being there yesterday, by the way. It was a DMS trap. Again. Do you have any idea why they're suddenly all up in our grill? They're normally annoying, but three traps in two weeks?"

"Bill publicity." Tension ran through his body, and he turned toward her, tapping his goggles to focus on her.

The room got warmer under his quiet gaze, but she shivered anyway. She answered the question he hadn't asked. "Yes, I'm fine."

"Team?" As always, the mechanical rasp of the voice changer disguised him.

"My friends all got away clean and uninjured too. Thanks for asking. So... what are we doing?" She tilted her head at him.

Her companion returned his gaze to the square below, adjusting his goggles as he did so. "Park."

Curiosity aroused, she picked up the binoculars and the paper, trying to follow what he watched out the window.

Shaped like a football, one end of the park was paved, with several hundred feet of green oasis before a farmer's market and a playground cut off the other end. It nestled serenely at the intersection of multiple large roads. Even at their height, the eternal cacophony of a busy New York City street still reached them, with car engines, sirens, and horns swearing at each other over the hum of conversation in the busy park below. The sidewalks were full of constant movement, with natives flowing around street hustlers and dawdling tourists. Several food carts had set up around the edges of the crowd, she noted with interest. Dull green privacy screens hid two large construction areas, one on either side of the park.

Their perch was closest to the paved end. At the base of the statue of a wigged guy on a horse, someone had erected a small stage with several folding metal chairs in front of it and enough patriotic bunting and small American flags to be a fire hazard. Supporters with signs filled most of the seats. Men in suits and sunglasses hovered near the podium, arms crossed and obvious handgun holsters on their belts.

Between the audience and the street, she saw a second group of people corralled behind a tape barrier that separated them from the temporary auditorium and what looked like a subway entrance. Most of this group seemed normal enough in shorts and t-shirts, save for the woman with butterfly wings, a man with a nest of octopus arms, and a white wolf pacing at the edge of the crowd.

A news team roamed around the outskirts, filming both groups, and occasionally interviewing people. Another pair of videographers intently recorded all the spectators, both those on the protest side and those in the seats. Zita frowned.

They shouldn't need that much background footage. Zita kept watching for why he'd chosen to meet here.

Under the shade of fenced-off trees, not too far from the protestors, a large Kodiak bear lounged on a blanket beside a triangular A-frame with something written on it. The bear wore oversized sunglasses, a green khaki hat, and a long tie attached to some sort of white collar. He appeared to be sleeping, one arm around a huge wicker picnic basket. At his side, an androgynous figure wearing an archaic khaki uniform with a wide-brimmed hat and black tie exhorted passersby. As Zita watched, he or she pretended to use a sign as a guitar. The combination of military posture, silly pantomimes, and almost manic energy identified the odd person, especially in combination with the nearby ursine.

Kodiak and Trixie. But why is she dressed like an old-school forest ranger? Is she acting as Vaudeville, the name she seemed to go by when she's doing mercenary stuff? Zita glanced at the paper, a badly copied notice of a counterprotest against a speech by a Senator Chivington supporting the metahuman bill. The presence of Freelance's team suddenly made a lot more sense. Zita asked, "Are you working right now?"

A shake of his head.

"Did you invite me to a stakeout?" Zita tilted her head toward her companion.

He nodded.

"Is our target your friends?"

Another nod.

She fought the urge to laugh. "Do you stalk your friends and loved ones often?"

A head shake.

How defined do you have to be to have your deltoids look so sweet despite all the gear? Zita locked her libido in a mental closet and forced herself to ask her next question, rather than continuing to fantasize about his impressively tight musculature. "Good to know. I'm assuming you're here because whatever they're doing is Vaudeville's idea then. Do they know you're here?"

One of his shoulders rose and then dropped. "Kodiak."

Perfectly understandable given DMS lately. She rolled with it. "Excellent. So, we're backup, not creepy? I'm cool with that."

A soft sound escaped him.

She couldn't decide if that was a snort or a chuckle, but decided it had definitely been some form of agreement. "Sweet. This proves I was right. Stakeouts are totally date activities! My friends and Remus both told me otherwise, but it makes sense to me, especially if you don't expect any real danger. Clearly, you're a dude with taste, and not just because of the fancy protein bars you favor. They almost taste like food."

Another sound, but this one was almost definitely amusement. Or a hiccup.

With a smile, Zita plopped into a seat, ripped open a protein bar, and snacked as she trained the binoculars on the square below.

Her peripheral vision showed him taking his seat across the table from her.

By the time she finished the bar, Zita was itchy to move. Following the antics of a pair of puppies in the dog run section distracted her for a few minutes but did not cure her restlessness. Remembering her time as an almost-statue, she surreptitiously wiggled her fingers and toes before loosening her shoulders. She glanced at Freelance.

He was motionless. As if sensing her gaze, he reached out, hesitated, and then picked up a protein bar. Even though he didn't seem to watch her, his body tensed as he pulled his mask out of the way just enough to take a bite, keeping everything hidden but his mouth.

Funny how just a glimpse of thin, ascetic lips and perfect teeth made her heart speed up and a certain giddiness run through her.

Stakeout. I'm supposed to be watching the park, not the man. She bit her lip, focusing on the small jolt of pain, before deciding to try a trick she'd used waiting for Wyn to get ready for the club. "Just about anyone's better than me at sitting still, but you got it mastered. I got to cheat a bit."

She set down the binoculars then did a partial shift to a hawk, stopping when her vision sharpened. Deliberately, she let the dim room lull her into an avian doze, where part of her brain watched for problems while the rest... rested. Or as much as she could with Andy's relationship racketing around her brain, refusing to let her relax.

Chingada Caroline Gyllen.

***

They had been sitting for almost an hour before she broke the silence. "So... you and your team. You been together a long time?"

His head inclined once.

She glanced sidelong at him and licked her lips. "You and your friends seem pretty tight. So, you've got to be a people person." By virtue of biting her tongue, she kept from adding anything about Trixie's obvious issues with sanity.

He twitched and stared at her for a long, silent moment, before returning his attention below.

After clearing her throat, Zita tried to phrase her question without giving anything away. She found herself pacing, though she didn't recall getting up. "If you had a friend who wouldn't listen when you try to warn them that a person they're spending a ton of time with is dangerous... how do you keep your friend safe? And how do you protect those around you when the inevitable destruction occurs?"

He tapped his gun.

"Not that kind of threat. The dangerous person is oblivious to the fact that they ruin other people's lives. When it goes bad, my friend and people around them are at risk of losing everything." The words were out before she had time to think, but she recognized—and disliked—the truth in them.

Light flashed off his goggles as he glanced at her. "Friend worth keeping?"

Mano. That she had no doubts about. "Yeah."

"Support but mitigate damage. Overwatch to avoid entanglement," he said.

Zita sighed. "So, I have to support my friend but figure out a way not to let...the human wrecking ball...lure me into their web of oblivious happy ruin. Even if that means increasing distance from my friend."

His head inclined slightly.

"Thanks, I guess. I'll think about that." She exhaled, sat back down, and resumed watching below. Streetlights had clicked on during their conversation, and the setting sun was an annoyance. After angling her chair to avoid having it in her eyes, she let herself lapse into avian somnolence again.

Several minutes later, in one of the drowsy glances she'd stolen at her companion, she noticed he'd tensed.

What'd I miss? She woke up and paid more attention.

A chubby guy now stood on the stage below. He appeared to be introducing a silver-haired man in a suit. Trixie and Kodiak seemed fine, though they both appeared to be awake and talking to tourists. Somehow, the tone of the crowd had altered, bodies showing more tension. Several among them had the distinctive gaits of military or former military. Two stood out.

Not good. Zita frowned. The wrapper of her protein bar crinkled as she shoved it into a pocket and focused on a couple of protestors. They'd been in the DMS prison just a few days ago.

She murmured, "What are they doing here? Tiger and Sheriff were in jail in another state as of Wednesday. Somehow, they don't seem like the socially responsible sort who run out to do a peaceful protest as soon as they get loose, especially together. Not to mention, DMS doesn't let people go. Ever."

"Powers? Who?" Freelance changed position slightly.

"Tiger's the tattooed dude who just shook his fist at the stage, and Sheriff's next to him, down among the protestors. He combines petty vengeance with poor business decisions, like using mass murder to advertise. His tattoos come to life and do what he says. Giant tigers and skulls with wings and flaming halitosis. Sheriff turns into an oversized honey badger with anger-management issues. She's had awful taste in besties in the past and got mind-controlled for it." A growl escaped Zita at the thought.

Her companion didn't reply directly, but said, "Construction zones not active. Armed crowd."

She huffed out a breath. "I noticed. The suit guys might step up though."

Freelance's silence spoke volumes, as did the glance he slanted at her.

"So much for quiet bondage time with you and all." She grumbled, realized what she'd said aloud, and coughed. "I mean, bonding. You're right, the suit guys probably won't try to help. I should go down there to stop them faster if they're going to pull something. Given Tiger's record, this has to be a setup for something bad. You want I should warn your friends?"

He turned away, checking his watch, and she heard a faint murmur. When he turned back, he nodded. "Tell them Code A retreat, 5."

"You got it... If it all goes bad, please don't kill nobody?" Zita pocketed her remaining protein bar and watched him as she slipped out of her shoes, cramming them awkwardly into her pockets.

"Necessary only." He stroked the top of his long gun once and began packing up.

"That's what my friends are afraid of," she muttered, running a hand over her hair, back and forth. "Seriously, hombre, don't kill nobody. You're going to set up a fast ride out for when things go bad?"

That got a curt nod in return.

Another thought struck her. "Will your friends listen to me? How will they know they can trust me? I mean, Vaudeville's wrapped a little different from the rest of us."

The masked man stared below and then transferred the weight of his gaze to her.

Do I have food on my face? She couldn't resist touching her tongue to the corners of her lips to check. "What? Do you know anyone else who fights using bubblegum cigars and fish? Effectively, no less? It's cool but weird."

"Tell them she can't touch Baby." His goggles bored into her.

Zita's little sister instincts hopped up and down, sensing a good story there. "Baby?"

He motioned to the pistol holstered at his side.

I think that's the gun I returned to him or a duplicate. Does he buy guns in bulk? Zita tried to smother her laugh, but a grin leaked out. "Right. It is a sweet pistol, though I'd rather use the grapple gun myself. More fun. Does it have a name, too?"

Freelance responded the way she expected. "No."

She had to try, so she held out her hand. "Can I—"

He shook his head.

Lifting herself up to sit on the windowsill, Zita sent him an arch look over her shoulder. She didn't bother to suppress her laughter this time. "Someday, you're going to say yes to me, you know."

Her laughter turned to a caw as she shifted to a crow and flew away.

Chapter Sixteen

While subterfuge was an option, Zita preferred to do something she might actually succeed at. *Direct it is*, she decided.

Just to be safe, she flew a few circles so she could approach from the park opposite Freelance's hiding spot. If it also allowed her to check for lurking DMS strike teams, that was a bonus.

New York had so much traffic that she couldn't tell if any of the vehicles she saw were legitimate or not. The men in suits definitely moved and placed themselves like obvious government security agents, but appeared too lightly armed to be DMS. They also seemed more interested in protecting the people onstage than interacting with the crowd. The chubby guy relinquished the podium to the silver-haired man. As he adjusted the microphone, she recognized the new speaker—the politician who had argued with Dr. Chaniclas.

Her stomach twisted. *DMS wouldn't risk someone they consider important getting hurt, would they? Then again, if what I saw earlier is an example of how he runs stuff, things might get deadly.*

Some of the audience could've been DMS undercover agents. Most were sitting, and several sported baggy shirts. Of those milling around, she spotted multiple people that had military gaits and even a few concealed weapons, including one guy with a hot dog cart. She could at least discount the group of bored tweens, the three harried adults attempting to control them, and the people entering and leaving the subway without lingering. The wolf was no longer visible, and Tiger stood chatting with a mulleted guy by the protestor's line. He'd found a bottle of liquor somewhere and swigged from it periodically. Under a streetlamp, Sheriff stared at the politician, her arms crossed.

No mames. I hope this doesn't go bad. I wish Wyn were here. She could probably talk them all into being friends or at least cordial to each other while they sang "Kumbaya" and held hands. Or whatever the Wiccan version of that is. I'll come in from this direction so I can drop Freelance's message, and then try to get Tiger and Sheriff out of here unnoticed. Zita shook her head as she landed behind a tree and shifted to her Arca form.

After sliding on her shoes, she got out her phone and called Wyn and Andy on their vigilante phones. Neither picked up. She put it away again with a grumble. She bounded out and onto the path.

A warm breeze wafted the scents of street food under her nose, along with warm asphalt, exhaust, and sweaty people congregating too closely together. More worrisome, she caught a whiff of Kevlar and gun oil. Even in human form, she could tell it wasn't the same brand Freelance preferred. As she crossed into the protest area, she heard a group debating if they could leave long enough to grab dinner.

Her stomach growled in sympathy despite the snacks she'd just eaten.

Four protestors fluttered over in a flurry of waving hands and laughter. All the young women wore costumes—one was a plus-sized Muse in sparkly nightclub wear, the second had the poor taste to imitate Caroline Gyllen, the third was an African American female Wingspan, and the youngest of the group, an obvious preteen... was dressed as Arca.

Trying to be polite even if she was deathly jealous that Faux Arca had the option of cargo shorts with nice deep pockets, Zita said, "Hi. Did you need something?"

Faux Caroline spoke first. "She even does the accent! Hi! Your costume is great! If you were just five inches taller, you'd make a perfect Arca. Have you thought about heeled boots?" She patted her high, blond ponytail and smoothed her skirt.

Fake Wingspan had a bawdy, contagious chuckle and none of Andy's usual reticence. "Boots can only do so much."

"Yes, but just think of what it'd do for her butt!" Faux Caroline giggled. She had the real woman's annoying bubbliness down pat.

Faux Arca gaped at her. She had a tiny, whispery voice, but an inch more than Zita in height. She plucked at her own clothes disconsolately. "Her costume is perfect. Mine isn't very good."

Zita smiled weakly at the girl. "I'm all about the authenticity. You look way more comfortable than me, though. Big pockets would hold shoes much easier."

After tossing the long, white hair of her wig over her shoulder, Faux Muse said, "Are you here for the protest or the costume contest later on Broadway? The speeches have been way boring, so we're heading out before it gets too dark. You can join us if you don't want to walk alone. We were just going to stop by the General Aetherics store to see if they have the latest Bug Invasion Game or any of those cute dog automaton pets."

"Not like that's likely. They haven't released it yet." Faux Wingspan snorted.

Faux Caroline said, "It's the flagship store, and Clockwork opened it himself way back in the dinosaur times. Like, the Seventies or Eighties or something. If anywhere has it early, it'd be here."

"Thanks for the offer, but I need to talk to some folks. Go on without me. Nice to meet you." Seeing a way out, Zita waved and strode forward.

"Likewise!" Faux Muse and Wingspan chorused. The four girls linked arms and strolled back to where they'd been before, chattering like a flock of birds.

She meandered over toward the off-duty mercenary pair. A trio of college boys surrounded Kodiak, all flashing hand signals of some sort, while Trixie took their pictures with a set of cell phones. The triangular sign beside the picnic materials read, "Support Metahuman Rights! Get Your Picture with a Bear!"

Laughing, the boys dug out the wallets and slapped bills into Trixie's hands as they reclaimed their phones and sauntered off, grinning.

"Seriously?" Zita said, gesturing to the sign.

The bear grunted and settled on his haunches, waving to the departing customers and to a curious family passing by.

As she tucked away the money, Trixie turned to Zita. Today she wore a black wig with the kind of conservative haircut a male news anchor might sport. She smiled pleasantly, but she'd done something to make her face seem like someone else's, more masculine and angular, and her costume hid any hint of femininity. The faint tang of metal and leather mingled with her natural scent, and her eyes were unchanged. "Great PR and makes a profit, supporting at least two metahumans. What's not to like? Did you come for a picture with the bear? You're Internet-famous, so only ten bucks!"

The bear gave a deep sigh.

"Don't spoil my fun," Trixie hissed at him. "Fine, Arca can have the family rate. Twenty bucks."

Zita narrowed her eyes. "That's higher."

A little smile playing around her mouth, Trixie buffed her nails on her chest. "I didn't say whose family."

Her attention split between the mercenaries and the crowd, Zita took a step closer.

Tiger and Sheriff had found their way to the very edges of the tape barricade where the tattooed man was heckling the politician. The badger shifter stared into space, her face blank.

While Zita knew the senator hated metas, whatever was being said had most of the protestors' posture changing to more aggressive, upset stances. *Not good.* "Your boss—"

Before she could say more, a beefy guy rushed away from the protestor crowd and intercepted her. He had the muscles of an active lifestyle, a naturally large build, and smelled like cheap drugstore cologne and wet dog. He flashed them a hard smile, the sort that wasn't reflected in his eyes. "Arca, for real?"

She tilted her head at him. "Last I heard."

"Fifty dollars for a picture with the bear, just for you!" Trixie trilled.

He ignored her, instead stepping up close to Zita, the way people always did when they wanted to use their height to be intimidating.

That approach never worked. Zita was far too used to others being taller than her. She rolled her eyes and wrinkled her nose. This close, the canine smell was even more pungent. "Personal space, dude. Doesn't matter how adorable I am, you don't got the right to hang quite so close. Or the breath. Eat a mint or something."

"You are not welcome in the Pack's town unless you are willing to bow down," the stranger announced, his tones ringing. He glared at Zita. "This is a peaceful protest, and we will not have your shenanigans here."

"What about wacky hijinks? I adore those, and demand you cut me in on them," Trixie said, clapping her hands together.

Zita nodded to the other woman. "Wingspan said we needed to have more, but he never explains why. Just giggles."

The man flexed his big shoulders and cracked his knuckles methodically. "Did you hear me?"

"Sí, my ears aren't broken. I just don't care," Zita snickered. *Oh, wait, maybe that wasn't diplomatic.*

Kodiak waved a huge paw and stuck his snout in the picnic basket, rooting through it. His butt wiggled as if he were dancing.

The other guy actually snarled at her. "You've been warned. The Pack has no place for your kind! Do whatever you are here to do and be gone."

Diplomacy. I got it this time. I'll pretend I'm Wyn. Zita smiled sweetly at him, and somehow all the things she'd decided not to say came out. "Your dog smells like it fell in a stagnant creek full of dead skunks. Give that poor thing a bath. It stinks almost as bad as your ultimatum."

The stranger's shoulders rose.

Mentally, she smacked herself in the forehead. To placate him, she tacked on lamely, "But I'm sure the pup's real cute and fluffy or something when he's clean."

He panted through his mouth and stared down at her.

Her back prickled, and she altered her stance to a more defensive one.

"Fine, fine, you got me. One hundred million dollars for that picture, just for you," Trixie said, grabbing his hand and giving it an exaggerated shake.

He yelped and pulled away from her.

A blank, genial smile was pasted on Trixie's face, and she tsked, swinging a key chain. A silver medallion hung between a bright yellow banana and a tiny rubber duck in camouflage in the hand she'd shaken with. "Are you okay?"

Kodiak snuffled and lumbered over, his big head swinging between the faux ranger and the man. He smacked his lips.

The stranger snarled at both of them and stomped back toward the protests. He stopped to whisper in the ear of a man near the front of the protest line. Neither seemed pleased with the conversation.

When he was sufficiently far away, Trixie turned back. Her face fell into more serious lines, and her eyes narrowed. "Funny how many wolf shifters don't like my silver key ring. By the way, the coronary waiting to happen over there, sporting the throwback mullet? He's the brain trust whose sign has human spelled with an 'o.' Word has it he's a wolf shifter who wants to unite all the New York metas under his banner whether they want it or not. Right now, he's talking to the sleaze with the tiger tattoos and the cheap booze. Is that the same guy that held up the nightclub?"

Zita snorted, glancing over at Mullet and then back. Beside him, Tiger had a gleefully malicious expression that made mental alarms ring.

"Somehow, I don't see that kind of unity happening, and yeah. Tiger's supposed to be in jail for that." While it was possible that a pair of hardened mercenaries happened to be selling selfies with a bear at the same time as a political rally, it seemed unlikely. The question tumbled out. "So, what's with the bear picture thing? Is this a regular side hustle or only when evil What's-His-Face is going to speak?"

Trixie cracked up. "Let us know what you really think. What if we're admirers of Senator What's-His-Face?"

"Well, you'd know his name, for one. I keep forgetting it, but I, umm, heard he'd have been happy if every meta just died during the sleeping sickness. You know, coma time." She scanned the audience and the protestors. While no one had acted yet, everyone's stances were becoming increasingly tense.

Tiger called out an obscenity at the speaker.

"Is that anything like Hammer Time?" Trixie cackled.

The bear buried his face in his paws with an exaggerated moan.

Zita stared at Trixie blankly. When the other woman offered no explanation, she said, "So why are you actually here?"

"Pocket money? Political statement? To piss off our mulleted friend there? Three wins in my book," Trixie said with a lazy smile. "So, why are you here? What about the boss?"

"I'm here because I think it's a DMS trap, and trouble's going to start any second now. Your boss said to tell you Code A Retreat, 5." Zita said.

Trixie's eyes narrowed, and she started digging through the massive picnic basket. She pulled out a clown nose, a huge fake beard, and a ham. "Well, that spoils our plans. It's getting too dark for more pictures, but I was hoping for a good bare-knuckle brawl. Not that I intended to fight without weapons, but it's convenient when others do so. I thought I packed everything I might need for this romantic picnic... where is that Uzi?"

The bear heaved a sigh. He might've shaken his head, but he started trying to put everything away again, huge paws clumsy despite the oversized basket. "Took it out. Needed room for the ham," he said.

"I'd say he shouldn't know where we are, but it's the Boss. How do we know you came from him, though? Maybe you want to hog all the barely veiled hostility here for yourself?" Trixie nodded to herself, as if that ridiculous stream of logic worked for her. She pulled out a string of lights shaped like tiny dinosaurs and a neon orange gas mask. After she tossed the lights aside, she stuffed the gas mask down her shirt, giving herself a strange potbelly. "Always handy to have one of these."

Zita eyed her. "Do you actually listen to yourself, or do you just say random stuff you think is funny? He said you still can't use Baby."

Kodiak cradled the ham protectively as he continued cleaning up the mess. "She got you."

The other woman pouted and started shoving items back into the picnic basket. "Fudgecicles! That's him. Also, Kodiak, I can't believe we didn't bring my Uzi. My grenades are still in there though, right?"

The bear whuffed. Took a bite out of the ham.

"Can we not pull out any weapons? This crowd has too many already," Zita said. The security guys were paying them more attention than she liked.

Trixie brightened. As she bent to fold up the blanket, she winked at Zita. "Later, you need to tell us exactly what you were doing hanging out with Bossman, since he's not big on answering questions or socializing. Just a note, it's never wrong to admit when you're being ridden like a pony."

Zita lifted her hand. "Wait, what?"

Before she could say more, Trixie laid a finger on her lip and mused aloud, "Then again, I guess you could actually be a pony, so perhaps I meant to say banging someone like a drum. We won't hold it against you if you are."

The bear nodded and batted his lashes at Zita.

Did Freelance tell them we were dating? What can I say without contradicting whatever he said? Or didn't say. She froze. Really not wanting this conversation to be caught by anyone around them, she whispered lamely, "It's not like that."

The other woman cocked her head, but thankfully kept her voice low. "I was just kidding, but... he is extra squirrelly about the phone to contact your team, even if you're not his usual type. It doesn't fit his usual modus operandi, either. What do you think, Kodiak?"

A snuffling sound came from the bear, along with slow, careful words. "She smells like a cinnamon roll."

"Well, sure, she's obviously one." Trixie stopped and turned to the bear. "Wait, you mean literally?"

He nodded. "Always has."

"Well, then, I can see it. At least short term, though I wouldn't have pegged her for the fling type." Trixie laughed for several seconds. Wiping tears from her eyes. she said, "For however long 'not like that' lasts, please bone him so I can ask him for a raise when he's in a good mood."

Zita stuttered, "We're not—"

A microphone squealed with feedback, and then Tiger bellowed over it, the volume making Zita wince. "Leave us alone! Or... bad...." The rest of his words were buried beneath the shouts of other protestors.

"Gotta go deal with that." With relief, Zita pivoted sharply and strode quickly toward the obnoxious tattooed man. *Punching someone has got to be easier than dealing with Freelance's friends.*

"You were told to leave." The man Trixie had pointed out stepped into her path and sneered at her. Despite the limpness of the rest of his sweaty hair, the top part of his mullet was fascinatingly stiff and bristly.

"If you're any kind of leader, get your people out of here and warn them. DMS is hunting metas. Tiger's probably in on it, so I hope you didn't give him your address," she said quietly.

"We're assembled legally with all the permits and like. They won't go after us." Mullet folded his arms over his chest, but didn't chase her.

Sidestepping him, she continued toward the two troublemakers. She didn't bother to turn around but called back, "I don't think DMS cares, and Tiger's a plant."

Someone thrust a microphone into her face at the same instant that a bright light stung her eyes. "Arca, I'm Reggie Washington with Goode News, New York. Are you here to join the protests against the metahuman bill?"

Another interruption? So much for getting Tiger and Sheriff out of here before anyone notices I'm here. She shoved away the microphone, blinking.

The reporter stepped into her path. Hazel eyes gleamed against the darker skin of a solid, middle-aged man with the nimble gait, slightly crooked nose, and thick shape of a retired boxer in a nice suit. Sotto voce, the reporter mumbled through the side of his mouth, "Help a brother out. They're trying to push me aside for someone younger, and I've got a kid in college."

"Oye," she said.

He repeated his question more loudly.

She sighed and didn't shove away the microphone when it came back. "I just stopped by to get a slice. Someone told me there was free food here, but I don't see any. As far as the bill, no, I don't support it. It gives DMS more power and money. They already piss off everyone they meet while swinging their current huge budget and lack of oversight around. Not to mention the way they lock people up and never give them trials or lawyers or phone calls or anything."

Reggie's eyes widened. "Really? None of their rights?"

"Not as far as I've heard. The DC metahuman business group—I think that speedy guy, Remus, runs it or someone like that—got court cases out the culo regarding that sort of thing, so they'd be good people to ask for proof," she said.

The speaker's words grew louder before the reporter could ask any follow-up questions. "We need the resources to identify dangerous metahumans and protect ourselves and our innocent loved ones from them. This is why we need this bill to pass. This what we need your strength to support! Look over there!"

Zita glanced around.

Onstage, the speaker was pointing at her. The suits she'd pegged as security had closed ranks, preventing her from having a clear path to the podium. All of the audience and most of the protestors stared at her. With delighted grins, the costumed girls were conferring among themselves. Kodiak and Trixie had stopped by a food cart on the outskirts of the protest area, close to the little triangular park. The bear now had a massive cotton candy and a ring of multicolored candy fluff around his muzzle. Trixie was still digging through the picnic basket near him. Tiger was rubbing the back of his neck and grimacing.

Sheriff finally noticed her. Shuddering, the other shifter's gaze met hers, and she mouthed, "Help me." Her face fell back into the weird blank expression she'd worn the rest of the day.

"A dangerous vigilante walks around in broad daylight, making a mockery of the police in this beautiful city! It's intimidation tactics like this that this bill and meta registration are meant to stop!" the speaker bellowed, still gesturing at Zita.

She pointed to herself and tried not to antagonize him. It made her brain hurt a little. "Me? I'm just getting lunch and answering this guy's questions because he's smart or something. Great guy to see on TV. I'm not threatening nobody."

Reggie and his cameraman grinned.

The senator continued, taking on oratory tones. "We're not fooled! Metahumans must be registered so the dangerous ones can be controlled, and our innocent loved ones are safe!"

"Registered and controlled? We're people, not guns. What, you going to make us all live in special camps or something, too?" Zita said, hands flying to her hips.

Leaning into his microphone, the senator stared at the crowd, his tone softening. "Let's be clear. The Metahuman Regulatory bill proposes common-sense regulations to help honest, hardworking Americans and provides reasonable funding to keep our communities safe. That's all. The only metas who would have to register are the ones with powers, abilities, skills, or attributes that could harm others or provide them with an edge over humans."

"Dude, did you say we weren't human? Did you just drop a little Nazi on this crowd?" She could feel her eyebrows rising.

Next to her, the reporter made a happy sound.

The senator leaned forward. "No, I did not. Do not put words in my mouth. Why are you protesting a registry? What do you have to hide?"

Zita ignored his question and barreled on with her own. "You said anyone with an edge. So, would your security team need to register? They look like badasses stuffed into suits and are clearly armed. This guy over here got a t-shirt on that says he's the best dad in the world. What about him? From what I know of kids, that sounds like a superpower. Good going, dude, unless you bought that for yourself." She waved a hand at a guy in the audience.

The man in question brushed crumbs off his shirt and straightened his shoulders. He beamed and nudged the woman next to him, who seemed less impressed.

"Don't be ridiculous," the senator said.

Zita didn't let him finish. "You said everyone who's smarter, more athletic, hotter, or anything other than average would have to register as metahuman. That just leaves, what? Congress and DMS? Got to say, that's fucked up."

That won some laughs, but it had a nervous edge to it.

The politician scowled and leaned forward. "I will not engage with someone who resorts to abusive behavior. What's important, now that we're done indulging the criminal, is that we protect the people of our nation, our innocent loved ones, from those who would harm them."

Sheriff ran to Zita's side and touched her arm. Sweat glistened on her face and pain showed in every line of her face. "Please, help. Listen, I know I've... been in the wrong before, but—DMS—going—kill me..." She screamed something unintelligible, grabbed at the back of her neck, and fell to the ground, arms and legs flailing. Fur rippled along one arm and disappeared again. One foot distorted into a hideous claw and then returned to human shape.

A man shouted, "She's going to change shape and murder you all! The revolution begins!" It might've been Tiger, based on the laugh that followed.

With an obscenity the microphone probably caught, Zita kneeled next to the badger shifter. Worry flooded her. While

Sheriff's previous shifts had taken forever and looked painful before, this prolonged, agonized flailing seemed somehow wrong. She shoved the microphone back at the reporter and waved them away. "Oye! This lady needs a doctor or a nurse or somebody medical! Stop filming her."

Zita tried to remember what her first-aid class had said to do for seizures, and rolled the other shifter to lie on her side. *Why would she be hanging with Tiger or even be here at all? If I hadn't just seen them in the same jail a few days ago, I would've assumed she had a rich friend who put up bail or leaned on highly placed officials to get her out. As is, given his presence, this stinks like a DMS...*

The walls of both construction sites burst outward with a thundering crash. DMS troopers poured out of the back of multiple vehicles, with riot shields and body armor, spreading out to loosely circle the protest and stage. Big cannons rose from the roofs of two of the vehicles.

A loudspeaker boomed out over the park. "This is the Department of Metahuman Services! Put down your weapons, lie down on the ground, and surrender!"

Just thinking about the jerks summons them now? Zita blinked. "Nobody was doing anything!"

Sheriff grabbed at her arms, one hand contorting into a claw and scoring Zita's skin with four long scratches. "Help," she gasped before another convulsion took her.

"If you want war, we'll bring it to you!" Tiger shouted, his face blank as he threw his bottle at the agents.

It shattered with a loud crash.

As she tried to keep the still-convulsing shifter turned on her side, Zita shouted, "Don't be idiots! If you fight, they get to arrest you. Go home. Go home the long way. Join a crowd. You're wolves and...and... whatever that tentacle dude is. You can outrun them. If you can fly, fly!"

"Kill DMS! Kill Chivington! Kill them all!" Tiger tore off one of his tattoos, throwing it at the ground.

A glowing orange tiger appeared.

Tiger pointed at the rapidly emptying stage. He wiped his mouth with his arm and smiled.

The park descended into anarchy, with the sheer number of people making it impossible for her to keep track of everything. Nearby, she heard more glass breaking.

Someone screamed.

Zita stood and stepped out of her shoes.

A group ran by between her and the tiger. Others held up their phones and began filming. One guy snagged a pair of abandoned backpacks and ran. Mullet stepped forward and howled, "We have permits!" Reggie's cameraman was filming it all while the reporter exclaimed into his microphone.

The tattoo tiger ran toward where a crowd of men in suits hustled toward the limousine she'd noticed earlier. The senator's silver hair bobbed up and down in the center, practically glowing under the streetlights.

Zita sprinted toward it.

A hail of bullets met the glowing tiger's approach, shredding it into nothing.

Guess they don't need my help. She skidded to a stop, reversing course to search for the tattooed man before he could do something else.

More screaming greeted the gunfire, and people streamed out of the park, sometimes knocking over others. Someone stepped on the flailing Sheriff.

DMS agents closed in, forming a rough circle around the stage and protest area, still shouting commands. They didn't have enough staff to cover all the gaps, but they tried. It didn't help that the people on the nearby sidewalks were actively participating, some leaving, some smashing things, and some arguing with the

DMS officers. A squad blocked off the subway exit so no one could enter or exit. Angry shouts came from within. Men on top of the riot vehicles aimed the big guns toward general area of the protest.

Zita couldn't find Tiger, but she could hear his voice, amplified over a bullhorn, calling for war.

Air guns popped nearby, and a shotgun fired as well.

Something roared. *Was that a bear?*

Sheriff's form jerked as a large dart pierced one leg. Her movements slowed and finally stopped.

From the corner of her eye, Zita saw Kodiak staggering, then leaning against the fence of the little triangular park area. It bent slightly under his weight as he toppled, crawling behind a small decorative stone wall. Trixie hovered by his side.

Please don't let anyone be dead, Zita prayed as she altered course to check the badger shifter and keep her from being stepped on again. After pulling out the dart, she took a second to check the woman's pulse. It beat strongly against her fingers, the erratic beat smoothing. Hefting Sheriff in a fireman's carry, she staggered once before finding her balance. She carried the larger woman to a now-empty bench near the stage, setting her on it carefully.

Smoke, thick and acrid, curled out of leaping flames in a trash can. Screaming and shouting and random, nerve-wracking sounds of weapons and things breaking filled the air.

Zita's mind spun, working to figure out how to calm the giant mess.

Mullet ran up and pointed at Zita. Since the attack started, he had grown big, frizzy sideburns. He growled, "This is your fault!"

A DMS guy with a net gun lowered it and aimed it at her or Mullet or Sheriff or all three of them.

More worryingly, Tiger had a knife in his hand, the large lime green one she'd seen before. He was creeping up on the agent.

"It's not me, dude! I didn't even know I'd be here. Watch out, DMS guy!" She ducked under the increasingly hairy arm of the angry shifter and ran toward Tiger.

Mullet shouted at her, "Hey! I wasn't done with you!"

The DMS agent aimed at her.

Zita zigzagged to the side and rolled past him toward Tiger. She heard the *sproing* of a net gun and an angry canine snarl behind her.

Horns blared. An APC roared up with an obvious machine gun turret on top, parking in front of the building where Freelance had been. More DMS agents poured out of it, even as sirens joined into the general cacophony.

"Because that's what this chaos needed, more government and heavy weapons," she muttered, picking up a folding chair and hurling it at Tiger as she sprinted to him.

It missed.

Tiger backed up, scraping at his bicep under his plain black t-shirt. He threw something in the air and shouted, "Kill her." Turning, he ran away.

Flames glowing in the mouth and eye sockets, a grinning skull appeared behind him. It opened its mouth and spat fire at Zita.

She jumped out of the way.

Behind her, flags ignited on the stage.

Eyes wide, the DMS agent backed up. He knocked over Reggie and kept going.

Zita circled the skull, trying to figure out the best strategy to get rid of the thing.

It floated, following her movements, until something—Reggie standing and wiping blood from his mouth—caught its attention.

It breathed fire at the reporter.

With a bit of tidy footwork that proved her boxing guess true, Reggie avoided most of it. Flames caught on his sleeve, though, wrapping around it. The reporter whipped off his suit coat and stomped on the flame. His cameraman retreated into the pungent smoke, bumping into a DMS agent in body armor and a gas mask.

The DMS guy snatched the camera and slammed it on the ground. Something cracked.

After a partial shift to a kangaroo, Zita grabbed one of the scattered folding chairs from the pavement and jumped up. She brought the chair down on the skull with all her strength.

It dipped closer to the ground, but its jaw fell open, readying for another fireball.

Zita landed, shifted to a gorilla, and whacked it, forcing it lower and lower until she finally battered it to the ground.

Previous experience had taught her that gorilla form wouldn't work to crush it. She turned into an elephant and trampled it. Vaguely, she realized she was bugling, and someone was... playing a vaguely familiar song in reply.

Her back prickled with warning, and Zita shifted to a great horned owl, flying straight up.

A dart clattered onto the ground where she'd been. No sign of the skull remained, other than an ache in her wings.

Zita rose higher and assessed.

On top of a DMS riot vehicle, Trixie was playing a bugle one-handed and using the enormous water cannon to knock down DMS men and hose down the closest shops and sidewalks. She wore broad grin on her face as she finished the song and hopped off the vehicle.

DMS men shoved Faux Muse, handcuffed and gagged, into the back of a vehicle, dropping a limp Sheriff inside as well. Orange smoke leaked out before they slammed the doors shut. An identical prisoner truck sat beside it, with a set of men in DMS armor standing guard in front of each set of doors. Both were inconveniently parked under bright street lamps.

Tiger was stalking someone, though she couldn't tell if they were a protestor or a bystander caught up in the madness.

On the ground behind him, motionless forms lay in pools of blood, one in DMS uniform, the other not.

Tiger lifted his bloody knife.

She dove, battering his face with her heavy wings and darting aside to land as Arca.

He stumbled, snarling.

Zita spun and kicked the weapon from his hand.

Tiger punched at her.

She danced back.

With an evil grin, he reached behind his back and pulled off another tattoo. A black and white skeleton appeared, wrapped in tattered robes. Its burning gaze held distant, red flames.

It swiped at her with its scythe.

Zita dodged, dancing backward in a fast ginga. She swallowed hard, gulping down nausea as the movement sent the inimitable scent of decaying human corpses washing over her. *Dead things. Why does it always have to be dead things?*

Tiger laughed as he retrieved his knife. "You're not so big without your friends, are you? How do you like being the one who's outnumbered?"

"Is that a short joke? Because I do prefer to think of myself as fun-sized," she retorted, pivoting so she could watch both of them. "Why don't you have tattoos of cupcakes or something happy? Just think, you'd never be without a snack. It couldn't hurt your disposition."

He snorted, getting a good grip on his knife while pacing around her, trying to get behind her. "There's no escaping the reaper!"

Zita kept turning, trying to watch them both.

Tiger ran forward, stabbing at her.

Jumping to the side, she kicked him in the stomach.

His breath whooshing noisily, Tiger staggered back.

Movement whispered at her back when the skeleton attacked again.

She turned.

It swung.

Zita dodged, skittering toward the slowly burning stage in mincing skips to avoid tripping over all the fallen metal chairs. Smoke stung her eyes and roughened her throat. She risked a glance back.

The fire had traced down the original flag and caught in the fabric hanging along the bottom edge of the stage and the wooden arch overhead.

She reminded herself Sheriff was no longer on the bench near the flames, and something inside her unclenched a little.

Cackling, Tiger charged at her again, followed by another swipe of the scythe from the skeleton.

They're herding me. She backed up more and grabbed one of the small poles. A flag burned at the other end. Ignoring the heat stinging her hands, she swung the pole two-handed like a staff to smack the knife from Tiger's hands when he tried to attack again.

It hit his forearm, right where his remaining tiger tattoo was. The odor of burning meat filled the air. Tiger backed up, howling and dropping his weapon.

Zita barely got her (now-bent) makeshift staff around in time to block an attack by the scythe.

The flagpole bent in half and hung.

Tiger growled, holding his injured arm to his side as he retrieved the knife.

After throwing the now-useless pole at him, she jumped backward onto a non-burning section of the stage to dodge the skeleton's next attack.

The scythe swept by, so close she got another whiff of the charnel scent. It buried itself in the wood.

Finally! Zita fell into a quick ginga to build up speed, and then did a martelo de negativa. With the full force of the momentum from her spin and body behind it, her foot connected with the side of the neck, right at the base of the skull.

Something snapped.

She dropped back, trying not to dance into any of the flames that crept across the stage.

The skeleton and scythe melted into black ink puddles, then dissipated.

"Carajo. I didn't think that'd work," she said, hopping down off the stage, landing with her knees bent. Her back prickled, and she spun to the side, grabbing a chair from the pavement and snapping it open in time to block Tiger's attack.

He lunged at her again with the knife.

Zita let the weapon slide through the legs of the chair, then closed it on his arm. She dragged it to one side, then the other, with the glowing weapon far too close for comfort.

Tiger staggered.

After releasing the chair, she tripped him.

He fell, dropping the knife.

Zita grabbed it. She barely had time to register the sting on her palm before she hurled it into the flaming part of the stage.

As she looked for something to tie him up with that wasn't on fire, a group of three DMS agents ran their direction. Two attacked Tiger. One came at her, a net gun in his arms.

Zita shifted back to an owl and flew up and up, out of reach. Her wings and claws held aches she bet she'd feel more later.

The agents forced Tiger onto his stomach, slapping cuffs on his wrists.

With a shake of his head, one of the DMS men directed the others, and they began hauling Tiger away.

Part of the overhang on the burning stage collapsed, sending another cloud of thick smoke billowing out. Most of the action was happening at the edges of the park, with DMS trying to corral groups of people. It was madness. People were running and throwing things, and someone even had what looked like a flamethrower.

Seriously? Nobody could bring a pizza but they packed a flamethrower? Crankily, she continued scanning the area.

The part of the park where all the protests and audience had been earlier was almost empty. Relief ran through her as she realized the audience had gotten away or joined the chaos on the outskirts. She could even see her abandoned shoes near where she'd left them. The truck where DMS had deposited Sheriff earlier was still there, but she didn't see any signs of Kodiak, Trixie, or Freelance.

The mercenaries must've gotten away. Well, since I have the chance, let's not give DMS any more of my DNA than what they might already have. Speaking of which, I can't leave Sheriff in DMS' hands if she was right about them killing her.

She swooped down and snatched up her shoes. Other than some dirt smudges, they seemed mostly unharmed. A shift to Arca on a nearby rooftop secured them in her pockets. *Sweet. Just saved a couple bucks.*

After switching back to an owl, she soared over the prison trucks. Two men stood guard at the rear of each vehicle with shotguns. Firefighters had finally maneuvered their engine to the curb closest to the stage. The fire now completely consumed the stage and had jumped to least one bush next to it. To her dismay, she saw a pair of DMS agents shove Trixie into a truck.

Pues, I guess it's going to be a two-for-one sale. After waiting for the agents to leave, she landed on the hood of Trixie's truck. A window was half-open, and she squeezed in as a raccoon. It had the same hissing sound and box with a switch as the one she'd seen in the tunnel, so she turned the box off, along with the cameras. The noise stopped. Hopping over to the driver seat, she was disappointed. The keys were not in the ignition.

Zita wriggled back out and scampered over to the other truck, where she made a mental note to learn how to hot wire a car someday. To her disappointment, the windows were all up, and no keys dangled from the ignition there either. She hid behind the tires and contemplated.

Firefighters began dragging hoses out. Someone in a tactical vest with DMS on the back of it appeared to follow around them around, yelling and flapping his arms.

DMS, making new friends everywhere they go, Zita thought. *Now, I need a distraction...*

Screaming drew her attention, and that of the guards. A huge, discordant crash sounded.

Disbelief in his tone, one man said, "Did a piano just fall on the APC gun?"

"Ricky! Ricky is manning the gun tonight!" A guard sprinted off.

His partner swore. "He's going to get both of us fired deserting his post like that!"

"We'll cover you. If you're not back in three, we'll call for backup to replace you and say a meta kidnapped a kid in front of us so you went to retrieve," one of the men guarding Sheriff's truck said. He walked over and took the sprinter's place.

"Thanks, man." The guard who had been worried about his job took off after the sprinter.

Two against one? Those are odds I can work with! Zita thought. *It just has to be fast.* Glancing around, she saw little she could use. She eased out from her hiding place and crept carefully to the side of the truck. After checking underneath, she noted the closest guard was only a few feet away, around the corner.

She switched to her Arca form. Regretfully, she pulled out her protein bar, held it to her heart a minute, and shifted to a gorilla.

She pitched it overhand so it would land on the other side of the trucks.

It hit one of the trucks, but at least it made a thud.

Praying the guards were distracted, she darted out around the corner of the truck, grabbing the closest guard from behind and putting him in a chokehold. Zita started counting seconds in her head.

The captured guard tried to smack her with his shotgun, but the angle made it nearly impossible.

She ripped it away with one hand, tossing it aside.

His companion wheeled and aimed at her, but with the her prisoner in the way, he couldn't get a good shot. He lowered his weapon. "Don't make things worse for yourself."

She hooted, still counting.

The guy she held went limp.

Zita hit her count and tossed him at his buddy.

The other guy stumbled under the weight of his friend and dropped his gun.

Shifting to Arca, Zita spun in a meia lua de compasso and kicked him in the face.

He went down.

She grabbed his keys, unlocked the closest truck, and pulled open the door.

Mullet pushed his way in front of the other men and paused right outside the rear doors. "I blame you," he said. Despite his words, he took the time to direct the other men away.

"Dude. Just go," she said, bending, she picked up the closest DMS guy who was already beginning to stir, and shoved him into the truck. She took a few steps to collect the other one and returned to the truck, staggering under a body more than a foot taller than her.

I got lucky that he has a glass jaw and my foot could reach his face. Talk about heavy!

Her luck ran out.

Three DMS men reached the truck, with Tiger struggling in the center of their tight triangle. Given Tiger now had a split lip and one agent had a black eye, she suspected they'd been delayed scuffling with their prisoner. One shouted, "They're escaping!" They grabbed Tiger and yanked him back, away from the truck.

Zita jumped back, slamming the doors shut, and putting the side of the vehicle between her and the men.

One of Tiger's captors uncapped something that spewed white smoke and rolled it at the truck.

Mullet bent double, retching, and backed away.

Despite the partial cover afforded her by the vehicle, her eyes began to burn, followed by all of her skin not covered by clothing—which was most of it, given her costume was little more than a mask, bike shorts, and a halter top. Tears streamed from her eyes. She tried not to breathe while she got her senses together. The men she'd freed were moving away.

Something crashed and crunched nearby. Car brakes squealed and crimson lights were hazy pinpoints nearby. A door rolled open.

A second later, a man coughed, a nasty, hacking sound, but just once.

Zita fumbled her way to the bumper of the truck holding Sheriff and Trixie, sightlessly feeling for the lock. She touched it, wheezing, and slid the key she'd taken from the guard in. It didn't work. *Different keys for different trucks. I don't know if I can pick it when I'm nearly blind and it's too distracting here to work the tumblers even with improved senses.*

Her instincts told her someone was close. She fell into a defensive crouch. *If they touch me, I'll turn into a bat and—*

Quiet and raspy, a male voice said, "Freelance. Freeze."

Zita froze.

A gloved hand tilted her chin up. Blessedly cool water poured over her face and eyes, and then something was held to her mouth. Rubber-scented oxygen poured down her sore throat.

She squinted, blurry images finally becoming clearer.

The quiet mercenary stood in front of her, holding an empty water bottle in one hand, and pressing a gas mask to her mouth with the other. His usual mask was torn, the beginning of a nasty scrape showing by a corner of the mouth she'd glimpsed earlier. Not too far away, by a destroyed wooden barricade, a black van idled, brake lights brilliant red, with a streak of orange along one side where it must've scraped something. A rear door hung open.

"You're here?" she asked. A reason presented itself. "Vaudeville?"

He nodded.

Her throat hurt too badly for more than a low chuckle to escape, and she searched her pockets. Found her lock picks. "It's her lucky day. I can help. Back up. Meta smoke, unknown effects," she rasped.

Freelance stepped to the side, taking his gas mask and holding it over his mouth.

The water and mask had helped. Even with remaining impairment from the gas, Zita had picked enough locks to get through the one on the truck with no problems.

The werewolf jumped out of nowhere at her with a hoarse, broken cry. "Your fault!"

She threw open the door, slamming him in the face with it.

The firemen exclaimed and lost control of the hose for a moment.

Water hit Mullet full force, knocking him to the ground several feet away.

Zita evaded most of it, but enough hit to soak her clothing and reduce the amount of pain she felt from the gas further.

Freelance avoided it all, stepping back behind the truck with a shake of his head.

Sputtering and fuming, Mullet waved a finger at Zita as he shakily clambered back to his feet. "You! Stay out of my city!" He spotted Freelance, froze, backed away, and then ran off.

Trixie hopped out of the prison truck. She'd pulled her fluorescent gas mask over her face, so her words were muffled. "About time. I'm not certain how much longer I had before their cameras noticed I had my mask on. Bear in the van?"

Freelance nodded.

After a two-fingered salute at Zita, Trixie ran over and hopped into the van.

Zita kneeled by the badger shifter. Her eye caught a colorful glint on the ground nearby. After scooping up the protein bar, she smiled. "Oye! It's a little squished but the wrapper's intact." After stuffing it in her pocket, she took a deep breath.

Freelance took a step toward the van, then paused.

Exhaling with effort, Zita hefted the unconscious woman in a fireman's carry.

"Friend?" His words were quiet.

"Nope." Zita shifted to a centaur, changing how she held Sheriff to better shield the unconscious shifter from errant darts. An overdose sounded like a terrible idea, even if the original hit had appeared to stop both the seizure and the flawed shapeshifting.

"Trustworthy?"

That made Zita snort. "Definitely not. She might be mind-controlled."

Even though he was almost lost in the shadows, she could practically sense him tilting his head.

"There! Catch them!" came a cry. Several groups of DMS agents approached from multiple directions.

"She asked for help, and everyone deserves a second chance. Go, be safe. I got a plan." *Sort of.* She glanced down at him. *So, this is what it's like to tower over others. Huh.*

"Foolish." He fell back toward the van.

Though she felt stupidly girly for saying it, she whispered, "Maybe. Text me!"

The van door slammed shut.

She scanned the area. The door gaped open on one of the larger storefronts nearby, with the security grill hanging battered and shoved partway up.

If I can get out of sight of all the cameras and people in this park...

Shouted commands and the pop of an air gun reminded her that she didn't have time to mull over her decisions as she darted to the side to avoid being shot.

She bolted for the shop, praying it was as dark and deserted as it looked. The loud clatter of her hooves on the pavement softened as she stepped inside onto carpet and picked her way forward trying not to knock anything over with her big body.

Whatever had been in the windows was gone, and all the pedestals near the entrance were toppled and smashed. A battered DMS helmet lay by the front door near a crowbar. The rest of the store, however, was untouched, with everything in white except for the merchandise, a few silver accents, and the dark gray floor. The handful of visible products had the slight disorder of hasty abandonment, but otherwise seemed untouched and distanced from each other as if they held contagious diseases. A wide, empty counter separated the show area from the back room. Two robot vacuums the size of Basset Hounds hummed as they sucked up dust and debris. Emergency lighting was on, tinting everything yellow. A woman, her face in shadow, sat at a desk near the entrance. Even if Zita didn't see cameras, she assumed they were there.

Something whirred as she entered. A pleasant woman's voice spoke. "I'm sorry, this location is temporarily closed. While we appreciate your patronage, please return during normal business hours. You have one minute to exit the store before security measures re-engage."

Zita chuckled and felt her tail swishing rapidly as her wariness grew. "Sorry, we'll be leaving in a sec. Here, let me close that for you." She set Sheriff down and yanked the security grill all the way down. She tried to secure it, but someone had snapped off the lock.

The DMS agents appeared to be taking cover behind their truck instead of charging in after her.

Praise Dios, she thought. *I finally caught a break. All I have to do is go out the back before they have a chance to surround the place. Or up to the roof. Somewhere with no cameras and no witnesses.*

"Thirty seconds," the woman said. The lighting in the store shaded to red.

"Sorry, your shutter's broken," Zita apologized, turning toward the woman. When she looked, however, she did a double-take. Her tail lashed through the air.

What she'd taken for a woman seated at a table... wasn't. The robot had smooth, silvery skin, magenta hair, and a face featureless save for two round eyes that shone crimson. Waist up, she was human-shaped enough to wear a store polo shirt, even if the articulation of her joints was visible. Below the table, her body was gleaming cube with the store logo on it.

"Fifteen seconds," the robot intoned. The vacuums cut out, their noise gone except for their wheels turning as they rolled to either side of Zita.

"I'm just going to go out the back entrance now." Careful not to trample Sheriff, Zita scooped up the badger shifter and walked toward the back. The storeroom door looked too small for her current form. Unease prickled her skin as the vacuums followed.

From outside, a man shouted, "Come out of the store now, and nobody has to get hurt."

With a hiss, the robot woman turned her head, appearing to watch Zita. "Your time is up. Enacting security protocols." Her mouth dropped open and an ear-splitting alarm sounded. The room lights brightened and switched to strobing red and white.

Zita stumbled, almost falling to her knees under the unexpected sensory assault.

The vacuums whirred closer, but now one wielded a long stick that glowed blue on the end. The other one's body opened with some kind of gun pointed at Zita.

Her instincts shrieked, and Zita bolted forward.

A gluey mass of something white flew through the air and stuck on a pedestal.

The other robot surged forward, stick buzzing as it attempted to hit her.

Her hindquarters whacked a stand as she danced to the side to avoid it and another glob.

Whatever was on it fell and crunched.

She winced and ran toward the counter.

The stick robot swung at her again.

Zita leapt.

The other one spat another glob of stuff at her, and it hit one of her hind legs. The stuff spread, locking up her hindquarters.

In desperation, she dropped Sheriff on the counter as she sailed over it, before she crashed into the (thankfully padded) wall behind the counter. Something cracked in the divider.

Zita groaned and shook her head. Her shoulder throbbed, and she struggled to stand on all four hooves.

Wheels whirred over the carpet.

She kicked, trying to free herself.

The vacuum came around the corner, prod buzzing.

Zita kicked again, this time managing to rip whatever it was off her legs. One hoof hit the robot and sent it crashing against a wall. After a quick shift to a gorilla, she grabbed Sheriff, hefting her and running into the storeroom. *I think I was safer with DMS than with the cleaning robots!*

After setting Sheriff down, Zita whirled and slammed the door shut before the vacuum could follow her in. Blissfully, the sound of the siren in the front was slightly muted and the flashing lights were gone, soothing her jangled nerves. She shoved a box in front of the door and scooped the badger shifter back up with a grunt.

The storeroom was far less fancy than the front, a small sea of boxes on shelves on a plain cement floor. A framed Employee of the Month photo grinned toothily down at her above a schedule near a small group of lockers. To her relief, she saw the exit sign and started walking that way, her entire body aching and Sheriff getting heavier and heavier.

To her horror, she heard a loud hum and saw a flashlight approaching.

She hid between two boxes and peered out.

A triangular robot with a single white light rolled around the corner, methodically covering every inch of the floor with a wetness that smelled of pine cleanser. It was taller and wider than Zita's natural form.

I don't need to know what party trick that huge thing is hiding. After waiting for it to turn away, Zita darted into the next aisle over.

To her horror, the light turned from white to an unpleasant red and white strobe, and more of the painful alarm came from the mopping robot. Through the shelving, she saw long, thin barrels protrude from the mop robot as it sped up.

No mames. And I got to keep carrying Sheriff until she wakes up. Zita bolted for the exit, climbing up a shelf and over it to avoid the robot. She landed hard, but at least didn't drop Sheriff.

The robot came around the corner.

Zita yanked open the exit, wincing as another alarm joined the cacophony.

Two DMS guys stared at her from right outside the door, one with a stun gun, and the other with a shotgun.

The robot wheeled up behind her.

Her back prickled. Zita jumped to the side.

The robot spat goop just as the stun gun fired.

While the gun had little or no obvious effect on the robot, bouncing off its metal shell, both DMS men were covered in a fine white mesh, much like what still probably graced Zita's behind.

She shoved the robot with her one arm. Even with her strength, she barely did more than make it wobble to one side for a second, but it was enough to get past it and over the struggling DMS men. The shop door banged shut behind her, mercifully muffling the horrible alarm.

"Backup!" someone shouted.

With Sheriff bouncing on her shoulder, Zita ran, turning down the first dark alley she saw. A fire escape, top layer of paint peeling to reveal orange flecks, hung on the side of a lower residential. Grabbing a dumpster, she used it to reach the bottom of the fire escape, and climbed to the top, still carrying the unconscious woman.

Still in gorilla form, she huddled down when she reached the roof, hiding below the ledge as her thoughts raced.

Where can I go with an unconscious and possibly brainwashed badger shifter who frenzies at the drop of a hat? It has to be someplace I can visualize clearly, but that would be empty right now. I can't take her to anyone's home without risking our identities. The old airfield would work, but DMS knows about that and might have cameras. Most of the places I can visualize clearly are iconic structures where there might be tourists. Ay... Someplace that would be empty and easily recognizable. Like one with a custom chandelier?

Voices came from below, and, for a second, she heard the ear-splitting store siren.

They're coming. She glanced around and huddled behind the stairwell.

Grabbing Sheriff's shoulder, she teleported.

Chapter Seventeen

Zita still couldn't tell if it was a squid or an octopus or the bizarre, alcoholic love child of both.

She pulled her gaze from the Danz Mizer chandelier. The wooden tabletops were just as uncomfortable as she had guessed. Despite it having been closed for the better part of the week, the stink of alcoholic sweat, rancid food, and warring perfumes hung like ghosts in the oppressive dark... broken only by the red glare of emergency exit lights. Scuttling sounds, like tiny feet on hard surfaces, only added to the abandoned feel.

She carefully set Sheriff down on the padded seat, checking for a pulse. After a second, she rolled the badger shifter to lie on her side in case more seizures started.

Heartbeat and breathing are steady. Good. Hopefully she'll be up again soon.

After shifting to her Arca form and a quick check to verify they were alone, Zita pulled her shoes from her pocket. She ran to the employee restroom. The sucking sound her cheap sneakers made as she ran was weirdly loud in the empty club. To her delight, she found a tiny shower of passable cleanliness. After scrubbing herself to get everything off, she dried under the hand dryers so she wouldn't drip everywhere. Sore, but clean and wringing out her long hair—an annoying aspect of her disguise—she sought out the manager's office where she knew the camera controls were located.

The door was locked, but not for long. After returning her lock picks to her pocket, she entered the room, leaving the door open so she could listen for intruders or Sheriff. The spoiled odor was less here, the room instead smelling strongly of Dmitri and spicy incense.

Dmitri's personal laptop was gone, but the one hooked up to the security monitors was still there.

Appropriating the vampire's cushy office chair, she flipped on the desk light and started erasing the footage of their presence carefully. Since she wasn't certain when Sheriff would wake, she carefully looped footage from the previous night. Her attention drifted, speculating on the number of codes Freelance's team had set up. A few preset plans with her friends might be handy, and she wondered if he'd be interested in discu—

"Are you sure we should be in here? Domina was gloating that DMS closed it indefinitely..." Sheriff asked, interrupting Zita's thoughts. The badger shifter leaned against the doorframe. Her face was red, and she had a nasty bruise darkening on one arm.

"Crossing police lines is probably the least of the charges against us at this point," Zita said absently, pulling her mind off her... Freelance. "Would you rather I left you in DMS' hands?"

"No, but I don't know if I like you." The other woman huffed.

"I get that a lot. It's okay," Zita said, pecking slowly at the keys.

Sheriff shook her head. "How'd we get here? And why can't I shift?"

Zita lied without any guilt. "I got you away from the park. Wingspan flew us here, but he had to go elsewhere to throw them off track. That's probably an aftereffect of the orange meta gas."

"Huh. Yeah, I remember that stuff. It shuts your powers right down. The junk they had at one of the DMS prisons made me sick to my stomach when I first got there, just like when I get seasick on boats. My stomach hurts, but I'm not queasy so it's probably the same as the nicer place."

Zita stopped her careful two-fingered typing. "You've been in more than one? We might have some questions for you later."

Shuffling a step or two farther into the room, Sheriff eyed their surroundings. "I was unconscious when they moved me between them, so I don't know what I can tell you other than one is much nastier than the other. Is this really Dmitri's office? Somehow, I thought it'd be bigger, and either all puffy red satin boudoir or maybe a kinky sex den. The wall of romance book covers seems about right, though. Being too good for the common folk, he almost always hid in here with Victoria or stuck to the upper floor before we turned meta."

While Zita felt an odd urge to defend the vampire, she also didn't think she should talk about the nearly fatal illness he'd suffered prior to his vampirism. "Probably more for other reasons than being stuck up. He's one of those weird people, you know, the ones who actually like hanging out and talking about nothing for hours with anyone. So, my guess would be that he has his reasons."

"Huh. Never thought of that. I guess my impressions were colored by Domina taking me under her wing when I first started here, and then helping me with my control. Of course, if I'd paid more attention, maybe she wouldn't have gotten her claws in me so deep," the badger shifter said. Bitterness dripped from her tones.

As she painstakingly changed time stamps, Zita grunted; her tone was curt since she couldn't find the right words. She suspected the other woman wasn't interested in pity. "It happens. Sorry. Next time, you won't be fooled so easy."

"Next time, I'll punch that vampire in her stupid face before she starts talking." Sheriff plopped gracelessly into the other chair.

A grin spread across Zita's face. Now that, she could agree with wholeheartedly. "That sounds like a plan. Maybe not in front of witnesses, though."

The badger shifter cracked a smile. "Or cameras. So, what are you doing now?"

While she was hunting for the right key, Zita bumped a button on the chair. It started vibrating against her back. *Nice.* "Right now, I'm looping the video footage for the next few hours so we have time to regroup and figure out where you can go to keep safe. I already erased the video of our presence, so no one should know we were here. I think I've about got it."

"It's a pity that my memory is not so easily erased." The vampire's voice was dry as he posed in the doorway. Today, he seemed even paler than usual thanks to his all-black ensemble: a long, ruffled sweater that hung to his knees, platform heeled boots, and a fancy coat with a wide fur collar too uniform to be real. His purple eyes almost burned against the deathly white of his skin.

"Is that a dress?" Zita blurted.

He glanced down, a strand of dark hair escaping his ponytail and dangling down to touch one cut-glass cheekbone. "Yes. As always, it is both a pleasure and a fright to see you, as your presence warms my heart, but trouble follows closely behind you. Had I known you were coming, I would have brought food since the kitchens here are in an unusable state. Why are you in my closed club? I assume not just so you can enjoy my massaging chair."

Guess this wasn't the best hiding spot I could've come up with. On the bright side, I was going to call him anyway to fix Sheriff's head. While she tried to think of a way to explain that would keep him innocent of any charges later, the truth fell out of her mouth. "Sheriff was hurt, and I wanted to stash her someplace safe since we're sort of on the run from DMS."

The vampire's brows arched. "Given how much they seem to enjoy raiding this place, another choice may have been wiser. I am only here to ensure it has not been vandalized further during its closure."

"Plus, we needed your help with vamp stuff," Zita added, waving her hand toward Sheriff. The rumbling and shaking of the chair were kind of soothing. *If only it could better apply a bit more pressure to that knot of tension in my lower back...*

The badger shifter flinched.

Dmitri sniffed and pouted, one fang peeking from his mouth. "How sad, you did not come for my company. This wounds me deeply. Am I somehow so dull that you spend time with all your other vampire friends rather than with me?"

Zita tapped her fingers on her hip. "I don't got any other vamp friends. Listen—"

"That speaks poorly of your social circle," he said, brushing imaginary lint off his dress.

She raised her eyebrows and scowled at the screen. "Dude."

He ruined his own mock upset... first by smiling, and then chuckling. "No, no, what did you need? If nothing else, this should be interesting."

"Domina messed with Sheriff's brain again. Can you undo whatever she did?" Zita said.

All of his studied nonchalance disappeared as he stood up straight. His fists clenched. "Domina is free and nearby?"

"No, she's still in jail, I think, but she's got to be trading favors with DMS or something." Zita wasn't certain how to explain without admitting to breaking into the prison. "I was at this protest. Somehow, Sheriff was there, but she was standing funny. She kept getting that blank look people had at Domina's evil little pool party, so I thought she might've, you know." She wiggled her fingers by her head.

"You guessed right." Sheriff leaned heavily against the chair. She closed her eyes. "While I was in DMS custody, they took me to Domina. She ordered me to pick out someone either very young or very old, shift to my badger, and destroy them. Then I was supposed to get mad and stay in badger form as long as I could until

DMS put me down... I really didn't want to kill anyone or die. There was a special phrase... Somebody said it. I tried not to shift, but it hurt so bad, and I was so angry, though I don't know why... everything's hazy."

Torn, Zita bit her tongue while she figured out how to reply. Her initial urge was to offer advice, but she'd learned with Wyn that sometimes people just needed comfort.

"I'm so sorry. While I knew her heart was foul, that is despicable. If you will permit me, it would be my honor to clear out any remaining compulsions upon you," Dmitri said gently.

Her face tight and muscles tensed despite her obvious exhaustion, Sheriff didn't look like being hugged, then offered ice cream and wine would help. More like it would make her shatter. Stiffly, she turned to Zita, her hoarse voice breaking a little. "Please tell me I didn't hurt a kid or someone's grandma? My entire body hurts, so something must've happened."

"You didn't hurt nobody. Mostly, you stood around making dopey faces until you asked for my help, fell down, and had a seizure. DMS hit you with some kind of tranquilizer dart, and you might've gotten a little trampled. Oh, and then you were exposed to the meta gas right before you were tear gassed." Zita thought back. "You might've gotten dropped once or twice when you were carried. Sorry about that."

Dmitri and Sheriff both winced.

"That would explain why I'm so sore. Why should I trust Dmitri not to fuck my head up more? I'd deserve it. Not only did I say awful things about you to everyone, but I helped Domina. Told her he'd be staying at Incubus' place and then she sent those thugs. I didn't know about that until afterward." Sheriff turned to face the vampire. "I'm sorry for all of it."

With a snort, he perched on the edge of the desk and crossed his legs, facing both women. "Undoubtedly, it was all praise for my roguish charm and the elegant yet dramatic way I carry off a cape.

And perhaps I am an idealist, but you made an honest mistake trying to help what you thought was a friend. Why would I punish you?"

Zita bit her lip. *She almost killed him, and he brushes it off?*

Sheriff squinted at him. "Because... you could've died?"

A smile touched the vampire's lips. "It would not have been the first time. Life and unlife are like that." He glanced at Zita. "Why did you bring her to me instead of Muse?"

Does he know about Wyn's telepathy? She fought to keep her face blank. "I thought since you're the better vamp, you could undo whatever Domina did. We don't know if they've got some other command laid in there. If it's magic or you fail, that'll be a future stop, but it could take Muse days to fix it once she finds it if she has to design new spells."

His eyelids lowered, sparkling with glitter even in the low light of the desk lamp. "That would seem to make sense."

Zita flexed her shoulders and hit the loop button on the screen. "Sí. I'm all about the logic."

Dmitri turned to Sheriff and slid off the desk. He held out his hand. "If I might have your permission? Sipping from you once would allow me the best and most painless way to verify what's been done. If Domina used a light hand, that should be all that's needed to remove her touch."

Remembering his giddiness when she'd allowed him to bite her, Zita raised her eyebrows at him.

"Only a sip, not a full drink, and Sheriff is not quite so strong a vintage as others," he said, catching her expression. Pink touched his cheeks for a moment before they returned to their usual pallid state.

The badger shifter stuck her chin out. "She drank from me too."

His fangs flashed as he frowned. "That complicates things. It's still possible she did that to amuse herself rather than to increase the power of her bite. If she's truly exerted herself, I may have to go deeper. It would be more of a mental intrusion, but I would not encroach upon your mind without your explicit permission and foreknowledge. Nor would I require any blood beyond the initial amount."

"You'll ask before going into my brain?" Sheriff said.

He nodded. "It pains me that it's necessary to specify that. Yes, I will ask first. Also, I must give you a choice. I can beguile you to feel no pain when I bite or you can take it without anesthetic, as it were."

Zita cleared her throat. "The pain's not that bad, really. Less than bullet ant bites, but more than a broken bone. Well, a small one."

After a deep breath, Sheriff stuck out her arm. "I've done enough bad stuff on her behalf without needing to add to it. I want to check on Nana without worrying that I'll murder her because Domina's a psychopath. Clean her out of me. Without pain. I've got a bit of a hair trigger and don't want to bite the hand that's trying to help me."

Dmitri nodded and withdrew a scarlet handkerchief from his pocket as he kneeled beside the badger shifter. He folded and unfolded it a couple times. It already bore a few tiny brown stains. "Arca, if you would witness so she knows I did nothing but what she requested?"

Zita opened her mouth to refuse but saw the plea in Sheriff's eyes. She swore in Spanish. "Fine."

"If you are ready, then, Sheriff. Gaze into my eyes," Dmitri murmured, picking up her arm gently. His eyes flashed red as her gaze met his, and he bit the meatiest part of her forearm.

Sheriff moaned, slumping in her seat. The husky sound did not hold any kind of pain. Her eyes were wide and dreamy as she panted.

Feeling like an unwilling voyeur, Zita popped out of the seat and began pacing. The chair buzzed behind her.

Without looking, Dmitri picked up his handkerchief and withdrew from Sheriff, maintaining only a single finger on her wrist. He delicately dabbed at his mouth, but never broke Sheriff's gaze. His eyes glowed red. "Curse that wretched woman."

Zita was pretty certain he meant his ex-girlfriend, not the one writhing in front of him.

After another couple of intensely uncomfortable moments, he sighed and glanced away. His eyes turned back to their usual purple. He said, "Sheriff, take a moment. Be calm."

The badger shifter smiled. Abruptly, she sat up straight, expression disappearing. Surliness crept over her face but didn't hide her flushed cheeks.

Dmitri fussed with his sweater dress, smoothing the sides. "You saw Domina recently, didn't you? I found strong new commands, but also older ones planted and reinforced multiple times. She must've found you an effort to keep under control and isolated. If you had a falling out with loved ones, that was at least her fault in part. I cleared away what I could without intrusion, but I fear I must invade your privacy to loosen any of the deeper bindings. Would you permit that? I would need to gaze into your eyes and touch you—a hand or your arm would fine—to do so. No more blood." He cleared his throat. "No more anesthetic."

If it were possible, Sheriff turned even redder. Her body shook a little. She rubbed her arms and scowled. Somehow, her hair bristled even more than before.

"Think about it." Dmitri said. "I would have to access your time with Domina. All of it, good and bad."

Turning away to grant the other woman the privacy to think, Zita gazed out the mirrored window and studied the chandelier. If she kept her body slightly angled so she could see if Sheriff attacked, who would know? "So, is that an octopus or a squid? Not knowing is killing me, but I wanted to know and figured you'd be pissed if climbed up there to check more closely."

Dmitri rose and joined her, turning his back on the badger shifter. He beamed and gestured to the light fixture. "I would, and it is nothing quite so prosaic as either. That, my friend, is the legendary kraken, terror of the high seas and fellow icon. They were known for dining on sailors and damaging boats, if they didn't just break the ship in half by wrapping around it."

Zita snorted and tilted her head. "It'd have to be huge to do that. It sounds like a bunch of sailors got drunk and chased each other around with their snacks telling ghost stories. The head seems more squid than octopus, don't you think?"

The vampire complained, something about poetry and souls that required a lot of hand waving, but she didn't pay attention.

From behind them, Sheriff's tone was firm, though it withered to a whisper at the end. "Fine. You can do it. I won't run around as a possible danger to anyone. Especially Nana. I think I owe her an apology."

Zita and Dmitri smiled.

While it may have only been ten or fifteen minutes, they were excruciatingly long ones. Dmitri again kneeled by the badger shifter and clasped her hand. Sheriff's mouth hung slightly open, and she kept twitching as if little jolts ran through her. The vampire's eyes glowed red, and his expression fell away. His whole body had that eerie stillness uninterrupted by breathing or any of the ordinary minuscule movements of the living.

Zita returned to the chair and tried to meditate while trying every possible combination of massage buttons and looking anywhere but at the others. As nice as Dmitri was, the whole undead thing still unsettled her. She checked the cameras. Still looping.

After releasing Sheriff's hand, the vampire took a couple of swift steps away. Deep purple once again dominated his eyes, which seemed a little sadder. "Domina's commands, which included several nasty ones meant to trigger you more easily, are gone, but you've had little practice controlling your shifting. Perhaps Arca could spare a few lessons in governing your ability? If she can bear to part with my chair."

Stabbing the off button, Zita shrugged. "Sure. You wouldn't be the first I've worked with. We need to set you up somewhere to rest and recover once we're done here. I'll see if Muse can do some healing as soon as I can reach her."

Sheriff winced. "I don't have anywhere to go. Club fired me after Tiger's attack. Before Domina got to me, I lived with my nana. I can't risk DMS busting down her door." Her breath came in short, sharp pants, but this time her voice held no pleasure, only panic and a hint of a growl.

"You did not quit, and I did not terminate you. I understand better than most how Domina can take the most innocent and twist them to her needs," he said, his mouth tightening. Red flashed in his eyes for a second.

The badger shifter angled her head to see him better. Gruffness mingled with surprise. "I'm still employed?"

Dmitri smiled, but it had an edge to it that it usually lacked. "You were never removed from the books. As DMS did not deign to tell us anything, and your grandmother did not know, you were merely placed on leave. Unpaid leave, because I've got a lot of bills to pay and suddenly acquiring a club was not in my fiscal plans. I may be somewhat overextended until Victoria's estate is settled. DMS knows this, and it's likely part of their plan to harass me. I had also hoped having a job waiting might encourage them to release you more quickly," he admitted.

Sheriff gaped at him. She blinked rapidly, tears welling up.

Zita patted her on the shoulder a couple times. Her voice was gruff. "Yeah, for a dead guy, he's all right. It's a little surprising, but you get used to it."

"Undead, Arca. Remember? Dating profile? Highly eligible vampire prince with his own nightclub?" Dmitri chided her, but his fangs peeked out of a smirk.

"Right, whatever makes the ladies like you," Zita said, grinning back at him.

He nodded in return. "Just so. One cannot underestimate the importance of a healthy night unlife."

Swiping an arm over her eyes, Sheriff sniffed. She grunted. "Thank you."

Dmitri bowed.

Uncomfortably, Zita pointed her thumb toward the showers. "How about we use the employee break room for the first few lessons? It doesn't smell too bad, and you can take a second to shower off any tear gas that's still on you. If that's okay, Dmitri?"

"Please, feel free. You already broke in. You may as well get full use of the facilities, such as they are," he said.

Sheriff's eyes widened. "Now?"

"Got someplace better to be? I'm going to try to reach my friends again, and then we can do a few lessons. We'll figure out our next steps after that." Zita flexed her shoulders.

"Yeah, I guess that works. Can I make a quick phone call on the house line?" Sheriff asked.

"Certainly. You know where the phones are, assuming DMS has not stolen them all," Dmitri said.

"Just in case, say you only stopped by for the phone and are leaving here as soon as you get off the line. They've probably bugged it by now. DMS has a hate on for this place, after all, and it'd be better if we didn't give them a reason to trash it more," Zita added.

Her step now a bit lighter, the badger shifter nodded. "I'll let you know when I'm ready for that lesson," she said and left the room.

As Zita paced, trying to allow Sheriff privacy and time, she paused by the vampire. She punched his arm lightly. "Thanks for everything, Dmitri."

"What's mine is apparently yours. I shall, however, require your support for our next movie night. You will be required to vote for my viewing selection," he said. "If you two reach a point where it would be comfortable, I would like to watch the lesson on control. We do sometimes get those who have difficulty managing their shifts here, and our current suggestions do not appear to work well."

"What've you tried?" Zita asked.

"The usual. Don't do that. Bad dog. The occasional newspaper to the nose."

She wrinkled her nose. "Does that ever work for you? I haven't had much success with it."

He shrugged. "You'd be surprised."

***

Somehow, Zita watched half of a vampire movie—albeit one with a lot of martial arts in it—before she realized how long Sheriff had been gone. "Pause the movie. She should've been done showering a while ago."

The vampire clicked pause on the remote, and the action on the screen stopped. "She's been through a lot lately. Perhaps she needed time to herself."

"An hour? Who takes an hour for a shower? Not even in a nice bathroom and yours is—" Zita caught herself—"perfectly fine for a quick workplace rinse."

Dmitri opened his mouth as if to protest and then closed it. "True, I suppose the very simple shower confines and lack of product would make it too unsatisfying to linger in. Really, the only reason we have a shower is Victoria didn't think staff should have to suffer for the uncouth who find it acceptable to throw beverages." Grief shadowed his face.

After an awkward pat on his shoulder, Zita escaped to check on Sheriff. She stomped back out, swearing in several languages. "She's gone."

"What?" The vampire lifted his head. "Truly?"

Zita held out a napkin with some writing on it. "Her nana is sick, so she ran over there to check on her. She'll call the club when she's ready for lessons, and she doesn't think DMS will bother searching for her."

Dmitri sighed. "You can lead a man to water…"

"But you can't push him in or it's assault," Zita grumbled.

The vampire laughed. "I suppose that is true. Do you wish to finish the movie? I believe the vending machine has a sealed bag of popcorn left in it."

"It's getting late, and I got work early tomorrow," Zita said as she ran through her to-do list. Her skin was still tender, and her throat hurt. She glanced up at the screen where Wesley Snipes was posed in mid-kick. Weighed her options. "But I think I can make time for him. The movie, I mean."

With a laugh and a wiggle of his perfectly groomed eyebrows, the vampire clicked the button. "Me too."

***

An hour and a half later, Zita wearily trudged into her apartment in her own form with a Danz Mizer t-shirt over her costume. It was dark, with only the little bulb on over the stove. She slapped her mail on the counter with a loud thwack.

With a startled cry, a lump on her futon jumped to its feet, revealing her brother Miguel. He waved a baseball bat threateningly in her direction as he blinked back sleep. To her amusement, his normally tidy hair stood up in every direction.

"Dude. How many times you going to hold a weapon on me in my own place?" Zita said, kicking off her shoes and glancing at the time. *It's after midnight. No more movies with Dmitri when I have to get up at five a.m., even if he did finally find a vampire flick with decent fighting in it.*

Miguel yawned, setting down the bat by his pillow. "Technically, I own the place. I called and left a message that I'd be here. You not checking messages again? Where've you been?"

"What, I got to report in to you now? I was out. Why are you even in town? You're based out of New York right now." Zita frowned.

Her brother sighed. "DMS has me filling in on an op tomorrow. I can't say any more about it."

She frowned. "I thought you were on desk duty because of the shooting? Have you been cleared already?"

With a scowl, he folded his arms over his bare chest. "They cleared me. As of tomorrow, I'm off desk duty and leading backup teams. As much as I hate being inactive, this was too fast. A man's life should be worth more than a week of desk duty."

Zita winced. "That does seem fast, though I know you wouldn't have done it if you didn't think he was murdering guys in front of you."

A little green light glowed from an unfamiliar phone charging next to Miguel's.

She patted her pocket to ensure it wasn't the one Freelance had given her. "Hey, whose phone is that next to yours?"

He hurried over and unplugged it, tucking it and the cable into his laptop bag nearby. "Not mine! An... old buddy... forgot it when we met up for drinks. I was charging it to... be nice."

Hermano, never try to pull off undercover work. Still, it's none of my business why you're lying about a phone, Zita thought, but instead she changed the subject. "Any word yet on those applications to go back to the FBI?"

With a grimace, he waved his hand. "I'm stuck at DMS for now."

"I can't help but notice you're staying on my futon again, when you could be curled up with your girl. Is everything okay with Linnea?" After a quick stretch, Zita flicked on the kitchen light.

Miguel flinched at the sudden brightness. "She's not real thrilled with me right now. I haven't told her about the poor man I killed, but she figured out that something was up."

Zita located a plastic cup and slapped it on the counter. "Why haven't you told her?"

"It's nothing she can help with," he said. His posture was strictly correct and military perfect, at odds with the crease on his face from the pillow and his rumpled sleep shorts.

With a sigh, Zita filled her cup with water and downed it before turning back to her brother. "Didn't we already talk about this? She knows you're keeping a secret that upsets you. If you don't say anything, she'll get busy imagining shit like you having a one-night stand with somebody else."

"I don't want her to think that I'd murder..." he began, letting his words trail off. Uncertainty made her eldest brother seem younger, more vulnerable.

"Oh, you're being a pinche idiot is all. Mano, if she's the one like you told me, she's not going to kick you to the curb. At least not forever. She's going to forgive your lame culo for holding out and make you promise not to pull that again. And if she splits over it, it's better it happens now before you got babies to get caught in the mess. You work SWAT teams and shit like that. It's pretty likely you're going to have to shoot somebody again."

He rubbed his eyes. "Way to lift a person's spirits."

"Pues, this is like talking to Wyn." Zita shook her head.

Miguel blinked. "What?"

"Fine, if that's the case, you don't want a solution. You just want to yammer about it and get some sympathy so whatever it is sits right with you. It's comforting or something." She pressed ahead, applying her hard-won knowledge until she reached a conclusion. "I'll give you hug and a pep talk if you want, but I don't think you really want to discuss this with me. You're worried about your chick and how she'll take it. So, go apologize and make things right about the keeping secrets. Maybe in the morning, after you've had some sleep, a shower, and picked up an offering. Wyn likes brigadeiros, so I recommend those, or Linnea's favorite ice cream or flowers or something. Then lay it all out and see if she's really the one or a pit stop you need to hurry out of."

He stared at her for a long moment. "That's remarkably sensible advice. It's only the comparison of my girlfriend to a restroom that convinces me that my reckless, bratty little sister hasn't been replaced by an alien."

"Bratty sister? You mean Quentin? He's probably at home asleep because it's late. You good now? I need to crash. I got work tomorrow," she said.

Miguel gave her a hug. Then sniffed repeatedly. His brow furrowed. "What is that smell? Where were you today?"

Zita dropped her glass at the sudden topic change but caught it before it spilled the last few drops of water. She refilled and chugged it to buy time. Plus, her throat was scratchy. The popcorn hadn't helped. "I was hanging with a friend tonight. It ran late."

He touched her chin, angling her face so the light hit it better. "And your face and eyes are all puffy and red... Zita, did someone pepper spray you? Were you at the New York protest that turned violent?"

"Me? Why would I waste my time there? I was climbing with Andy earlier." She remembered he might not back her up on that. Her voice was far too fast and shrill when she corrected herself. "I mean, by myself."

Her brother seemed on much more familiar ground now that the focus was on her. "You don't know if Andy was there?"

"We were supposed to climb, but we argued, and he left. Then I was awesome on my own until I went and hung with someone else," Zita said. "That's what I meant."

His former self-assurance back in place, Miguel raised his eyebrows. "It must've been some fight to have you so upset you'd cry. How could you have insulted him so much that he left? Andy's practically in the dictionary under patient."

"He's mad I don't like his new girlfriend. You know, I'm tired and need sleep. Don't you have groveling to do tomorrow or something?" Zita snapped.

Although he still looked suspicious, her brother said, "And you not liking her was enough to make him storm off?"

"I may have said some things," she admitted.

He sighed. "Just when I hoped you were finally managing to keep normal friends. Did you compare her to a toilet? Has he changed from bro status to a romantic interest for you? Are you jealous?"

She gagged, nausea swirling in her at the thought of that kind of relationship with Andy.

"Clearly not. Is she a criminal?" Miguel answered his own question and launched another at her.

Zita snorted and tried not to blurt out who her friend was dating. She scrubbed at her plastic cup, cleaning it far more than water warranted, before setting it in the dish-drying rack. "No. She's law abiding, but she's all kinds of entitled and is going to walk all over him. She'll break his heart and not even notice... Anyway, I said some shit. He got pissed and stomped off when I wouldn't pretend to be happy for him."

Her brother slapped her on the back. "I'll tell you what I frequently tell myself whenever I hear about your escapades. Sometimes, you have to let others make their own mistakes, even when they're idiot family. Just be there to help them up when they fall. So, sleep on it, and do some groveling, unless he's not worth keeping as a buddy." He paused and grinned a little. "Maybe buy him some brigadeiros and flowers. He might be the type."

"Whatever. Night, Miguel," she said.

As she walked toward the shower, her brother called after her. "Remember, Z, it could be worse. At least he's not dating an axe murderer or Caroline Gyllen!"

She shuddered.

Chapter Eighteen

The next day, Zita was late. She hated being late. Impatience was an insistent, unscratchable itch to do something, even though only Dmitri had arrived before her.

"Do you think we missed her? Did Sheriff say she'd come back?" she said.

"As I said before, she texted to wait here for her," Dmitri muttered, his attention glued to his phone screen.

Warmth ran through her mind as the mental connection opened with Wyn. *Did you need something? I would've thought you would be in bed by now.*

"Finally!" Zita said. She pulled out her phone and held it to her ear. *I wish. I don't know why everything has to take place late at night, like at midnight, instead of a decent hour like five a.m..*

That hour would qualify as cruel and unusual punishment. Even most serial killers are kinder than to run amok in the predawn hours. What's up?

Dmitri glanced up. "Did I miss it ringing?"

"Dog whistle ringtone," Zita lied.

He nodded and returned his attention to his phone.

She spoke aloud, her words echoing what she sent. "DMS set a trap at a protest in New York. Sheriff and I were there, and she's willing to talk to all of us about the DMS prisons she's been staying in. We were supposed to meet earlier today, but Dmitri didn't get her message until after dark, and I didn't get his until twenty minutes ago. Anyway, we're at Danz Mizer, so how soon can you collect Wingspan and get here? Hopefully, Sheriff will be here soon."

I'll check with Andy and see if he's available. Did you invite Jerome?

Zita glanced over at her companion, but he was ignoring her. She spoke both aloud and on party line. "Yeah, I texted. He said he was on his way and to wait for him. Asked who else would be here."

Her mental voice unexpectedly sharp, Wyn sent, *Excellent. I'll be right back. Normally I'd just add Andy to party line, but your inability to act with maturity regarding his relationship means it's far more comfortable for everyone if I don't. It comes from a place of deep love when I say y'all need to handle your issues soon. This can't go on.*

Party line dropped.

Zita blinked. Grumbled. Honesty compelled her to admit the truth of her friend's words, and she resolved to try to be better. *Whatever that meant.*

Absorbed in whatever he was doing on his phone, the vampire just grunted.

The mental link returned before she could even lower the phone.

We might be a little late. Andy's in the middle of something right now, so I'm waiting for him to come get me, Wyn sent.

The words slipped out despite her good intentions, a sneer twisting around the words. *Can't bear to leave his new girlfriend?*

Wyn's answer held less warmth than Antarctica did when Zita had practiced being a penguin. *No, he's on stage being presented to the rest of the faculty with some other new hires. He's been worrying about it for days, which you'd know if you could quit being ugly about Caroline. As soon as they're done with the speeches, he can slip out of the reception. Is it an emergency? Do you need to come and get me?*

Ignoring the poke, Zita spoke aloud at the same time she sent the words mentally. "No, we can wait for you guys to get here. Sheriff's not here yet. Don't get caught slipping in."

Wyn's confidence vibrated over the line. *Illusion will make us the souls of discretion.*

That worked well so well with the movie disguises at the hospital, Zita sent. "Uh-huh."

Hush your mouth. The rebuke was accompanied by a wave of amusement. *I'll alert you when we're on our way.*

"Got it." Zita snapped her phone shut. "Wingspan and Muse are running late."

The vampire glanced up from where he seemed absorbed in his phone. Both the table and the man seemed overdressed for the abandoned club. Ivory cloth hid the top of the table, and a stack of plates, ornate silverware, and cloth napkins sat in the center of the table beside two buckets of chicken tenders, eight dips, cheese biscuits, and four containers of sides.

"Phone games? Can we do something useful while we wait instead? We could at least sweep in here." She wrinkled or nose. "Or take out some trash?"

He sniffed. "DMS has declined to release the club. They claim it's a crime scene. As far as efficiency goes, I'm outlining the first in a spin-off book series. My deadlines wait for no man or shapeshifter. Last time I texted, Sheriff replied she'll be here in a few minutes and to leave the back door open. I told her to buzz and we'd let her in, as one never knows who might take advantage of an open door."

Zita grunted and walked over to the table. When she came up behind him, she could see rows of brightly colored candies on his screen. "Looks like a game to me."

He pocketed the phone. "I assure you. It was vital research."

"If you say so." She scooped up a chicken tender and a biscuit, then took a big bite out of each.

A buzzer sounded.

"Ah, that's the back door! Let's see if it's your friends or if I forgot to cancel a delivery. I am lost without Incubus to tell me these things," Dmitri said, going into his office.

Zita snagged a napkin and followed him into his office. As she entered, she saw him switch the security camera view to the back alley. She chewed as fast as she could while she studied the man outside the door.

His build matched Jerome's, but she didn't know the large African American at the door. The brim of a ball cap and a pair of sunglasses obscured his face, and a baggy t-shirt and jeans completed his outfit. His posture and balance were all wrong as well.

The vampire reached for the computer mouse. "Is this someone you were expecting? Why is he wearing sunglasses at night?"

"That's not anyone I know. He looks similar to someone I was expecting, but the dude I know goes for tight t-shirts that show off his guns, among other things." Zita studied the screen, noting the way the fabric of the loose shirt bunched at his shoulders. "Wait... I think he's wearing a bulletproof vest under there!"

His fingers curled for a moment, and then Dmitri reached for the mouse. "You have quite the sharp eyes. Let's check the other exterior cameras."

Zita polished off the rest of the food she carried while he flipped through. While no one stood too close to the front door, she caught flickers of movement at the edge of the camera feeds.

From the expression on his face, the vampire had noticed as well.

"They're at both doors. Do you have roof access?" Zita choked down a too-big bite.

Silently, Dmitri clicked to another camera view. This time, they could see men in armor right by the door.

"Well, somebody thinks we're badass. Secret tunnel?" She wiped her fingers on the napkin and tossed it into the trash.

"An obvious oversight in my renovations. I'll set the computer to erase security tapes for the past hour." The vampire set the security system to switch between the different cameras and typed a command.

The buzzer to the back door rang again.

"Window it is, then. Come on!" Zita snagged his arm and pulled him out the office and to the closest one. She threw an arm out, barring his access until she did a partial shift to an owl. Holding a finger at her lips to hush him, she peeked out. A glint of metal and a glimpse of movement on nearby rooftops caught her attention. "Good thing this is an older building with working windows, not just glass panels. We must be seriously scary for them to pull out this much firepower."

After throwing open the window, Dmitri peered below. "I fear they've caught a vampire. Hopefully, I can escape if they leave me alone with only one or two people. Shape change and fly before they catch you!"

Fearing DMS had brought snipers, she tugged him away from the glass. "Careful, we need to go out fast. Change to a bat and fly away with me. We'll meet up at that building with the tower a couple blocks down."

Doors banged open below, and people shouted. "DMS!"

"I can change into a bat, but I didn't say could fly as one!" he hissed.

"Seriously? Am I the only person who practices their superpowers around here? Fine. Shift, and sit on the ledge. I'll grab you and fly off," Zita said.

He glanced at the ledge. "I've really only hung upside down a couple of times from a closet rack, and someone lifted me up and held me until I got it right."

She smacked her forehead. "Buey. Shift!"

Rapid footsteps and shouting came from below.

He changed shape to a large black bat that wobbled unsteadily on tiny feet.

"Don't fall or bite me," she said, lifting him.

Feet thundered up the stairs. "There's one!"

Zita slid onto the window ledge, shifted to a barn owl, and flew off with the bat in her talons.

He squeaked.

***

Now that the vampire had sunk his fangs in their business, he had no interest in disengaging them. "I will not cower in Brazil while you attempt to solve my issues."

Half an hour later, Zita and Dmitri met with her friends in the closed Greek restaurant. To be certain the illumination from the camp lantern lighting their clandestine meeting would not leak out the window, they'd drawn all the shades and moved a pile of snowy linens to the table to block them from view. Wyn and the vampire shared one side of the same back booth they'd met in with Jerome previously. Andy pulled up a chair and scooted it to the witch's other side. Zita sat alone in the wide booth seat directly opposite the others.

Andy's quiet rejection stung. Zita tried to concentrate on dissuading the vampire and the DMS issue instead. Somehow, it seemed easier. *Maybe I should've asked Dmitri for advice, too. Given how he regularly manages to convince people to let him drink their blood, he has to be good with people. I didn't mean to call Caroline a tool in front of Andy again at breakfast, but it just slipped out.*

He glanced around, folding his arms over his chest. Other than raising an eyebrow at Andy's choice of seating, Dmitri either hadn't noticed or had been too tactful to ask about it. "For once we are not literally in my business, but the raids and my missing employees remain so. Why are we in this place anyway?"

"It was the only joint I could think of to bring you on short notice that DMS wouldn't expect." Zita sighed and nudged Wyn mentally, hoping her friend could do the eyelash flutter trick or something and convince him. Dmitri had shown no interest in hiding safely in Brazil or in a cave full of bats—assuming she could teach him how to fly and hang upside without someone placing him on his perch—while they somehow found a way to stop DMS' campaign against him and metahumans in general.

The witch pinched the skin between her dainty eyebrows. "Dmitri, you don't know the entire story. In this case, ignorance is not only bliss, but safety."

The vampire cocked an eyebrow and leaned against a nearby table. "Do not think me naive. When I went to warn my court of the danger to metahumans, three had not been seen since arrests for minor violations, and one had a missing granddaughter. DMS has resorted to mind control and staged outrages to hide their unsavory actions. I also saw the prisons when I assisted Sheriff with Domina's latest mental violations against her. They have captured a large number of people and are holding them against their wills. The conditions at the hidden prison are particularly appalling. They have food and water, but little else. They've no privacy unless they end up in solitary, and then they are in a dark box for days with a bucket for their personal needs."

Zita and her friends gaped at him.

Finally, Wyn spoke. "While we didn't know the full extent of it, your information confirms our suspicions. It puts someone who requires accommodation for their abilities, such as yourself, at special risk. That's why we suggested temporary relocation until the danger passes," Wyn said.

Dmitri laughed, but the sound held little humor. "The sensible recourse would be via the courts. It would not be dangerous, but would be costly, time-consuming, and, frankly, long odds for you to win as vigilantes with little money and no legal standing. They certainly will not accept the sworn word of a vampire about what he saw in someone's mind. Something must be done to rescue those in DMS' clutches, and I will be part of it, however long it takes. If you thought this had a fast resolution, you would not be trying to stash me in another country or with rodents."

"Hey, the bat cave would keep you closer to your family. It's not a bad option," Zita protested.

He ignored her. "I have a standing invitation to shelter with the Count, so I will stay with him until this resolves. He is not a metahuman, so DMS should have no recourse should they violate his rights."

"The Count? Does he like to count?" Andy said. His mouth twitched as if trying not to say more.

A half smile touched Dmitri's lips. "He's the club accountant, so one presumes so. However, I have yet to observe any thunder or lightning when he works on our taxes."

Andy howled with laughter, wiping his eyes. "Sorry. It's just..."

The vampire surveyed him and chuckled. "Yes, I understand. I had much the same reaction at first. He is the only one in the entire court who chooses to be called by title rather than name. While I would have chosen a different rank for that reason alone, Victoria did as she wished, and all of her beaus had the same rank in our court."

"All her what?"

Dmitri shrugged. "Her lovers."

The word slipped out before Zita could stop herself. "¿Neta?"

"Age does not preclude romance," Dmitri said, frowning. "If one's best friend chooses an unconventional love life and all involved are adults consenting of it, how arrogant would it be to stand in the way of her happiness?"

"Indeed," Wyn murmured in agreement, steadily eyeing Zita.

She shook her head. "It wasn't about her age. She just seemed too—"

Someone kicked her under the table. Based on the lack of strength and pointy shoes, she assumed it had been Wyn, a guess confirmed with her friend's mental words. *Hush. Please don't insult the woman he thought of as a second mother. You've precious few friends left that you haven't already irritated this week.*

"Don't kick me! I was going to say conservative! She dressed like a bling-loving nun in a lacy mantilla!" Zita wrinkled her nose at her friend. Belatedly, she tacked on, "Not that there's anything wrong with that. I'm just saying. Expectations."

Dmitri laughed. "In many ways, she was the more daring of the two of us. So, my departed friend's love life aside, let us continue. You clearly aren't going to simply stay in your secret identities until DMS policy changes. By the process of elimination, you'll be taking illegal action. The most logical is a prison break of multiple persons or a heist to retrieve the proof required to unequivocally prove DMS' wrongdoing. Possibly both."

"Oye," Zita said intelligently. *I swear I didn't tell him anything!*

The vampire lifted his hand and made a graceful gesture. "By all means, convince me that I know nothing."

Andy chimed in. "Right now, you haven't done anything wrong and are a victim of DMS. Joining in with us will risk your, uh..."

Dmitri leaned forward, ticking off points on his elegant fingers. "My what? Unlife? A quick death would be preferable to a one chosen by Domina or life as a laboratory experiment. Reputation? I am the prince of a court of monsters. Infamy can only aid me there, and the publicity might sell a few more books. My home? I've been fortunate enough that DMS missed me in their recent raids on my club and the one they performed on my house earlier tonight. They're clearly hunting me, and whether their intention is to capture or kill, I cannot go anywhere familiar. Thank you for the interesting trip to Canada to call my mother and ascertain my parents' safety, by the way."

Even beneath his olive skin, the red flush in Andy's skin was visible. "No problem. You know that you could go to jail with what you're suggesting."

"While I'd prefer not to leave any evidence that would result in my name on a wanted list, this is bigger than you and your friends. As the Prince of DC who would dictate how others act—how they feed, which is intimate for many of us—I have a responsibility to act in the best interests of my people. Incubus is also not just my club manager, but my best friend. Sheriff has been taken not once, but likely twice given her failure to appear this evening. We know DMS has them. How many more of my people have they stolen away? How is this not my fight?" Dmitri raised his brows and stared at them.

Wyn's eyes were huge, and her lips parted as she watched him.

Zita frowned. "We may have to do it during the day."

The vampire batted his lashes at her. "While flattered, I'm not that kind of vampire." When she didn't respond, he sighed. "No appreciation for my fine humor. You know I needn't sleep all day. Trust me. I have been constrained most of my life by my health. Now I may act provided I take sufficient care, and I intend to do so."

"Dude, I've hung with you in the daytime. You're pretty much dead until someone punches you or sets off an air raid siren in your ear, and then you fall asleep whenever you sit down. Will you stay awake if you're on watch?" Zita pointed out the cold, undead truth.

He opened his mouth and then closed it. "If nothing else, they're using Domina to implant suggestions. I can remove those and add my own powers of persuasion to make this as bloodless as possible, if you will pardon the pun. You cannot take all the risk by yourselves. I can also assist in another way as well. Some of my court may be willing to join their numbers with ours to assist. With at least a few more people, your identities would be less obvious. As it is, a shapeshifter, a witch, and a thunderb—"

"Giant golden eagle shifter," Andy interrupted.

"As you wish. You are a distinctive trio. This would create a level of deniability, at least for the ladies. I fear no one comes close to your avian form in size though, Wingspan, save the Dragon." Dmitri arced his brows at them and held out one pale hand.

Wyn steepled her fingers. She mused, "I could create some short-use disguises for us that would hide us even from Dmitri's recruits."

"We might not be able to avoid them finding out who we are. We could only accept help from the ones we could trust not to say we were there," Zita pointed out.

"That does limit who I can bring. Of course, if it is too risky, all I ask is you stay out of my way while my people and I rescue our own. One way or another, I will not tolerate this. It would be far better for us to join forces. All I ask is that we retrieve the six or however many of my court who have been stolen," the vampire said.

When Zita opened her mouth to refuse him, Wyn raised her eyebrows and spoke over party line. *Would you rather he tried to do something on his own? He's determined, and we could use his aid and the extra manpower.*

Wyn touched Dmitri's arm. "Are you certain? If so, you will be welcome, but there is no turning back. We'd also request that you not tell your volunteers who we are, and if they guess, they are to never speak of it. There is also something of a time issue. A precognitive foretold the deaths of thousands if we don't act in time."

The vampire touched her hand with his own. "No pressure, I see. Positive. I will not hide if I can help, and I know at least four who chafe against inaction, could not be suborned, and previously served our country's military. Now, what is the plan?"

Andy's shoulders slumped. "We don't know."

Clearing her throat delicately, Wyn said, "A hacker was helping us, and he was working on both a plan and retrieving schematics. However, his house was swarming with DMS when we stopped by earlier, and we saw no sign of him."

"We're guessing they have him, given the amount of police tape and the computers they were removing from his home," Andy added.

We lost Jerome? Zita swore. "I was hoping he was just off with yacht-loving models and missed our texts. He had a whole happy plan of some kind he was working on."

This is bigger than the three of us. You should see if the mercenaries would help. Assuming they'd agree to work for free and not to kill anyone, they'd be used to creating strategies for situations like a prison break. Wyn bit her lower lip as she sent the message.

Zita started to chuckle at the idea, but then Andy's next words destroyed any humor at the idea.

Andy nodded. *Agreed. Let Dmitri in on it, and contact Freelance. We need help. Not just the mental help we normally need either.*

You're actually serious? I don't want to drag them into this. We've already got too many people at risk. Zita folded her arms across her chest.

The vampire watched them. Pulling out a tiny notebook from his pocket, he jotted down a few notes.

Wyn kept her opinion matter-of-fact. *We need the help, and they undoubtedly have tremendous experience at this sort of thing. They're already operating illegally or nearly so, given their clientele. It's not like their reputations will be ruined.*

Zita growled out loud, sending an apologetic smile toward Dmitri. *Contrary to Wyn's prejudice, they're not criminals. They're probably legal and will lose out on prime jobs if they're wanted by law enforcement. Trixie and Kodiak don't usually even wear masks. They depend on gear that needs replacing, plus transportation and lodging *costs. So, in addition to asking them to risk their lives, you're asking them to shell out what might be prohibitive amounts of money.*

Wyn tossed her hair over a shoulder. *Dmitri's friends all face that too, and we don't know that any of them will actually be of any real assistance. Having people who know what they're doing might be the difference between saving the port city and our kidnap victims... or losing all of them. Besides, do you really have the right to decide for them what is too dangerous? Trixie and Kodiak are metas, so they have a stake in this too. It can't hurt to ask.*

Can't it? And Freelance is a meta too. Zita managed not to make any noises out loud this time, but her fists clenched under the table.

Andy sent, *Is his power being scary or popping up from nowhere? I'd somehow feel a lot more comfortable if it were.*

Please. How would you feel if Freelance left you out of a big, dangerous mission to save thousands of people, including your family? For all you know, they've got relatives trapped in that prison or living in that city. Wyn arched her brows at Zita, her expression implacable.

The last comments hit, and Zita flinched. *I don't expect to be invited on mercenary missions, but I get your point. Fine. I'll ask, but I'm not going to push.*

Wyn subsided. *Fair enough.*

Struck by a thought, Zita narrowed her eyes at Andy. *Are you dragging her in too? You know she wouldn't stay quiet about our involvement.*

He glanced away. Anger leaked with his reply. *I won't force Caroline to choose between actively trying to arrest us or betraying her oaths to serve her country. No one should be forced to choose between two things they love.*

His jab made her heart hurt and fanned her annoyance. *But the risk is fine for us? For Freelance and his team? For Dmitri's buddies? What about when—*

"Do let me know when you're done communicating magically with each other and wish to speak to me again, though I'd request it happen before the sun rises," Dmitri said, glancing between them.

Enough, you two. Let's not revisit that issue. Wyn cleared her throat. "I had hoped Sheriff could have told us where the primary prison is. We could've worked from there. I don't suppose you caught something useful? Domina's prison only holds a few captives. They must have the others elsewhere. Also, we'll need to give you a phone with a special app to contact us with. DMS is probably tracking yours."

Dmitri glanced at his hands. "That does explain why Arca demanded I remove the battery from my phone once we left the club. Unfortunately, I do not recall all of Sheriff's memories, merely impressions. I do not think she knew the locations. DMS prefers to move metas both unconscious and restrained between places, and none of her cages had windows or views. She recalled being held two separate places, both quite warm."

Wyn tossed a lock of hair over her shoulder and sighed. "I'll try to reach our hacker again when we're done here, but it's unlikely he is still at large. Without his computers, he may be unable to do anything anyway. I can also cast a spell to locate him, but I'll do that soon. If you know Sheriff's full name or have something of hers, I can cast it on her as well. I've found that nicknames do not work nearly as well as birth names."

"Accessing personnel records at the club might be an issue right now, but I can speak to her family and find out. If her grandmother's illness was not a DMS ploy, I'd like to ensure someone looks in on her to confirm she has what she needs, anyway," Dmitri murmured.

Wyn nodded at him. "That's an excellent idea. If she's unwell, let me know. I'll cast a healing spell on her if it's something that can be cured. Unfortunately, I cannot undo genetic issues, only mitigate their negative effects."

The vampire tapped his chin. "I suspect Sheriff has returned to the DMS prison, perhaps with your computer-loving friend. The timing of her messages was strange. She has known me long enough to know the futility of attempting daytime appointments with me, let alone expecting me to convey said meet to someone else."

Slowly, Zita said, "She might've been trying to tip us off. We need to make a couple calls. Or at least one."

"What's that?" Wyn said.

"DMS is kidnapping supers left and right. If they've taken, um, our computer friend, raided Dmitri, and have been trying to catch us, they might also go after other open metas. I happen to have overheard that they called in extra team members from out of state." Zita pushed a lock of hair from her face.

Dmitri said, "You seem to have your ear at a lot of doors."

Zita kept talking. "We need to warn Remus and his lawyer, if it's not already too late. They're both open about their abilities, and them disappearing would allow a win by default on that legal case they're part of. The one where you guys kept explaining how important it was like I didn't hear you the first time?"

Wyn paled. "Oh, yes. We should definitely do that. I'll do the location spell on our hacker friend, and you call Remus' lawyer. He requested we not contact him directly, if you recall. His attorney's personal cell phone number is on the back." She reached into her purse and drew out a business card and a cheap phone marked with a tidy "Police" label.

Zita took both items. "I'll do a quick flight as soon as we're done here and try calling while you're casting. Wingspan, you'll guard her during the spells after you drop Dmitri off at the Count guy's place, right?"

Pursing his lips, Andy nodded.

"That does bring up another issue. With our computer friend missing, we don't have access to the data that was collected about DMS, so we can't release it to the media like we'd hoped." Wyn pinched the skin between her brows and sighed.

"Not like we know anyone with the kind of serious pull we'd need for a story that big to not just seem like yet another Internet conspiracy theory," Andy muttered.

"Some of those are true, you know," Zita shot back.

He snorted. "Don't worry. I know you have your own unreasonable collection."

"Dude, I'm just saying the truth is out there," she said.

Both men snickered.

"You know, perhaps I will leave our hacker one more message before we get distracted again." Wyn withdrew her phone from her purse. She glanced at the screen. "Someone contacted me via our app?"

"You left that on? We're going to have to find another meeting place all over again," Zita sighed.

Her friend shrugged and swiped at the screen of her phone. "I keep it in my purse. It can't be tracked there. I won't stay on it long here. J—our computer friend texted! DMS doesn't have him!"

"Is he okay?" both Zita and Andy demanded.

"Yes, he's boarding a plane for Switzerland on the advice of his attorney," the witch answered, eyes on the tiny screen.

Again, Zita and Andy spoke in unison. "What? Why?"

The vampire mumbled to himself, but Zita caught his words. "My lawyer never suggests anything that amusing."

After she'd finished reading, Wyn giggled. "Apparently, he snuck out of his house this afternoon for an intimate social engagement he didn't want his DMS watchers to interrupt. When he returned home, DMS had invited themselves inside, so he called the police and reported a home invasion. While the cops dealt with

DMS, he decided to go ask his attorneys some burning questions. Their advice resulted in the airplane ticket."

"Ask if he has the data?" Zita said.

"And ask if he has the video on him, please," Andy said, almost at the same time.

Wyn's fingers flew over the phone.

After an interminable and silent wait, broken only by the rumbling of Zita's stomach, Wyn's phone began beeping with the steady cadence of a metronome.

Snatching it up, Wyn read it. "If we can figure out who to send the information to, he has the video and a handful of interesting tidbits from our prior scouting run that he or his lawyer will release to the media if we can figure out which outlets are the best choice. His contacts are primarily gossip or technology columnists, so they're suboptimal."

With a snort, Andy said, "When would optimal ever describe anything we do?"

"Speak for yourself. I'm awesome," Zita said.

The witch rolled her eyes and scrolled down. "Unfortunately, he didn't have time to go through all of the data. Roughly three-fourths is locked up in the computers that DMS has confiscated. However, to provide an abbreviated version of his prodigious gloating, his machines are heavily encrypted. If DMS attempts to force their way into his files, the entire contents of his drives will be erased."

How fast can Jerome type with those big hands on a little phone? Zita wondered.

Wyn continued scanning, an almost constant stream of beeps coming from her phone. "And now he's saying not to get into any trouble without him. He says we need to either join him or pick him up so he doesn't miss any of the action. Apparently, he left one of his toys watching the show prison. However, since he'll be unreachable for the next ten hours or so, he's posting the feed on a private online site so Wingspan can keep an eye on it."

Andy squeaked. "Me?"

"One can only assume he's concerned that Arca's mere proximity might damage their delicate electronic workings. I'll ask," Wyn said.

Zita rolled her eyes. "I'm not that bad. Don't be a hating hater."

"How am I supposed to sleep? What if I miss something because I have to use the bathroom?" Andy said.

"No answer. Given his last message was just 'Boarding,' we can assume that any further communication won't happen for several hours. Since I'm canceling tomorrow's plans anyway, we can meet at my place so we can trade off watching."

Zita thought wistfully of the work she had to do for her brother's business tomorrow. "I could come over too and help."

"The two of us have it. You probably have more important things to do," Andy said.

Delicately clearing her throat, Wyn dropped her phone into her purse. "Any thoughts on how we can disseminate the video and whatever else he salvages?" Wyn said.

Dmitri tapped the table to get their attention. "This may be an avenue where I can assist. All three raids on my club were highly publicized, and DMS has released my name as a metahuman of interest who has had contact with many others. Two or three reporters have been besieging my known contact information since the raid Saturday. We can only hope that one of them has sufficient influence to keep the story from being buried. Up until now, I've been disinclined to make a statement, but that has changed. Surely one—or all of them—would be interested in the inner workings of the churlish DMS? Especially given the recent speculation following public appearances by a vigilante alleging DMS is not only denying basic rights to metas arrested, but also attacking anyone unfortunate enough to be between them and their prey."

Wyn and Andy looked at Zita.

Zita shrugged. "They asked me questions. I wasn't going to lie about it. Speaking of which, I met a New York reporter who'd love nothing more than to embarrass DMS. They busted up his camera when he was getting an exclusive inside look at the New York riot, and he's fighting being replaced by a newer model at his job."

The vampire all but purred. "Excellent. Give me his information and I will see to his inclusion. Hunger is a wonderful motivator. I should know."

Zita's stomach rumbled. She groused, "It certainly is. I wish I'd thought to grab some of the food we had to leave behind. Maybe a few of those cheesy biscuits—wait. We know someone who does PR on the big scale."

"Who?" Wyn's brow knit.

Andy and Dmitri leaned forward.

"Camembert! No, Bleu. You know, Rani's bouncy cheese girl. Brie! You got her card in your bag, Muse?"

Reluctance showed in the slow movements of her pretty hands as Wyn dug out the card and set it on the table. "It does say she's the Public Relations Vice President for General Aetherics Energy Division. Do we really want to drag her into this, though? The more people that know about this, the harder it'll be to keep it secret. Still, the information our friend saved might be proof enough for her to do us a favor in conjunction with Remus' lawsuits and the public records of the raids on Dmitri's home and club."

"The senator dude pushing that bill is counting on the secrecy hiding his slimy trail. You know that video was creepy as all get out. If we can convince enough people, they can't pass the bill or get away with as much while we work on finding proof of the rest of the stuff they've been up to. Nobody will take my word alone over the senator's about what went down in New York, but a lot of people had phones. One's got to show that it was mostly DMS and Tiger attacking. I could search our hacker friend's house for his danglies too to see if DMS missed them. He could keep sorting through info while he's stocking up on cuckoo clocks and chocolate."

Dmitri held up a too-pale hand. "His... what?"

"Arca has mental blocks against technology and common courtesy. Don't push her for details or we'll be here all night while she's misnaming thumb drives," Andy said in an aside to the other man.

The vampire nodded. "Ah! I had noticed. Now that is settled, what's next?"

"First thing we need to do is find where they're stashing everyone. We found one DMS prison, but it was mostly for show and to allow Domina to compel folks for them," Zita said.

Dmitri growled.

Wyn sighed. "I've tried casting spells, but it's not working. With the exception of Domina, I cannot find most of the missing. Every time I try to cast the spell, I get the same fictitious result. My theory is that someone else cast some form of magical obfuscation over wherever they're keeping all the metahumans."

"You're certain they're not dead?" Andy jumped right to the most cheerful choice as usual.

The witch nodded. "If they were, the spell would fizzle in a specific way and point to the corpse. I tested that back when we first started looking for her by searching for known dead people. Elvis is, in fact, buried at Graceland... if you were curious."

Dmitri leaned forward. "Pardon. I am new to this, but what result is the spell giving you?"

The witch threw her hands up in the air, and her face soured. "Incubus and Sheriff are at the faux prison facility. For everyone else, it redirects my spell so the results put them in the waters of the Bermuda Triangle between San Juan and Bermuda."

The vampire considered her thoughtfully. "What if it's not being redirected?"

"It's the middle of the ocean. No islands are marked or anything on the maps. I checked." For all her denials, Wyn sounded intrigued.

That reminded Zita of an offhand comment the badger shifter had made. "The real little ones aren't on general maps. It's possible. Sheriff said something about the orange gas at the one prison making her nauseous, but not at the other. Maybe it wasn't the gas. She could've been seasick if they got there by boat."

"Muse, as the magical expert, I ask respectfully what would be the easiest? Creating and maintaining this obfuscation or hoping that anyone who found the address by accident would think it was either a joke or a cover-up? Allowing others to think what they wish is the best way to lie without lying about petty things like life and death." Dmitri smiled.

Zita added, "Or undeath?"

Fangs flashed white as he smiled at her. "Just so."

Andy offered, "What about a boat? Could they have a big, converted cruise ship or something? What he said makes sense, and they could move it if they suspected a problem. Then again, somebody might notice a large boat hanging out there all the time."

Wyn frowned. "You really believe that a super-secret prison facility is just floating around the Bermuda Triangle on a boat? That area isn't even technically in the United States. It's international waters."

The vampire shrugged. "It seems insane to have a government correctional facility outside of American territory, but legalities seem to be irrelevant to them. Then again, they may never have expected anyone to track them, either. If they use the false prison as a staging facility to ensure only metahuman prisoners are taken there, and then ship them..." He whipped out his phone and began tapping at it.

"You said the Bermuda Triangle. Does it appear to move around or does it seem consistent in location?" Dmitri asked.

The witch pursed her lips. "It stays still."

Andy pursed his lips. "The town by the faux prison has a pier, but I doubt they could be regularly docking a ship there of the size necessary to hold every metahuman that's gone missing. The Atlantic would make a good dumping spot for the bodies, though."

Wyn still seemed unconvinced. "They'd still need to resupply. Someone would notice what would have to be an unusual vessel taking on that much food."

"The dock wouldn't be a big deal. The Caribbean has lots of ports with the capacity to supply and refuel cruise ships, so it's possible they're using one of those for fuel and smaller ships for other supplies like food. Ferrying passengers or objects via small boat is cheaper for big ships and a great income source for the supply ship. If it never moves, then we might be looking for a small island or something manmade. Non-military ships don't usually refuel at sea. It's dangerous if you don't know what you're doing," Zita said. She dug out a protein bar and took a bite.

When no one spoke, she glanced up, chewing.

They were watching her.

Swallowing hastily, she said, "What? I dated a guy whose family had a little boat. They did diving tours and ship supply runs during the tourist season and fished the rest of the year."

"Fun and Arca aside, guys, what are we going to do?" Andy asked.

Zita frowned at him. "You say that like I'm not fun."

Wyn pursed her lips. "Well, if they're in the Bermuda triangle, and we want to remain unnoticed, we'll need to secure a boat. That will be a challenge given our funds."

"You have funds? That is a relief, given my finances are too precarious to assist much," Dmitri said.

Andy snorted.

With a toss of her pale hair, Wyn replied, "Not really. We have the remains of a very small reserve, but it is certainly insufficient to rent a boat. Unless Arca has shoved more cash down her cleavage since then?"

"One time. I did it one time. It was a distraction. It's not my fault I forgot the money was in there," Zita muttered.

The vampire chortled. "Given your... general demeanor with people, I had thought the news reports were mistaken in claiming you were a stripper, but I would assume your actions attracted sufficient attention of whatever kind."

She rolled her eyes. "I'm not a stripper or a gang banger. We just haven't corrected the news reports because it's easier to go with the..." An idea hit, and her lips curled up in a smile as she remembered something one guard had said.

Zita leaned forward. "Guys, I think I have a plan, but we'll need to act fast and soon... it needs to be Sunday."

Everyone groaned, except Dmitri who whipped out a notebook.

"I had plans for this weekend," Wyn said.

Zita nodded. "Me too, but now, we'll have to delay at least some of them. We start later afternoon on Sunday."

The vampire frowned. "Can we move that back a couple hours to at least past sunset?"

"When we were doing some scouting, we found out they move prisoners Sunday afternoons from the base they use as a front for their secret prison." Zita shrugged.

Dmitri seemed startled. "We did? I am late to the party, as it were, then. How much of this have I missed?"

Andy gave a little cough. "A bit."

Zita nodded. "What he said. Plus, we have security codes good until Monday and access cards, if they haven't cancelled them yet. We can take some pictures while we're in to get more proof for the PR stuff, but our goal is to get Dream Auntie and Elle out."

"And my people," Dmitri said.

"It'd be better to do it all legal-like," Zita said.

The vampire nodded. "Incubus will starve in isolation, and if he only has access to one cellmate, he might take too much and accidentally harm them. They've already tried to weaponize Sheriff once. The four missing from my court have similar needs or possibilities for misuse, so they require release as well."

Zita exchanged glances with her friends. *Incubus was pretty close to starving when I saw him,* she admitted.

Wyn spoke. "Those are good points. Fine, they're out... but they may have to accept relocation to another country or something if they want to stay free. If they go home, DMS will just reacquire them."

He nodded.

With a deep breath, Zita continued. "Hopefully, the drones our friend left will let us know if anything happens, but we'll plan for Wingspan, Muse, and myself to wait at the prison tomorrow. Everyone else will gather on the boat, which is one of the details we'll have to figure out after everything opens on Saturday."

"You mean later today?" Andy asked, nodding toward a clock on the wall.

Zita groaned at the hour. "Sí. We need someone who'll rent us a boat without asking too many questions or expecting the kind of money we don't have, plus we need to line up the reporters or whatever."

"Why do you need a boat anyway? Wingspan can carry everyone," Dmitri asked.

With a sigh, Wyn admitted, "My spell can tell us where we need to go, but not where we are in relation to it. Wingspan can carry people in bird form, but it's some kind of interdimensional space. That means GPS is unreliable and there's no landmarks to memorize at sea. Given that we don't know where we are—"

Andy grunted. "I always know where I am. Just not where we are in relation to our target."

Wyn nodded at him. "Right. Wingspan can get us home at any time, but we don't know how close or far we are to, say, Bermuda versus San Juan. We'd basically have to fly circles hoping the spell's pointer would budge enough to let us locate it. If it is a boat and moving, that further complicates it. Once we have them, we'll need a place to put all the rescued people, unless they can fly or teleport themselves home once freed?"

Dmitri shook his head. "A couple can fly, but not over that much water."

"Not to mention, Wingspan's unique. If they see him, we give up any hope of getting plausible deniability to keep our butts out of prison. So, I got a great plan. You ready for the rest?" Zita added.

The others all wore dubious expressions.

Without giving them a chance to argue, she continued. "We go to the faux prison Sunday, late afternoon. Wingspan, you monitor those drone messages so we know if something happens before that."

He winced. "That's going to suck."

Wyn touched his arm. "I'll take a shift for you," she promised.

"Anyway, the three of us will follow the prison transfer transports. They might even have Sheriff and Incubus in them, which would make freeing them easier later. Once we find the prison, Wingspan and Muse can go get the ship. Muse will board while Wingspan brings in Dmitri's buddies and our computer friend."

"And Dmitri," the vampire said.

"You too, I guess, but you'll need a disguise. It should be after dark by then given that it takes a while to boat places. I'll scout out the prison while I'm waiting. Then we free Dream Auntie to avoid the people dying in the city, and Elle so she can get proper medical care, plus Dmitri's friends. When we're there, we take pictures that we can release to the PR folks." She dusted off her hands. "See? Simple. Efficient. We got this."

"And if the prisoner exchange doesn't happen?" Dmitri asked.

Zita shrugged. "Muse uses her spell while Wingspan sticks to man form and carts her around in a spiral to narrow down the location. It's a time suck, but we can try. If that fails too, we switch to plan C—try the original plan again next Sunday. It'll just be harder to scout because the code will have changed and all the key cards will be dead, if they're not already."

The vampire tilted his head. "Perhaps vigilantism is not as complicated as I had thought. This does sound simple."

Wyn groaned.

Andy moaned, "Famous last words."

Chapter Nineteen

Her wetsuit was giving her a wedgie.

Zita wiggled in place, her bare toes curling over the edge of a cliff. Thirty-five feet below, waves chopped the river's surface into myriad tiny peaks, sending salt spray upward, though none of it reached the woman standing above it. To her left, a handful of guaraná bushes hid what she knew was another drop, a less safe one onto rocks. Heat from the sun had her sweating in her rubbery garment.

"Why am I hesitating? I've made this dive before. And where's my partner? I don't cliff dive alone," she said, her attention returning to the drop.

A door appeared in the bright blue sky, and a woman stepped through. Clad in a soft orange dress suit and a matching hat, Dream Auntie looked around, drifting over to stand on the ground away from the edge of the cliff.

"Oh, if you're here, then I'm dreaming. That explains why I'd be considering a cliff dive without a buddy. Well, at least you're not interrupting a sex dream this time," Zita said.

"You can only imagine my relief at the same thing," Dream Auntie said. "I have come to—"

Zita waved a hand. "You need to bring my friend in on this. You know her. Magical girl. You've visited her dreams before, but you prefer to harass mine."

Dream Auntie harrumphed. "My energy is low these days. To walk her dreams requires a great more effort."

"Well, I'm not talking unless you're telling me something direct." The water drew Zita's gaze again, and she watched it until the other woman growled.

With a gesture, Dream Auntie opened an archway beside herself, white cane covered in tumbling roses. "I will invite her here, then, but it is not me to blame if she doesn't come."

"That's what he said and why it didn't work out for them," Zita joked.

Dream Auntie stared at her. The landscape around them faded. "If you are done, may I speak now?"

Zita grumbled. "Fine. You could've let the cliffs stay. I'm almost certain that diving would've been safe."

"Not until you know what you leap from," her companion replied. "Now, I must tell you—"

Wyn stepped through the portal in her Muse guise. "Hello? Ah, I had been hoping to catch you! Can we have a name to call you?"

"Are you actually my friend or a figment of my brain? If you're a figment, Dream Auntie here will probably make you go away like everything else," Zita said.

Throwing her hands up in the air, Dream Auntie said, "My name is Linda! Linda Mwangi. I have little time and you people do not allow me to speak! Will you and this stubborn woman listen now?"

"Yes, it's really me. It should be fascinating to compare notes on our respective interpretations of this shared oneiric experience." Wyn grinned at Zita, eyes twinkling. Turning to Dream Auntie—Linda—she continued. "Of course. Though I am curious if Mwangi is a common surname? We met one not long ago."

Her eyes dark and intent, Dream Auntie glanced at her. "Did you now? It is not uncommon."

"Big words. It's you. I don't think like that. Chido," Zita said.

Wyn shrugged. "Technically, we saw two Mwangis. One was the doctor, and the other was a grave."

"A doctor! My sister always wished to be such. Tell me of them. Who was on the tombstone?" Linda leaned forward.

Her voice gentle, Wyn said, "The tombstone said Patricia Wanjiku Mwangi." She listed the dates carved on it.

Closing her eyes, Linda put her hand over her heart and bowed her head. "That was the name of my sister and our birthday. Tell me of the medic?"

Wyn replied, "Dr. Mwangi runs a free medical clinic in the Brazilian mountains for the local indigenous people not too far from the grave. We do not know if Patricia was related or not."

Zita's memory sparked. "He has a similar accent to yours when he speaks English. It's a lot less noticeable in Portuguese for some reason."

"Can you tell me any more of him?" As she lifted her head, Linda dropped her hands to her lap, curling her fingers into tight balls.

Her eyes distant, Wyn shrugged. "We spent very little time together, and he was not chatty. Nor welcoming. He wanted us to leave before we brought trouble to his quiet clinic, as he said that metahumans attract other metahumans and misfortune."

"He is not wrong," Linda said. "Would you know the full name that this wise doctor is called?"

Wyn stared into the distance, her gaze unfocused in a way that meant she was accessing her prodigious memory. "His medical school diploma gave his name as Patrick Irungu Mwangi."

Her gaze distant, Linda drifted from the ground. "It is possible. He could be... I wish I could see him."

Wyn shrugged and snapped her fingers. An illusion of the doctor formed.

Linda inhaled. Her eyes seemed misty.

"How do you do that?" Zita asked. "It's not even your dream. It used to be mine, but Drea—Linda here's been messing with it. As usual."

Her friend shrugged. "This is like lucid dreaming. We can do what we think we can do. Please don't test it out."

Zita wrinkled her nose. "You're no fun. I can wait, though."

"Ah. I do not know for certain, but he greatly resembles my late uncle, brother of my maternal parent. Tell him… tell him that Linda Nyambura Mwangi says he has grown into a fine man. If he wishes to meet with me, I would welcome him."

Zita bit her tongue and exchanged a glance with her friend.

As if sensing what she was struggling to articulate—possible, given her friend's telepathy—Wyn's tone was very gentle. "We can do that. What if he doesn't want to meet you?"

"It was my wrongdoing that drove my twin from me. If this doctor is who I think and would forgive me for my slowness in understanding, I would walk across a million dreams to speak with him. If he will not, then nothing will change from the current future. Either you will fail and I and those of the port will die, or you will succeed, and I will become a tool among the machinery until I too break." Linda hung her head.

"Okay…" Zita said.

Linda held up a hand and intoned, "My time runs short. Listen closely. When the road forks, you must not choose between them, but take both. Manacles are not necessary when the mind is enchained, and only horror can follow that road if freedom comes while the shackled walk. The boxes are important, and if you miss them or do not trust enough, sharks will feast among the wreckage."

She speared Zita with a glance.

"I will be direct. If the song ends before you reach the box or you jump more than twice with it, there will be more death than just yours." With each word, Linda faded more and more until she disappeared at the end of her dire pronouncement.

As the dream fell apart around them, Zita managed two words. "Drama, much?"

***

A few hours later, sweat trickled down her spine as Zita climbed up the partially constructed wall of a two-story house. For once, her attention wasn't with the exercise or on the man who had been outpacing her for the past hour. She'd suggested a quick free run, hoping to enjoy the movement and ask him questions, but she found herself curiously unwilling to broach the topic.

Given the option to choose their meeting place, Freelance had chosen an empty construction site in New Jersey. A two-story building stood partially erected, the bones in place, but the marks of weather on the wall studs told her that no one had worked on the building for a while. That said, it had a nice screen of trees and enough walls up to hide them from curious eyes... Any that were up in the pre-dawn hours staring at abandoned sites, anyway.

With a sigh, she boosted herself onto the floor and got to her feet. Before she'd gone any farther on the mostly complete flooring, she saw him waiting for her. "I thought since I have to go soon, we were doing up to the attic and down again one last time, winner gets to pick the next location?"

Clad in his usual monochromatic armor, Freelance tilted his head at her. "Distracted. Problem?"

When even the man who rarely spoke made you talk about something... Zita braced herself and tried to think of a way to ease into the topic. So, of course, she began babbling. "Yes. So, you can say no to this because it's a long shot. Which you're good at but that's beside the point. This doesn't have anything to do with you and me, and I know it's a big ask."

His body angled sideways, tension seeping into it.

She forced herself to focus, "Anyway, I was wondering. Do you know somebody who could loan us a ten-person boat on Sunday? And maybe drive it around the Bermuda Triangle, afternoon and nighttime frame? Backup that doesn't kill people would be good too."

Utter stillness came over him. She could've mistaken him for a strangely sexy Kevlar statue were it not for the faintest movement of his chest as he breathed.

Great. I get to be a wanted felon and possibly lose my… whatever he is all in the same weekend. She swallowed. "If you can give me the name of someone who'd loan us a boat without bringing you guys up, that'd be fine. I think you should say no to everything else."

He tapped his goggles, and they whirred. "Why?"

Without meaning to, her fake accent came out thick in the words. "If we get identified, and we probably will, our reputations will be trashed. We'll be at the top of the US Most Wanted list for very illegal actions. As opposed to now, when we're close to the bottom of the list. We'll definitely be making some very big enemies. You don't need this kind of trouble, and I don't want to bring it down on you. Oh, and it doesn't pay, either."

Something in that tangled mess of words stole some of the tension from him. "What crimes?"

"Technically? We don't know, but we're trying to keep things as legal as possible. If we're unlucky, it'll be assault, plus kidnapping, destruction of government property, maybe treason, plus possibly a bit of international piracy? If we're lucky, we'll at least have plausible deniability." Zita shrugged.

"Target?"

She hesitated before answering. Finally, she admitted, "A DMS prison. We're pretty certain they're operating illegally, but we don't have time to let legit channels catch up, especially since they got somebody highly placed to hand-wave it all."

The heat of his gaze, even through his goggles, seemed to burn her. "Plan?"

"We have several different plans, but not enough information about our target to narrow down which one to use. We got a more legal route we're hitting up, too, but we're on a tight timeline to avoid the explosion. So, we're trying to lessen the risks where we can."

"Explosion?"

"Crazy but true, there's this metahuman who sees the future and gives super vague warnings. If we don't do something, a big port is going to go boom and a lot of people will die. Other than telling us who we had to rescue, that's all the detail she gave us. We're also saving a few others. One's someone I promised to help a while back, and the others are the price for another person's help."

He grunted. "Too high risk. No pay. On standby anyway. Sorry."

Although part of her wondered what someone kept mercenaries on call for, she exhaled in relief. "Gracias a Dios. I didn't want to drag you and yours into it, but you're a grown man and can make your own choices. I wouldn't have asked but we need a boat and our original backup had to bail. He also had our plan and most of our scouting details."

"Foolishness," the mercenary said, turning toward her.

"I know, right? No worries, we'll figure something out."

Her pocket buzzed raucously. Zita checked her phone.

Wyn had texted. "Your brother sent you a message about a last-minute job he needs you on now, code bad decisions?"

"Carajo. I guess I got to go. Something came up at work and I'm going to need the funds if we get in as much trouble as I think we will." She paused. Hated that she wanted to ask. Loathed the way the words stuck in her throat. "We're still okay, right?"

He nodded.

Zita set her hand on his arm. Without thinking, she gave his bicep a light stroke with her fingers. "Thank you. Hasta luego, I hope."

Freelance glanced down at her hand and then at her face. "Buccaneer Fortress Marina. Bermuda. Gator De Rocher. Boat. Bribable."

"Gracias." She stepped back, shifted to a golden eagle, and flew off.

* * *

Assistance came from unexpected, cheesy sources.

Squeezing a meeting in between Zita's work appointments, Wyn and Zita paused on the docks near a seafood restaurant overlooking the Chesapeake Bay and a marina of expensive boats. Water rustled and reflected painfully bright sunlight. Four figures waited on an outside wooden patio, though only one table was set up for dining.

Her expression drawn, Brie shredded some kind of biscuit over a tiny porcelain plate, a napkin in her lap. She was clearly a masochist, as she wore one of those narrow skirts that lacked pockets and didn't allow any freedom of movement, coupled with another pair of very high heels. The silky, short-sleeved blouse seemed sensible enough. Brie's companions were three very obvious bodyguards; they wore bulletproof vests under jackets that didn't hide their shoulder holsters. They had to be sweating to death, given the heat.

Cautioning Wyn to hang back, Zita scouted briefly. The area was less busy than she would've expected, but no one seemed out of place. A sign on the restaurant announced it was closed for a private party. Only a few cars were visible in the parking lot. Most seemed the kind of battered vehicle parked far enough from the entrance that she assumed they belonged to the staff.

"It's weird meeting somewhere in the daylight in a public place," she muttered to Wyn as they finally approached the patio.

"You'll get no argument from me on that," Wyn said. She smoothed her clothing—unnecessarily, as her illusion never showed wrinkles or dirt.

As soon as she caught sight of them, Brie stood, striding forward and opening the door to the patio. A golden bracelet winked in the sunlight, shaped like a metallic spider wrapped around her wrist. "Thank goodness you contacted me! What have you heard about Rani?"

"Rani?" Worry broadcasting over their mental link, Wyn hurried to the other woman. "What about her? We haven't seen her since the club."

Her face crumpled. "You didn't know? I'd hoped you were calling to tell me you'd rescued her."

Zita had a sinking feeling she knew what was coming. "From?"

Wyn reached out and put her hand over Brie's. From the stricken expression on her face, her friend shared her suspicion. "Goddess, we had no idea. What happened?"

"She got separated from us at the club. When she didn't join me or contact us for bail, I started calling around. Headquarters verified that she's been arrested, but they've been unable to get lawyers or anyone else in to see her. They can't even confirm where she's being held. DMS is claiming she participated in a terrorist action and aren't allowing anyone to speak to her," Brie said.

"No manches! They might be able to push it and claim that drink she threw was assault, but they did shove her first," Zita said.

Wyn moaned. "Oh, no! I knew we should've taken you with us. DMS is why we wanted to meet with you."

Brie made a gesture to the bodyguards, and they retreated, two standing by the path Wyn and Zita had arrived from, and the third remaining by the restaurant door. After offering them seats at the only table set for dining, Brie coughed delicately. "Before we begin, I should tell you that given your unique position at the time, upper management at General Aetherics reviewed the security tapes from the New York store on the night of the riot. They have elected not to pursue any actions against you for the damage done to the store—assuming your cooperation with the Rani issue—of course."

Wyn frowned. *Why does everyone try to manipulate us?*

Too much awesome in one place? Zita narrowed her eyes. "My... what exactly do you mean by that?"

Brie rubbed her bracelet. "We need Rani released sooner rather than later. It's not just because I care for her. She's one of only two SNARC ball technicians in the world, and General Aetherics does not take her kidnapping lightly. They actually paid for this meeting and suggested the location so we can all flee more easily if DMS attacks."

"What do you mean we can all flee?" Zita asked. "You're probably safer away from us."

With a roll of her eyes, Brie said, "DMS has reviewed enough club footage to decide that I am a dangerous metahuman who assaulted multiple people. They're demanding that I surrender to their custody, despite the sworn statements of my bodyguards about what happened. Given my position and the lack of cooperation with Rani, General Aetherics is not inclined to allow this. I'm only still in the country because I'd hoped you would call, and I'm supposed to leave following this meeting. So. We're all in trouble together. What did you want to meet for if not to help Rani?"

"We'd hoped, given your position, that you'd be willing to release some information that was passed along to us about what DMS is doing. Failing that, suggest some contacts who would be sympathetic enough to take our data and disseminate it," Wyn said.

Zita added, "We know a reporter or two, but we figured you'd have, like, real resources and contacts."

Brie sniffed. "Is that all? We regularly send out press releases and so on. I can have every major news organization on it in a heartbeat. It'd help if they could interview some sympathetic people and see some of the abuses upfront. Assuming there are some. What is this story you want me to put out there for you?"

"DMS is kidnapping metahumans and searching or seizing their belongings with no warrants. They're also instigating events to manipulate press around metahumans to make it seem like we're all criminals. Once they're in custody, they disappear. No lawyers. No phone calls. No visitors. You've experienced this yourself. Poor Rani's a victim of it now," Wyn said.

The bubbly woman steepled her fingers. "Before I use my contacts, however, I have to have data that won't get us sued if it's discovered we're the source. Do you have any evidence that can be given to the press? I don't have any I can publicize as I don't wish to announce my powers nor do I have any of the recordings from the club to back up my innocence."

Wyn tapped a finger against her lips. "We might be able to get you copies of those videos."

"That would be a help. So, what else can you give me?" Anticipation lit Brie's expression.

Zita went for the big event first. "You know the recent New York protest that they said turned into a riot? It was all a trap. They had DMS agents waiting and a ringer in the crowd who started trouble. Nobody else even joined in before DMS kicked down their hiding places and started arresting and tear gassing everyone."

"Do you have proof? I believe you, but General Aetherics can't seem to support conspiracy theories or rely solely on testimony by an illegal vigilante. Were there any coherent videos?" Brie raised her brows.

Thinking back, Zita frowned. "There was a reporter, Reggie with Goode News or something like that. His camera got broken in the scuffle, but they probably got footage before that. A bunch of people were waving their phones, so there's that too."

Brie typed something into her phone. "My staff can follow up on that. Is that all?"

Withdrawing a business card from her purse, Wyn set it on the table. "You may or may not be aware of the lawsuits brought by Remus Arroyo Guzman and his nonprofit organization for metahuman business professionals regarding illegal violations of civil rights by DMS. Those would be a matter of public record, and his lawyer's willing to talk about it. They've also been repeatedly raiding the Danz Mizer nightclub and the owner's home. Here's the information for the lawyer representing both. I've also heard rumors that a third party will be speaking up soon about illegal search and seizures as well."

Wyn cleared her throat and continued. "I spoke briefly earlier to Remus' attorney, and she agreed to give you a thumb drive with that and our other evidence so far on it. I have to warn you though... we may have found a copy of a call between a senator and a DMS scientist, discussing what sounds like human trafficking."

Color fled Brie's face. "And they have my Rani? They can't be allowed to sell her. Do you know where they're keeping her?"

Wyn and Zita exchanged uneasy glances.

"We can guess," Wyn finally said.

Brie closed her eyes for a second before pulling out her phone. Her fingers flew over it. "Great, I'll go with you and bring a camera-person so we can get some footage of the conditions or at least an establishing background shot to help pique interest."

"That's going to be hard to do. They have a faux prison that they use as a holding facility, but Rani's probably already been shipped to their main penitentiary," Wyn said.

"So?" Brie didn't glance up from her phone.

Zita said, "We'd need a boat to take anyone there other than ourselves. Wingspan's not exactly subtle when he's transporting people."

Brie's eyes widened, and she stared at them for a moment. "You know where both prisons are?"

Zita bit her lip. "Roughly?"

Holding up a manicured finger, Brie said. "Give me a second." She typed furiously on her phone.

Somehow, Zita's knee was jiggling again. *Who's she texting?*

Wyn touched her knee and returned to sitting serenely, hands folded in her lap. *I don't know, but I don't want to scan her if I don't have to. It seems rude.*

Zita bit her tongue to keep from commenting.

"I'm just checking on something," Brie said, still typing. "I can rent a boat for you and even crew or captain it for you. However, I've got two conditions. One, I'm coming with, and I'm bringing a camera person and our bodyguards. Since I'm no fighter, I'll happily stay with the boat, and my guards will protect me so you can focus on whatever you'll be doing. Two, you have to promise to find Rani."

"You can't. It's going to be dangerous and, uh... questionable?" Zita said. *Why does everyone want to come on the stupid dangerous missions? How did an attempt to find a missing girl snowball into jailbreaking eight people from a federal prison?*

Let me handle it, Wyn soothed. The witch smiled at Brie. "Your PR expertise is invaluable, and if you can turn that toward helping our cause, that would be the greatest aid of all, though the funds to rent a boat would also be appreciated. Given your position, you can't afford to risk your job or anything else given the delicate nature of this particular mission. However, we can promise to do our best to find Rani. You have my personal promise on that."

Brie glanced up. Her face and words were icy business, the friendly bubbliness gone. "Rani is not only very important to my company, but she's also my girlfriend, and I couldn't bear knowing that I failed to help when I had the option. The cost-benefit analysis is mine to do, and I am the one who decides what is too expensive. While I will review their efforts later, I have complete faith in my very excellent staff's ability to see that your information gets to all the appropriate persons. In contrast, I'm not giving a blank check to a bunch of masked vigilantes with no surety behind you."

For once, Wyn blinked. "But your job…"

"You'd be surprised how often someone decides kidnapping a SNARC ball technician is easier than waiting their turn in the queue and paying the bill. While it's generally not within my purview, these are not unforeseen circumstances, nor are my actions out of reasonable bounds. Security staff and upper management discussed acceptable measures prior to this meeting. General Aetherics permits considerable latitude with adequate justification, and I'm using mine. However, I concede that it will be dangerous. I won't bring a camera person, and I will request only bodyguards who are also qualified ship's crewmen." Brie tapped her foot.

Wyn bit her lip.

Sí, I can see how you're handling her, Zita sent. She wasn't certain how to react, but she was pretty certain laughing would get her in trouble.

Brie's phone chimed. She peered at it. "Ah, the gears are in motion. I need to see the rough area we're going to, though."

Wyn sighed. "Fine. I'll check for Rani's location, since we should verify that before we drag you into anything." She unrolled her map and spread it over the table. After anchoring the corners with salt and pepper shakers, she sighed. "Hold the edges on your side, Arca. It's a bit windier here than I'd like, so it might blow the arrow off a little."

Eyes wide, Brie nodded.

Zita held down the corners.

After a few murmured words, Wyn dangled her now-glowing arrowhead over the map. It pointed to the same spot in the Bermuda Triangle.

Something clicked, and Brie lowered her phone. "Sorry, it'll help me estimate gas and stuff. Probably best to pick up a boat in Bermuda to minimize time getting to there." Her fingers flew over the phone. "Incoming."

The air snapped.

Remus appeared on the patio. He glanced at Zita and Wyn, and took a step back. Dismay shone on his too-pretty face. "I know my lawyer told me to expect this job, but..."

Her face like stone, Brie held up a hand. "Did you bring me an envelope?"

He nodded and handed her a manila one from a large pocket in the front of his shirt, hidden by the cut of the opening.

"Thank you." Brie pulled out a memory card and took a picture of that and the business card. After stuffing both into the envelope and sealing it, she handed it and another business card to Remus. "Please take this to that address, for Montrez in Marketing. He'll know what to do and see that your invoice is paid as usual."

The speedster paused, his gaze not quite on Wyn and Zita. "My apologies that I haven't been able to do more, but... I can't afford another lawsuit or to be put in prison."

With a snap of air, he was gone.

Brie exhaled. "Expensive, but worth it if it gets us to Rani faster. How long do we have?"

"Not long enough," Wyn said, and they got back to planning.

Chapter Twenty

If the tarty forty-something cougar in the lingerie didn't back off with the disparaging remarks, Zita was going to lose the battle to hold her tongue.

Elbow-deep in a wall, Zita double-checked her fixes to the wiring with a flashlight while silently grumbling to herself. Since the old alarm—installed less than a year ago—showed every sign of having been yanked out, she had no wish to have Quentin's company blamed if the house burned down, no matter how annoying the homeowner was. She didn't want the woman dead, either, just not hovering nearby questioning every movement. Without interference, she would've finished up the previous day instead of having to come back again Sunday morning.

If I get this done soon, I should have time for a couple hours' nap before I have to break into the DMS prison. As she finished her examination, she pulled her arms out of the wall and was fitting the new control panel into place when she heard high heels approaching.

Again.

Wonder what her problem will be now? I'd call in someone else, but she'd get the wrong idea about them since they're all ex-Marines. Quentin owes me so big for this. I can't believe he slept with this person. Zita braced herself.

"Are you certain you're qualified to do this?" came a whiny voice behind her.

"Yes, I have all the appropriate certifications. You saw my ID yesterday and earlier today, a few times," she said through gritted teeth as she tested the connections were tight.

A sniff. "Do you?"

Zita swallowed the first several comments she wanted to make and swapped her tools for the items she needed. As she repaired the wallboard, she said, "Yes."

Warmth flooded her mind. Wyn spoke over party line. *They're moving the prisoners early! How fast can you get to my place? Andy's already here.*

Biting her lip, Zita thought as she smoothed the wall around the new panel. *I'm twenty out from your house, and I have to dump Quentin's van somewhere friendly. This house doesn't qualify as that. Do we have the time for me to get there? Or do I need to ditch it somewhere closer to here?*

There was a pause, and she had the impression her friends were probably discussing how to answer before Wyn finally spoke again. *My place is fine. The drone showed transport vans arriving. I doubt they can load them before you get here, but to make sure, Andy and I will go now. I'll leave the surveillance drone feed showing on the laptop in my basement so you can teleport right in. Since we'll be following the vans, and there's only one highway in and out, I'm certain you'll find us if we need to follow them.*

Sold. She hopped down the ladder and folded it.

"Are you certain you should be doing this without adult supervision? Maybe Quinton should come check your work." the woman behind her asked. She tapped her foot.

Zita was still steaming. She tried to modulate her tone. "Lady, I'm almost thirty and have been doing this for years. I'm sure *Quentin* is busy."

The homeowner blinked. "Really? You look like a teenager."

After picking up her tools, the trash, and ladder, Zita headed out the door. She congratulated herself mentally for being polite. Over her shoulder she called out, "I get that a lot, but I heard older people can't tell the ages of younger folks very well, especially once they hit sixty. So you've got lots of company. The new panel should be pretty good, but I want the wall to dry before we test it too much given how the last one fell out. I'll come back tomorrow, but it should be usable after that. See you then, ma'am."

From behind her, she heard a hiss, like an angry cat.

***

With a little driving that even Zita had to admit was aggressive, she reached Wyn's house in fifteen minutes. After parking the work van, she stripped off her coveralls and t-shirt, leaving those and her tools locked up in the vehicle. She put on the mask she'd stashed in a pocket, then teleported to Wyn's basement. Once she took off her shoes—unfortunately, the ones she'd worn for work were too big for her pockets—she shifted to a golden eagle and teleported to the sky visible on the computer.

Heat and humidity made each flap take extra effort until she found a thermal comfortable to ride on, well above the drone's view. She scanned the ground below for signs of activity.

I'm here. Scouting, Zita sent.

Wyn replied, *Good. Can you keep watch? We cannot monitor the drone feed from here. By the way, I finally got through to Dr. Mwangi before we saw the transfer. I didn't mention her abilities, but he said he'd take her in and make sure she gets the appropriate care for a coma patient. He thinks she might be family.*

Excellent, Zita thought, before movement below drew her attention.

Her first circle took her over the fenced compound of the faux jail. One van was parked by the kitchen of the aboveground prison. The open doors of the loading dock let her see another van's nose protruding, and a third one idled outside that building. A fourth vehicle, an SUV with blackened windows, was parked but running in the lot nearby. Smoke leaked out of the top of one window in a thin stream.

As she widened the circle, lifting higher up still, she found her friends, huddled in a grove by the only road in or out.

No hay bronca, I got this, she replied. Movement caught her attention, and she lost some altitude to ensure she was identifying everything correctly. She swore mentally.

Even though she hadn't meant to share her annoyance, apparently her friends heard it.

Andy asked, *Any reason for the swearing?*

Zita glared at the men sliding the long, rectangular steel boxes into the van by the kitchen she'd escaped the other day. *They're loading coffins into one of the vans.*

Dismay and exclamations came back at her words. Wyn sent, *Can you mark the vans so we don't lose them if they hit traffic?*

Get out my climbing chalk. I'll come by and pick it up. Zita dove, as if chasing prey, and landed by her friends. She shifted to her Arca form and held out her hand. "Two coffins. They closed the van door afterward, so I'm guessing they're done with that van and should move out soon."

Andy kept a careful watch on the road. Wyn handed Zita the chalk and sighed. "I couldn't reach Jerome or Dmitri, but Brie said her people are ready. Jerome sent her more goodies to release. She's also got the boat."

"Not much choice but to go without the guys, then. Hopefully, we'll get a spare minute later to get them," Zita said.

Without looking, Andy snorted. "Not likely with our luck. So much for having a plan."

After shifting, this time to a crow, Zita launched herself skyward. She banked and darted through the trees toward the buildings.

A minute or two later, she was on the roof of the van idling outside the below-ground prison, dropping the chalk on it. The van roof burned under her claws as she laboriously drew a squiggly shape on the roof. Bird claws were not meant for art, but the cameras nearby meant she couldn't risk shifting. Peeking down, she glanced through the windows into the interior.

She sent a quick update. *The ones by the loading dock have metas loaded in the back. They all look stoned, plus they're chained and the orange gas is everywhere. Tiger's in one and he has special steel mittens. I marked that vehicle with a star.*

Noted. So, the vans by the loading dock are the live prisoners, and the other one has the dead. What's in the SUV?

Bored DMS guys smoking, based on what I saw flying past, Zita sent.

Once she'd finished there, she flew to the vehicle containing the coffins. She landed. The cameras here didn't seem angled to catch the roof, so she risked shapeshifting to a raccoon. She'd gotten one long, straight chalk line done before the wind threw hot smoke over her.

As the reek of rotten eggs, chemicals, and blood rolled over her, Zita gagged. Her eyes watered and her stomach roiled.

The chalk fell, broke, and rolled.

She scampered after it, scooping up the bigger chunk.

Engines revved. The vehicle jerked forward.

Startled, she staggered, releasing the chalk in favor of staying upright. She switched to a crow and fluttered off. *They're moving. I marked the coffin one with a single line, but I didn't have time to do a good job. Also, I lost the chalk.*

Fortunately for you, Wyn carries a supply of it for me. You can use the orange kind, Andy sent, his voice dry.

Once she got high enough, she switched back to a golden eagle. Zita scoped out the area, altering her path so she could follow the vehicles.

All four were in motion, proceeding in single file toward the exit, with the SUV in the lead. The loading dock door was closed.

She sent, *They're moving out. You're ready?*

Yes, we're going to follow. Andy will carry me, and I'll have an illusion up so we look like clouds, Wyn replied.

Zita's beak fell open, and she chirped with amusement. *No shortage of clouds here. Keep off the storms, though, Andy, since I didn't get to mark the vans particularly well.*

He sent distracted agreement.

At least this part of our plan is working, Zita thought.

***

Fluffy clouds flying suspiciously low and a tiring golden eagle stalking them apparently went unnoticed by the people in the DMS vehicles. Even without Zita's marks on two of the roofs, they were easy enough to follow, first as they sped down the paved rural road, and then when they clung together in a group on the highway through the Everglades.

The real issue came when the coffin van peeled off from the other three and took an exit leading south thirty minutes later.

Wyn sent a flurry of commands. *Follow the coffins! We'll keep after these three. If they split up, we'll try to follow the one you marked with the star. Once we come to a stop at the boat, we'll let you know. I can use my phone to send a short live stream that you can use to teleport to us from my basement again.*

Never split the party! Andy argued. *It never ends well.*

Too late now. Zita had already broken off from the highway, praying that this road had a slower speed limit so she could coast more.

Andy swore.

***

When the van blew out a tire and rattled to the side of the road twenty minutes later, Zita sent up a silent prayer of thanks. She might be fit, but her bird forms weren't built to allow travel at top speed indefinitely, especially against the wind. Quietly, she landed behind a tree, switching to a mottled tortoiseshell cat. Her stomach growled.

She was still sore from the long flight but running as a cat stretched different muscles than just her arms and back. She eyed the DMS vehicle.

The back doors were shut, but one of the two men in the vehicle hopped out and removed tools from a small space in the rear of the van. He grumbled as his plain blue workmen's uniform darkened with sweat in the heat of the Florida summer sun. The guy started working to replace the destroyed tire with the spare.

If I can sneak inside when he opens the doors again, I can hitch a ride wherever they're going and hide behind the coffins. As much as it'll be creepy to hang with the bodies, I can't exhaust myself now. I've still got to scout out the prison once we're sure where it is. She snuck closer, until she was concealed in a riotously blooming firespike bush.

She sent a quick update. *Guys, we got a delay here. A tire blew out on the van, so I don't know how much longer before they hit the burial ground. If it is burial and not a dump-in-the-ocean situation. I'm going to hitch a ride when I get a chance. Birds aren't the best form for a long chase, but anything else would be too obvious. How are you guys? Are they at a harbor yet?*

They seem disinclined to speed. Right now, their route leads toward a major population center, so perhaps they are taking them to a large ship that requires deeper ports, Wyn sent back.

Andy spoke. *I still think we shouldn't have split up.*

Locating their cemetery will literally allow us to show the press where the bodies are buried as well as granting families closure. Not to mention, Linda said we needed to take both forks when we came to them. That could refer to the vehicles separating, Wyn sent.

I still have a bad feeling about this. Foreboding filled Andy's end of the link.

That's because this is probably the riskiest thing we've ever tried, Zita sent. *I got your back, mano.*

His tone was bitter. *Unless I'm with Caroline.*

Buey! Can we not argue about the tool right now? Zita tensed, switching to a hummingbird and gulping down nectar from the flowers while she waited for her chance.

The guard finished putting on the tire, and attached the remains of the old one to the rear door of the van. Finally, he picked up the jack and other implements and opened the van.

She zipped into the dark interior.

Even though she'd been nowhere near him, the guard swatted at his head as she passed, but didn't look up.

Zita hid in the narrow space under one of the coffins. To keep from exhausting herself as a hummingbird and to allow movement in the dark interior more easily, she switched to a raccoon. The air had a thick quality to it and an unfamiliar scent. To her surprise, she couldn't smell the dead at all.

Once the tools were stowed, the guard slammed the door shut. It clicked.

Heaving a relieved breath, she took a moment to assess her ride.

The interior of the van was painted white on all sides and lacked any padding. The floor vibrated slightly with the motion of the vehicle. Road noise and the humming machinery obscured whatever conversation was happening in the front seat, reducing it to the low rumble of male voices. Four special racks were built into the reinforced sides. The coffins sat in two of them, wrapped in thick, industrial chains bolted to the floor and secured by heavy padlocks. The boxes themselves were plain metal, with utilitarian handles and several long scratches and small dents on the outside.

The incongruity bothered her. *You'd think if they're worried about the coffins rolling around, the chains would go to the walls instead. That won't hold them in place, though I guess it'd keep the lids from popping open. You'd think they'd be sealed well enough to avoid that, though. The racks have stuff to hold the coffins in place anyway, but maybe it's a safety thing for crashes? In any case, are they reusing the boxes to move bodies? They aren't new with all that damage to them.*

Unsettled at the oddities, she frowned and kept examining the interior as the vehicle began moving.

Copper pipes ran from a large, humming black box near the front and connected to the two coffins, with the pipes for the unoccupied racks covered by hinged white plastic caps. Above the box, floodlights were dark and separated by a tiny black bubble of glass. A tiny LED threw a bloody glow over the interior of the vehicle.

Her eyes went back to the coffins. *With those chains, I can't pick the lock without shifting back to Arca, but maybe the little paper at the end can tell me what—who—is inside.*

With a deep breath, she belly-crawled beneath the coffin to the marker. Her nose wrinkled and her throat itched. When she reached the end, she wiggled the top half of her body out, intending to climb on top.

Brilliant white lights flashed on, blinding her, and she darted back under cover. The light on the camera turned from red to green.

With the extra illumination, she could see the black bubble was a camera. It also revealed the orange mist seeping from the capped pipes where they connected to the coffins. The gas pooled on the floor of the vehicle. Around her.

Zita swore internally and squeezed herself between the wall and one of the boxes, trying to lift both her head above the level of the gas and maintain her balance. Her mind whirled as she tried to keep each breath shallow. *Of course. There's no need to use meta gas on the dead. The coffins are a ruse. This is why Sheriff didn't remember how she got from one place to another.*

She paused to focus on party line, *Guys, what if there's more than one prison? Or multiple boats? The people in the coffins are alive.*

Are you serious or are you just bored? Andy sent.

She kept herself from growling with effort. *I wouldn't joke about this. Not while we're in the middle of it.*

That's awful. I hope they're at least asleep or something. Horror tinged his reply.

Probably. I haven't heard any movement or yelling from the boxes, so I'm hoping they're out cold, she answered.

He sent back a wash of concern and discomfort. *As much as I hate to go against gaming wisdom, splitting up earlier was the right call. We need you to find out where they're taking those prisoners in case it's wherever Linda is. We have to find her before the port goes boom.*

I'll skim the men we're following to see if I can figure out their destination. It might take a few minutes if they're focused on anything other than that. Are you safe for the moment, Zita? Wyn sent.

Her muscles, already tired from the hard flight earlier, protested the unnatural position she had to keep to avoid falling into the fog. *Uncomfortable, but okay. At some point they'll run out of Florida to drive to,* she sent back.

Wyn sent acknowledgement. Party line disappeared, leaving Zita alone in her own mind.

The lights shut off as well, the LED changing from green to blinking red.

I didn't get to tell them that I got a face full of the gas. Will I turn into me if I breathe too much of that stuff? I've never fallen out of animal shape before from exhaustion, so it's possible I could be stuck as a raccoon for a while. Well, I'll make a run for it as soon as they open the doors. Zita huffed.

Horns blaring, the van slowed suddenly and took a hard turn to the right.

She scrabbled to keep her grip, her tail lashing.

The floodlights flared to life again. The red light changed to a blinking green one. This time, there was a loud click and the caps on the top pipes fell open. Orange billowed out with a whooshing sound, rising higher and higher until it covered both the coffin and the top of Zita's head.

I can't move without being seen. Maybe if I stay still, the lights and the extra gas will cut out and then I can risk doing something. Teleporting is out. I'd never find the van again, she thought with dismay. She buried her face in her fur to filter as much as possible.

After a minute or two of waiting, her arm didn't feel as sore. It was delightfully fluffy though. Almost pillow-like. Zita fought to focus and breathe as little as possible.

Her eyelids drooped. *That flight must've really taken it out of me.*

Her paws slipped, and she was distantly aware of her body falling to the floor, the sudden pain jolting her awake for a few seconds.

Flopping awkward onto her side, Zita panted and stared through the shifting fog at the blinking light of the camera. *I need to move. Get out of here.*

Her eyes slid shut and she slept.

Chapter Twenty-One

The world was fuzzy and smelled distinctly like a day-old Cubano sandwich, rancid mayonnaise, and cheap printer toner.

"Wake up, and hurry. Remember others' talents may soothe the savage heart and stop the fiery flow." The soft, African-accented woman's voice faded as Zita fought her way through a horrible headache to consciousness.

Who puts mayo on a Cubano? And why does my mouth taste like sweaty feet smell? Need to move, Zita thought hazily. She tried to move, but she was stuffed into an unnatural position in a tight place, with her feet crammed into her stomach. A dark, hot place. She caught herself panting to try to cool off. When she wiped her sweaty paws on the walls, they felt like thick, coarse plastic. Whatever she was inside was narrower at the bottom than at the top, and shaped elliptically.

The world shuddered and bounced along unevenly.

As she fought to kick her sluggish brain into action, her struggles to move became more frenzied until she got her feet down so she no longer kicked herself with every motion and could move more freely. Zita squinted and was irritated to see that everything was black, save for where painfully bright light leaked in from somewhere above. She growled. *I'm in some kind of cage!*

"It's waking up!" someone said.

Another person growled, "Move faster!"

"You try carrying it up this hill fast! It's heavy!" the first voice protested.

The second one growled, "Fine, let's use the cart."

The bouncing sped up, jostling her from side to side and adding a layer of nausea to the pain before subsiding as her plastic prison was placed on a flat surface. A moment later, an engine roared to life, but it had the higher-pitched, unconvinced growl of a golf cart or motor scooter.

Pushing herself onto her hind legs, Zita reached up to see if the top would come off. It appeared to be both anchored solidly and of the same plastic as the rest of her prison. Jagged, uneven holes the size of a dime were punched at irregular intervals a few inches down from the top. Carefully bending down the jagged, inward-pointing edges of the holes, she inserted her front paws to stay in place as she rose on her hind legs to scope out the area.

Behind them, a couple of utilitarian buildings and what looked like a guard post squatted at the edge of a dock. All of them had the kind of ridged, water-conserving roofs she associated with Bermuda. Desultory tropical vegetation clung grimly to life around the buildings. Given that and the sea breeze she could catch through the air holes, she assumed she'd slept through whatever boat trip had been necessary. Seabirds screamed high overhead, but otherwise it was quiet.

Her plastic prison tilted slightly as the vehicle ascended something, the engine developing a whine. She switched to another spot to try to see their destination.

They were ascending a steep trail up a pitched, rocky slope with the kind of dark rock she associated with volcanoes. Partway up the mountain, a high wall corralled a series of buildings, decorated with barbed wire along the top. White clouds streamed from the smaller group of buildings; she assumed it was a power plant based on the electrical grid tower. The bigger edifice looked like someone had transplanted the ugliest prison they could find onto a slope too small to contain it. Half of it jutted out over the ocean, supported by five long pillars, above a hundred-foot drop where part of the volcano must have sheered away at some point.

On either side of the gate, machine gun turrets posed menacingly, with a man seated at each. One spun to point at them as they approached. Incongruously, striped umbrellas in cheery primary colors shaded the gunners. Weirdly, at both corners of the visible exterior wall, a truck was parked, pointed toward the ocean. Tarps covered box-shaped cargo. Above everything else, dark gray smoke trickled from the summit, confirming her earlier guess about the type of mountain.

Guess I found the secret prison. Why did they build it like that? It's already on the side of a volcano. Does it need to be any more unstable? Wyn can find Andy and me anywhere on the planet, so I just have to delay anything bad until they get here to help. Experimentally, she prodded the emptiness in her mind where party line usually dwelled. *Guys?*

No answer.

The vehicle entered the outer walls.

Her container jolted as she leaned forward to try to see better.

"I see paws! It's trying to get out!" The first guy yelped far too loudly before something hit her cage.

The container tilted, falling from the cart.

It hit the ground or a rock or something hard and rolled, throwing Zita around in the close confines.

A yowl escaped her. She curled into a ball to try to keep from throwing up and protect herself as much as possible.

The first voice said, "Are we certain it's a meta and not rabid?"

"The doctor said a real raccoon would've died from the amount of knockout gas it inhaled. If Chaniclas wants the animal, she can have it. Pick it up carefully, and let's find out where she wants it before it busts out. You can carry it once we're there, but I'll keep an eye on it to ensure it behaves." The second person sounded much calmer and more reasonable. She really didn't like him.

Despite the battering she'd taken, she forced herself up and tried to pry the lid off. All she managed was to bend one tiny bit enough to find that something secured the lid to the rest of her cage, and it was securely fastened on all sides.

Second speaker sighed and showed her enmity was well placed. "Here. Let me."

In dizzying motion, the container was righted, throwing her back down to the bottom. Just as she tried to recover, it was violently shaken from side to side.

Zita hissed, gulping down nausea.

Based on the amusement in his voice, second voice was a sadist. "Be still and quiet, or we'll shake you up and let you roll down the whole damn hill before we pick you up again. That was just a short drop. You understand?"

She growled.

"Good creature," Sadist said.

Her cage was put back into the vehicle, which began moving again with a jolt.

Zita closed her eyes and plotted her escape. *At least the headache is receding. That'll help.*

Minutes later, something beeped. It sounded like the same sequence she'd heard at the other prison, though she couldn't be certain without looking. She was so busy mentally high-fiving herself that she almost missed the pneumatic hiss of what she guessed was a door. Her cage rocked in a regular pattern.

They haven't changed the codes yet! That'll help. Wonder if any of the key cards I have in my pockets still work? Let's hope they didn't deactivate them, assuming I can shift to get them later. I'd try, but I'd rather wait until my friends contact me. Easing to her feet, she stretched to peek out.

Cement walls and a long, metal staircase greeted her eyes, along with the arm of someone in DMS uniform.

"Remember, we'll shake you up and kick you down every step if you don't get your fingers out of there and sit down. Give it a little shake to remind it," Sadist said.

Whoever was carrying her cage complied, throwing her around the interior of the container. While the close confines kept her from serious injury, it still hurt.

She released the air holes with a growl and miserably braced herself on the walls instead. Something squished disconcertingly under her paw, releasing more of the spoiled mayonnaise scent. In her current form, it smelled delicious, and her stomach rumbled. *Of course. My fur is probably filthy, too. Ugh.*

In her new position, she couldn't tell much about outside the plastic prison. The few odors she got smelled like misery, chemicals, and cleanser. Voices murmured, their tones unhappy. She caught glimpses of guard posts and cells, but couldn't quite crane her neck high enough to catch details. Either no one greeted the two men carrying her, or she somehow missed it.

Counseling herself repeatedly to patience, she contented herself by resuming her plans to escape. Zita gradually eased into a new position, so she wouldn't be shaken again, and prepared to spring out once the top was removed. If they left her in here, she'd have to risk shifting to a much larger shape and hope it was sufficient to break open the thick plastic. She glared at the walls keeping her in place.

Several interminably long hours or possibly minutes later, they stopped.

"Ma'am. We brought the raccoon," Sadist said.

Heels clicked across tile, and a woman spoke. "Interesting. We haven't heard of too many vermin shifters other than the mad squirrel man and possibly Arca. We're certain it's a raccoon and not a squirrel? Even though we ensured the island is vermin free in case of his capture, he would require slightly different handling. I'm surprised it hasn't returned to human form yet. A trash can would certain not suffice had it done so."

After a second, Zita recognized Dr. Chaniclas, the scientist she'd eavesdropped on at the faux prison. The shape and composition of makeshift cage made sense now. *Trash can? I need to get out of here before party line connects again, or I'll never hear the end of this.*

Sadist and whoever was carrying her said nothing in response to the doctor's words.

"Fine then. We have plenty of shifters to study, but another sample couldn't hurt since this one has held animal shape an unusual amount of time. All the others return to human shape during unconsciousness." Chaniclas paused, but heels clicked against a tile floor.

They do? I like sleeping as an animal. It's cozy, Zita thought. She crouched, preparing to enact her escape as soon as possible.

A cabinet door opened and closed, and someone, probably the scientist, clacked over by the trash can. "Perhaps the lack of shifting is a consequence of the tight confines? Nonetheless, the meta gas will have reduced their powers and should force it to return to a humanoid like all the others any minute now. Hold it still for a moment."

Abruptly, a hole was punched through one of the walls with a screwdriver or something else pointy, hitting one of Zita's legs and stopping, but not before puncturing her.

At the sudden pain, she yowled and yanked her leg off the screwdriver. Warm blood welled up and dripped. She tried to edge away from the hole as much as possible.

It withdrew.

A needle darted in and pierced lower down on the same limb.

Zita kept herself from moving to avoid making it worse. *One more thing to make certain they don't keep. I don't know what my*

DNA looks like right now, but I won't leave any clues leading back to my family.

Finally, it withdrew as well.

She hurled herself at the lid. It didn't budge, but someone grunted and staggered.

"That's sufficient. Dump it into the Pit and return to your regular duties. We'll handle the creature from here," the scientist said.

"Yes, ma'am," Sadist said.

Tearing and ripping sounds commenced. And continued for several minutes.

How much duct tape did they use? Zita thought, bracing herself to leap. *At least I rated more than one or two quick strips.*

Her world was abruptly upended and shaken roughly.

Choosing to jump rather than just fall, Zita landed on her stubby little feet and chittered angrily, looking around. Her tail puffed up and lashed of its own accord. Her injured leg ached with the impact, and she had to stop herself from licking it, as her animal instincts suggested.

She'd been dropped onto a textured metal floor, oddly sectioned like a child's drawing of a daisy, with a center circle surrounded by a series of other circles, all the same, boring gray. The walls were a mix of thick transparent plastic and white concrete, and the ceiling was unbroken concrete, probably fifteen feet up, with harsh white floodlights embedded flat in the surface. Unlike the mostly empty faux prison, here people were crammed two and three into tiny cells with blankets on the floor. Flanked by a pair of roommates, Rani peered out of one. Chillingly, a rare empty had the chair-toilet combo in the middle of a series of runes. In a few of the rooms, pipes spat the miserable orange mist over listless inhabitants. Incubus was alone in one. His face held that hungry, starved expression again.

Other than where she stood, the only room that wasn't a cell was a wide, antiseptic white room by the only visible door. It had the cabinets, computers, and tables of a medical exam room crossed with an office. Her stomach clenched at the sight of a battered steel coffin open on a wheeled cart and another of the sadistic dentist chairs, only without padding. In addition to the door to the arena area, it also had a barred, heavy steel exit labeled CELLS and a smaller, normal one with a glass window and LABS sign.

A man in a DMS uniform pushed something, and the arena door closed. Bars descended on the lab side. Two other guards stood in the room, and someone in a lab coat and ridiculous heeled shoes was kneeling by a small fridge. At one of the keyboards, a man in a lab coat focused on whatever he was typing, paying no attention to her.

After setting something inside—probably Zita's blood sample— the woman turned around. Dr. Chaniclas picked up a clipboard and gestured toward the computer screens.

A guard hurried to one, and the biggest screen displayed several squares with a different scene in each. While she was too far to see most clearly, Zita could make out the distinctive shape of the prison squatting half-off the volcano.

The scientist nodded to the guard and surveyed Zita. She walked over to the window overlooking the cells and pressed a button. Her voice was made scratchy by the intercom. "At least those morons can correctly tell the difference between a raccoon and a squirrel, so you're probably not the madman. Now, what will we do with you? Quite frankly, our space limitations demand we unload some of the more useless specimens of your species. Recording on. New intake, prisoner designation 24601. Full name unknown. Raccoon, shift!"

Around the circular ceiling, the LEDs brightened, with a ring of little green lights flicking on around them. The extra illumination revealed a ring of dome cameras that she'd missed spotting before, the dark shapes hidden against the shadows of the curved ceiling.

Unwilling to play along with whatever the scientist was doing, Zita scurried to the edge by one of the walls and pressed against it. She could smell ocean water here and saw a small gap where the wall and the floor met. Even though she knew it was probably pointless, she pried at the spot to see if she could widen it or at least determine the dimensions. *If I can shift small, I can squeeze out of that gap later. With bird shape, I can get to the ceiling, but the walls go all the way up, and there's nowhere I could perch except for maybe the air holes to a few of the cells, but that'd be a short-term solution only.*

"Enough of that. Let's see who you are." Chaniclas pressed a button.

A faint vibration came from the metal circle under her paws, and a soft buzzing sound started.

Instinct howled a warning. She yanked her paw out and tried to jump to the next section of flooring, but her current form couldn't leap far enough. Zita slammed into the ground belly-first in time for an electrical charge to race through her, like a giant Taser. A long, thin whine of protest escaped her as she lay immobile, muscles painfully locked and singing with agony from the jolt. *Dying would be worse, but I really hate electrical shocks. For once, I'm happy that I haven't eaten lately or this would be even more embarrassing,* she thought. *Also, I feel way better about pepper-spraying Chaniclas before and leaving her chained up.*

"That was quarter power. For a human, that would've been merely a painful jolt. For something your size, it must've been far worse. If you can shift, I'd urge you to do so. You reptilians can't maintain animal form forever, especially if one applies sufficient pain for long enough. You've marinated in our lovely meta gas recently, so that should also encourage you back to at least your human disguise. I understand you received quite the dose while you were napping," Chaniclas said, her voice conversational. She wrote something else on her clipboard.

Zita stared helplessly at one of the cells while she waited to regain control of her body. It was one of the few that had only one person in it, and to her shock, she recognized Elle. The teen's body swam in an adult-sized orange prison jumpsuit. The fit, streamlined muscles that had marked her as a swimmer before were gone, leaving her seeming very young and very frail.

After a minute or two, Zita managed to twitch one paw toward the girl. Then the other.

The scientist stared down at her, waiting. Once Zita staggered to her feet, Chaniclas made another note. "Mildly interesting. Initial electrical stimulation failed. Subject shows mild pain tolerance."

Zita opened her mouth.

Chaniclas pressed a button.

Another shock ran through Zita, and she collapsed again.

When she recovered enough to turn her head to see the lab area, she caught a guard pointing to something on the computer screen.

Chaniclas glanced over at him, and frowned. Gesturing to a guard, she said something, hands moving. When she returned to the intercom, her tone was brisk. "Shift as soon as you're able! My time is limited, so use it wisely. I have to go oversee extermination of a wind-up drone infestation and go speak to idiots who think complicated real estate transactions can be performed overnight. Apparently, no one is capable of making decisions around here without me, even when it's their job. You'd think it wouldn't be that hard to keep a bunch of test reptiles in cages, but no. I must be constantly vigilant."

Zita made a high-pitched sound as she tried to regain control of her body. *Why do they always have to talk at me?*

Tapping her pen against the scarlet slash of her lips, Chaniclas pressed the intercom again. "Don't bother playing stupid with me. I know what you are. This... metahuman ruse is ridiculous, and it'll be the one that ends the reptilian infiltration of human society. As if anyone would believe that someone could fall into a coma and wake up with powers! What do you think of that?"

Unable to speak in her current form or do more than prop the top half of her body up, Zita blew a weak raspberry.

The scientist scowled and tapped a foot. "Reptilians don't get to comment on the validity of scientific methodology. My genetic sample database of your people is probably the most complete repository of DNA records of your kind on the planet, and I will find the key to identifying you in your human forms. Then there'll be nowhere to hide, and we will crush you underfoot!"

Someone's got a cause, and it is way out there. Well, if I'm going to get shocked again, I might as well earn it. Zita tilted her head. And then made a rude gesture with both paws.

"Mock me if you will, but I will end your people's world domination and return Earth to wholly human hands. I don't know why I'm even bothering to tell you this. Of course, your little bit of crudity informs me that you've recovered. Do shift before I shock you again." Her gaze wandered to the split screens.

Zita panted, waiting to regain control of herself.

"Or perhaps I shall resolve our overcrowding issue and exert a different pressure. It's very irresponsible of you to waste my valuable time like this." Despite the content of her words, Chaniclas' tone was diffident. She could've been talking about the weather.

The door to Elle's cell slid open.

Anticipation dripped from Chaniclas' voice. "Into the Pit, little monster."

"Please don't make me," Elle whispered.

"Did I ask your opinion? Do it, or I will have to punish you," Chaniclas said.

Shoulders drooping and head lowered, Elle stepped onto the metal floor.

The cell door hissed shut. The prisoners watched with a variety of expressions, though the majority seemed forlorn. A couple shouted encouragement, but she couldn't tell for whom or what.

"Now, raccoon. You can turn human or reptilian, I don't care which. If you do not, I will shock all of you on the full human charge. Mind you, that might kill the girl. At your size, it might kill you as well. It definitely won't improve anyone's mood. Really, it's no loss for us. I've gotten all I can out of her, and one more shifter, more or less, doesn't matter. If you survive, I'll simply add another useless lizard every time you fail to shift."

Zita glared at Chaniclas and shifted to Arca. She had to push herself to do so, and it took longer than expected, like trying to walk through waist-high pudding. And now that she thought about food, she was hungry. So hungry. Her injured leg burned, and all of her muscles ached like she had the flu. "Don't hurt the kid," she rasped as she got to her feet.

Chaniclas' smile was toothy enough to be sharklike. "Subject 24601 identified as vigilante known as Arca. Won't it annoy General McCarten to know that two idiots with a trash can and duct tape did what multiple of his elite military strike teams failed to do? Have my personal boat prepped. While she's the most likely to be about on her own, I somehow doubt her friends will stay away forever."

After a nod, the other scientist—Lab Coat Guy—collected a tablet and slipped through the LABS door.

The scientist began, "Now that we've established that, we can all be reasonable—"

Before she could say more, her phone must've buzzed because she looked down and pulled it out of a pocket. She put it to her ear, her face growing progressively crankier. Although she replied, the intercom wasn't on to reveal the words.

Her gaze on the scientist, Zita edged toward Elle. She whispered, "Hey, you doing okay, kid? I been looking for you!"

The girl frowned as if she'd suddenly started a spouting nonsense. "Why?"

Zita frowned at her. "Why wouldn't I? I said I'd help you, and I'm not going to let some jumped-up science nerd hurt you no more. Irene said to tell you she misses you."

For an instant, Elle's face lightened. "Really? She okay? I haven't heard from her."

"She was on house arrest last I heard. I'm guessing they're not real good at giving prisoners their letters here," Zita said.

A bitter laugh escaped Elle, one too old for a someone her age. She rubbed her too-thin arms with her hands. "No, they aren't real concerned about us. You'd have been better off if you hadn't come looking for me. If you get the chance to run without me, take it. I forgive you. I hope you can forgive me."

Zita took a step toward Elle. "What? Why?"

Before they could talk further, Chaniclas spoke again. "Am I interrupting? I can spare only a few minutes, so let's get to fighting. I can only assume your companions are on their way here, so we'll want to prepare their special accommodations and some surprises before they arrive, in addition to my already heavy workload."

"You got time. I was kicking around on my own when I saw some dudes with a busted tire that I thought I'd help. They might not know I'm missing for days." After throwing together that collection of half-truths and lies, Zita glanced at Elle. She kept her gaze away from the magic user cell. *If the meta gas is why my shapeshifting is sluggish, I don't know how many of my powers I can count on. Maybe I can delay long enough for it to wear off or my friends to get here. I know they're coming, but I wish I knew when I'll have my powers back.*

Retreating to the center of the room, Elle whispered, "Don't make her mad, Arca! Please!"

To buy time, Zita cast about for something to keep the scientist talking. "So, I noticed you set up this place on a volcano. That's an interesting real estate decision. Any reason or do you just like risking random fiery death when you're running a prison/lab/torture chamber house of crazy?"

The kid smacked her forehead.

"This location is ideal. Anyone who sees it believes it to be a false address, the volcano provides free energy to power everything, and it isn't subject to the petty strictures of any legal— No, I won't answer questions for your amusement! I will tell you what's going to happen. You are going to fight to the death. The winner gets to continue living in a cell." Chaniclas gestured toward the wall of prisoners.

"That doesn't sound like science. I thought scientists did science. School has betrayed me," Zita said. Remembering Elle, she turned to the teenager. "Stay in school. Even if it's wrong sometimes, it's better than working in fast food or fights to the death."

"I'm not eight, but fine," Elle said, though a ghost of a smile touched her lips.

"Right, so yeah, hard pass on the fighting to the death. It's a lose-lose," Zita said.

Chaniclas was back to smiling. "It sounds like a win to me. If you kill her, then I've got footage of the famous vigilante killing a child. If the youth kills you, I've got proof that even the youngest reptilians are a threat. This will be a lovely addition to the collection that'll accidentally get leaked to the Internet and... how did you get me talking again? You're clearly one of the less intelligent lizards, given that atrocious accent. It sounds like every Mexican buffoon in American movies."

The little sister in Zita couldn't resist making her accent thicker. "My friend says villains gotta monologue. It's stupid, but required or something? You've been making prisoners fight and taping it? Including a sick teenager? What is wrong with you?"

"You're invaders and this is war. Humanity won't go down easy. I won't let it, and I will do everything necessary," Chaniclas said

With a shake of her head, Zita said, "You're not worried that someone will realize you're forcing these battles?"

"I'll remove the sound and label it subhuman fight club or some such nonsense. It should go viral fairly quickly." Her scowl deepened, and the scientist dismissed Zita's arguments with a flick of her hand.

Zita stared at the woman. "You do realize I'm not going to fight her, right? And us sitting around isn't going to have a chance against porn and cat videos. They're what the Internet was made for. Pues, I bet you would like that cat with a face that's all nope all the time? Maybe you should spend more time watching that instead of torturing people."

A guard must've made a sound, because Chaniclas wheeled around, her gaze furious. After a few seconds, the scientist pressed the intercom again, once again calm. "You have no choice. Get to fighting."

Wide-eyed and miserable, Elle whispered, "If you take some damage and drop, I'm pretty easy to fool in my monster shape."

"It's more like a giant stuffed animal shape," Zita said, pretending the kid's alternate shape wasn't weird and creepy.

"She hasn't made me kill before but you're not the first— AAHHH!" Elle fell to her knees, grabbing at the back of her neck.

Zita ran to the teen. Leaning protectively over her, she said desperately, "Shh, Elle, remember our lessons. Hang on. You control the shifts, they don't control you."

The girl gave no sign if she heard Zita or not.

Chaniclas lowered her phone. "Less chatting, more murderous reptilians. And remember. This is for the Internet, so make it good."

In rude Spanish and English, Zita told Chaniclas where she could put her stupid fight club idea.

The scientist didn't bother to reply out loud, but she pressed a different button.

As another of the cells opened, a tall, rangy woman strutted through. She had a confident walk that lacked the balance of a trained fighter, but also had rolled up the sleeves on her jumpsuit to show off the kind of muscles that came from lifting. Her gaze assessed Zita and apparently found her lacking, as scorn crossed her face. Hairless hands, tipped with long, flesh-colored talons, and clawed feet revealed at least some of her metahuman powers. "Speak for yourself, loser. I've got no problems killing you both."

Zita glanced at the third prisoner. "Have I punched you before or something? That's a lot of anger for somebody I haven't talked to yet."

"You knocked over my motorcycle and got me locked up here!" The woman methodically cracked the knuckles of her hairless but clawed hands. She jogged in place, revving herself up for something.

Unfortunately, Zita had a pretty good idea of what the other woman—Zita named her Grumpy—was gearing herself up for. Swearing internally, she stayed between the newcomer and Elle. "Doesn't ring a bell. Can you narrow it down? Maybe describe the bike? That part I'm sorry about."

The woman screeched a long string of especially foul profanities at her.

"Hey! Young ears!" Zita said, waving the teen's direction. When the threats descended into the desecration of animal corpses, she shook her head. "Some people got no class."

Elle writhed on the ground in convulsions suspiciously similar to Sheriff's at the protest. "Pain," she said, the words trailing off into an agonized whimper.

That's what was wrong with Sheriff's shifting. It was forced, and not just by Domina's compulsion. Zita swore internally. She glanced around for something she could use. "Elle, that pinche doctor messed with you. Don't let her win. Come on, practice your breathing and shit."

Although tears ran down her face and her body arched, the girl choked out a half laugh. "Still... cussing..."

"You bet your ass. Control the shift," Zita replied. She hesitated near the teen, unsure what a reassuring adult figure would do. Since she personally hated it when people patted her head, she ruled that out. *Shoulder pat? Big hug? Mix of the two?*

Grumpy acted first, charging at Zita while swinging her fist in what would've been a brutal hit had it landed.

Zita ducked easily, retreating a couple steps to lure her attacker away from Elle. Her ginga was pure habit. *Being comforting will have to come later.*

Chaniclas tapped the glass and pressed something on her phone. "Hurry it up. Skip your usual hesitation and just shift, little monster."

Elle screamed and babbled incoherently. Her body shivered into another series of convulsions. For a second, pink fur shadowed her gasping face.

Instead of following Zita, Grumpy lunged for the teenager.

Without hesitation, Zita darted forward to intercept with a spinning kick that knocked the clawed woman away before she could touch Elle. "Seriously? That's a kid!"

The teen moaned.

For the lack of anything else to help, Zita bent and eased the girl onto her side. It was made more difficult by the need to avoid flailing limbs and to keep an eye on Grumpy. Leaning protectively over her, she said desperately, "Breathe. In. Out. You got this, Elle. It's like making yourself do the last few laps for swimming practice. You keep going. Hang in there and take control."

"Really, you're just hurting yourself now, little monster," Chaniclas commented.

The girl gave no sign of whether she heard the words or not.

Grumpy got back to her feet, flexing her hands.

With a loud clunk, the floor wrenched itself from the wall, receding about a foot from it. All the circles except for the center one began to lower.

The clawed woman swore and tried to pounce on them.

Zita grabbed Elle and rolled, propelling them both to the central circle and out of Grumpy's reach. "Sorry about the rough handling, kid."

The rest of the floor descended with a motorized whirr, the hiss of hydraulics, and the huff of forcefully expelled air. A second level of cells, just as crowded at the first, was revealed, and then a third as the floor continued downward. Sheriff was in one of the cells on the bottom level, sharing it with another woman.

Stuck two floors below Zita and Elle, Grumpy ran to the base of the center pillar and shook her fists at them, "Come down and fight me!"

On the center pillar, Zita hugged the shuddering, thrashing teen, stroking her hair once, and then released her. Balancing on the balls of her feet, Zita stood to better scope out the arena. "No mames. What now? Stay calm, Elle, I'll figure a way out somehow."

"Get away before she shifts! She won't have a choice! They've done it before," Sheriff shouted. Her palms flat against the clear panel of her cell on the bottom floor, the badger shifter's eyes were wide.

"I'll have to trim out this bit. Get to the fighting. She's going to hurt you, little monster. The only way you can make it stop is to make the others go to sleep," Chaniclas said.

Sleep. Others' talents. Something tickled at her memory. Pausing, Zita tucked one of Elle's arms closer to her body so it didn't dangle in midair or get cut off if the floor came back up. "No way. Remember me? I never hurt you none."

The floor jerked.

Grumpy was less fortunate, stumbling to one knee with the movement, whatever she'd been about to do interrupted.

Slowly, the metal flooring revolved, each section spinning at a different pace than the others. The center was the slowest, a minor blessing Zita was grateful for.

"Dizzy! Hurts!" screamed Elle. Her voice held an inhuman timbre, and her body arched.

Grumpy staggered like a drunk to the center pillar and appeared to be hugging it when Zita peeked below to check on her.

Returning her attention to Elle, Zita whispered, "We'll figure this out...We'll figure out something to get you back to Irene. And her pies. Breathe."

The girl's breathing slowed, but tears ran from her eyes.

"Caramba, kid, you've got balls of steel. Hang on," Zita said. She touched her forehead, finally remembering what she needed. Her eyes caught on the people watching them. One she vaguely remembered from Dmitri's club, and another sparked recognition, like she'd seen a picture... "Hey! Which one of you is the kindergarten teacher from DC who's buddies with Remus?"

A short, skinny black man in his fifties came to the front of a cell. His face was haggard, but he didn't appear injured, and his cell didn't have any of the orange mist in it. "That's me."

"Sing the girl to sleep or do whatever it is you do, quick. Everyone else, shut up," Zita ordered.

A scrabbling sound came from below.

The room didn't quiet, but it was less noisy. Enough so she could track Grumpy by the rasp of nails on metal. She glanced down.

The other woman was trying to claw her way up the metal tube to reach them with moderate success.

The teacher waved his hands. "But that only works on children."

Zita gestured to Elle. "Kid! Right there! Por fa, she needs help!"

Scratching and scrabbling came from the pillar below her. It sounded close. Something huffed behind her, and clawed feet scraped on metal.

Pivoting, Zita ducked low and swept out a leg, hoping to discourage Grumpy from attacking. "Come on, I don't want to hurt you, but you need to stop all this foolishness."

A shaky lullaby came from somewhere nearby. It was nearly inaudible.

Grumpy tumbled backward, but managed to grab a handful of Zita's long hair. She yanked it maliciously.

Involuntary tears sprang to Zita's eyes as she was pulled to the very edge of the platform, the revolving flooring throwing her off balance. She turned her stumble into an attack, striking hard at the forearm pressure point. *Stupid to not focus on her. Wish I'd never given this shape such long hair, too.*

With a yelp, Grumpy released her.

The teacher's voice grew in strength as he sang about sleepy sheep or sheepish sleepers or something.

Elle's breath seemed to even out, and the thrashing lessened. With a relieved sigh, she slumped into a boneless sleep.

Worry over the girl lessening, Zita shoved her hair out of her face and let herself return to a ginga. Her scalp ached, but she disregarded it.

Grumpy snarled, standing up and shaking several long strands of hair off her hand. She turned and drew her foot back to kick the unconscious girl.

The warmth of party line flooded Zita's mind, distracting her enough that she almost tripped as she pushed Elle out of the way of the attack and slid under the clawed woman's kick with a negativa.

Wyn squealed, *You're awake! Are you okay?*

A little shaky as the world spun around them, Grumpy tried to stomp on her.

Don't bring the boat close! They got big-ass guns that can maybe reach the shore! Zita rolled out of the way and bounced back up in her ginga. One foot touched empty air and she stopped backing up. She held up her hands in a placating gesture and tried to sound soothing, or at least calm. "Can you chill? I apologize for the bike, especially if it was a sweet ride."

Since he sounded like himself rather than a chorus of male voices, Andy had to be in his human form. *We were worried. Glad you're okay, Z. Sorry we were held up so long. DMS set the metas on the vans we followed loose and triggered something to make them start attacking people. We had to catch them all, like Pokémon in AethXP, where science is fun.*

He's talking about the General Aetherics amusement park, the Aetheric Experience.

Grumpy growled and turned toward Elle again.

Busy! Zita sent. Stepping forward, she spun into a high kick and hit the other woman in the face. Something broke under her foot.

We're close to you! Something's up, though. Brie's trying to convince them we're lost tourists with some kind of engine emergency so we can get to their docks, but our ploy is apparently failing. They also have a lot of drones flying around. Can you put the guns out of commission? Wyn sent.

With a scream, Grumpy fell back, bending double and bringing both hands to her face.

Later. When I can. Zita rolled into an esquiva but followed up this time with a vicious kick to the back of Grumpy's calf that had the clawed woman crashing to the floor. "Stay away from the kid!"

Andy sighed over party line. *I'll smash them if I have to, but the whole flying under the radar thing will be a wash if I do that. We'll give Brie another minute or two to try to convince them to let us in closer before I do. Can you hide or hold out that long? What's going on anyway?*

Zita kept an eye on her attacker, hoping the other would give up. *The usual. Forced cage match where the floor spins and shocks you. Got dosed with meta gas. Found Elle, Sheriff, Incubus, and Remus' teacher bud though.*

Grumpy lunged for Zita, one hand still over her face.

At her words, her friends burst into all sorts of exclamations that Zita tuned out as she danced aside.

Carried by the force of her attack, Grumpy teetered at the edge.

The floor stopped spinning.

Elle slept through it.

Zita staggered.

Grumpy fell.

Jumping forward, Zita lunged, landing on her stomach in time to grab Grumpy's arm. Her body was dragged out over the edge an inch by the larger woman's weight. Her arm ached. "Oye!"

Grumpy hung suspended two stories above the floor.

We'll be quiet, Wyn sent.

Something thunked, and the bottom panels started coming back up.

Zita braced and prepared to lean back so she could pull the much bigger woman up before the rapidly rising floor could injure her.

Her opponent had other ideas though. Grumpy slashed at her with her other hand.

Pain shot through Zita's arm, forcing her to release the clawed woman.

Grumpy fell, landing with a small cry.

Swearing, Zita held her injured arm against her body and peered over the edge.

Her opponent was getting back to her feet as the floor rose again.

Zita stepped away from the edge as the floor connected with her pillar. She took advantage of the moment to grab her hair, twist it, and shove it down the back of her sports bra so it wouldn't be an easy target again. It itched terribly.

Grumpy's gaze fell on Zita. Her face was a bloody mess. She screamed something unintelligible.

"Can we quit now? We both drew blood, no reason to keep going." Zita held up her hands and stayed between her attacker and the slumbering teen.

Despite having an obvious limp and staggering from the spinning floors, Grumpy attacked again.

Zita slid under the blow and grabbed Grumpy's leg with her good arm, using the clawed woman's momentum to throw her up and over her shoulder.

Grumpy thudded into a wall and shook her head, her expression dazed.

Something clunked under their feet, and the floor vibrated.

Please, Dios, not another electrical shock. The kid wouldn't survive. Maybe if I pick her up, she won't get as much of a hit from it. Zita's instincts screamed, and she leapt toward Elle.

Half of the floor disappeared, retracting into the center column with startling speed.

Zita landed on one of the sections that remained in place.

Less lucky, Grumpy disappeared with a sharp scream. It cut off with a splash three seconds later.

Zita ran to the edge and looked down.

The reason for the prison's odd elevation over the water suddenly became very obvious. With the floor gone, this section opened up directly over the ocean. Gray fins slashed through the waves, converging on a pale form that disappeared as multiple sharks ate in a white, gray, and red frenzy. The water boiled with activity, the foam crimson. In the distance, she heard a loud boom and distant automatic gunfire.

She winced and felt sick.

The intercom came on. Chaniclas' unruffled voice said, "Well, at least we won't have to feed the sharks tonight. I suggest you not play nice. There can be only one, you know!"

"What kind of drugs are you people on to think this is okay? Who thinks of this kind of chingado shit? Wasn't the forced fight enough?" Zita said, waving at the missing section of the floor. Her stomach roiled with nausea. *This place!*

Wyn said, *You're speaking to us again? Are you out of danger?*

What? Andy sent.

The floor just disappeared and dumped someone into sharks. Pretty certain she was dead before they got her, but I didn't have time to save her. Gulping down the acidic taste of her disgust, Zita twitched her shoulders and forced herself to look at the lab area.

Anger and dismay vibrated over their connection.

Finally, Andy sent, *I'm appalled, but have to ask... Do the sharks have lasers? Maybe on their heads?*

Why would they have those? I'm not fighting anymore but I haven't gotten loose yet. Zita cleared her throat. "I'm the last woman standing. Going to let me out of this Pit now?"

The scientist was next to the intercom with a wheelchair, a guard beside her. "There's still two of you living, so I think not. We've had a change in plans, and you're no longer necessary. This needs to end now."

We've got our hands full here too. If you need us, though, let us know and we'll break off for you, Wyn sent.

"I thought the point of this was that I was never necessary. So, what's changed?" Zita said. She strode away from Elle, hoping the distance between them would make the girl safer. *Has the gas had enough time to wear off?*

"True, but I've no more time to waste on PR measures. I'll edit what I've got to get the narrative I want. Right now, I need to get the shock troops out. Odd. It is surprisingly cathartic to share one's secret successes with another, even one of limited intelligence. Enjoy your death. It'll probably be horrible, but in either case, you won't be my problem anymore," the scientist replied and tapped something.

Something clunked.

Zita tensed to leap.

The floor dropped out from under her.

She jumped and grabbed one edge of the center platform. The metal bit into her hand as the rest of her dangled over the long drop. Bringing up her other arm, she got a grip with her bloodied hand.

A grinding sound and click came from the lab area.

Before she pulled herself up, Zita checked to see what they were doing now.

A guard leaned out with a gun, aiming it at her.

"No, that could ricochet!" Zita called out, gesturing to the cells filled with people even as she swung around to put more of the column between her and the lab. She quickly put her hand back. "You'll kill someone!"

He fired.

The bullet missed her but hit the edge of the thick metal plates and broke, scattering fragments. One embedded itself in the column, not far from the sleeping teen.

Carajo. I don't know the depth of the water, and this is deadly high, not just risky high. I don't think you guys can get here in time, Zita sent.

The guard aimed at her again.

Hope the gas wore off. Dios save me. She glanced at Elle, exhaled, and pointed her toes.

That sounds like a Zita cue to do something stupid. Please don't, Andy sent.

Wyn's worried comment followed. *How can we help?*

You can't. I'll be fine. Probably. Zita let go.

Chapter Twenty-Two

As far as ways to die went, falling a hundred feet or so into shark-infested water from the fighting arena in a secret prison was at least interesting.

Not that Zita had any intentions of dying.

She focused on shifting, and doing so quickly as the water loomed.

Her powers stuck for a panicky second, slower than usual, but as if she'd blown through a barrier, she was a brown pelican.

After flaring her wings for a moment to slow her descent and angle herself away from the cluster of feeding sharks, Zita bled off the rest of the momentum by diving the remaining several feet into the water, hoping her avian instincts would help.

Her body split the water cleanly, and she fluttered her wings underwater and kicked until she surfaced. Her injuries burned and ached, but she ignored them. Paddling as fast she could, she swam away from the hungry fish.

Already, gray fins stalked her, undoubtedly drawn by her blood. They were fast. Too fast.

Wrong bird choice. She flapped to take off, her wings lifting her in short hops, but not quickly enough. Her webbed feet dipped into the water at the end of each skip.

A shark leapt at her, jaws wide.

She yanked her feet up out of its reach at the last second. *Time to change tactics.*

The animal crashed down and oddly, abandoned the chase. Another glided closer.

Before it could launch itself at her too, Zita threw herself into a shift. This time, her powers complied without delay.

Her body elongated to a fully grown orca, and she came down in the water in a huge splash. As she clicked to figure out the number of enemies chasing her—poor Grumpy's body must not have lasted long with so many—the sharks milled in a confused group.

Praying her bluff would work, she turned toward them. *Get lost*, she tried to tell them. It came out as a mournful call, interspersed with the brisk clicks.

The sharks fled.

Zita let herself sink deeper into the water, continuing her warning sounds to scare off any lurking wildlife. *Apex predators are fun to bluff with. I'm going to make sure no more sharks are lurking around here as much as possible without beaching myself. After that, I'll scope out the island when my view isn't limited to the interior of a trash can.*

What was that? Andy sent.

Nada. Nothing. You guys doing okay? she sent back. Her echolocation told her that her noise had scared most of the larger sea life away or into hiding. The cliffs rose abruptly through the water like a wall, rather than the gradual drop of a beach. A metal plate covered part of it—perhaps to strengthen it?

The water was deep under the prison. *Deep enough that it was remotely possible I could've survived the fall if I did everything right and Dios had mercy on me. That's serious world-record-diver territory, and I'm not that practiced.*

She circled the support pillars, winding her way around them until she surfaced near the center one. Underwater, they were identical sturdy concrete structures. When she bobbed to the surface, they rose to meet the bottom of the prison, with long notches about sixty feet up from which something black and boxy was inserted. The center column was the exception, as it followed the pattern of the others until the sixty-foot mark. Above the notch, the pillar ballooned out, with the bottom of a metal tank of some sort showing.

I guess that's where the floor hydraulics are. Well, enough swimming. Elle and the others still need help.

After one last burst of echolocation, Zita leapt from the water, shifting seamlessly into an albatross. Joy burst from her beak in a discordant cry, buried under the sounds of gunfire: the rumbling roar of the machine gun turrets, interspersed with the sharp cracks of individual firearms in between bursts. *Thank Dios my powers are working right again!*

She circled under the prison, getting her bearings.

Offshore, a large ship—a warship or a smaller cruise ship?—appeared to stay in one place. Hordes of people lined the railing with big, bulky items she couldn't quite make out at this distance. A gray yacht that was likely only small in comparison appeared to be waiting miles offshore, with a white yacht a short way from that. From a third direction, a much smaller passenger boat chugged along, with most of the deck taken up by a multi-windowed cabin and only few people on deck.

Did you guys bring friends? I got to say, I never expected to see so many boats in the Bermuda Triangle, Zita sent.

Wyn answered, *Just Brie, her lawyer, her favorite bodyguards, and us. The lawyer mentioned the Bermuda Triangle actually includes multiple busy shipping lanes, so perhaps the others are unconnected. You noticed the cruise ship?*

We asked her to limit the people at risk, so she brought her lawyer? Never mind, I don't want to know. Yes, I noticed the cruise ship. You must be the small ship with the windows. There's a pair of yachts too, and I haven't checked the docks yet. Zita clucked and flapped sideways in surprise.

A pair of silvery bowling balls with camera eyes and helicopter propellers flew by slowly, scanning the land. Both had odd notches in the back and a single arm underneath that held what looked like a cattle prod. An oddly familiar one, similar to what she'd seen in the store during the riot.

Once she could tell they wouldn't attack her, Zita followed the weird drones. Not that there was much to see besides the concrete support pillars, waves, the upper half of the metal plate on the side of the volcano, and the black cliff. From her experience as a climber, she knew scaling sharp volcanic rock like that without gloves would result in shredded hands. The only camera on the prison down here was pointed at the cliff.

When the robots appeared to be filming every inch of the underside of the jail, she turned aside to find the source of the noise.

Cautious of the weapons, she rode a thermal higher, assessing the prison as she emerged from under it. It was nearly windowless, and the upper floors appeared to have obvious camera placements by the few visible windows. Men in DMS uniform manned the walls, long guns held ready, though they seemed to be content to let the machine gunners do most of the work.

The flying balls were all over the island. The machine guns at the prison shredded any that came too close to the forbidding walls, leaving odd metallic debris scattered over the steep path to the prison. A few soared over the prison anyway, having either flown high or agilely enough to avoid being destroyed.

The docks, out of range of the machine guns, had more frantic activity and the majority of robots, as if they were waiting for the machine guns to stop. Wads of white stuff trapped a handful of people in place in the street nearby. Logos on the couple of docked ships declared them to be DMS vessels. The smaller one had a few people trapped under the odd webbing on the deck. Something that looked a lot like a pair of jet skis bobbed by the docks, each one attached to a large box on water skis. Two humanoid robots—she'd mistaken them for people until she drew close enough to see sunlight reflecting off their skin and the jerkiness of their movements—sat by one of the containers, assembling arachnoid-shaped robots with inhuman speed. Each wore a gold wristband on one wrist, like a spider wrapped around their artificial limb.

By one of the buildings, a uniformed guard burst out of a door and attacked a ball robot with what looked like a shovel. Even though he battered it down, another came up behind him and poked him with the stick hanging beneath it.

Light flashed.

The man stiffened, then collapsed.

A spider-like robot darted over and spat webbing on him.

Stunning people is the new "in" thing, I guess, she thought. *Can you guys see this?*

The boat's parked, and we're watching through binoculars. It's a mile or more away from us, Andy sent.

Amusement tempered Wyn's rebuke. *Parked? Seriously? Anchored, I believe.*

Desert rat. No apologies, Andy sent.

Where'd all the robots come from? Zita asked.

We thought they were your doing, since they seemed to be attacking DMS, and you were concentrating earlier, Wyn sent.

Seagulls didn't snort, or she would've done so. *Concentrating on not dying, yes. What do I know about robots?*

Andy grunted over their shared link. *Nothing, but we figured there was a big red button marked with "Don't Press" or "Unleash Robots," and you had to hit it.*

Not saying that wouldn't be tempting, but the only buttons I've been pressing have been on people. If I see one that says "Make Robots

Go Nuts," should I go for it? Zita flew a little higher to check what was happening on the prison grounds.

Both of her friends replied at once. *No!*

A variety of people in neon orange prisoner jumpsuits shambled around the prison grounds holding dull black batons. A pack of wolves accompanied them, led by a familiar white wolf. None of them moved naturally. If any of the flying robots got too close, the prisoners swarmed them and hit or bit them until they stopped moving. Above them, on the walls, machine gunners rotated and sent another burst of bullets toward the robots outside the gates.

If I can turn off the machine guns, can you two get close enough for Wyn to put the wolves and the people in orange to sleep? I think they're brainwashed like Sheriff was, and who knows if the robots will tase them too or actually kill them. Remembering what they'd said about both the meta gas and the electrical shocks when she was a raccoon, she added, *The wolves are especially at risk. If the robot stun sticks are calibrated for humans, it might be too much for them.*

Of course, but I mourn for the part of our plan that allowed us plausible deniability. Wyn sighed mentally, but her mind was clearly already planning. *Andy will have to bring me in once the guns are down and protect me while I do it, since I can't shield and cast. It'd also help if they were all herded into a small area or something. Brie and her companions can bring the boat in when it's safe to do so. They're doing all the sailing anyway. It's a shame it's daylight. Dmitri would have been perfect to deprogram those people.*

Andy sent, *He would've. Our entire plan would've been great if, you know, anything ever went the way we planned it. Why didn't we plan for that? See what you can do about the guns so I can bring in Wyn safely.*

Zita circled, eyeing the chaos below. *Everybody's a critic.*

Let us know when the big guns are down, Wyn sent.

One of the parked trucks whirred as it tilted its box upward. The tarp fell off, revealing long white tubes.

As soon as she realized what was happening, Zita was shouting over party line. *Rockets! They got huge rockets pointed at the boats! On trucks!*

A whoosh sounded, and light flared as a missile shot out of one of the tubes, skimming the water in the direction of the big ship or her friends.

Andy sent, *On it!*

A sonic boom ripped through the air, followed by a flash of light and a large explosion over the ocean.

Even with the distance, Zita spotted a small figure dropping into the water out by the boats, landing with a splash.

Careful to avoid machine gun barrage, she flew around to the truck that had fired. It was unmanned.

My cape! The explosion pretty much vaporized it. Andy mourned. *Can you get my spare out, Wyn? Maybe I can use it to dry off.* A person shot out of the water and flew slowly toward the smaller boat.

Despite knowing he was nearly invulnerable, Zita had to release the breath she'd been holding. She turned her attention to examining the truck and its deadly load. After landing on a side view mirror, she peered through the window at the vehicle controls. Zita shook her head, hopping onto the rear half to examine the tubes holding the missiles.

That was your extra, the witch replied. *Remember? Your original one was sucked into the cotton candy machine. Then it got dunked in the deep fat fryer and burned when you were chasing the tentacled gentleman through the concessions cart. I'll see if anyone brought a towel.*

Aww, man, Andy grumbled.

Perching on top of one of the tubes, Zita sent the bad news to her friends. *The rockets are remote controlled. The outsides don't have any obvious electronics I can disable to get rid of them, either.*

While I could switch to a bigger form and try to crush them, that could make them explode, and I'd rather not end the day as chunks of meat.

Absolutely no dying! Wyn sent.

Andy concurred. *What she said.*

Motion on the water caught her attention, and Zita launched herself that direction, coasting down below the cliff edge to stay out of the line of fire of the big guns. Absently, she sent, *Doing my best. I'll look for a control room so I can disable them from inside or something. Unplug the computer controlling it or steal the joystick or something. I need to get back to Elle.*

The machinery whirred again.

Rocket getting ready to fire! She warned her friends.

Beneath the prison, a pair of small motorboats drifted in. Fit shapes cast aside the blankets that had camouflaged them in the water. One boat had several men with wiry, rangy builds, matching gray body armor, and a mismatched assortment of weaponry. The other boat had only three individuals in it. One was lean with a military stride and wore a peppermint-striped suit coat over body armor, topped off by a straw hat and cane. The second was a Kodiak bear. The last was hidden behind black armor and a pair of goggles, but she'd recognize that body anywhere. She'd certainly spent enough time stealing surreptitious glances at it. His weapon looked more like an air rifle than his usual long gun.

Well, I know they're not with DMS, and now I know what they were on call for, she thought.

Another rocket blasted out, heading toward the boats.

Getting together gear—including gloves, she was gratified to see—the small groups headed toward the cliff. Remembering the camera, she glanced at it. It appeared to still be working, so she swooped toward it.

Another sonic boom, followed by a louder explosion and flash of light.

Taking advantage of the distraction, Zita whacked the camera with her wings until it recorded only rock, not the people from the boats.

When she finished and looked below, Freelance's goggles were trained on her. While Trixie lingered at his side, the others were nearly at the base of the cliff already.

Gazing at him, she flared her wings.

His head inclined.

Not a fan of those missiles, Andy sent. *Pretty sure the local fish are tired of seeing my butt hit the water too. I'm done waiting for them to stop firing. You said they're unmanned, right?*

Sí, Zita replied, ignoring her silly tremble at Freelance's acknowledgement.

Andy's grim satisfaction filled the link. *Physics for the win. I'll be back for you once the guns are down, Wyn. Zita, concentrate on finding Linda, Elle, and as many of our original targets as you can. I'll get the big guns. They fired at a civilian ship, and I won't have people dying because I can only stop so many missiles at a time.*

Both women murmured their assent.

Something zipped by overhead. A second later, one of the trucks with the rockets flew by, supported by a man flying beneath it. He flew out over the water, and dropped it near a big rock. It submerged, sinking below the waves. Andy hovered for a moment before zipping by overhead.

Zita bobbed her head with glee. *Go, Andy!*

The machinery circling the central pillar rumbled and a section of the prison floor opened up. Even though she tensed to catch anyone falling out, nothing happened.

Chaniclas' words came through clearly, however, her high-pitched tones carrying. "You two guard the geothermal power plant. The robots only attack people in uniform, so take that off first. Kill anyone who tries to get to the control room. They can't be allowed to take it. You six, come with me and the two prisoners. The rest of you, defend this place."

Zita fluttered closer to the opening, hoping to see what was going on. They'd either chosen to stop talking or were doing something else, because all she could catch were scuffling sounds.

Another truck flew by overhead and ended up beside the first one.

Missiles handled. The machine gun emplacements are next, and then I'll come get you, Wyn, Andy sent.

Wyn sounded happier. *Great! I'll have Brie bring us closer to the island then, so we can retrieve our people more easily.*

The merciless voice of Chaniclas rose again. "Now that's settled, I have more than sufficient genetic samples to consult to determine why the girl's adaptation to human form was flawed and hopefully duplicate it in others. Feed her to the sharks, so we have an open cell. I need to see whether those idiots have managed to sink any of the boats yet."

No mames, bitch. Zita spread her wings and rocketed through the gap and back into the arena.

Chaniclas' strident voice echoed as the scientist shrieked. "How do you lose two trucks filled with missiles? They don't just walk off! Do I have to do everything?"

Inside the thick plastic walls of the lab area, a small group of men was leaving, and a glimpse of orange and drab red suggested Chaniclas and a prisoner accompanied them. While three guards clustered around the monitor, a man in a lab coat kneeled beside two shivering DMS guys who had been propped up against a wall near the door to the arena. Said door was open.

When Zita got to the arena, it was still at the top level, the one with the lab. Two cells gaped open—Rani's and the one beside it— and Elle still slept in the center. A big, burly man in uniform was trudging across the floor toward the teenager.

Kid! He's big, need surprise. Shifting to Arca in midair, Zita landed, knees bent to absorb the force of the impact, behind the big guy threatening Elle.

His foot drawn back to kick the sleeping girl, the guard paused and glanced back at the thump.

She hooked her foot around his ankle, grabbed the back of his uniform, and yanked him away in a smooth, practiced motion.

He sprawled on the still-solid part of the platform.

While he was down, she darted forward and snatched his Taser. "Hey! Loser! Why don't you pick on someone half your size?"

He sat up.

She zapped him. While he was out, she grabbed his badge, helpfully hanging from a lanyard. Zita hung it around her own neck. At the sound of a bang from behind her, she spun.

A prison guard had slammed shut the door to the lab while she'd been handling the one about to attack Elle. Four sets of eyes stared at her from the laboratory; Lab Coat Guy made notes in a tablet.

"Oh, hi! No, I'm not dead yet," Zita said, stuffing the Taser in her pocket. "I'd wish you better luck next time, but I'd be lying, and I'm all about the truth. I don't suppose you all want to give up now?"

A guard lunged toward her and pressed something on a console.

The floor vibrated.

Zita scooped up Elle, shifted to a bear in mid-step, and ran for an open cell. She jumped.

With a buzz, electricity crackled across the section where they'd been.

They crashed into the cell, but Zita was careful not to land on Elle. Setting down the girl by Rani's cowering roommates, she ran to the door before they could close it and leaned all of her prodigious weight against it.

The door hit her, but was unable to move her bulk. She squinted, trying to make out what was going on with her bear vision.

Still stunned from being tripped and then tased, the poor guy on the floor took another round of electricity.

As soon as the charge faded, Zita sprinted over and grabbed him.

Vibrations began again.

She tossed him into the other open cell, shifting in midair as she jumped to hang off the open door as a large howler monkey, using the air holes as anchors for her fingers, toes, and prehensile tail. The badge hung long on her small frame, but didn't break off.

The floor lit up again and the door shut, but she was on the outside and none of the electricity touched her.

She grinned at the anger on their faces. Instead of crossing the floor again, she climbed across the cells. *It's not even all that challenging given the regular spacing of the air holes.*

"You have to come down sometime," Lab Coat Guy told her. After releasing the intercom button, he turned away to speak to a pair of guards who sauntered into the room.

Zita continued climbing until she hung from the holes closest to the lab. She studied the door. It was a heavy, clear plastic one, with retractable bars on the other side. A key card reader and a number pad were embedded in the wall beside it.

Something happened outside that had the lab staff rushing to the monitors.

Figuring they were busy, Zita pulled off her lanyard with her tail and stretched it out. She slapped the guard in the cell's keycard against the reader. The door snicked, and she pulled the handle, leaving it ajar.

Lab Coat Guy watched the monitors with the guards. "Chaniclas needs to know the machine guns are almost down and the robots are taking out our wall defenses. Get rid of the monkey while I talk to her so we can give her some good news."

Zita jumped over and punched in the code. The bars withdrew. Desperate to get into the lab before they could shock her again, Zita wrenched the door open.

A guard started her direction, and she roared in his face, the loud howl the animal was known for.

He took a step back in surprise.

She shifted into a bear and barreled into him, slamming the guy against a wall.

He groaned and went limp.

Something hard hit in her in the back, and she whirled, finding a man wielding his baton and a woman with a Taser. They gulped. Behind them, Lab Coat Guy fled down a hall, clutching his tablet.

Judging it to be the biggest threat, Zita slapped the Taser out of the hands of the woman. She tried snarling.

The female guard backed up a couple steps.

"It's just Arca!" The man hit Zita with his baton.

It stung.

She cocked her head at him. Growled.

He offered her a sheepish smile.

Zita lifted her paw and swatted his hand.

Something cracked, and the baton went flying.

The man screamed and bent over his hand. Both guards ran.

Something clicked in the arena area. Grappling hooks attached to the floor.

A straw hat on a cane rose and waved in the air, followed by Trixie. She slid the hat back on her head and used a hand signal, then pulled her weapon, training it on Zita. "What have we here? Bear envy? While you're fluffy, and I'm flattered, there's no comparison with the real thing."

Most of the people from the boats fanned out around her, advancing on the lab. Their weapons lifted as they approached the open door, except for Freelance, who brought up the rear. His long gun hung on a sling in front of him.

Zita had little doubt that he could move his long gun and fire it long before she could reach him, were she inclined to attack. She shifted to Arca and waved as she scooped up the lanyard with the key card and stuffed it back in her pocket. "Don't shoot. I'm harmless."

Shifting to a bloodhound, she sniffed the lab coat hanging on one of the chairs. Fixing the scent in her memory—she was pretty certain it was Chaniclas—she looked up.

Trixie had lowered her weapon, but the strangers still had theirs pointed at her.

Freelance made a gesture, and the remaining guns dropped. He pointed toward the lab. Two of the men ran in and grabbed the computer keyboards. They began typing.

"We should've expected this once we saw your buddy breaking all the fun toys outside. Does he know how much expensive machinery he's just ruined? So why are you here? What brings a little cinnamon roll out here?" Trixie leaned on her cane—a wooden one with a curved handle—and tilted her head, grinning.

Zita whuffed and then froze as she caught another scent. After sorting out the odors, she followed the newest one to the LABS door. It was very fresh, only minutes old, and mingled with the scientist and several other scents. *Chaniclas wouldn't take Rani out of a cell for no reason, even if her ability is inoffensive.*

She glanced back at the cells and shifted to Arca. "Rescue. Do me a favor and open the cell with the sleeping kid there, please, if you're opening cells. Don't scare her. She's got a bad heart and a scary second form."

Before she could point out which cell, one of the computer users interrupted. "Opening the designated cells for the targets."

The cell Rani had been in and the one where Zita had stashed the stunned guard in both opened. Now awake, the man started to limp out, a hand on his baton.

"You might not want to let that guard out. He's had a rough day and isn't in the best mood. Leave the other one open. If the kid wakes up, tell her I'll be back for her," Zita said.

Freelance pointed a handgun at the cell with the guard. His head turned to survey the man.

Caught in the act of creeping out, the guard stopped, took one look at Freelance, and stepped back, closing the cell door behind himself.

Zita nodded. "Good call, buddy. Those cells were empty when I got here. Speaking of which, they're running off with at least one of the people I came here for, so good luck with your mission. You on rescue, too?"

One of the men at the computers glanced up, but Trixie answered first.

"Pansy rescue, where our pay gets docked for every person we kill," Trixie snorted.

Zita couldn't help a smile at that. Using the guard's badge, she got through the card reader, punching keys on the numeric pad with very little thought. "I got to go chase those people down. They don't get to leave with her."

"Her?" Trixie glanced at Freelance.

The mercenary leader nodded and made a couple hand signals.

Zita slipped through the door, not arguing when Trixie and one of the strangers followed. Shifting back down to a bloodhound, she raced after Rani, down a hall filled with doors.

The helpful sign-maker had struck again, so she didn't need to check the rooms to know that they passed by a blood analysis lab, a morgue, an autopsy room, a surgery, and a chemical lab before the scent stopped in front of the one labeled DR. CHANICLAS.

Excitement ran through her. Zita filled in her friends. *Chaniclas took off with Rani for some reason—it's not kinky, Rani smells too scared for that—but I think we've cornered them. The scent's getting stronger. We're catching up! Pan comido, we'll at least be able to get Rani, Sheriff, Incubus, and Elle out of this pit. If Sheriff and Incubus recognize any of Dmitri's other folks, we'll try to grab them too.*

Good. Poor Rani hates this kind of thing. She just wanted a quiet life. The boat's almost at the island, Wyn sent.

Andy had an update as well. *I've got one more machine gun to take down. They know I'm here, so I have to move carefully to avoid either having bullets or shrapnel ricochet down onto the prisoners wandering around down there.*

After flattening herself against a wall, Trixie used a bunch of hand signals that culminated in a rapid game of paper, scissors, rock. When she won, she smirked and pointed high.

Zita scooted over to hug the wall as well, and hunched down.

The stranger kicked the door open and swept in high.

Trixie stepped in low.

An air gun popped and the guard inside the room dropped, a dart sticking out of his shirt.

After a second, Trixie called from inside, "Clear. Are you certain this is where they were?"

Zita poked her nose in.

The room was smaller than she'd expected, but held all the usual office paraphernalia except a computer, and she could see where one was supposed to be. The office had bookshelves stuffed with medical journals, a big wooden desk, a rolling chair, a fancy phone, and stacks of papers. A hideous brown rug covered the same speckled white tile that ran down the rest of hallway and (presumably) throughout the entire lab complex. Other than the way her scent had seeped into everything, as if the woman almost lived in the room, the only signs this was Chaniclas' office were in a small photo of a smiling young man, half-hidden behind a stack of papers, and a plain white coffee mug with purple lipstick on the rim.

Other than the downed guard and the pair who had come with Zita, no one else was there.

"Carajo! The trail stops at the wall!" she swore, not even realizing she'd shifted back to Arca until she heard her own words.

Proving she'd worked with a tracker before, Trixie eyed the wall and then brightened. "Oh! It's a secret door! We should find the trigger. Maybe it's a book in a bookcase or a light fixture that turns to the side!" She started pulling books off the shelves.

Her teammate started working on another bookcase.

After a shift back to the dog again, Zita checked to see if any of the recent trails had veered off from the others. She followed Chaniclas' and another person's scent to a corner behind the desk.

While the two mercenaries kept decimating the bookshelves, Zita stared at the rug. The second person's trace was only on one portion. She pawed at it. A floorboard was loose under the carpet. Switching to Arca, she pulled it up and spotted a big red button underneath. *Wonder if this will make the robots go crazy? Why would anyone have a button for that anyway?*

She pressed it.

The wall opened.

"Oh, hey, I found it!" Trixie said. Despite her light tone and cheery smile, she had a gun in her hand and was cautiously checking the tunnel entrance.

Letting the floorboard fall back into place, Zita shifted back to a bloodhound and raced down the newly revealed corridor.

***

As it turns out, barreling down dark tunnels with no lights was hazardous to your nose.

After an embarrassing mishap with a turn she'd missed because she'd been too wrapped up in the olfactory information, Zita shifted to a jaguar and continued on. Odors were lessened but still trackable, with the aroma of saltwater growing stronger as they traveled through the damp stone corridors. While she'd hoped the others would've missed the small collision, Trixie's smothered guffaw had made it clear their night-vision goggles were working.

"What do you mean I can't come?" A man screaming told her when they were close.

They emerged into a natural cavern, where a small, white boat rocked on the waves as a metal door ground open in the cave wall. Her face decidedly green beneath the warm tones of her skin, Rani was being hauled up from below deck to stand bent over the side. Her shoulders heaved as she grabbed onto the railing. Another pair of guards stood by Chaniclas. Lab Coat Guy was in front of her, his body shaking.

The scientist sniffed, the sound carrying despite the distance. "I told you to defend the prison. You're here instead?"

"I did everything for you, and you were going to leave me here with the bombs?" the man shrieked at her.

One guard noticed them and whipped out his gun. "Company!"

Zita dodged behind the closest boulder.

The guards fired. Chaniclas ran below deck. One guard tried to pry Rani from the railing. Lab Coat Guy attempted to follow the scientist, but she wouldn't allow him in.

Trixie and her teammate weren't as fast, and the stranger got hit in his shoulder, dropping the gun he'd been about to shoot. As she tended his injury, Trixie hissed, "Get Rani to tell a bad joke. Doesn't matter which one. Trust me."

Zita frowned. Licking her lips, she peeked out from behind the rock and gave it a try. "Chanclas! We meet again! How you doing? I heard you been kidnapping people again. Is that like a hobby? Get your dudes to stop shooting so we can talk! Hey, is that Rani? You got a joke for me, my friend? You should tell it right now."

"Clearly, your intelligence has been overestimated if you believe this is the time for humor. And it's Chan-i-clas, you moron," Chaniclas said from her hiding place. "My men'll shoot anyone who moves, and that includes any kind of animal. Speaking of which, someone get rid of Igor. He ran from his post. Humanity doesn't need a coward defending it."

A pair of guards steered Lab Coat Guy to the railing and pushed the unlucky man off the boat.

Trixie was hidden behind a rock, but her twirling cane was visible enough that a guard shot at it. She withdrew the cane from their sight. "Let one rip, Rani!"

Zita frowned. Lab Coat Guy hadn't come back up from beneath the water yet. "Why don't you just give up, and we can all talk this out or something?" She was really proud that her true opinion of the woman hadn't slipped out. "Get you some medicine for those delusions."

Oops.

"Joke now, Rani!" Trixie called out, clutching her cane to her chest and peering out.

Tensing as she prepared to run, Zita shouted, "Tell the chingado joke, Rani, or Vaudeville will just keep nagging us until you do!"

Rani shrugged and choked out, "What kind of dog does a mad scientist have?"

"A lab! Boo! Get off the stage!" Trixie shouted and made a gesture with her cane.

A massive hook came out and yanked Rani off the boat, somehow dragging her through the air and to the mercenary woman without touching the intervening water or injuring her.

Trixie beamed and patted Wyn's ex-girlfriend on the shoulder. "I wasn't certain that would work, but I should never doubt my own hilarity! Yours, now... You need a better repertoire of jokes."

Rani gaped at them.

Trixie's teammate pulled her behind a rock with them.

One of the guards shouted, "Clear!"

Zita ran forward, zigzagging to avoid the potshots being taken at her, and dove into the water, shifting to a dolphin as she went. She swam over to where Lab Coat Guy had disappeared and searched for him.

When she surfaced a few seconds later, dragging the hapless man by his shirt and keeping his head above water, the boat almost hit her as it zoomed out the now-open entrance.

As they passed, Chaniclas cupped her hands over her mouth and called out, "Choose wisely, Arca. You can chase me down, or you can do something about the bombs that are going to go off in ten minutes, killing everyone on the island."

The boat accelerated away.

Zita shook her head and dragged the guy to land.

Trixie was talking on her earpiece.

"CPR him!" Zita called out. "You guys bring any bomb experts? Bombs go off in ten minutes, and she says they'll kill everyone."

Trixie made a face. "We were paid to rescue Rani and one other, not this loser, but I suppose."

Before she could do anything, Lab Coat Guy gasped, coughed, and rolled to his side, vomiting water.

"I'm so good that just the promise of my CPR saves lives!" Trixie cheered, before returning her attention to her earpiece. "Right, Bossman. She said ten minutes."

Rani gulped. "I don't know about the bombs, but Chaniclas has another prisoner she calls Youth below decks. Some poor woman in a coma. She's supposed to be almost eighty, but she looks like she's forty."

Trixie stiffened. Dug out a photograph. "This woman?"

"Maybe? Hair's different, no makeup, hard to say," Rani said.

Zita swore. Focusing, she sent her thoughts over party line. *Chaniclas might have Dream Auntie, and she set bombs on the island. We have probably nine minutes now to find and clear them all. I'm going to try to open all the cell doors so the prisoners can try to get out of the building before it explodes.*

We should try to call her Linda. Remember her warning about mental shackles? The mind-controlled prisoners are still running loose. We can't risk them tearing apart any prisoners you release or forcing the freed people to murder them to survive, Wyn sent. *I don't have a spell for bombs.*

Andy offered, *If you can find them, I can try to carry them away like I did the tanks. Unless that'll make them blow up?*

I have no idea what moving them will do. The mercenaries are here for Rani, so she's already got a ride off the island. We can always find her again later. Trying to get info on the bombs. Zita ran to Lab Coat Guy and propped him up. "Tell me about the bombs!"

Lab Coat Guy gasped and coughed a little more. Despite his dip in the water, he was sweating profusely. "I can't believe she'd do this to me."

Zita managed to keep herself from commenting on that. "Dude, is she telling the truth about the bombs?"

With his arms wrapped around his knees, Lab Coat Guy muttered, "Yeah, sure. It's a last defense against letting anyone free the metas. I can't stay here. Why would she do this to me?"

"Concentrate. Where are they?" She resisted the urge to shake him.

Lab Coat Guy curled up into a ball. He wailed, "What has she done? I'm going to die!"

She pried his arms away so he could hear her. "Dude, you need to chill. You don't have to die if you help us. Where are the bombs?"

"On the prison support columns! I can't stay here! I have to get somewhere safer!" Lab Coat Guy said. He leapt to his feet, staggering a little, and ran off down the tunnel.

Zita passed along the information to her friends. *The bombs are on the prison support pillars. Check the notches. I think I saw some black boxes in them.*

With a muttered curse of her own, Trixie took Rani's arm. "Come on. You and Gimpy here are getting in the boats."

"Hey!" her teammate objected.

All of them hurried toward the tunnel.

Conscious of the presence of both Rani and the injured man, Zita asked Trixie as they jogged along, slowed by Rani's blindness in the dark, "Can someone on your team defuse bombs? Or make it so they don't explode if moved? Wingspan can get them somewhere they won't hurt nobody, but we don't want to set them off if moving them does that."

Trixie snorted. "We're under orders to retreat and try to follow the boat. Boss says he'll see if he can defuse or at least make them so your buddy can get rid of them. Try not to drop them on the missile trucks. That could be very bad."

Tamping down her urge to ask more questions, Zita sent, *Freelance is going to either defuse or make it so the bombs can be moved. He'll tell Andy when it's safe to move them.* After a second, she passed along Trixie's comment about the missile trucks.

I'm on it, Andy sent. *And yeah. Bombs on missiles could be a bad combo.*

Her mental voice unhappy, Wyn sent, *Should we go after Chaniclas? We see her and can give chase, but I think her boat is faster than ours. If she has Linda and goes to a port city...*

Zita ran a hand over her hair, back and forth as she ran. *We don't know if Jerome's explosion still happens. Carajo. Can you put an arrow over her boat or something? I think I can stop it if you can show me where it went.*

When they got back to the arena, the rest of Trixie's team was already gone.

She paused by Elle's cage. The girl was conscious. "I'll be back as soon as I can." Running to a still-open section of the floor, she peered below.

Hanging from a climbing harness, Freelance had the box open in one of the column niches and was examining it with his goggles, wire cutters in one hand. Kodiak waited in a small motorboat at the entrance to the cove under the prison.

"You sure you can get all of them done in the time?"

A nod.

"Certain?" she asked.

He glanced at her.

"Sorry," she asked.

Andy flew down and hovered by the mercenary leader. "Are you disarming or just making it so I can move them to a safer spot?"

Freelance snipped something, closed the box, and shot his grapple gun at another spot. He unhooked his harness and pointed to the box he'd been working on. "Move."

With a wave, Andy snatched the box and carefully flew away with it.

"Right, so I need to chase down Chaniclas."

Chapter Twenty-Three

The boat was easy to spot, given the glowing red arrow and words "Genocidal Maniac" hovering above it.

Clearly, Wyn shared Zita's opinion of Chaniclas.

Shifting to a golden eagle, Zita soared up. Men in DMS uniforms stood on the deck, and she thought she'd spotted Chaniclas through the window.

She circled. *I see them. Come help when you can.*

With pleasure, as soon as I'm not carrying bombs into space. Freelance can only deactivate the motion sensors on them so fast, though, Andy sent.

Wait for us! How will you stop them when you're alone? Wyn sent.

You're on a rental tourist boat. They don't usually come with boat lassos or whatever people use in situations like this. Once I stop it, you guys can catch up and put them to sleep. Everyone but Chaniclas, anyway. We need to make sure she doesn't have any other nasty surprises, though she should be far enough out that she shouldn't have enough signal to trigger anything else back on the island, Zita sent back.

True, though I don't know what armaments the bodyguards brought, and Brie is wearing some very strange armor. Extremely cute boots, but it's possible she has something else stashed that I don't know about. I'll do the sleep spell as soon as I can, Wyn sent.

After shifting to a peregrine falcon, Zita stooped to catch up to the boat, enjoying the speed as she sliced through the air.

Someone pointed and shot at her.

She rolled aside, pulling up until she hovered only fifty feet above the water.

The men on deck lowered their weapons to aim at her again.

Again, she dove toward the boat, splashing into the water instead of hitting it.

Once underwater, she let herself sink down a several feet and shifted again.

In her new shape, she sensed rather than saw the disturbances as they emptied their weapons into the water. Keeping pace with them, she jetted along below their boat until the attacks stopped.

Then she rose and wrapped five of her arms around the boat, careful to avoid the propeller. The water shivered as she knocked someone overboard accidentally.

If the boat were much bigger, I couldn't pull this off.

The boat stopped moving, and the man in the water seemed to be sinking rather than swimming.

With a mental sigh, she brought up a tentacle to seize the man underwater and lift him up into the air. She dumped him on the deck, careful not to catch him on the hooks of her appendage.

Her tentacle stung a moment later, and she withdrew it.

Rising up from the water, she swiped across the deck with a tentacle, knocking down the remaining standing guards. If one jumped into the water and another fell, she didn't worry once she verified they seemed able to swim. When the one she'd rescued from drowning went for one of the dropped weapons, she clacked her beak at him.

He stared at her.

Chaniclas shouted, "Kill it!"

Zita flexed a tentacle.

The dripping guy lifted both hands in the air and sat down, back to the wall. "Nope, I'm done."

While the scientist shouted, Zita used an arm to sweep all the weapons to the front of the boat, as far from the cabin as possible, along with a bucket and anything else on the deck other than people. *The boat isn't going anywhere right now. I might need a little healing though, nothing too major, but I don't want to risk shifting back and having the injuries be over an artery or something.*

Understood. We're close, Wyn replied.

"Turning off the engines! We don't want to burn out the motor," someone shouted.

When the boat engines cut off, Zita unwound one of the arms that had been holding it in place. Underwater, she wrapped an arm around the propeller and twisted until she felt it break. That done, she glanced around. The guards who had fallen into the ocean were trying to climb back aboard, so she scooped them up and set them by the smart guy.

Another sharp pain stung her, and she eyed the deck. Chaniclas stood there with a harpoon, preparing to strike again.

Who packs a harpoon in their emergency kit? Irritated, she whipped her other tentacle over and grabbed the scientist's leg. Zita hoisted her upside-down into the air. When Chaniclas clung grimly to the weapon and insisted on attempting to stab her again, Zita shook her gently until she dropped the weapon.

A boat roared up beside them, and a wave of water slapped against Zita.

Brie's delighted squeal was the first sound she heard from the newcomers. "She's enormous, but so cute and colorful with the bright purple and orange and blue! I think I saw something similar on the cover of an adult coloring book!"

Zita sighed in disgust, which resulted in her blowing large bubbles in the water. She glanced over. Several bodyguards surrounded Rani's girlfriend. Brie had found and put on form-fitting armor, complete with heeled boots and a short skirt. Wyn, in her Muse guise, stood beside her, lips tilted upward.

The lawyer tsked. "No, don't set foot on the boat, Brie. We're here to render aid to a vessel having issues. Can you keep holding them afloat, Arca?"

I have a few owies. Can you fix them? Zita brought her injured tentacle up and slapped it onto the deck of the rental. A line of bright red blood ran from it, mingling with the seawater dripping from her limb.

"Ugh. She can, yes." Despite her words, Wyn had her healing spell going and relief ran through Zita's battered body. *Interesting choice of form. I wouldn't have expected a giant calamari.*

Calamari? We've only got two more to go, but one's the central pillar. It's more complicated than the others. At least, that's what I'm interpreting Freelance's grunt to mean. Interest came through Andy's end of the link.

Zita snorted, blowing more bubbles. *Don't get any ideas, bird brain. I'm a kraken. It solved a problem, and I'm a problem solver. Dmitri assured me they were terrifying, but people keep stabbing me anyway, so it wasn't quite as successful as I'd hoped.*

I was just joking, Z. Even if I wasn't staying in human form, we had dinner when we were sailing to the island, Andy sent.

Her stomach rumbled. *Lucky you.*

For someone who was upside down, disarmed, and with her escape boat disabled, Chaniclas seemed awfully interested in her wristwatch. And smug.

Brie noticed too. "What's with her? She seems far too pleased with herself."

"Perhaps all the blood's rushed to her head. How long has she been upside down?" Wyn asked.

Zita lowered Chaniclas and dropped her. Suspicion flaring, she came up with a way to verify whether she was right not, one that had the added benefit of being something that the scientist would hate. *Have Brie use her power on Chaniclas. Once we have our answers, put everyone on this boat to sleep. I think I need to get back to the island.*

As she pushed herself back up, the scientist's smirk grew wider. "You just proved my point about the ruthlessness of your species. You came after me instead of trying to save the others of your kind on the island."

"You mean the bombs on the supports? They're all being defused by demolitions experts," Wyn said.

If anything, Chaniclas' smile grew wider. "Is that so?"

Zita narrowed her eyes. *What isn't she telling us? What'd we miss?*

"Where's Rani?" Brie leaned over the railing of her rental boat, her expression worried.

Rani's in a boat being protected by the mercenaries. Someone hired them to save her. I'm guessing General Aetherics, given some of her comments earlier.

Eyes wide, Wyn nodded. "Brie! Use your power on her! Rani's safe and offshore."

The lawyer shook his head. "If you attack them, it could count as an act of piracy."

Wyn tilted her head at him. "Is sharing her love of music really an attack?"

"That usually only works if they want to talk," Brie said.

"The way she's gloating, she's dying to tell us. We need to know why!" Wyn said. The second sentence came out like a song. She seemed to dance, but the movements of her hands were too precise.

Concern flashed across Chaniclas' face followed by confusion as music swelled. She wiggled, but it was rhythmic. "You're all fools," she sang. "Fools, fools, fools!"

Behind her, the guards sang backup. One by one, they yawned and slumped into unconsciousness. They snored in an almost syncopated rhythm.

Pursing her lips, Wyn opened her mouth and sang back, "Why? What have you done?"

"It's not me. It's what you've done! Or haven't done! You think you're so clever, but you're almost out of time. The bombs on the supports were backup for the main one in the power plant. It'll set off the volcano and everyone on the island will die."

Zita remembered. *Chaniclas put guards on the control room, and then tried to send her assistant to protect it as well. It's in the control room.*

Again, Wyn's part of the conversation came out as a sharp soprano trill. "It's in the control room."

The scientist's smile wavered, but the words finally tore from her in a wash of wavering notes. "That may be, but you'll never get there in time to do anything about it."

Sleep them. I got to go. Zita released the boat, jetted a short distance from the crafts, shifted to a dolphin and leapt from the water, switching to an albatross again and flying as fast as she could back to the island.

And Chaniclas just fell asleep. Brie's singing her big finale, and her bodyguards will board to "help" and rescue Linda, if necessary. Hurry!

Doing my best.

***

Given the time constraints, Zita cheated. She combined flying speed with short range teleports to get to the power plant in record time.

Fortunately, the spider robots had knocked out most of the guards on the power plant, leaving only a couple of out-of-uniform guys inside by the two main doors.

Zita let herself in through a window then shifted to a swift to avoid them. The helpful sign maker had struck here as well, and she blessed whomever they were as she flew straight to where she needed to go.

The control room had its own hydraulic door with the ever-present badge reader and number pad.

After a switch back to her Arca form, Zita swiped the guard's card she'd grabbed in the arena.

The door buzzed loudly, remaining red.

She threw it aside, digging in her pockets for the ones she'd gotten at the faux prison. The next one also failed with another loud noise that seemed to echo through the plant.

Shouting came from the direction of the outer doors.

Last thing I need is to fight them on a time limit. If I can't get in, we're chingada. Praying she was right, she sorted through the badges until she'd found the one she'd taken from Chaniclas at the fake prison. She swiped it.

When the light turned green, she punched in the code and into the room. The beeps seemed to echo in the empty plant.

Busy watching camera feeds of the spider robots patrolling on the exterior of the plant, the woman inside didn't even notice her.

Zita seized the back of the woman's chair and whirled it around before the other woman could speak. "Don't get up. Where's the bomb?"

With a squeak, the control room operator said, "What are you talking about? Bomb?"

Snatching the woman's badge off first, Zita shoved the chair out the door with the technician still in it. "Security's cranky, so I'd just run home!"

She slapped the button next to the door.

The hiss of the hydraulics closing the door cut off whatever the woman was saying and the heavy footsteps running down the hall.

Zita snorted and focused on finding the stupid bomb before it went off or someone figured out a way in.

She scanned the control room. It was filled with a mix of computers and machinery, ranging from intimidatingly industrial to rusted relics from someone's basement to mysterious and glowy. A few cheap rolling chairs rested in front of computers, but no one was there. Nothing looked definitively like a bomb.

While she searched, she used a desk lamp to take out the camera in the room. Spotting a big black box on the wall, she rushed over and opened it, picking the flimsy lock with ease even as she swore at the time it cost her. Breaker box. She kept searching, panic rising.

Was I wrong to come here? Wyn, borrow my eyes and project what I see so Andy can tell me what's a bomb and what's supposed to be in the control room of a power plant! she sent.

Darn it, Zita, I'm a physicist, not an engineer! How would I know? Andy paused. *Look for something hidden. They wouldn't want people finding it while maintaining the power plant, but they'd want it in an important spot. Maybe a box or a hidden door somewhere right up against the volcano or a pipe junction.*

Zita spotted a door half-hidden behind one of the consoles. Darting over, she yanked it open. Buckets, a small toolbox, and a mop fell out on her. Janitorial supplies were crowded into the tiny room along with a small selection of basic tools, and there, at least, she recognized everything. "Wrong door," she muttered.

She frowned and paced. *You guys better try to evacuate this place... I don't know if I can find it.*

Andy sent, *You could just start opening everything. Freelance is still doing the central pillar, but we got the rest.*

Can you sniff it out? Wyn sent.

Zita stared around. All the computers looked like computers. The other stuff was tangles of wires and a big, glowing, glass pipe with red blobby stuff cascading inside of it like an oversized lava light, throwing a crimson hue over the entire room.

I only know the scent of a couple types of explosive. If they used anything else, I could miss it. Wait. Lava would melt through pretty much any material, right? Or is that too much of an engineer question? Zita asked.

Andy's voice slipped into the happy professorial tone he used when talking about science. *That's a question I can answer. There's a few metals that can withstand lava, though not unscathed. By the way, if it hasn't been expelled from a volcano, technically it's magma.*

Glass or plastic? She pressed.

No. Metals. Titanium or tungsten, definitely. I don't remember the others offhand.

I have an idea. She examined the tube, and glimpsed a shadow behind it. Careful not to touch it—extreme heat radiated from it— she edged behind it and found a black box, roughly the size of a suitcase, fitted into a notch in the stone wall and against a tangle of pipes. It was chained in place and held with a combination lock.

Found it. She snorted as she finessed her way through the combination lock and tossed it aside. Moving as fast as she could, she pulled the chains off until she could open it.

A digital timer glowed at her.

25 seconds.

She swore.

24.

Nobody else can get here in time. Zita exhaled, her eyes on the cameras. *If I can, I'll get back as soon as possible. Save the kid.*

With a deep breath, Zita grabbed the bomb and teleported with it to the very edge of the one camera feed.

She appeared in midair above the island.

The box clicked.

Zita teleported again, straight up.

The air was cold and her lungs burned from the lack of air as she threw the box.

She teleported just as a wave of light and pain hit her.

Reappearing hundreds of feet below, she forced herself to shift to an albatross, despite the agony burning in her.

Something boomed, and smoke poured from beneath the prison. It... sagged.

This time, the pain was more than physical.

A cry escaped her, as she spiraled downward, not completely in control of her descent.

Chapter Twenty-Four

"You're an idiot," Wyn ranted.

"Sure," Zita said amiably. An hour after disposing of the power plant bomb, she balanced on the railing of their rental boat, trying not to wonder too loudly. She worked to put her thoughts into coherent order, walking back and forth in an effort to quiet her discordant mind. In the distance, she could see the prison jutting out over the water, an odd sag to the center section.

Of the six bombs that Chaniclas had ordered planted, only one had gone off on the island, destroying the central pillar of the prison floor. Since Andy had stopped the prison from collapsing, the prisoners had been largely unscathed, mostly protected from flying debris by the thick plastic walls of their cells. Wyn had found and healed Zita. Once her injuries were better, her friend had put the mind-controlled supers to sleep, and Zita had freed all the others. Sticking close to Elle, she'd escorted them down to the dock area and as far from the damaged prison as possible.

Andy was stuck holding up the weakened section of the prison for now. Uninjured himself, he had said Freelance had given him a two-word warning before jumping away from the central pillar and diving into the water immediately before the blast. Even though the mercenary had made it out of the immediate blast radius in time, he had still been underwater for several minutes before Andy finally saw him come up and get into a boat steered by the bear shifter. They hadn't spoken to Andy, and he'd been unable to follow them.

Whatever DMS guards weren't already stuck in webs around the island wisely had not interfered with any of their actions. None had fought when a very militant and still-armored Brie and her bodyguards had turned a warehouse into a temporary jail for Chaniclas and any other DMS personnel they'd disarmed and rounded up.

Zita focused on watching the churning water as the large ship's tender—a General Aetherics Cruise Line vessel—passed by, heading toward the small dock that currently held the now-empty DMS boats and a Coast Guard ship. People in uniform scurried in a bustle of activity that swirled around the larger grouping of orange-clad former prisoners; not one of the uniforms belonged to DMS personnel.

Wyn gestured emphatically at some point she was making in her diatribe. At least her friend had waited to unleash her tirade until after she'd healed Zita's injuries from the blast she hadn't entirely escaped, and they'd done everything they could for the prisoners. Now, however, having removed themselves from the island—to avoid distracting the Coast Guard with their presence and the possible need to arrest them—she was having her say.

And then some. It's not like I had any better choices. Zita snorted.

"Are you even listening to me? If I hadn't gone ashore to put the mind-controlled people to sleep, you might've been mistaken for a dying seagull and put out of your misery! Do you know how injured you were? Broken bones! Burns over—" Wyn said.

"Ladies!" Rani strolled over, beaming. She'd worn that expression since Brie had dropped her off on the boat following a long and very thorough kiss. Somewhere, she'd also traded in her prison uniform for regular clothing. "Good news! Since General Aetherics had applied for the prison contract previously and their cruise ship is already here, the US government is negotiating an interim contract to allow them to evacuate and hold all the inmates until a more formal contract can be finalized. Apparently, US prisons aren't ready for an influx of several hundred metahumans, especially given that some of them are children. It's also the quickest option. The Coast Guard will take Chaniclas and the DMS staff here into protective custody." Something in her expression implied she would have relished the scientist and her henchmen being trapped on a ship with their victims.

"What will happen to the prisoners once they're on the ship?" Wyn asked.

Zita tipped herself into a handstand on the railing.

"Isn't that dangerous?" Rani lifted an eyebrow at Zita, but allowed her attention to be drawn away. "Last I heard before I left, military police from the closest bases will supervise metahuman containment until each case can receive an independent, formal review to determine if they're actual criminals to be rerouted to prison for trial or simply DMS victims who need to be sent home. Minors and the medically unstable will be top priority. It'll take time though, as DMS has all their records in the damaged building, so everything needs to be moved and reviewed by experts."

"Elle?" Zita asked, going upright again.

Rani nodded, her expression softening. "That poor girl. Elle and a couple other prisoners with serious medical conditions will be moved to the closest military hospitals via helicopter so they can be evaluated and receive any necessary treatments. Once they're stable, they'll either be returned to the cruise ship or released to their families. In Elle's case, that'll be her foster mother, and Brie promised she'd follow up on it and exert any pressure she could. While I was there, I saw more than enough to justify letting the girl go home."

"Since they know the sick crap that was being pulled here, what about the other prison?" Zita asked.

Rani shrugged. "No idea."

Wyn suggested, "My best supposition is that some other branch of the federal government will commandeer it and use it to hold supers like Tiger and Domina, whose abilities require special handling. Perhaps they will finish the construction that was begun and turn it into the prison it was meant to be, instead of a holding station."

After correcting her foot position—she had almost slipped off the rail, and that would just be embarrassing—Zita said, "So this place will just hang in limbo?"

Wyn glanced at the island. "They don't know about the continued stability of the building given the one bomb that did go off, plus apparently there's legal issues around holding American prisoners on foreign soil, so it may be evidence. The press Brie rounded up are having a field day, and even though they're being kept as separate as possible from the prisoners, I expect we'll see a ton of interviews over the next few days."

Rani's eyes sparkled. "Technically, General Aetherics owns the island as of this morning. They might have to negotiate on how much equipment the US government can remove from it, but they'll probably convert it into something useful once they've had the time to assess it."

"Like a super expensive fixer-upper that might blow up at any time?" Zita shook her head. "Buey, Brie arranged all this in a day and half? You got a hell of a girlfriend."

Rani smiled smugly. "I do."

Wyn touched her shoulder and smiled, though her eyes seemed a little sad. "Told you I approved."

Her ex-girlfriend smiled, and the pair shared a gaze, something unspoken between them.

Maybe I should go somewhere and let them talk it out now. It beats being yelled at here, Zita thought, hopping down to the deck.

A small yacht zipped by, and a familiar rangy woman on the roof threw something white into the air. With a hoot, the smaller boat circled just out of range of the larger ship's wake.

The object spiraled upward, looped, and, improbably, swooped to the deck and lodged in Zita's hair. Hope and fear warred in her throat. "Oye!"

"Arca, open me?" Curiosity on her face, Wyn plucked it out and unfolded it. Her smile died. *Himself needs your shapeshifting prowess? No companions.*

Zita glanced around, a wide smile breaking out. *That's what Trixie calls Freelance. That or the Boss. I need to see what he wants. He can't be too injured, or they'd want you.*

Rani's forehead furrowed. "Did that mercenary seriously use a paper airplane to send you a note?"

"Yup," Zita said, popping the P and vaulting off the railing. "She's special like that. They're probably being paid to rescue a shifter stuck in an alternate form or something."

"That doesn't seem like an effective way to contact you. They'll have to wait. It must not be important if they're indulging her need for physical comedy, plus we need to get the boat back. I also promised Brie we'd let a couple of the reporters interview us," Wyn frowned. *Remember? We set up the interview specifically so you could be at home on the phone with Miguel while Arca is interviewed live.*

"My phone's off, and if they're resorting to Vaudeville's tricks, it's important. If someone needs my help, I'm going to give it. What if they're in trouble and the mercenaries are trying to peaceably handle them?" Zita glanced around casually, checking for people watching. Rani's bodyguards lingered close, of course, pretending to do something on the deck, and Rani was watching the interchange curiously. At least the military folks were ignoring their boat.

Her friend continued frowning. *But...*

"I'll meet up with you before the interviews." Zita craned her head, trying to see where Trixie's boat had gone. She spotted it, lurking farther out. *They came to rescue a couple people, not go after the bombs. Freelance did it anyway and almost died doing so. Keep party line up, and I'll call for backup if I need it. Alternately, that way you'll notice if they gas me. Besides, the cruise ship buffet line is way too long, and they're out of crab legs.*

Andy cleared his throat. *She's right about the mercenaries and probably about the buffet, though how she'd have had time to check it...*

Zita buffed her nails on her chest and blew on them. A grin tickled her face. *Mad skills, mano. Just kidding. With the time they've had to throw it together, it's probably just a cold cuts, chips, and soda on some tables.*

Andy sent laughter over the connection at her comment. *Or something. Where'd the robots go, anyway?*

I don't know. They all cleared out before the Coast Guard got here. Brie and her people were pretty evasive about them, Zita sent.

A speck on the horizon seemed to grow bigger.

"I suppose." After tossing a lock of hair over her shoulder, Wyn sighed. *Is anyone else thinking that Clockwork isn't as retired as he's supposed to be, given the automatons that were overrunning the place at one point?*

Andy added his opinion. *The spider-shaped ones seemed awfully similar to the ant robots we fought in Vegas last year, and the humanoid ones at the docks were pretty close to the ones at AethXP earlier.*

The Aetheric Experience, Wyn corrected.

Whatever it's called, I want to go back there sometime. It looked like fun. Zita, they have a giant laser tag area you might like, Andy sent.

Cool. I don't know much about the Clockwork dude, but it wouldn't surprise me if he keeps his hand in. It's not like General Aetherics can't spare the funds to indulge him if he wants to build a bunch of robots. Rocking on her feet, Zita nodded, squinting at the rapidly approaching shape. "Something's coming."

Sunlight glinted off the blond hair of a person flying above the water. For a moment, the figure paused, turned to the side, and patted their own shoulder.

Zita groaned. "Oh, look. It's a tool. Just what we need."

Wyn shot her a dirty look. Rani just seemed confused.

In a swirl of wind that ruffled her perfect ponytail and stirred her skirt-shorts but didn't flash anyone, Caroline came to a stop by the boat. She eyed the women and the others visible on the boat as she floated in midair, one leg drawn up, the other extended.

Struggling to keep her annoyance out of their link, Zita sent, *Your girlfriend's here.*

Andy's response was similarly controlled. *Thank you for letting me know.*

Rani gaped. "Oh, Brie is going to be so sad she missed this. I'm a huge fan! I had your posters on my wall for years!"

Very deliberately, Caroline pointed to a small black box clipped to the front of her navy tank top, near a small Air Force insignia. "I seem to be having issues with my body cam. Perhaps it's the sea spray? Pleased to meet you, Miss. As you know, I'm Caroline Gyllen, civilian metahuman support currently attached to the United States Air Force. Is it just the two of you vigilantes here today? Or is your third here as well?"

"Actually, there's a lot of people here today. The Coast Guard, DMS staff, several hundred of their victims, and a boatload of reporters and General Aetherics people." The words slipped out before she could stop them. *Now she's going to turn us over to the authorities and it's going to take forever to sort out—that or we'll have to break out and that'll just increase all the charges against us.*

"Wingspan's holding up the prison until all the prisoners can be safely evacuated and the computers retrieved for records of what went on here," Wyn said. All she said over party line was, *Have faith. She's not as bad as you think.*

Caroline's posture softened slightly.

Rani whispered, "I didn't realize you two knew her? I'm so honored to meet you!"

We'll see. Her voice flat, Zita said, "We've met."

Andy didn't send anything, but frustration and annoyance leaked from his end of their connection.

After a glance between them, Rani said, "I'm just going to go below decks and check something. It was a pleasure to meet you."

"You as well." Caroline stared for a long minute as Rani scurried off. She pursed her lips and spoke slowly. "You know, there's a lot of people calling for you to be arrested for invading a federal institution without provocation."

Smoothly, Wyn said, "I'm sure they'd change their minds once we explained to them how we happened to intervene only because we were in the area searching for one of us who was missing when they attacked a ship filled with innocents."

The floating blond nodded. "It's a shame I won't run into you when I'm on the island and get a chance to ask your side of things, then. I must've just missed you with all the people and the confusion."

"That's a pity," Wyn said. Her face was serene, though one corner of her mouth seemed to turn upward. "I'm certain we would've had a good chat if you'd run into us."

Zita frowned. *She isn't going to try to arrest us or something?*

Not to gloat, but people change, Zita, Wyn sent.

"Good luck." Her face easing, Caroline nodded. She turned and flew away from the ship.

Wyn called out, "To you as well!"

Pausing in midair, Caroline lifted a hand in a wave. She then tapped the box on her shoulder, resolutely facing away.

They watched her go. She seemed to head directly to the prison, skipping the dock area.

Zita broke the silence first. "I'm out to see what the mercenaries need. I'm guessing that means keep a low profile?" She repeated herself over party line for Andy.

But our interview? Wyn tried.

Andy sounded distracted. *Can we do the illusion trick and pretend Arca shows up at the last minute? If we give her a sandwich or something, anyone who's ever met her would believe she went off to grab a bite to eat.*

I could eat, Zita agreed.

Duh, Andy sent. I think the Coast Guard got almost everyone. It's just computers and such they're trying to remove now. They are scary good at evacuating the place. You think they rescue people from mad scientist labs often? Be careful. I'll join Wyn as soon as I can so she's not alone.

Wyn frowned at her. *Our interview is on the cruise ship in an hour. It will be the farthest thing from being alone possible.*

Zita snorted. *You both be careful too. You're the ones who are going to be on a ship full of half-starved metas who've been held prisoner for Dios knows how long. I'll call if I need backup.*

***

Following a shift to an albatross and a quick flight, Zita landed on the gray yacht, taking care to do so behind the cabin. She shifted to Arca.

"Finally! You know, I wanted to hit them with flaming Jell-O shots or something but Bossman said it was too dangerous. Like we aren't mercenaries living la vida danger-a already." Trixie pounced on her the second she emerged from her landing spot, grabbing her arm.

Zita didn't fight as she was dragged toward the cabin. "How'd you guys find the island anyway?"

The mercenary doctor laughed. "You rented a boat. The guy who owns it has satellite trackers on all his ships, and our client told us you'd lead us to the targets."

"Makes sense," Zita said. Spotting a sleepy-seeming bear at the controls, Zita waved.

Even as he lifted a paw, Trixie opened the door and shoved her into the cabin. "Get to it!"

Zita found herself in a small room that held a minuscule kitchen, a tiny three-sided sofa that surrounded an even smaller table, and a silent mercenary leader. An open door led to a bedroom where she could see a long gun laid out on the bed along with a cleaning kit.

The mercenary stood very still by the window, pivoting to face her. His head nearly touched the low ceiling. As usual, his only movement was the slightest whisper of breath, though the way he held that magnificent body was wrong. Too tense. Too tight, like over-compressed springs about to break rather than his usual alert readiness. He smelled odd, too. In addition to his usual mix of woodsy male and gun oil, a pungent chemical reek pricked at her nose, like oil mixed with something astringent.

She shut the door behind her. "You rang? Or paper airplaned, anyway?"

Trixie's curious face pressed up against the glass, the slats of the window blinds casting lines across her like a modern, not very complicated puzzle.

With a curt movement, Freelance snapped them shut, hiding his teammate.

"So, what's the problem? Vaudeville's note only said you needed me to shapeshift or something?" Zita asked.

He held out his hands. For once, he wore no gloves, but his hand had the dull shimmer of metal. "Stuck."

"Oye. Guess I won that discussion we have on and off about whether or not you're a meta." Zita ran a hand over her hair, back and forth as she thought.

"Fix." Fingers flexing, he lowered them to his side.

"You think I can help? That's... I mean, I guess I've worked with a few others before if you count Elle, Sheriff, and that mermaid at the swimming pool." She stopped to collect her thoughts. "Órale, let's start at the beginning. Is this the first time you've shifted?"

He nodded.

Her next problem was figuring out how to ask without sounding like a proposition in a porno. Though a corner of her mind really, really wanted to know. "Is it just your extremities or is it your whole body? Has anything changed since you first shifted?"

A brusque head shake. "All. Gills, webbed hands, went away out of water."

"Everything everything? Even your—never mind." She held up a hand and took a moment to focus on the matter at hand rather than speculating about his anatomy. One or twenty deep breaths later, she said, "So what happened?"

"Tangled in debris. Got gills, webbed hands. Blast leaked chemicals into water. Hydraulic tank ruptured. Changed again, metal skin." His shoulders were a bit too high, with his left side turned away slightly as if he would attack at any second.

She stared at him and stepped forward, hands extended to him.

After a pause, he offered her one of his.

Gripping his wrist gently, she ran her fingers over his skin. It was like touching a fine metal mesh and didn't feel human. His pulse was too slow, though it sped slightly under her touch.

Funny how his hands still have calluses from his guns... and what I'm guessing are other weapons. Zita bit her lip and released him with one last stroke of her fingertips over his palm. "I have no idea what to tell you."

"You teach others." He lowered his hands.

Zita snorted. "I doubt those tricks would work for you. Most of my students have control issues. They need practice and maybe therapy. You... you're probably the most disciplined person I've ever met, so teaching you some yoga and breathing exercises isn't going to work. The mermaid, however, she changed when she hit the water..."

His shoulders twitched.

Her mind kept running down comparisons, and she began to pace, speeding up as she concentrated. Not that the tiny room allowed her more than a few steps in either direction. "I think you're more like I was, back when I couldn't control my changes. Your skin changed in reaction to the poisoned water, sí? I'm guessing that's the odor on you, the stuff that leaked from the elevator and whatever else in the column that exploded?"

He nodded.

"You smell off, so you might still have some of those chemicals hanging out on your body. You need to get naked and hose every last bit off." She paused, trying not to let an image of that distract her. Stupid close quarters. Stupid sexy man scent.

"Maybe you'll shift back once all the nasty gunk is gone, just like the gills went away when you were out of the water. Did you bring a change of clothes or just every gun known to man and then some? Putting on gear polluted with that stuff afterward might undo all the good of the shower."

After a moment of silence, he touched his ear and murmured.

Following a perfunctory and oddly syncopated knock on the door, Trixie barged in, her face alight with mischief and glee. It fell when she saw Freelance by the bathroom, and Zita in the narrow space between the sofa and table "Well, shit. Doesn't anybody have inappropriate sexy fun times anymore? So much for hoping you'd get laid so I could ask for that raise."

Despite her words, she held out a black backpack to Freelance, who took it wordlessly and retreated into the bathroom. Despite his lean form, he had to stand in the shower to shut the door.

Zita tried not to be offended when she heard the lock click. *Not like that could keep me out if I were going to be a creeper and invade his privacy,* she grumped internally.

Trixie shook her head and sighed, eyeing Zita. "Kids these days. No fun. You might as well hang out and wait for him to come out. He's armed, of course, but I'd rather leave you to guard him. You know, while you're alone in a room with a bed, you could sex him up so I can ask for my raise? I'd rather you guys did the deed so you stop infesting him with your hero cooties. I signed up to earn money as a mercenary under a good boss, not to be jobless with a dead idealist."

Squelching the part of her that thought it was a great idea, assuming she could get him back to his normal form, Zita folded her arms across her chest. "That's not why I'm here."

"Of course not, my little cinnamon roll. Apparently, none of us are getting lucky today." Tapping the bathroom door in a staccato pattern, Trixie called out, "I'm leaving Arca to watch your back out here. Or wash it in there. Not judging, though as your doctor, I will say it'd be good for you to get some. Kodiak and I will be eating our feelings at the all-you-can-eat buffet when you're ready to emerge from your cocoon. I'll grab you a plate of nuts, berries, and whatever the most expensive leaves are."

"You have a buffet on this boat?" Zita couldn't help asking, licking her lips. Her stomach rumbled. To get her mind off Freelance being all naked and soapy and... naked in the next room... she concentrated on the idea of food and started jogging in place.

Trixie heaved a dramatic sigh. "I want to say yes, but no, we don't. We have a bunch of MRIs that Kodiak doctored with some spices while we were eavesdr—waiting for a sign that you two were done."

Zita glanced at the closed, locked bathroom door and sighed. "Guess I'm waiting here then."

"Do everything I would do, including locking this door when I leave. I think there's cherries and whipped cream in the mini bar," Trixie advised as she slid out the door.

Zita locked it. She glanced toward the bathroom, noting the steam leaking out from it.

After spending a long, boring minute sitting still, she contented herself doing body weight exercises to pass the time.

Zita, are you okay? Wyn broke into her thoughts.

It took a moment for the words to penetrate the focus she had on the exercises. *Yes, fine. No danger here.*

Curiosity from both of her friends came over the line even before Wyn asked the question. *What did they need help with?*

Instinct told her that Freelance wouldn't want his problem known. *They wanted advice on a shapeshifting thing.*

Oh, is Kodiak okay? He's a very nice man, even if he does spend a lot of time in his bear form around us. I can do a healing spell if he needs it, Wyn offered.

Andy chimed in. *Yeah, let me know if I can help.*

He's fine, thanks. I got this, Zita sent back. *What'd you need? Or were you just worried that they'd decided to go for the lowest bounty of the three of us?*

Wyn replied, *I'm glad he's well. Our television interview will be live in a little less than an hour. Can you get away, so you can go home and phone Miguel while it's on? Proving you and Arca can't possibly be the same person is the point of this interview, after all. Illusory you will be eating, which is my excuse for the delay in your answers. You'd just have to transmit your answers to me after I send you the questions.*

She eased into a yoga position that she could easily hold. Her stomach complained again. *I'll go home as soon as I'm done here. Shouldn't be long.*

***

Several minutes later, Freelance emerged from the bathroom. For the first time, he wore no armor, though a black hood hid his hair. His spare goggles, the ones she'd tried on in Brazil, hid his eyes and the upper half of his face, leaving only a strong chin and thin, ascetic lips visible.

She couldn't help but notice the grapple gun at his waist was missing and the way the damp fabric clung to his defined muscles, even more perfect than she'd imagined... Zita forced herself to focus.

He gestured to the lower half of his face. Belatedly, she realized his skin still held a faint metallic tint, though less so than earlier.

After a cursory sniff, she crossed the tiny cabin in a few steps. Fine, white scars under his chin and ears were visible from her current angle. She inhaled deeply and retreated. "I don't smell the chemicals anymore, so maybe we just need to get your system to reset now. Try to think human things. What makes you feel human?"

"Talk." Even without the voice changer, his voice was little more than deep rasp of a whisper.

Suppressing a shiver that had nothing to do with fear, Zita blinked. "What? You want me to just babble about whatever?"

Freelance simply nodded once, apparently having run out of his allotment of words.

"Well, I suppose I could come up with something. You want to hear what happened in the DMS prison? That was some messed-up shit." When he didn't reply, she launched into a carefully edited version of events.

The tint was gone from his skin by the time she finished. He slid a photo over to her.

She glanced at it. Linda Mwangi stared up at her from it, dressed in a jumpsuit even Zita recognized as being from the Seventies. Someone had written "Jane Doe" at the bottom of it.

He regarded her steadily.

"You weren't just supposed to rescue Rani? You were supposed to save her too?" she asked, heart sinking. She shoved the photo back at him.

After a pause, Freelance nodded.

"Did you at least get paid for Rani? The lady in the photo's name is Linda. We're taking her home to her family. I don't want to stand in your way, but I can't give her to you. She's been missing from her family's lives for too long as it is, and I know they don't have the money to hire you," Zita said.

He nodded and tucked away the photo.

"Is she why you tried to defuse the bombs?"

After a pause, he shook his head.

Zita tilted her head at him, considering. "Is it a secret?"

Another head shake.

She started to ask again, but stopped. "Vaudeville said you guys found us because the rental boat guy had trackers on our rental. Did you know when you gave me his name that your on-call job would require you to follow us?"

"No." The word was little more than a whisper.

One of her hands rose to touch her collarbone. Zita swallowed. "Did you have names that wouldn't have allowed us to be tracked that you could've recommended?"

Slowly, his head inclined.

"So... you gave me this guy's name because you could track me later if needed?" Her nerves danced.

He looked away.

That was enough answer for her. She inhaled. At a loss for words, she hurled herself at him and hugged him.

At first, it was like holding a magnificently sculpted, if damp, statue, but the tension in his body left in an exhale and his arms went around her gently, almost tentatively.

Giving him a squeeze, she released him and smiled. "Thank you. You're a good friend. All those people would've been really chingada if all those bombs had gone off, and it's nice to know you'd consider having my back."

His grip prevented her from backing away, and he gazed down at her. "Not just friends."

Another tremor ran through her and her mood turned. She licked her lips and searched what little she could see of his face. Now her heart was racing. "No, not just..."

Freelance leaned down, far enough she could feel the heat of cinnamon-scented breath. "Yes?"

Zita rose on her tip toes, her hands clutching his shoulders. "Less talking."

Warm air, like a silent laugh, brushed her lips a second before his mouth came firmly down on hers.

Her fingers clenched the fabric of his shirt as she luxuriated in the taste of him, and she leaned up, pressing against him.

His grip was tight, too tight for a second before he loosened it and freed her, far too soon.

Even as she stepped away again, Zita knew she had a loopy smile on her face. "We should go, sí? And, um, you want to try free running and dinner sometime?"

Hefting the backpack, he crossed the small room and held the door open for her.

She stepped through.

"Soon," he whispered.

Zita grinned like an idiot and didn't care.

Epilogue

Her apartment was invaded while she was in the shower.

As soon as Zita stepped out of the bathroom, the steamy air rich with the scent of vanilla soap, she heard the low murmur of familiar male voices. She scrubbed a hand over her head, back and forth, setting her short, wet hair standing on end.

The interview's about to start, Wyn sent.

"Oh, joy. I thought I had more time, and I'd been hoping not to do this on an empty stomach," Zita muttered, not relishing the idea of trying to talk to her brothers and answer mental questions as well.

Footsteps came down her hall.

Before they could speak, she lifted her voice. "I just got out of the shower. Unless you want to chat while I'm naked, I'll be out in a sec."

The footsteps retreated, faster than they'd come.

She grinned to herself. *Definitely Miguel. Quentin wouldn't care.*

After throwing on some clothes, she padded into the living room, her feet silent on the thin carpet.

Unsurprisingly, her eldest brother was poking through the mail that she hadn't had a chance to deal with for the past few days. Quentin had her fridge open and was peering inside. Neither was paying a great deal of attention to the TV she'd left on, set to the channel that would be airing the interview with her friends and illusory Arca.

"We need to talk, Zita," Miguel said, setting down her mail. With a frown, he gestured toward her chairs. "Please have a seat. I hate talking to you when you're bouncing all over the room."

She wrinkled her nose and leaned against a wall instead. "And I hate discussions where I have to sit still. So, what am I in trouble for? Whatever it was, Quentin probably did it."

"Don't drag me into this. I'm just here for the free grub," Quentin said without changing position. A plastic lid ripped open, and then another in the depths of the fridge.

Miguel frowned at her. "Do you have to be in trouble for the three of us to have a nice sibling chat?"

Raising an eyebrow, Zita nodded. "Yeah, pretty much. I mean, usually you tell me not to do something or that something I've done is too risky, and I roll my eyes and mostly ignore you. It's not really a chat so much as you nagging and us ignoring you."

"Us?"

She shrugged and plopped into her usual glitter-encrusted chair. "Me and Quentin. So, what's wrong this time?"

"Your fridge doesn't have nearly enough food. It's Sunday. You always make food on Sundays for the week. Where's the food? Now I'll have to make my own lunches. Also, none of your containers are labeled. Why don't you label them?" Quentin mourned, closing the fridge. Despite his complaints, he had a homemade protein bar in his hand.

Zita laughed. "If I put labels on everything, Miguel'd be happy, and you'd eat everything in there. This way, you both suffer. Two for one for the win, mano."

Quentin grinned. "Probably true."

Miguel cleared his throat uncomfortably.

Another thought struck her. She bounced right out of her chair and over to her eldest brother. "Is Linnea preggers? Am I going to be an auntie? I'm going to be the fun aunt. I will teach your little rug rat to climb mountains, and jump out of planes. Plus, I'll hold their hand when they get that awesome but inappropriate tattoo that you said they couldn't get... you know, the one Quentin paid for because you know I never got the cash for that."

Quentin blinked. "Are you ratting on me in advance? I mean, I'm not saying you're wrong, but not cool, Z."

His face reddening, Miguel opened and closed his mouth. His gaze fell on the envelope in his hand. "Why do you have a letter from the Department of Homeland Security?"

"Beats me," she said.

He lifted his eyebrows.

She rolled her eyes and snatched up the letter. "Fine. It's probably a bill for when they stuck me in quarantine or something stupid like that."

"Well?" Miguel waved his hand.

Zita ripped it open and read the letter. Surprise and delight ran through her. "They found it!"

Even Quentin stopped rummaging through her cupboards at her tone. "What?"

"Papá's Saint Jude medal! And the other crap that was stolen when I was locked up in the quarantine hospital!" She grinned. "They want me to set an appointment to pick my stuff up."

A smile broke out over Miguel's face. "Seriously? That's amazing! And they don't need it in a court case?"

She kept reading. "No, they say it was stored offsite due to a lack of space and recorded improperly. However, when the storage unit came up for renewal, they investigated and located all the missing boxes." Something about that tickled her memory. *Jerome said something about hacking storage unit records for a client. Could it be related?*

After a second, she scoffed at herself. *Who would steal boxes of personal belongings only to give it all back? Then again, they didn't say everything was returned, just that all the boxes were. Someone could've taken everything of monetary value and left the rest. My stuff would've only had value to me and maybe my family.*

Quentin cheered. "Three cheers for government incompetence! Just think, if they'd done their jobs right, your stuff would've burned up with all the other records and stuff in the hospital."

Miguel sobered, his eyes suspicious. He frowned. "That's a very odd sequence of events, but I'm thrilled we—you—are getting his medal back."

"I'll schedule an appointment to pick it up as soon as possible. My locksmithing boss will reschedule anything I have if it's during those work hours, right?"

"Yeah, he won't have a problem with that, especially if you bring him a lunch or two," Quentin said, filling a cup with some fruit juice.

She grinned at him. "I won't do that, but I will get the container with the leftover bean stuff out so we can throw them into tacos."

He raised his glass to her and drained it. "Sold!"

A moment later, Miguel picked up the topic she most wanted to avoid. "Now that you two have settled the dinner issue, where were you today, Zita? It's pretty interesting how you're never home whenever Arca shows up somewhere."

After returning to the fridge, Quentin got himself a refill. He sipped it. "Did I need to be here for this?"

"Yes," Miguel bit out.

Zita's spine prickled, and she forced her body not to tighten up. She picked her words carefully, trying to be as truthful as possible. "I don't plan my schedule around some vigilante. I just get around a lot."

Quentin snickered, and her other brother gaped at her.

She amended her words, realizing what she'd said. "Not like Quentin did. More like I go out lots doing cool stuff. Since I didn't leave the country this year, I've been doing lots of little trips. Besides, I'm sure I'm here sometimes. You don't visit often enough to see when I'm home or not."

Miguel relaxed a little, but his face still had a narrow, calculating expression.

Despite that, Zita smiled, pleased with herself. *I'm getting better at this diplomatic stuff. All that was true enough. Planning is nearly impossible. Look at how hard it's been to line up meets—dates with Freelance? Not that I'm going to share that with my overprotective big brother. He's going to flip when and if I ever start sleeping with the man.*

Her eldest brother struck. "Yes, you do. So, if you weren't engaged in illegal vigilante activities earlier today, where were you all afternoon?"

"Working?" Zita's mind whirled, praying Quentin wouldn't contradict her.

"I checked your schedule. You weren't scheduled today," her eldest brother said.

To her surprise, Quentin stepped up and lied. "She was on a job for me. I might've slept with a client once, and she's... persistent in wanting a replay. So, I sent Zita to do the job on the down low. If I remember, it was a complete house alarm wiring job, so it would've taken a while."

"Not a quickie," Zita agreed.

Quentin choked, turning away for a moment.

"Why didn't either one of you say so?" Miguel put his hands on his hips, deflating slightly. Something that looked a lot like relief crossed his face.

Quentin grinned at their eldest brother. "I just did. And I asked her not to say anything."

"Why didn't you speak up earlier when I was going off about her being missing again?" Miguel scowled.

"What kind of brother would I be if I missed an opportunity to see you flip out like that?" Quentin's grin faded. "Besides... I'm not real proud of some of my past behavior."

Miguel rubbed the back of his neck. "I was... I thought... Never mind. Good. Next time tell me sooner."

Muse's silvery laughter broke in. They turned to the television, where the interview was finally starting. Illusory Arca was really enjoying a sandwich.

Zita's stomach rumbled. She got the beans and other taco fixings from the fridge.

Quentin laughed. "See? Not her."

Relief spread across Miguel's face as he nodded, his attention caught up in Wyn's explanation how they'd been trying to have a day off at The Aetheric Experience when things had started going wrong, starting with the attack on the park. She made it sound as if they'd been innocently searching for Arca when they'd seen missiles fired at a civilian vessel and had to intervene.

Fortunately, with her brothers wrapped up in the interview, it wasn't hard to answer the questions for Wyn mentally.

By the time the clips started airing, including a piece of the conversation between the senator and Chaniclas, Miguel's phone was almost constantly pinging with texts. The one he'd claimed belonged to a friend.

He grimaced and typed something, tucking the phone back into his pocket. "I have to go. All that"—he waved at the screen—"sped up the timetable of things I was working on."

As soon as Miguel was gone, Quentin tapped Zita's arm. "So, who is the mystery man? He's one of mine, right?"

"He?" Zita blinked and shoved a plate of food his direction.

"I know you took off early today. The homeowner called and complained about you several times. Miguel's wrong in his reasoning, though. Clearly the crazy at DMS affected our boy if he thinks you could be a vigilante. You don't even watch the news. No mames, you'd miss all the crimes because you'd be off in the woods or in the gym ignoring the rest of reality. I doubt you even know the name of the President?"

She opened her mouth, wanting to protest, but couldn't remember. After a second, she chomped on a taco.

Her brother took a bite and talked around it. "So, who's the guy?"

Zita took a deep breath, knowing that if she said it, the rest of her family would know by sundown. Miguel might be back with more concrete demands. *Screw that, they'll know pretty much as soon as my back is turned. Quentin can't keep a secret to save his life.* "Umm, I'd rather not say. It'd be nice if you didn't bother digging up someone to date this month though. I already got a date."

Quentin stopped eating, his taco halfway to his mouth, for all of a few seconds. "You got a second date? You go, girl! When this one goes crying away, make sure you tell me right away. The guys in my therapy group love to hear the funny stories about your dates. You be extra... you with him."

That made her set down her food. After taking a large bite and chewing it quickly. She was, after all, hungry. "Be extra me? Nice way to support your sister. Is that why you sent me so many losers, because you wanted to make them angry?"

He shook his head. "No, no, I sent you a lot of nice guys who aren't picky. You know, buds who could handle a few dates with you and that you might like well enough to sleep with. They're the ones I figured wouldn't give you anything itchy that required medication, anyway. We all know you aren't seriously looking for a boyfriend."

"Oye, are you trying to piss me off?"

He grinned. "No, so where's Miguel's pick taking you? Rubber chicken dinner?"

The words shot out. "We're going to do some free running, and he's not Miguel's pick."

His eyebrows rose and delight shone. "You circled back for one of mine? Which one? Iggy? Luis? I bet it's Iggy. You can't resist the bad boys, and once you look past the forgettable face, he's got that vibe."

She took a wolfish bite of her taco and let him babble on about his buddy for a minute. "No. It's a guy I asked out. I met him playing paintball a while back, and we ran into each other again, so... Anyway. No big."

"You picked someone out, and he said yes?" His mouth fell open.

Narrowing her eyes at her brother, Zita said, "Sí. It happens. Choose your words carefully or only part of you will show up at your next therapy session."

Perhaps because he knew she'd never act on the threat, Quentin made a production of stroking the stupid goatee he'd been cultivating. "I suppose it's possible. We do share genes, so it's conceivable you might occasionally not scare someone off. Is this a first date?"

Forcing herself to act casually, Zita shook her head. "No, we met up before. I told you. Paintball."

"And this guy still wants to date you?" Quentin eyed her. "You're not nearly relaxed enough to be getting any on the regular. What's wrong with him? Would I like him? More importantly, how would Miguel feel about him?"

She grimaced before she could stop herself. "Nothing, he just isn't local and travels a lot. Miguel would be fine with him...eventually. He's clean, no record or anything." *I hope. Even if he isn't, he's more than competent enough to get away with most crimes.*

Quentin snickered and relaxed. "I saw your face. Miguel'll hate him. Poor doomed guy."

"You don't know that," she said. "He's a—" nice stuck in her throat, so she substituted one she could mean—"good man with a very sensible world view."

Quentin snarfed down the rest of his taco. "Is he in law enforcement? Or the Church?"

Reluctantly, the answer left her lips. "No."

He nodded. "Miguel will hate him. One, Miguel didn't pick him. Two, you picked him. Three, you know Miguel's going to hate him based on your expression, and four, you don't exactly have a record of making good choices with men."

She made a face at him. "You're supposed to be on my side. My track record is perfectly fine. And I feed you!"

"¿Neta? You must be in denial. Let's look at your choices so far. First, you had the fisherman who wanted a woman to stay home and have his babies. When you ditched him, you hooked up with that acrobat who married someone else, and then got you chased out of your favorite aerial gym when you refused to be his side piece." Quentin shook his head.

Zita straightened, drawing herself up to her full height and trying to look down her nose at him. It was mostly wasted effort, given her snub nose and his height advantage, but she tried. "I rejected all those losers you and Miguel fixed me up with, though, so that's got to count for something. Come on, Quentin, you know if Miguel hates him, I need your backup."

He took a long drink and nodded. "Fine. I'll back you up and won't arrange anything. And I won't even ask his name. You know what else? I'll tell Miguel so he knows not to schedule anything for you."

Not like you wouldn't have told him anyway. She relaxed. "Thanks, Quentin." Zita took a big bite.

Her brother grinned and added, "After all, I'm hooking you up with someone next month after this guy crashes and burns. Miguel has to wait his turn to find someone for you to piss off." He cackled.

Zita nearly choked. "Quentin!"

He grinned. "Just keeping it real, Z."

***

"Caroline chingada Gyllen," Zita muttered under her breath, parking her motorcycle by Andy's ancient sedan the next day. Once she'd hung up her helmet, she went to the door of the basement apartment where he lived.

She took a deep breath, touched the newly recovered saint's medal at her throat, and knocked. A curtain twitched in the main house, and she waved to Andy's dad or stepmom, whoever was watching.

Andy opened the door, his long hair loose and rumpled. He had on pajama pants plastered with smaller versions of the logo on the matching t-shirt. When he saw her, his body tightened and his face closed down. The big bowl of popcorn he held gave a little crack. Somewhere behind him, his cat meowed loudly. "Z?"

Her heart gave a painful twist when she took in his defensive posture and angry expression.

"Come in." He stepped aside.

She entered, glancing around.

His living room hadn't changed any since she'd last seen it, though it was cleaner than when she'd briefly stayed on the sofa. Weird costumes hung on the dark wood-paneled walls. Spaceships were frozen mid-battle on his big television. Since the video game controllers glowed in their recharging stations, she assumed he was watching a show rather than playing a game. Papers still covered his desk and bookshelves threatened to either explode or collapse due to the excess of contents.

Hope trickled through her when she spotted the spare snack bowls on one shelf, the same place he'd kept them for her during her brief stay.

Sprawled on the overstuffed sofa like a battered feline king, Cupcake eyed her. Someone had spread a plain navy blanket over the faded orange, purple, and cream plaid pattern of the brown couch, but gray and white cat hair covered it. The massive cat's raggedy ear flicked a few times at her, and he began grooming his nether regions.

Even the cat's a critic. She stared at her feet.

Andy appeared absorbed in contemplating his own.

She broke the silence first. "Dream Auntie get to Mwangi okay?"

"Yeah. After Caroline took over, Wyn and I got her to his clinic. He was pissed. Some because she'd been in a coma that long, and some because they took more blood than he deemed safe and hadn't hydrated her properly or something. He had a buddy there though, a big guy with a Jersey accent. Anyway, his friend cooled off his temper, and they said not to worry about Linda any longer. Actually, Mwangi said that if we'd just forget their existence, that'd be even better." Andy gave a half laugh.

Zita rocked slightly on her feet. "Chido. Sounds about right. Wonder who they're hiding from? Clockwork, maybe? General Aetherics or whoever hired Freelance wanted both Rani and Linda."

He shrugged.

Awkward silence fell again.

She cleared her throat and forced out the words. "Here's the deal. I get what you've been saying. You and Caroline are a, a serious thing. It upsets you when I dis her or the two of you."

Andy nodded.

Zita took a few steps one direction, then another, finally returning to her original spot. While she could feel her shoulders tightening, she couldn't stop them. "You get that she seriously screwed over my family, right? Even if that wasn't her goal?"

His face dark, Andy nodded and opened his mouth to speak.

Interrupting, she crossed her arms over her chest and hurried before he could defend Caroline. "Don't. I just wanted the acknowledgement. I still think your relationship is a huge mistake, but it is what it is. Caroline and me got too much history, and I'm not forgetting it. I got that right."

He tried to interrupt again, but she held up a finger. "Let me finish first. You're my friend. I'll support you, if not her. So. Don't expect me to be buddies with her, and don't tell her my identity. Even if I won't hang with her unless I have to, I'll stop insulting her. When our paths cross, I'll be nice. You need me to cover for a date, I got your back."

He started to speak again.

She took a deep breath and let the next part tumble out. "I'll try to be more open-minded that she's changed if you let me keep some space from her so I can breathe. Maybe things can be different someday. I'm trying to let that happen. However, if I think she's screwing you or us over, I am going to speak up."

His smile was tremulous. "I know she won't hurt us, so I can live with that. Thanks, Z. Wyn told me what went down with the Olympics, and... I understand at least part of it. Hard not to. When I got cancer, I had to go live with my dad for the insurance, and I had only met him a few times before. It's not the same, but I get it."

Zita twitched. Her voice was gruff with relief. "Chido. You got any chili powder for that popcorn?"

Scooping up the untouched bowl, Andy poured half of his popcorn into it and handed it to her.

Her fingers closed around it.

He jerked his chin at the spice container next to his television, and then sat down. Reaching over, he set his own popcorn aside and hauled his big cat into his lap.

The sofa was still warm from the animal as Zita plopped down on it with her snack.

Five seconds of spaceships exploding was more than enough.

She had to speak. "Thanks. What are we watching? Have you ever seen the *Blade* movie? Dmitri and I watched it and it seemed like something you'd like."

His eyebrows rose. "Which?"

"There's more than one? How's the fighting in them?"

He laughed and bumped her shoulder with his. "Ah, padawan, you have so much to learn."

"Pada-whatever yourself. Pick one. I'll trust your choice, but I reserve the right to complain." She bumped his shoulder back and ate some popcorn.

Languages Glossary

These are definitions of the words as Zita uses them in the book, and may not include all possible variations. The Spanish is primarily Mexican in usage and slang. Needless to say, anything marked with "Vulgar" should not be used in polite company.

amiga: Spanish. Friend.

arca: Spanish. A chest or ark. Zita originally used it referring to Noah's ark in *Super*.

ay: Spanish. An interjection, similar to "Oh."

brigadeiros: Portuguese. Truffle-like Brazilian chocolates.

buey: Spanish. Dude.

cállate: Spanish. Shut up.

capoeira: Portuguese. A fast, fluid Brazilian martial art known for its acrobatic and dance-like kicks, spins, and other techniques.

carajo: Spanish. Shit. Vulgar.

caramba: Spanish. A mild interjection of surprise or dismay.

chanclas: Spanish. Flip flops.

chido: Spanish. Cool.

chingado/chingada: Spanish. Fucked or fucking. This has other meanings as well, but this is how Zita generally uses it. Vulgar.

culo: Spanish. Ass. Vulgar.

de verdad: Spanish. True.

diga: Spanish. A standard phone greeting. Literally "Tell."

Dios: Spanish. God.

esquiva: Portuguese. A dodge in capoeira, typically followed by an attack.

ginga: Portuguese. The most basic capoeira footwork, a moving fight stance.

gracias: Spanish. Thank you.

gracias a Dios: Spanish. Thank God or Thanks be to God.

hasta luego: Spanish. See you later.

hermano: Spanish. Brother.

hombre: Spanish. Man.

la vida: Spanish. The life.

mamá: Spanish. Mom.

mano: Spanish. Bro. Abbreviated form of "hermano" as Zita uses it.

martelo de negativa. Portuguese. A capoeira move that begins with a hop that flows into one leg kicking high while supported by the other leg and an arm.

meia lua de compasso. Portuguese. A capoeira kick where a front handspring and a spinning reverse roundhouse kick combine to hit someone with both feet.

momentito: Spanish. Just a moment.

mujeres: Spanish. Women.

nada: Spanish. Nothing.

negativa: Portuguese. Capoeira defensive move where the practitioner drops low to dodge an incoming attack.

neta: Spanish. Really, for real, you know.

no hay bronca: Spanish. No problem.

no mames: Spanish. No way or what the fuck? Literally, don't suck. Vulgar.

no manches: Spanish. No way.

órale: Spanish. An interjection. Can be used like heck yeah, right on, listen, hey, or hurry up.

oye: Spanish. An interjection that can be used as hey, listen, or yo.

pan comido: Spanish. Piece of cake, literally "eaten cake."

papá. Spanish. Papa. Dad.

pendejo: Spanish. A jerk or asshole. Vulgar.

pinche: Spanish. Sucky or fucking. Vulgar.

por fa: Spanish. Abbreviated form for por favor, please.

por supuesto: Spanish. Of course.

pues: Spanish. An interjection, equivalent of well, then, or since.

sí: Spanish. Yes.

tía: Spanish. Aunt.

verdad: Spanish. Right. True or truth.

From the Author

Thank you for reading!

All prisons and legislation in this book are imaginary, much like DMS, General Aetherics, anything attached to them like AethXP, my characters, and chocolate that leaves you thinner than when you started eating it.

Please consider leaving reviews for any books you've enjoyed, positive or negative. Reviews assist other readers in finding books and let authors know what they've done right (or wrong).

For the latest on past and future releases, monthly chatter, free short stories, and the occasional other freebie, subscribe to the newsletter on my website, https://www.karendiem.com/. You can also use the website to contact me, browse free content (cut scenes, sample chapters, my abbreviated autobiography, and more), or find me on social media sites (Twitter, Facebook, etc.). Since I'd hate to read the same stuff everywhere, I do try to put different content in each place. New release notices are the exception and go everywhere.

Arca Chronology

This list only includes novels completed as of the publication of this book. For the most complete and up-to-date chronology, including short stories, see
https://www.karendiem.com/chronology.

Super
Human
Power
Monster
Toga
Party